# TRUTH IS NOT SUGARCOATED IN THE CANDY FACTORY!

**Mary**, whose romantic dreams ran head-on into naked erotic reality . . . **Daphne and Danny**, bedmates who went as far as uninhibited lust would take them . . . **Brigitte**, a woman-libber betrayed by her body . . . **Sam**, a male chauvinist whose dream of sexual conquest turned into a nightmare . . . **Eve**, a chic older woman with a growing hunger for young boys . . . **Charles**, rich, handsome, powerful, who discovered that having any woman he wanted was no longer enough . . .

These are some of the men and women whose intimate secrets you will share in the boldest novel by the most brilliant woman novelist in Canada today—Sylvia Fraser.

*"OVERWHELMINGLY POWERFUL . . . PULLING NO PUNCHES . . . IT WILL BE CONTROVERSIAL . . . AND PROBABLY WILL BE THE BEST CANADIAN BOOK OF THE YEAR!"*
—HAMILTON SPECTATOR

# SIGNET Titles by Bestselling Canadian Authors

---

# THE
# CANDY
# FACTORY

Sylvia Fraser

A SIGNET BOOK

**NEW AMERICAN LIBRARY**

TIMES MIRROR

PUBLISHED BY
THE NEW AMERICAN LIBRARY
OF CANADA LIMITED

*As before.*
*Plus Anna, Doris and Randy.*

# Contents

# 1. The Legend
# of Mary Moon

Mary Moon was just one of those things that sometimes happens in a large and expanding corporation.

Once she had been Hunter Confectionery's chief accountant. Now she worked nine to five in a dingy basement cubicle, squashed between the Hunter Museum and Computer Control, making entries in a ledger entitled Special Accounts, as she rubbed her silky bosom against her desk, and hummed the lovesongs of a few decades before: "Pagan Love Song," "Beautiful Dreamer," "Moonlight and Roses" . . . often running down at the end as fhey did on her Victrola.

No one knew what Mary Moon wrote in her Special Accounts book.

No one cared.

No one at Hunter's knew or cared a tic about Mary Moon. She had the sort of unmarked face that slips in and out of everyone's mind like the moon through clouds. No one ever really "saw" her, though occasionally someone would notice the strong rose sachet she wore and would ask: "What's that perfume? Does anyone else smell roses?"

For thirty years Mary had lived in the loft on the third floor of the original red-brick building called Old Factory, with her mother Mariah and her father Philip, a retired man-of-the-cloth who paid the rent by once-nightly stints as a watchman.

There were four rooms in the loft—a linoleum kitchen with a gas stove, a bathroom with an iron tub, a bedroom partitioned off for the elder Moons, and a large parlour with an alcove containing Mary's brass fourposter.

Though Mary had misty memories of a time that had once seemed happy, life in the loft had year by year faded with its mothy rugs and mouldy hangings to the same dismal hue.

On a typical day the elder Moons would sleep till noon when their daughter would rouse them for lunch, centred on coddled eggs and soup. As the daughter returned to work, Mariah would take out her needlepoint altar-cloths and coloured threads, and Philip would take out his journals and assorted pens; and Mariah, in her rocker and Philip, in his leather chair, would prick and jot their way through a lifetime's justifications to a boiled supper, an hour of prayer, and an evening of TV, ending at ten o'clock when Philip—or, latterly, Mary—would go downstairs with keys and a flashlight to inspect the Candy Factory.

That was the "set" of life in the loft.

The emotional spoils had always belonged to the elder Moons.

All week the air between them would snap and sizzle like a dry storm, full of lightning and undigested thunder without possibility of relief, until Saturday night at 9.30 when one or the other would turn on TV wrestling from the Hamilton Forum. Then, Mariah, riding her rocker, would align herself with the white trunks. Philip, puffing his pipe, would align himself with the black trunks. With her, shrilling in a high whine, and him, pounding his armchair with a low growl, they would punch and jab their way through a life that should have gone one way, but, instead, had gone another, with the daughter between, humming to herself and making up stories for her Special Accounts book through the lens of her own outdated romanticism ... a moonstone rubbed smooth by abrasions.

It was from her parents that Mary had learned the discipline of silence. Since no one in the loft ever listened to her, she stopped speaking. Gradually, the persons with whom she had worked at the Candy Factory passed into retirement, and if new ones ever thought of engaging her in conversation, she was always so surprised they rarely did so again. Nods, vague smiles, fleeting hellos were the coin of Mary's existence. That she was not quite real became a polite but mutual convention.

Mary was never sure, during all those years in the loft, what her parents quarrelled about—failures, infidelities, disappointments, weaknesses, betrayals—who could say? Their grievances, first stated decades ago in the innuendo used in front of children, had become more cryptic with the passage of time, so that an issue that had once been fought out in paragraphs was later dealt with in a sentence, then in a word or a syllable. The Moons could refight, in a single Saturday night, every mortification of their married life, with snorts, whinnies, and wheezes, the very quintessence of bitterness, swinging back and forth in time with the ease of bell-ringers on coarsened ropes, without ever uttering an intelligible word, and still have enough voice to pray for each other on Sunday, a day set aside for prayer and fasting.

On Sunday, October 15, 1972, Philip Moon was, as usual, preaching a sermon to his congregation of two, standing erect, white coxcomb bristling from clerical robes tinged green, when he collapsed into the fine print of Revelations. Mariah took up the text where her husband left off, and it wasn't until the service was completed, with Philip's hand growing cold across the page and his pipe burning *ashes to ashes* in his elephant-foot pipestand, that a doctor was called.

Philip Emmanuel Moon (1889-1972, "What he sows let him reap") was buried in St. Peter's Cemetery and Crematorium, amidst much confident talk of eternity and rows of marble obelisks that must have looked tall before the public highrise went in across the street. Present at graveside were Mariah Moon, her daughter Mary, six boys from the stockroom pressed into service as pallbearers, and President Charles X. Hunter himself, grandson of the founder, dominating with easy grace this scene, as he did so many others, the habitual sadness of his face imparting the hallmark of mourning to proceedings that otherwise would have seemed dreary.

After a month of tears and fasting, life in the loft returned to what would now be normal. Mariah locked her needlepoint in its chest and, henceforth, spent afternoons embroidering on the revised legend of Philip Moon's sainthood. In the evenings—caustic of tongue and short on sunlight, her daily bread spread with gall and her cup running over with self-pity—she would expand her physical needs to take up as much of her daughter's time as possible, dividing each hour into pills of every hue, a bitter rainbow ending in the chamberpot. However, without Philip's rage to goad her, she often fell asleep when she least expected it, so that life slithered away from her like a ball of yarn, and the harder she pulled on it, the more it unravelled.

One ritual in the loft remained unchanged. At 9.30 every Saturday evening, Mariah would turn on wrestling from the Hamilton Forum and, aligning herself as always with Good vs. Evil, she would harangue the villain in black trunks exactly as if he had been her Philip.

On Saturday, March 24, while riding her rocker like the last horse of the Apocalypse and punching air with her marital rings, Mariah saw Bulldog Black catch Angel Face Angus in the ropes and begin to twist. Clutching her own throat, eyes bulging, her face a gasp of outrage circled in grey thistles, Mariah slumped forward in her rocker and fell to the mat. Mary, faithful to family tradition, waited for the match to be awarded before turning off the set and calling the doctor.

Mariah Peacock Moon (1891-1973, "Into the arms of Jesus") was lowered on cranky chains to her final respite on top of her Philip, with one space left for Mary.

It was a bleak, black-and-white day, with the gaudy reds of the carnations adding an intemperate note like scarlet lipstick on a corpse.

Mary stood pebble-eyed at graveside in the Girl Guide hat and coat she had worn to her father's funeral. As the minister pronounced "dust to dust," dropping lumps of clay on the coffin, like two shoes falling, a gust of wind sent her hat spinning through the tombstones. Another seeded her hairpins over the raw earth, wounded by her mother's grave. Laughter clotted in her chest. Pressing her hanky to her lips, she tried to convert it into hiccups, the way she used to in church when the soprano sang off-key. It was only when her mother did not arise from the coffin to reprimand her that Mary Moon realized both of her parents were at last dead.

The days of April lengthened, softened, and elided into those of May.

Mary, in the first gush of freedom, tore down the muddy curtains that smothered the four windows of the loft and replaced them with yellow organdy. She rolled up the musty rug, faded to the colour of mouse dung, painted drab wicker furniture white, and scraped the sooty paint from the skylight. She softened the Calvinistic lines of her mother's daybed with cabbage-rose chintz. She planted flowerboxes with petunias and painted the frame of the mirror, in which three generations of Moons practised their sermons, a free-thinkers' lilac.

As Mary was pushing the mirror across the room, its card-

4

board backing fell off, uncovering a full-length portrait of herself.

Mary stared at the portrait.

She felt a sharp twist of pain in her chest and her eyes filled with tears.

The painting—done when she was a young girl in Paris—had not been finished. The face was blank.

Mary hastily shoved it against the wall.

That night she dreamt of the artist.

She dreamt she was chasing him through fetid yellow fog on the ravine side of the Candy Factory, begging him to fill in her face for her, and pursued—*thump thump thump*—by her mother, on her rocker, with her father's false teeth snapping at her side. Once she caught up to the artist. Once she actually held the forked tongue of his coat, glossy and sinuous, in her hands, but it hissed like a snake and she dropped it.

May warmed and spread like maple syrup into June.

Mary found it increasingly difficult to sleep in the muggy loft. She would spend the spirit-hours with her head thrust out her alley window, her breasts tumbling indiscriminately from her satin robe into the velvet mouths of her petunias while cats tore the cellophane silence with their yowls and mated in garbage cans, her mind tortured by images of violence and eroticism and memories that bubbled up from hidden wells primed by the accidents of the dark ... herself a child ... lying in a tangle of buttercups and daisies on her grandfather's farm, watching butterflies with sooty wings ride other butterflies with sooty wings ... watching dragonflies with shivery blue bodies ride other dragonflies with shivery blue bodies ... watching her grandma's cat writhing in a fit in the twitchgrass, eyes glittery, tongue lolling, yowling from a place far back in her throat in agony wrapped in molasses. Mary followed the cat through the twitchgrass, scarping her belly like the cat's along the ground as she wriggled, haunches held high, tail on-the-beg to the sky howling experimentally from a voicebox deep in her belly, following the cat's split red nether-eye, moist with tears, till she felt something papery crunch beneath her ... *hornets!* They were buzzing ominously under her belly! They were tearing out hunks of flesh! They were divebombing her. Up her nose! In her mouth! In her hair! She was rolling in the twitchgrass, screaming, trying to protect her face! They were burrowing between her fingers, forcing apart the fleshy knuckles, sticking their barbed stingers into her eyes. They were up her dress, inside her pants, depositing their black eggs between her legs with stingers hot as fire! She was trying to beat them off but her dress was sticky and sweet, and she was twisted in it, bound up in a sugarweb, and it was dribbling into her mouth, choking her even as she was screaming.

As a sot to restlessness, Mary spent more and more time inspecting the Candy Factory.

Each night, girding her waist with her father's ring of keys, she would follow her puddle of light through the darkly twined corridors of Old Factory, built by Xavier X. Hunter in 1896—first through the renovated executive floor, then the business floor, then down into the basement, past her own tiny office and the Hunter Museum, containing hand moulds dating from the time old Xavier presided over the Production Line in his shirtsleeves, then on to the great steel door leading to the new Production Sector, built by Charles X. Hunter in 1954 and covering a city block. Using the largest and shiniest of her metal fingers, she would travel through the concrete corridors of the Production Sector, clotted with the smell of roasting chocolate, riding her own shadow through patches of moonlight as she caught this or that form in the incandescent eye of her flashlight, with her imagination expanding to fill all the dark and silent places.

The more Mary learned about the Candy Factory, the more real and familiar became her fantasies about it and, hence, the entries in her Special Accounts book. Whereas before she had written about martyrs and maidens and unicorns, now she wrote about the people who worked in the Candy Factory, incorporating the privileged information she found in drawers, or overheard in washrooms, or read in people's faces by studying them discreetly as a servant who is considered a part of the furnishings, noting the small gestures that indicate what a person really thinks and feels apart from what he says he thinks and feels, and setting all this down in the loops and coils of that person's own hand, for a talent in penmanship was one of the few in which Mary prided herself.

6

Mary inevitably developed favourites among the employees of the Candy Factory. Usually she fixed on one person or another because of some imagined connection, or parallel, or resemblance to persons or incidents in her own past, so that in making up entries about them she was actually making up for the mistakes and disappointments of her own life ... becoming in a spooky way a whole book of characters in a timeless dance with the lost possibilities of her own life.

Mary saw Daphne Foster of the Public Relations department and her boyfriend Danny Steel of Ads as herself and a boy named Michael to whom she had been engaged all one summer until they had quarrelled at a church picnic. Mary would sit at Daphne's desk, her feet rooted in the comfortable loafers Daphne always wore to conduct the daytime tours of the Candy Factory, reading through Daphne's letters as if they were her own, reliving that bittersweet summer up to the climactic scene which, more than any other, had sentenced her to spinsterhood, wondering what would have happened that day if Fate had intervened to wipe out the barrier of fear and pride and stubborness between herself and Michael—to give love another chance.

Morgan Jones, a black youth who worked in the Chocolate Department, drew on some dark guilt in Mary which she couldn't quite get hold of—a long-forgotten act of casual prejudice which had become a sticky lodestone for other anonymous guilts, now collected inside her in a sludgy pool of regret. Mary would stand on the steel parapet that gridded the ceiling of the Chocolate Department, and she would shine her light down into one or the other of the bubbling vats of chocolate that Morgan tended by day, and she would imagine for herself an act of baptism which, through serving Morgan, would lead to her own expiation.

Sam Ryan of Sales provided Mary with comic relief, for he seemed to play out as farce the sort of events she had been taught to consider as high tragedy. Mary would go through the pornographic literature Sam had sent to him in plain wrappers, and the latest gags in his "joke" drawer, and the newest addition to his whodunit library, and she would concoct bawdy adventures for him in his own flamboyant style, though always adding the sort of moral instruction at the end that befitted a minister's daughter.

Beau Whitehead, an industrial researcher who worked at

Hunter's on a government grant, aroused Mary's motherly compassion because he seemed so much like herself, full of psychological knowledge he was unable to apply. Mary would shine her light like a halo, round the face of the statue of the Virgin that Beau kept in his basement office and she would imagine herself as that statue come to life, reaching out a gentle hand to the head placed for comfort on her alabaster lap, tracing, with the pulse of life, Beau's dry scholastic markings ... brackets around the mouth, quotation marks on the nose, dashes across the forehead, circumflexes over the eyes.

The bitter feud between Eve Martin, Mr. Hunter's senior secretary, the Brigitte Young, his junior secretary, rebuked Mary with a memory of the petty jealousy that had festered between herself and her own sister Julie, depriving them both of a friend. Mary would read the women's lib pamphlets Brigitte circulated throughout the Hunter office, with their plea for honest confrontation and womanly understanding, and she would wonder: why couldn't Julie and I have liked each other better? And then, thinking of Eve and Brigitte: why can't they?

Charles X. Hunter reminded Mary of her own father, both men of exceptional charm and ability, pressed by family tradition into positions to which they were not, in their gut, committed; men who mistook the approval of others for the approval of themselves; who hid self-doubt under easy external success. Mary would sit at Charles' desk, smoking the brier pipe he was trying to give up, watching shadows creep across his office, and imagine him in confrontation with his past ... as the man he might still become.

Celeste Hunter—Charles' beautiful socialite wife, whom Mary had observed at Hunter functions and especially at her annual Valentine tea—reminded Mary of her own mother at the height of her ambitions when she still hankered to be a bishop's wife—queenly, overbearing, convinced of the rightness of her own privileged claims on life, committed to surfaces, the shinier the better, with the view that anything that can be forced to look good must be good. In conjuring a fate for Celeste Hunter, Mary borrowed heavily on the trappings of fairytales with their fondness for swoons, spells, pricked fingers, and snowqueens in crystal palaces.

The trouble with all this was that while the characters in

Mary's Special Accounts book, guided by her own clear view of things from the loft, worked their way through the daily labyrinth of surface detail to a sense of inner wonder, optimism and growth, their counterparts, in real life always seemed to miss themselves and each other in the darker corridors of habit and pessimism. They would fail to see what was right before their eyes; or seeing, fail to trust; or trusting, fail to make a commitment; or committing, fail to risk, thus always falling short of what, on paper, seemed their potential.

Mary worried a great deal about this discrepancy. It seemed to her that it all came back to the popular belief that God was dead. It seemed to her that, in killing off the old God of Good and Evil, people had mistakenly, at the same time, killed off their faith in the Mystery of Life, which meant the difference between their living in a room with an open skylight, through which anything from a dove to a griffin might fly, to their living in a prison. Thus, life for many people in the Candy Factory had become claustrophobic, unheroic, repetitive, and purposeless, devoid of such human miracles as the power of love to change, of madness to heal, of insight to release, of intuition to perceive, of compassion to rescue. Sometimes one or another of Mary's people would seem so close to such a discovery that she was tempted to add to their eyes the beam of her own light, but though she had the vision, she lacked the experience, the practical courage to intervene. . . . Mary's life, too, withered for want of a small miracle that would release her.

Mary might have gone on endlessly weaving her word tapestries from shadows on walls—like the Lady of Shalott, like her own mother with her altar-cloths, like her own father with his journals—had she not been tortured nightly by the artist. He would descend upon her from the nimbus of her own brass bed, one eye in a wink, the other suspended like the full moon over her desires, and he would dangle before her face marzipan fruits from Hunter's Sweets of Life collection, offering them first between pinched fingers, then between pursed lips, then rolled in his tongue, sticky with saliva. But though she ached with hunger, she would not reach them for she had no mouth . . . she had no face.

It was on the first day of July, while she was eating lunch in Hunter's park opposite the Candy Factory, that Mary first saw the other artist. He was on his hands and knees drawing a street scene of Paris, his outfit a collage of lifestyles from high to low, beginning with rubbertire sandals and progressing up through a swallowtail coat and vest to a workman's cap laid on the beg for coins.

There was something about him—some air of bristling self-absorption—that drew Mary's attention. As he dipped into his right pocket for chalk, and his left for a bottle of liquid that he drank from a brown wrapper, Mary fingered a quarter in her change purse, torn between compassion in the coin requested and feelings more complex.

The artist finished his picture and signed it: *Renoir*. He sat back on his haunches. He adjusted his black eyepatch. He rolled his single eye craftily from person to person like a squirrel twirling a nut, testing for a soft spot.

He looked at Mary. She flushed.

She had so perfected the art of watching others without seeming to that she hadn't noticed she had pierced her own anonymity by staring directly at him.

The artist's eye shifted from Mary to her handbag, agape beside her on the bench. Still fixed on that, he picked up his cap and climbed with exaggerated precision to his feet. He limped to the bench and slumped heavily upon it. Mary felt him as an accumulation of sharp angles and abrasions at the end of the bench. She resisted putting out her hand to snatch back her handbag.

The artist, still ogling the bag, took an oily postcard from his pocket and set it on the bench beside her. He spread the coins from his cap across his palm and counted noisily: "Five, six, sixteen, twenty-one. . . ." Again Mary felt the insolent probing of his single black eye as he challenged: "That's not enough, lady. I don't have enough for a sandwich and coffee."

Mary had eaten only one section of her chicken sandwich. She extended the rest on its waxpaper platter, faltering only slightly as she said: "You're welcome to what I have, sir."

The artist looked at the sandwich with ill-concealed disappointment. He picked up one square, with thumb and finger wielded like silver tongs, then jammed it into his mouth as if stuffing a gangrenous wound with cotton. He swallowed, without chewing, belched, then helped himself to the rest.

Mary studied his drawing—the usual sentimental sludge served up to tourists with this exception: the faces of the flowersellers had been grotesquely twisted into those of gargoyles.

"Did you study in Paris?" she asked, curiosity overcoming reticence.

The artist snorted. "You *might* say that, lady."

He rolled his one good eye melodramatically up to the heavens: "Actually, I studied with Life."

He tapped a gimpy leg: "Bullets."

He tapped his eyepatch: "Shrapnel."

He tapped his throat: "Gas. All of me went to Paris, lady, but only half of me came back."

The artist took his bottle from his pocket. He brought it up to his eye and looked down it. Pantomiming reform, he tossed it from himself as a thing accursed. *Lips that have touched alcohol shall never touch mine!*

"I myself have visited the continent only once," continued Mary, drawn in by his odd behaviour, unable to resist the compulsion of that single black eye. "I travelled with my Aunt Elvira who, as it turned out, had quite a yen for the artists. She must have commissioned her portrait seven times! One handsome young man offered to do mine as a gift. It's a surprising thing but I came upon that portrait just the other day. Unfortunately, it wasn't finished."

Mary glanced sideways at the artist.

He was glowering at a poodle, leg up, about to despoil his drawing.

Mary leapt from the bench. She shooed the dog, garnering the hate of a wispy young man at the end of the rhinestone leash.

She returned to the bench. The artist was gone. So was her change purse.

The postcard had been stuffed inside her handbag.

She examined it—the same scene the artist had drawn on the sidewalk, even to the signature, which was as good a forgery as she herself could accomplish.

Mary shifted uneasily. *Was it her imagination or could she still feel the artist's prickly eye raking her from the bushes?* Feeling herself under its hypnotic effect, she took a Hunter ballpoint pen from her handbag and scrawled across the postcard, in a hand so unfamiliar she judged it must be her own:

"To the Artist—I have an unfinished portrait in need of talented completion. If you are interested in this com-

*11*

mission, please come to my home, tomorrow night, over Hunter's Confectionery, at 8 o'clock, and we will discuss the matter as to terms and price."

She signed the note: "Miss Mary Moon, Special Accounts," with a P.S. "Please bring samples of your work."

Mary slid the note on the bench, then fled home ... back to the Candy Factory.

# 2. The Tramp

The tramp crawled out of his sewer, yawned, squinted up at the sun, now leering over the roof of the Candy Factory, and made his prediction: *Hot and humid with a high of 82. Cloudy by eight. Storm warning.* He was never wrong. Or, if he was, he never noticed, which amounted to the same thing.

He crawled back into his sewer—part of the original Candy Factory drainage system, now plugged and abandoned.

He unrolled yesterday's newspaper, used as a pillow, and pawed its contents: a plug of chewing tobacco, a teabag, a hunk of salami, a bottle of vanilla extract and liniment, and—he grinned—one suede change purse.

He held the change purse in his hands.

He fondled it. It was soft and creamy, with a pink-silk lining and a tight silver clasp.

He opened it.

He found the postcard inside, where he had stuffed it. He crawled out of his hole into the sunlight. He read, mocking and mimicking: "If you are interested in this commission . . ."

He sniggered, squiggling his fingers inside the silky lining, thinking of the silky little woman who owned it, thinking of her creamy-pink cunt. He looked up at the Candy Factory seeming to tower over him from his rat's-eye position down its gully side. *Well, why not? They occupied the attic and the bowels of the same building. It was time they got acquainted!*

The tramp, laughing, stuffed the purse into his trousers.

He swigged from his bottle. He ate his salami.

He looked across the gully to the freeway where cars slid by—sixty to the minute, faster today than yesterday because it was Friday and the suckers wanted to get the day done with.

He untied the cord of his trousers and dropped them.

13

He exposed his wasted flanks, front and back, to the cars. Nothing showy, nothing taunting—just the boredom of any man checking himself in a mirror, without looking. Someday, he hoped, a set of eyes would give him back a shocked reflection of himself and then maybe there would be a screechy pileup, with gore smeared all over the highway, and he would be hunted down as a Menace to Society. The thought amused him. If Helen's face could launch a thousand ships, why shouldn't his arse stop a dozen cars? Besides—he cast his good eye on his drainage hole which, for all its slimy squalor, was divided into eating and sleeping areas—a man, no matter how disgusting he made himself, was seldom more than one dank deed ahead of selling out his honest pain to the bourgeoisie.

The tramp squatted. His kneecaps plugged into his armpits, he rocked from heel to toe, giving himself over to the rapture of defecation.

Defecation was his greatest pleasure.

He liked the tickle of the wind on his bare behind, and the teasing dangle of himself in the coarse wet grass. He liked the titillation of that first air globule as it squashed itself, like a fat warm grape, through his sphincters, to waft back to him in a spattered bouquet of his own flatulence. He liked the pusling grip and release of his muscles, as they stroked their long brown eggs through his bowels, and the steamy clash of hot turd with cool earth mould. Far better than jacking-off. More like childbirth, he imagined. A true act of creation, accessible to every man—God's wonders, mixed with a man's juices, passed through a hazardous course of tubes and tribulations, then offered up, once more, to God: *Give unto Caesar that which is Caesar's and unto God that which is God's.*

The tramp rolled his buttocks, coiling his spoor. He wondered what colours he had produced today: russet? mahogany? puce? maroon? khaki? dun? fuscous? saffron? purple-flecked? green-tinged? The possibilities were as endless as the colours in oil, as the patterns in fire. Even when he had taken the art of the bowel so seriously that he had eaten with tones and textures in mind, he had often been fooled, and now, with an aging and leaky system. . . .

The tramp chuckled. *Hee hee hee!* Well, he had had his triumphs, when life and art had, for him, briefly coalesced. He recalled that time, a couple of decades ago, when bored with painting a bowl of cherries in the style of Cézanne, he

14

had eaten the cherries, then moulded his excrement into a bowl, which he had entitled "Life Is Just a Bowl of Cherries" and sold at an ad hoc Greenwich Village show to a Dallas matron who thought it "just cunning" for peanuts.

He recalled the time when he had produced large smeared canvases, entitled "You Are What You Eat," for a New York show regarded as Significant. The canvases were highly praised, by those who claimed to know about such things, for the boldness of their metaphor, while the artist's solemn claims that he had never been less metaphoric, or more realistic, were patronizingly dismissed until opening night, when the air-conditioning broke down in a heat wave and the flies restored to a stunned art world the forgotten wisdom of Solomon.

The tramp chortled. *Ahhh, the lost arrogance and ambition of youth!* Now he just pooped for pleasure.

The tramp pinched his sphincters, flicking his buttocks a little pridefully to create a serpent's head. He imagined the serpent's tongue, flickering its way back up his rectum, creating in reverse all the pleasures he had just experienced, plus the added titillation of wilful penetration. He turned on his heel. He evaluated his pile: carbuncle, with a touch of ochre pleasantly glossy but with the coil broken toward the middle—not enough roughage for the length, or had he let his concentration wander?

The tramp sniffed his spoor. He felt the usual craving to devour it, but resisted—not out of revulsion, but out of moral responsibility. He believed the day he dined on his own spoor would be the last day of his life, and—since everything in Creation was but an extension of his own imagination—the end of the Universe. It would be the Devil swallowing Himself by the tail. God feasting on His own body, in remembrance of Himself. The supreme act of solipsism.

The tramp reached for yesterday's paper.

He had had his morning devotional. Now the world was awaiting his political statement.

He turned the pages, still squatting, and decided hastily on a picture of Nixon.

He disengaged it and, folding it face out, thoroughly wiped his ass. It wasn't that he was anti-American. It could have been Trudeau or—neither was he sexist—Indira Ghandi or—neither was he pro/anti Arab/Israel—Golda Meir or Anwar Sadat.

The tramp placed the newspaper on his spoor, like a butterfly. Nixon looked at him, reproachfully, from his rusty moustache. The tramp felt a flicker of self-disgust. He was becoming too crude, too obvious. Time was when a political smear from him had meant something. He had got Hitler *before* the Beerhall Putsch. He had got McCarthy when most people thought he was a ventriloquist's dummy. He had got Stalin when he was still smoking Churchill's cigars. Once, following the tramp's bumswipes across the earth had been like reading tomorrow's newspaper. Now he scarcely remembered who ruled what country, let alone how badly.

The tramp stood up.

He tied his trousers and crawled into his tunnel.

He emerged, wearing vest and swallowtail coat, fastened with a system of cords and pins as complex as any used in the hautest of couture.

He checked his pockets with the brisk efficiency of a businessman checking his briefcase.

It was a magician's coat, organically renewed, patch upon patch, with secret compartments, false linings and trick sleeves through which flowed the items he had found most useful in persuading a gullible public to pick its own pockets and to thank him for it.

The tramp was very good at his trade. He would have been rich many times over had he not protected himself with rules and vanities.

He did not, for example, accept government handouts. A man of pride did not bite and suck at the same time, and the tramp was no sucker.

He rarely stole—always preferring to make an exchange.

He never accepted charity, unless he failed to qualify for the charity being offered. He never accepted charity for which there were no qualifications. He was a tramp, not a bum. He did not like dead faces around him.

He begged only from people who found it distasteful to be asked and painful to give.

He never accepted payment unless he could fail to do what he was being paid to do while convincing his employer he had done it, and even that made him uneasy: how—truly—did such a position differ from that of the average wage-earner?

He seldom carried over one day's profits to the next. In the old days, he had always paid for himself by noon, but now that his tastebuds were burnt out and his prick more-or-less just another appendix, he didn't mind letting the business of survival consume his day: what would he do with more leisure? *Play golf at The Toronto Hunt Club? Hee hee hee!* For the tramp, the perfect day was one that kept him sober enough to earn enough to get drunk enough. Anything less was suicidal. Anything more was . . . suicidal.

The tramp set himself one more hazard. In milking the cow of guilt and the goat of greed, he always insisted on being fashionable. National guilt, he knew, established the long vogues in "charity," so that during a war he always carried a full line of crutches, slings, and veterans' ribbons, whereas during a depression he stocked high on dark glasses, hearing-aids, and other items suggesting congenital impairment and reminding even the indigent—to his profit—that at least they had their health. During boom times it was the diseases of excess that society—and, therefore, the tramp—took a noisy interest in. Though he had never been a drug addict, he had been cured twice at public expense. Though he had never been a convict, he had been rehabilitated three times. Though he had never lived in Cabbagetown, he was a favourite interview subject of TV crews doing poverty studies there, at the usual commercial rates. And—perhaps his crowning achievement of the sixties—he once spent a week at a resort in Muskoka in something called the Blue Project, as a paid schizophrenic.

The tramp started up the slope to the highway, favouring the lame leg he described variously as the result of Nazi/Communist/police/black/Mafia brutality, depending on the presumed prejudice of his listener.

His needs were twofold: food and drink. Food had never been a problem for the tramp. When he had kept himself clean, he had often dined out at conventions, weddings, and funerals—never so small they expected to know you, never so large they checked invitations. More recently, he had snacked on the politics of the left, which he classified as one of the diseases of excess. During the plummy days of leftist discontent, he had dropped down to the U.S. embassy, as casually as a tourist to his American Express office, for free coffee or soup, shouting "fashionable pricks!" only slightly less loudly than others were shouting, "fascist pigs!" Now that leftist movements had deteriorated to mere politics, the tramp was waiting for the excesses of the right to morally rearm themselves. When Billy Graham had made his well-publicized walk through London parks, splashing through semen bogs up to the clocks of his blue socks, he had been behind the times—which, of course, meant he had also been ahead of them. Now if Graham should slip on a condom at Time Square and break a leg . . . well . . . the tramp would be ready with knife and fork for the fatted calf of Righteousness to be carved up and served. Christo-o-Ramas in ballparks! Manna rained down from heaven, courtesy of the late Cecil B. DeMille! In the meantime, his tastebuds had skidded with his station. He was not a fussy man.

The tramp paused for an old man's moment on the dusty shoulder of the Don Valley Parkway, feeling the cars swish by on their way to King and Bay. It was the need of drink—meaning money—that sometimes kept him more alert than he wanted to be.

This was a time of unprecedented middle-class suspicion. People who used to feel guilty if they didn't shell out had now been made to feel guilty if they did. The men were afraid their taxes would go up—it all came back to that. The women were afraid to trust a man with broken shoelaces with the price of the foam on a beer lest they grease his slide to perdition. . . . He'd even had one old biddy remove the dime from a piece of kid's birthday cake before giving the cake to him!

It was the legacy of the stupid "anti-heroes" of the sixties who had made everyone nervous.

Just let one of those jerks panhandle fifty cents, and the fool would use a dime of it to phone the local paper to brag about it. The tramp spat in a long phlegmy stream: *Ripoff artists, bah! Now they were all insurance salesmen in $7.50 haircuts.*

The tramp limped along the gravel, feeling it burn through his sandals. The inadequacies of those who had ruined business made him recall, with chagrin, the one humbling period of his own vagrant's life . . . that time he had spent in India. No matter where he had gone in that country of bottomless poverty, or how he had divested himself, he had remained a rich tourist to the pathetic mutants who grovelled at his feet, kissing his sandals and sometimes thinking, in their ignorance of such luxury, that the thongs were part of his toes. Benares, the Holy City where Hindus go to die, had been the worst. At night, it shimmered in the redglow of funeral pyres. By day, lines of reechy beggars clawed at the faithful as they went to the Ganges to bathe. Disease was rampant. Festering bodies—armless, legless, rotting—lay in the sun and moaned. One trunk-with-a-head had chosen the tramp as his "wealthy" patron, rolling after him wherever he went, like a gruesome dog, his abscessed stumps padding the earth as he turned over and over, his smile stretched wide and unwavering as it bit into the dust then turned heavenward into the fly-specked sun, enduring a hundred days and nights in as many yards to the corner. He came at the tramp out of the stench of alleys. Or he was that foul heap of rags in a marketplace that suddenly blinked an eye. Or that dead cow in the gutter, twitching with lice. Or that barrel propped against a sycamore tree, scratching itself. The tramp had withstood as long as he could. Then, overnight, he had broken. Bilking a group of tourists who had wanted to see a *real* sacred cow, he had showered the beggar with their coins. Then he had robbed and killed a British colonel and, kissing every hand and foot of Shiva, had fled with the money to Bangkok. In India, the tramp had been in mortal danger of valuing his own life.

Now the tramp squinted through the triple line of freeway traffic. A white dog was caught on the boulevard, afraid to cross and unwilling to go back. It was a very thin dog, a puppy, with bones pushing through its hide like ribs through a rotted hull. The tramp had seen him around for a couple of weeks. The dog, recognizing him, wagged his tail, straining forward and whimpering in the heat from the wheels.

The tramp picked up a stick and tapped his shins, trying to coax the dog to risk the traffic. The dog whined, pawed the burnt grass, but would not budge. Were the dogs getting smarter? Or was he losing his touch? Often in the past, he had whistled dogs to a splashy release-from-misery, then shed real tears over their carcasses while guilt-ridden motorists peeled off dollars for their funerals. Once he had parlayed a skunk into five dollars from a trucker with a screaming kid who thought it was a cat. Once he had carried a bleeding mutt through a village, collecting twenty bucks for medical expenses before roasting the corpse in the field on the other side. It took a war—and especially a holy one—for people to feel sentimental about death. Now the highways were red-streaked and fur-lined, and nobody cared. What value was a man's life if no one was trying to take it from him?

The tramp started down the hill. He heard a howl through the traffic. The white dog had paralleled him along the boulevard and was preparing to dash through the cars to his master. The tramp, on sentimental impulse, hurled his stick at the dog, slapping him smartly across the forelegs. The dog, yelping, turned tail and dashed to safety through the empty lanes on the far side.

Rummaging in the muddy creek the tramp found a popbottle—*bah disposable!*—and exploded it in a splintered star against a bridge abutment. He picked four strawberries and ate them, then half a mildewed hamburger probably left by a construction crew. He felt something lick his toes. It was the white dog, tail wagging. It had crossed the freeway through a drainage tunnel. The tramp tossed a rock, hard, into its snout, watching it burst like an overripe pomegranate. The dog, wailing, ran back to the tunnel.

Travelling by mudcreek and road through the ravines that were smuggling summer into Toronto, the tramp continued south and west into the city, startling the occasional bird, squirrel, lover; nudging into a lunchbag and finding an apple; swigging from the emergency flask he kept in his coat where the magician had kept his rabbits; finding one-third of the morning's *Globe and Mail* and forming a quick prejudice for tomorrow's rites of passage; trekking under a bridge and noting—with a connoisseur's hauteur—the sort of illiteracy that posed as graffiti these days, then turning up a gravel road and coming upon the city by way of St. Peter's Cemetery and Crematorium.

He liked cemeteries and especially the tiny ones. St. Peter's, wrapped in its black iron fence, was like an exclusive suburb with all the right names on its mailboxes; WELLINGTON, SMITH-HAYES, WINDSOR. The Tramp's favourite was a twenty-foot obelisk recording the nativity, nuptials, and demise of a John WORTHINGTON and a Mary WELLBORN. He tossed his cap to the top of John WORTHINGTON's pink finger. It pleased him to cap *that* performance.

The tramp saw an open grave on the far side of the cemetery. He shuffled towards it, over the heads of the departed, each decaying shamelessly under the weight of its own boldly engraved lies: "Beloved father of.... Devoted husband of...." *Indeed, indeed!* Some of the older residents had inscriptions stapled by quotation marks to their mouths. These the tramp read aloud, making his voice placating, hopeful, threatening, ingratiating, as the script suggested: "I *trusted* you, oh Lord!" "At rest, at last!" "Till *He* comes." "But for the body, present with the Lord."

The newer headstones were noncommittal. Just the dates of birth and death—the hard covers between which a life had been lived—with no hint of content. Why couldn't the dead be more generous with their experience? Why not one single *true* statement from every person now *lying* here as the price of admission?

The tramp struck a pose before an open marble book with only "his" side filled in, and improvised: "My life was an open book, except for the footnotes I kept tucked in that dirty hotel room on Jarvis Street."

He passed on to a grey cathedral-like structure, and prompted: "In another month they would have found I was dipping into the collection plate."

A spinster, under a cross, confided: "I was only happy when I masturbated."

The tramp picked through flowers mounding a fresh grave, selected a lily, saw the stem was broken, and threw it down with disgust. Today's "fresh" flowers were so trussed with wires, intravenously fed on preservatives, and prolonged in freezers that they rarely got to the cemetery in any better condition than the corpses. It was an act of euthanasia to let them die and the tramp, though a tramp, had his finer feelings.

He settled, instead, for an artificial wreath, denouncing as he did so the trend to plastic which he interpreted as unconscious cynicism on the part of the bestower that the other things they had planted here weren't going to be sprouting up again either. He replaced it with his listerine bottle, containing one dandelion which he thought . . . *more hopeful.*

The tramp had a profitable morning.

He traded the plastic wreath for a bottle of homemade gin from Jarvis Street bootlegger with Mafia connections.

He sold an "I am deaf and dumb" card for seventy-five cents to an unemployed actor who wanted to Xerox them as business cards for certain of his favourite CBC producers.

He sold a "hot pussy" phone number for a buck to a pock-faced lout outside the Warwick Hotel which, when dialled, would bring him Dial-a-Prayer.

He sold another plus an obscene password to a Royal York Shriner for two bucks, which, when dialled and whispered, would net him the wrath of the Chief of Police.

That gave him $3.75, which he converted into three bottles of Derby sherry at the Lombard Street liquor store, before hopping a laundry truck to City Hall.

The tramp liked City Hall with its graceful walkways, its reflecting pool, its council chamber like a flying saucer flanked by stone scrolls. He sat in a marble planter containing a dying birch and watched the air-conditioned mausoleums give up their dead—at first in a trickle of those sneaking out early, almost colliding with the stragglers back from lunch, then in a gushy stream, with the girls blowing like wilted flowers over the concrete, and the men, wan as corpses in their sombre suits, with their stiff necks and flaccid cocks.

The tramp checked his watch—rather he checked a pawn ticket at the end of a gold chain, which he found served him better, since it didn't require winding or incite the envy of other Soldiers of Fortune.

It was 4.30.

He collected six newspapers, almost complete, from benches and bins and resold five of them to subway patrons for fifty cents.

He filched the wallet of a tourist taking pictures of Henry Moore's Archer, and returned it for a reward of two dollars.

As a treat the tramp decided to ride the subway.

Committing himself to the hot democracy of a crowded car, and with his own reeking body pressed against the bodies of fussier patrons beyond their endurance or recall, he indulged his taste for flatulence, recalling how at the height of his powers, he had been able—by shifting weight as if pumping an organ—to emit nether yips and toots in a fair rendition of "Yankee Doodle Dandy," but having to settle, now that dysentery had ruined his muscle control, for a rough approximation of the C scale.

The tramp got off at Bloor Street, trailing curses as a wayward bride her torn wedding veil.

He hiked east on Bloor, back to St. Peter's Cemetery.

He went to the fresh grave, covered with green matting.

He had been thinking about that grave since morning.

He lifted the matting like a man checking a hotel bed. With a sly glance about, he crawled inside.

The smell of the moist earth rose to meet him. The grave

was snugger than they used to dig them, and certainly the new tenant was not going to be six feet under. In the funeral business these days that was considered air rights. In the indecent economy with which relative toppled in upon relative, a man's slot in perpetuity quickly shrank to a couple of feet, and then—as fast as the worms could handle it—to mere inches.

The tramp chuggalugged the bottle of Derby. Colours rippled through his mind, at first in misty undulations of pink and mauve, then in spasms of eggyolk and blood, with pitch and khaki and puce vomiting up through the rainbow on the back of his eyes. He began to shake. The earth shook. Memory spewed over the tramp, overwhelming him . . . himself a boy, age five? age six? . . . digging with an old man he thought must be his grandfather through the snow of a battlefield, his hands bound in rags, looking for his stepbrothers. . . . He stopped digging. There was something in the snow. He picked it up. It was a man's eye, one eye, staring, glassy, without a face . . . one eye, with all the bitterness of a soldier's short brutal life packed into its ogling glance. The boy quivered, holding the eye in his palm, knowing, without words, that he was holding—as his first memory of life—the futility of life. . . . His grandfather turned. The boy, guilty to have seen so much, popped the eye into his mouth. He sucked on the eye, finding its mate, spattered in pink beads in the snow.

The boy found other eyes, in other snowbanks, fierce, accusative, set like macabre jewels in faces frozen in terror and hate. Still sucking on the eye in his cheek, as evil to ward off evil, crying, corrupted, but unable to spit it out, he kept on digging, finding each man's face a diary of his last wretched thoughts . . . a hand, severed, still cocked on a gun with the wrist trailing wisps of tendon . . . boots, sticking out of white mounds, like black arrows pointing to the grisly deeds below . . . hearts, congealed in a puddle of their last tears.

The boy pulled on a green rope, and found it to be an intestine, unwinding from the bowels of his step-brother Anson, without a head. And then he found his brother Metro, petrified with his horse, half-man half-beast. And then the youngest son of the miller with his hair turned white . . . each snowbank adding to the boy's store of death, when he was still milky with his own birth and unable to withstand the imprint of so much evil.

23

The snow began to melt. The soldiers were still fighting, trading his village back and forth, like a harlot won and lost at a gaming table, and now it was worse, with the white gone, the mercy of God removed, so that each man was steeped in his own gore ... *nauseous, nauseous,* like vegetables in a rancid stew ... green cabbage-faces stuck together by their stench ... corpses fat with gases that made them hiss and moan as he turned them over in their wriggling nests of white worms ... hands bulging from khaki cuffs like black sausages in too tight casings ... *putrid,* their mouths a-twitch with bluebottle flies, tongues like purple balloons, four times their size. The boy vomited into the carrion, not even noticing, as he dug, no longer surprised to step on a snake, rippling its way through a brain cavity, and to have it spatter into a column of ants ... seeing birth, now, as a soldier's belly bloated with rats, their furcoats sleek with blood as they gnawed their own birth canal up through his rectum ... digging through a handful of something green, and a handful of something yellow till he found the faceless face of his stepuncle Gervais, the ear by which he turned him having come off in his hands ... crying, but not noticing his tears, just a wet appeasement to despair ... digging out of habit, not knowing anything else, the old man he thought to be his grandfather dead now through unnatural natural causes, his hoary head having sunk lower and lower over the bodies of his line till once the old man happened to look up to see the dangling boots of his favourite, Anatole, only fifteen, hanging from a tree, with crows in his eyes and a bull's-eye painted on his back, having been used for target practice.

No relatives of the boy's were living now, but still he dug, picking out the faces of those he recognized—the school teacher with the only glasses in the village ... guessing what arms and legs belonged to him ... where one stump left off and its neighbour began ... sometimes just wrapping in a hand or two from another corpse, then hauling that on his wagon to the edge of the field and trading it for food to whoever came for it, finding they paid more if they seemed to get most of the parts and if he stuck back some teeth or sewed on an arm in a jacket—doing the only thing he knew to survive ... too stupid to leave the flesh and take the guns, the boots, the buckles.

The people of his village and the next hid their eyes whenever they saw him now, the angel of muddy death eating with the stench of putrefaction on his hands, his boots slippery with another's flesh so that in the end it was like eating the corpses, munching cheek-to-cheek with the rats through another man's vitals. Why, then, go to the trouble of hauling and cleaning and sewing when he could feed direct? Why deal with a middle man who despised him, thus gypping himself of half the profits? Why not, when he found a plump thigh, dripping with sweet blood, just roast that up, instead of converting it to pig flesh at the butcher's?

The tramp convulsed in his grave, sucking on his bottle. He didn't know if he'd ever done that—eaten a corpse—it was too far back to remember, but that's what his nightmares said, full of dead eyes on sticks and maggoty mouths shouting at him, accusing him, hunting him down, pursuing him from village to village until he learned his talent to drown them in paint, to slap upon their ulcerated flesh the masks of the living—portraits of innocence, of beauty, the lovelier the better, so that one day the wealthy were lining up in the capitals of the world to be flattered by the artist's golden brush as he did, cosmetically, for the living what he had once done for the dead ... until no matter how elegantly he turned a painted cheek, the other face underneath would begin to ooze through, and he would pile white on white on white, each portrait more dazzling in its technical purity than the last, so that looking into it was like looking into an ice crystal, but now, no matter how thickly he piled his paint, or how skilfully he banked it, the hot black faces of putrefaction ate like acid through the drifts ... the faces those beautiful faces would soon become ... *what's the use? oh, what's the use? what's the use? what's the use? what's the use?* The tramp heard traffic. There was spittle on his mouth. The grave smelt acrid, defiled by fear. He downed his last bottle of Derby, holding it so tight his hands ached, sucking on the glass mouth long after it was empty. He laughed, a sound beginning in a sour belly but erupting up into his throat in harsh relief. Others drank to forget. The tramp drank to remember, to put a pitchfork into the eyes of his visions so they'd leave him alone for a while.

He lifted the green matting.

Daylight struck him in the eye. He recoiled. He lay back, panting, in the grave, recovering himself.

He got up on one knee—still unsteady—and yawned, as if trying to convince himself he was just waking up for the day.

He arose, melodramatically, from the grave, his coat in a cone like the cape of Dracula, making a mockery of the last of his nightmares.

The tramp limped heavily, hastily, to the exit of the cemetery, putting distance between himself and his nest of bad dreams, tipping his hat to the groundskeeper, forgetting it was on the end of John WORTHINGTON's marble finger.

He retraced his steps along Bloor Street, towards Yonge, feeling lighter and better, but not yet ready to go home. On impulse, he turned up Park Road into Rosedale.

The tramp hadn't been in Rosedale for over a year.

It was a dangerous area for itinerants, full of high-laced widows with blue hair on the lookout for able-bodied men to fix screens at depression prices. They didn't ask either. They *ordered* from an upper casement. The tramp pinched his nostrils (and, to get the tone just right, his asshole): "My good man, would you be so kind. . ." And if you would not "be so kind" they'd set their bulldogs on you, or call the police: "Officer, there is a shabby man of quite distinct odour asleep in my sweet allysium. I should think, with taxes we pay, not to mention the danger to my pubescent granddaughter, due home from Taylor Statton. . ."

The tramp swigged and giggled.

He noted—with delight—that it was garbage night in Rosedale.

Garbage night in Rosedale had once been important to the tramp. He used to do all his shopping here.

He remembered now, through the rosy fumes of nostalgia, the anticipation of lifting a dinted lid as if it were a silver salvo and discovering . . . an antler? a broken peacock feather? the lid of a Chinese lacquer box? The tramp nudged an anonymous green bag, feeling an anonymous green squish. That was when people of the best sort packed their cans as if they were packing for Europe. Now, since Mr. Glad . . . Well, who wanted to spend an evening untying plastic knots just to find a few hundred pounds of potato peels?

The tramp turned from Park onto Avondale.

He saw an ebony cane sticking from a carton. He investigated. It belonged to a black umbrella of the Neville Chamberlain sort, with every spoke broken. He hooked it over his arm and continued up Avondale, enjoying the smell of cobwebs and rotted silk. That was the thing about Rosedale garbage: it had a bouquet and a patina like none other. Each piece smelling of the closet where it had hung a decade before being moved to the attic, then the basement, then the garage, then back to the closet to be argued over a dozen more times before being discarded. And then never in its entirety: overcoats with the buttons cut off, lamps with the cords removed, corduroy pants with the good parts cut out to mend somewhat better corduroy pants with the bad parts cut out. Rosedale garbage was for connoisseurs—a challenge of the best sort. You had to wait as long for a full suit of Rosedale rejects as for the finest Saville Row tailoring. It always came feet first, the trousers minus the zipper, neatly folded, and last in the can as if the discarder was trying to pretend—so as to make such waste bearable—that she was just packing it into a drawer for the night. Two weeks later, the faded jacket might appear, tossed into the can with the lid jammed on crooked, as if after tormented self-debate. Three weeks, maybe six, and it would be the ulmost-new vest, with the lining razored out and—lo, at the stroke of midnight—an apparition in nightgown and haircurlers, materializing to snatch it back, having just been told in a vision that there was a distant relative in Winnipeg who might yet grow into it!

The tramp passed an antique laundry tub, covered with a mended linen cloth. He waited discreetly for a woman in a babushka to pass, for that was another thing you had to watch about Rosedalers—they frequently went around disguised as their own cleaning persons and gardeners. In fact, the greater their prosperity the more they felt obliged to hide it. Let the Dow Jones rise fifty points in a week and not even old tennis shoes were discarded in pairs!

In this Rosedalers were opposite to their Forest Hill rivals. Forest Hill garbage was a disgrace! Whole sets of dishes with a bit of colour worn off from the dishwasher! Wrong-colour scarves with the price tags still on them! And the tougher the times the more Forest Hillers competed to throw out! Last recession, the tramp had to stop going in there. The profits were turning him into a greedy tradesman!

The tramp lifted the linen cloth from the antique tub with the tip of his umbrella. He found . . . a single brown parcel, butler-tied, like a roast ready to pop into the oven. He undid the knots and discovered a dog food tin full of coffee grounds! Chuckling, the tramp exchanged the clean white cord on the parcel for the frayed one holding up his trousers. He retied the parcel, as if for resale, recalling another Rose-

dale Axiom of Discard: the larger the house, the more consti-
pated its head and bowels and, hence, the smaller the pile of
garbage. With one exception: when a house changed title to
someone not a relative then the new owner felt obliged to
purge.

The tramp turned from Avondale onto Rosedale Road and
shortly thereafter found himself confronted by just such a
purge: trunks, bags, cartons, heaped to the size of a modest
dwelling! He picked through the lot with the spike of his umbrella, wielding it from his wrist like the Count of Montecristo his sword. He turned up a set of frayed white cuffs, a
pair of powdery kid gloves, a battered art portfolio and one
mouldy spat. The tramp put on the cuffs and gloves. Then
reaching into an inner pocket and imagining the roll of
drums, he withdrew a second spat, estranged brother of the
first, and a collapsible top hat. He put these on.

The tramp strutted along Crescent Road toward the bright
lights of Yonge Street, enjoying the sprightly ra-ta-tat of his
umbrella as it struck the pavement. Posing at the entrance to
the Rosedale subway station like John Barrymore under a
Broadway marquee, he checked his pawnticket and then,
more furtively, the change in his pocket: $2.40. Just enough
to make a one-drink assault on one of the city's snootier—
and darker—restaurant-bars! The tramp hadn't done that in
. . . how long? Over three years!

He crossed Yonge Street, chortling to himself, already sa-
vouring the high point in the drama when the maitre d'—his
nose twitching through the smoke and garlic of his cut-above
establishment—begins to suspect that he has not just seated
the Prince of Wales *hee hee hee!*

A small van drew up beside the tramp and stalled in the
traffic with one of its doors flapping. How could the tramp
resist? He stepped nimbly inside and seated himself on a
packing case as if it were the jumpseat of a Rolls Royce.

The van turned left on Bloor and sped east to—*small
world!*—Hunter Street. It parked at a defunct travel bureau,
with its sidewalk a litter of cartons and travel posters, four
doors down from the Candy Factory.

The tramp slipped from the van. He crossed the street with
a bouyant *ra-tat-tat* to Hunter Park. The fountain, with its
twitter of sparrows, looked cool and inviting. What better
place to dally till the sun went down than his own front
yard?

The tramp uncapped his spell-blinder gin. It was still too early for fashionable drinking, but not, perhaps, for the *unfashionable* sort?

He swigged, holding the raw liquid in his mouth, enjoying the suck and burn.

He looked for his chalk drawing: It wasn't there. *How fleeting is fame!* He reached in sudden recollection into his pocket and drew out the suede change purse ... *soft and warm and creamy with a pink-silk lining*. He thumbed it, playing with the tight silver clasp ... thinking of an old-maid school teacher he once got three fingers up inside before she fainted in gratitude *hee hee hee!*

The tramp folded his hands over his chest with his thumbs inserted in the change purse.

He dozed in the last brassy rays of sunlight.

He dreamt about . . . the little white dog.

He dreamt the little white dog was waiting for him, tail wagging, at his slimy sewer hole. He dreamt he was fondling the little white dog, *nice doggie doggie doggie,* nudging him, with an indulgent finger, behind the cocked ears . . . stroking him down his bony ribcage . . . patting the narrow flanks and feeling the thin hide quiver with requited happiness.

He dreamt he was drawing the little white dog between his knees, squeezing inwards with his kneecaps till he could feel the jump of a pulse between his thighs.

He dreamt he was tickling the little white dog, down the long velvet line of his throat with one hand.

He dreamt he was undoing the white cord of his trousers with the other.

Now he was slipping the cord around the neck of the little white *nice doggie doggie dog. . . .* Now he was tightening the cord, twisting it, drawing back the head of the little white dog, feeling the ripple of tendons and the drool of saliva from the silky jaws as the little white dog gasped for life and protested death, his paws paddling the empty air.

He dreamt—breathing heavily now—that he was reaching forward with one hand and breaking the paws of the little white dog, first the right and then the left.

He dreamt—feeling violence surge up through his cock, now—that he was pressing himself against the back of the little white dog. He dreamt he was taking a knife and plunging it deep into the bowels of the little white dog, with blood spurting from both ends as he imprisoned the little white dog against the thrash of his own convulsions.

He dreamt he was burying his cock to the root in the blood and excrement of the little white dog, riding each shudder of death as it heaved through the frail, still-disbelieving body ... feeling the ribs cave and crack as he thrust and gasped his way to a climax, his muzzle of fingers denying the agonized beast the relief of his own death rattle ... the tail still wagging in hopes of finding love and succour, if only he could get through this last cruel line of traffic to the other side of the road.

The tramp was flying, now, with his forked coat stretched wide to catch the breeze and his curved yellow beak deep into the gurgling carcass of the little white dog. He carried the little white dog to a spit of black rocks, washed by the ocean. He dropped the little white dog. He watched the body impale on black shards, as sharp as spears. He saw the waves boil and eddy around the body of the little white dog, churning to wine, crested with pink foam.

The tramp swooped low over the little white dog, tearing carrion from the chest cavity of the little white dog with his curved yellow beak, sucking up the entrails of the little white dog, gorging on the little white dog ... except that now it is *not* the little white dog. Now it is the little white lady.

The tramp awoke.

He had bitten through his own lip. He was tasting blood.

His hands were locked in a fleshy collar around the gin bottle, squeezed between his thighs.

He unhooked them, with difficulty, cracking them, knuckle by knuckle.

The bouyant mood of the afternoon was gone. The regurgitation of his past had left the tramp dissatisfied. It had not been *enough*. He felt the need for an act of profit and violence—something to separate him from the smug security of the life he had been leading. Another escape from India.

The tramp looked at the creamy change purse.

He looked across the street to the Candy Factory. He looked up at an oval window, fluttering with organdy like a frilly nightgown.

The tramp opened the change purse.

He drew out a small scroll: "To the Artist—I have an unfinished portrait in need of talented completion. . . . P.S. Please bring samples of your work."

The tramp snorted: *In lieu of one decaying British colonel?* He rolled his black eye across the street to the pile of rubbish outside the defunct travel bureau, then scowled toward the horizon. Thunderheads were collecting. The air twitched with undischarged electricity. The storm he had predicted was certainly coming.

Humming to himself, the tramp washed his hands like a surgeon, in the fountain of Hunter Park.


Mary Moon sat in the sultry loft, feeling shadows creep up on her from all four windows.

She was listening to the tick of the clock.

She was listening to the drip of a tap.

She was listening to the rattle of the wind.

She was listening to her own heartbeat.

Mary assured herself that the artist would not come, even that he did not exist—that she had invented him as she did everything else. Afterall, hadn't the chalk drawing disappeared by the time she had gone back to look for it? Could that have happened in a single day's downpour?

What's more, even if the artist *did* exist, chances were good he would never find her note.

What's more, even if he *did* find her note, chances were *better* he would never accept her invitation. He was an itinerant, *a common tramp.* By now he was probably a hundred miles away, in a different city.

Mary looked at the mantle clock: It was 8.15.

She thought of playing her Victrola to make the time go faster, picked up "Pagan Love Song," then put it down again as too suggestive.

She thought of making another entry in her Special Accounts book—something about a common tramp—but decided that was too large a temptation to fantasy when she needed her wits about her.

She thought of peeking once more through the organdy curtains. She decided, instead, to light the candles.

It took three matches for three candles.

Mary felt the moisture on her lip heat up in the spurt of flame. She felt sweat trickle down her rose-powdered armpits, and the insane flutter of a pulse in her eyelid.

Mary looked for reassurance into the lilac-framed mirror in which three generations of Moons had practised their sermons . . . *seeing not herself but the blank-faced girl in the portrait on the other side, seeing herself as she had been when—*

Mary's hands flew to her cheeks. They were burning.

She must stop this nonsense, this confusion of the present with the past! It was all right when she was conjuring up stories for her account book but ever since she had seen this man, this stranger in the park, the other artist had been *intensely, intimately* on her mind. She had been acting like a green girl waiting for her beau instead of a down-at-heel artist whom she might be able to help with a commission. Mary stole a look at her mother's rocker. What would *she* think of her silly behavior? Then at her father's armchair. Or he?

Mary sat primly on her chair, hands folded as if seated on a church pew. She darted her eyes around the loft, taking comfort from familiar items freshly dusted and polished, casting her mind back to the last time she had waited for visitors and having to go all the way back to the manse, imagining herself, now, to be her mother, taking one last look about the drawing room before opening her door to nothing more menacing than the Woman's Auxilliary. She was safe in her own home, afterall. She need never open the door!

Mary's eyes caught, and snagged, on her table, set with her best china for two. She flushed in embarrassment to see everything so coyly set out that way. *What could she have been thinking of?* She would just forget that idiocy! She must have been daft—completely out of her mind—to imagine such a thing!

Mary heard a gurgle of thunder, like laughter caught deep in the throat. She glanced through the skylight at livid clouds, thickening. A storm? Her hands felt sticky. Her chiffon scarf clung in a gooey coil to her throat. She could smell the mustiness of its years in a trunk even through her rose sachet. Her thighs were wet. Her hair was stuck in kiss curls to her forehead. Her whole body, ever since she had exposed herself to that artist's single black eye, felt fleshy and cumbersome, not her own, the victim of sensations she hadn't had since—

Mary looked at the candles. She shouldn't have lit them. It was too hot. It was too soon. They were burning down.

She stood up, feeling wicker rip from the flesh between silk stocking and silk pants. She pinched out the candles, her thumb and finger darting through the flames like a fleshy moth. She held too long to the last wick. She recoiled, sucking her fingers. *How stupid!*

Mary looked about her in the muggy loft. Now it was as if she were cowering in shadows.

She repeated: *How stupid!*

She started toward the light switch, then jolted. *A clang? a slamming? the outside door? the wind?*

Mary strained toward the door. *Another muffled thud?*

She heard it again—*yes*, in the shape of a foot ... one foot, then another, ascending her vestibule stairs.

She felt a clammy prickling.

She recalled a horror story her Cousin Annie once told her, their heads shivering under a pillow: "*Now I'm in your mother's room. Now I'm in your father's room. Now I'm coming up your stairs ...*"

Mary clapped her hands over her ears.

Why had she remembered that alarming story?

Why had she invited a stranger to the loft after her years of seclusion? She wouldn't open the door! She'd pretend she wasn't in!

Mary held her breath.

She caught sight of herself in the lilac mirror, eyes wild, features twisted into those of a gargoyle. *Oh—!* Her hands began to twitch. They flew up to her hair and tangled. Her heart was yammering.

Mary collapsed in a long exhalation of air. She began gulping air, moistly, hoarsely.

She heard two feet collect in ambush outside her door.

She tried to calm herself, remembering the better qualities of that other artist in that other time—the elegance of his swallowtail coat, the rakish tilt of his tophat, the debonair *ra-ta-tat* of his ebony walking stick.

It was no use: she could not get control of herself.

She put her hands to her eyes and pressed inward. *What is happening to me? Why do I feel so queerly? What power does this stranger have over me? Why have I invited a thief to my home?*

Mary heard a throat being cleared on the other side of the door—a rusty, phlegmy sound.

She felt her own throat parch.

She looked toward her mother's rocker, then at her father's armchair as if seeking instruction.

She looked at the porcelain doorknob: SHE WOULD NOT OPEN THE DOOR!

33

The tramp stood outside the loft door, cocky, confident, safety pins glittering like a chestful of medals. He could hear breathing, thick and wheezy, on the other side, as if the door itself were a membrane heaving in and out.

He rapped with the crook of his umbrella—a sharp reprimand.

He waited, tapping his moist palm.

He listened. The breathing had stopped.

Smiling coyly, he slipped the head of his umbrella inside his spare glove and nudged it against the door in a powdery caress.

The tramp listened again. The air stood on tip-toe on the other side of the door. He reached for the knob. He heard a swishy slither. He laughed. No mistaking that sound: *silk thigh kissing silk thigh!*

The tramp slid his fingers into the silky lining of the suede change purse. He licked the blood from his bitten lip, toying furtively with the silver clasp. He heard the fleshy rustle stop, inches away. He cleared his throat. He adjusted the new cord in his trousers. He heard the brass bolt slide as if through grease. He saw the doorknob tremble, like a porcelain egg. He saw it begin to turn . . . stop . . . then turn again.

The door cracked, one inch.

The tramp inserted his spatted foot and, ever so gently, pried.

Miss Mary Moon, Special Accounts, glowed in the dark like a waxen figure from Mme Tussaud's. She was swaddled in a flimsy white gown of antique lineage, slashed low to reveal milky shoulders and a slender neck, exuding the heady scent of crushed roses. The tramp smirked. A still-moist virgin all dressed up fit to kill!

The tramp tweeked up the corners of his smirk into a polite smile.

Mary Moon smiled, hesitantly, back. The tramp extended his smile into a friendly grin and slid on the wet ends of it into the loft.

"I'm so glad you found my note and decided to consider my commission," said Mary Moon, trying to sound both formal and welcoming.

The tramp removed his top hat and kissed her hand, feeling it tremble . . . tasting flesh. "I was so embarrassed to have missed you yesterday in the park. I was gone, but for a moment, to seek out a policeman to change your dollar, so we might complete our transaction. When I returned you had vanished!" He placed fifty cents in the scented palm he had just kissed. "Madame, your change."

Mary Moon blushed, folding her white palm around the coin. She took the tramp's top hat and umbrella. He removed his powdery glove, torn-finger by torn-finger, sending his one black eye scuttling like a rat about the loft. It reared back, ogling the table set for two: *complications?*

He handed his hostess his gloves but retained his art portfolio. "I see I had better keep this and be brief, since you are expecting company."

"I?" Mary Moon spun round. She saw the table, *a deux*, stammered, then blurted: "Oh ... I had thought ... that is ... if you have not yet dined?" She caught her lip as if hastily tacking a too-loose garment, and flushed from pink to crimson.

The tramp looked out the window, calculating. *Darker would be better, though not too late.* He shook his head. "I'm sorry, Miss Moon, nothing would delight me more, but I cannot accept. You see, considering my plans for the evening, I would have to insist we eat immediately, and I would not allow myself to be that rude."

Mary Moon smiled, a little tremulously. "But that is not a problem. Everything is ready, and I'm not used to being so fashionable as to dine much later."

"Well—" The tramp inspected the table. He rubbed his knuckles, narrowly resisting cracking them. "Since you are expecting no one else—"

"No one ..."

The tramp chuckled.

He gave up his portfolio.

Mary Moon laid it, along with his umbrella, hat, and gloves, on the brass bed in a dusky alcove. Returning to the parlor, again with the slither of silk thigh, she gestured to the table. "Since your time is so short—?"

The tramp strode toward the table, the thought of the night's work making him ravenous. He drew out his chair, saw his hostess hovering behind hers, and remembered: *Ahhh, yes, the amenities.* He slid with exaggerated gallantry to the other side of the table, head swivelling, as if trying to see what could be detaining the maitre d'. He seated his hostess, noting, again, the long luminous line of her throat ... delicately blue-veined ... circled in pearls. He assessed the pearls. *The kind a young girl might receive, birthday by birthday—probably real.*

The tramp seated himself.

Mary Moon lit the candles.

She bowed her head, amidst much fussy adjusting of scarf, releasing more succulent white flesh. She began to pray. "For what we are about to receive . . ." *Indeed, indeed!*

The tramp picked up his knife. *Bah, silverplate!* He hefted the candelabra. That felt better—heavy, like the kind used on altars. He tipped it toward the papery skull opposite, imagining he were cracking an egg. *Heavy heavy heavy hangs over thy head. What must this person do to redeem herself?*

A tear of hot wax fell on his hand.

He looked at the hand. It was shaking. It was a long time since it had killed. It was a long time since the tramp had felt that much greed . . . or that much compassion.

The woman opened her eyes—a filmy blue, as if she were looking at the world through a veil of her own weave. Not the sort of eyes with any hauntings in them.

The woman lowered her glance, seeing herself so intensely regarded, drawing around herself that coy vagueness too-old virgins use to hide from themselves their true intentions.

She reached for her napkin.

The tramp did the same, slipping the silver ring into his pocket—*a little something on account.*

She ladled soup from a Blue Willow tureen into two Blue Willow bowls. "I hope you are fond of chilled soup? I thought . . . something cold for a summer's night?"

*"Charity* is always *cold,"* said the tramp, so charmingly it sounded like a compliment. He smiled his reassurances as he added to himself: *As cold as chastity, and with the same generous rewards.* He hooked his finger, in sardonic imitation of his hostess, then dipped and sipped. He almost gagged. He was tasting—*straight*—the only liquid he despised: *milk,* with a sprinkling of parsley.

The tramp spat daintily into his napkin.

His hostess leaned forward with the anxiety of all great chefs. "Is there something the matter?"

The tramp waved a declaiming hand. "Certainly not! It's just that I wouldn't *dream* of taking another drop of *this elixir* without the appropriate accompaniment." He withdrew from his emergency pocket his spell-blinder gin, wrapped in brown paper.

"Ahhh, the wine," said his hostess ruefully. "The one thing I have forgotten!"

She fled to the kitchen.

The tramp laced his soup, then hers.

She returned with what looked like two eyeball glasses from a medicine chest. "Will these do?"

"But of course!" exclaimed the tramp, neglecting to add this particular brand would stand up by itself.

The tramp filled one of the glasses. He broke off a piece of cracker, chewed ceremoniously, and swallowed. He drank his gin neat, rolled his good eye and, smacking his lips, pronounced: "The *sunny* slope . . . a *vintage* year."

They clicked—to a "memorable" evening—and drank.

Now it was Mary Moon who coughed into her napkin. "Oh, dear! I'm afraid I'm not used to alcoholic beverage."

"A pity," said the tramp, drinking in the liquid heave of her bosom: *Yours is the sort of flesh that should be marinated in it.*

Mary Moon served the rest of the meal: Tinned salmon, which she billed as smoked salmon; liver paste, posing as *pate de foie gras;* roast chicken, social-climbing as pheasant; Jello caramel pudding tricked out as sabayon . . . seeming, from her disjointed conversation, to be dipping out of the compelling memory of the past, looking at him with surprise, from time to time, as if she expected him to vanish.

The tramp scraped back his chair. He dabbed at his mouth: "I haven't dined so well since I was in France!" he exclaimed, adding to himself: *In the trenches. . . .*

His hostess, giddy from the "wine," served him tea in eggshell cups. She gave him a cigar, celebrating the birth of some young scion he now adjudged to be of college age. She played "Beautiful Dreamer," "Moonlight and Roses," "Pagan Love Song" on her Victrola, her eyes pellucid with the memory of loves he was sure she never had. She served him brandy from Hunter's Connoisseur Cordials, six drops per chocolate.

She told him, in a babbling gush, about her father: "A passionate man of the cloth whose fires grew cold."

About her mother: "A woman of the most ardent faith, but, in the end, a bookend to him in bitterness."

About her sister Julie: "A great beauty and a great wit. Oh, how I envied her . . . in a sisterly way, of course!"

About her Aunt Elvira: "Quite a flibberty-gibberty sort of

person, my mother always said. She married well and then was widowed. Of course, it was *Julie* Aunt Elvira really wanted to go with her to Paris, but Julie was so busy with all her beaux my parents said I could go if I didn't neglect my Bible reading."

The tramp watched the lick of fire across the humid breasts and the beat of a pulse at the base of the shadowy throat. He watched his companion fan herself with an old Parisian menu from which she fancied she had taken the evening's dinner. He watched the smoky trail of her scarf, back and forth through the flame. He listened to the grumble of thunder through the loft windows, and saw the crack and sizzle of lightning through the skylight. He gummed the creamy suede purse under the table. He was becoming restless. It was time for the night to reveal itself.

The tramp let his eye rove to, then fix upon, his portfolio on the woman's brass bed.

At length she caught his direction. "Oh, but I'm forgetting myself in the pleasure of the evening." She arose—unsteadily—to her feet.

The tramp stood up, catching her tightly by the arm. He picked up the candelabra and steered her toward the bed. "My work requires space, and there is more room in here."

They paused at the bed, with the woman reaching, unexpectedly, for the candelabra. "I'll hold the light."

The tramp, reluctantly, gave it up. "Very well." He would play out the amusement a little longer, a bit of sport to recall on a winter's night. He opened his portfolio and spread the contents across the bed ... Trevi Fountain ... The Matterhorn ... The Eiffel Tower ... all rifled from the travel bureau's garbage pail.

"Since I had nothing unsold on hand, I had to take these from a public collection about to go on tour," he announced, wallowing in gleeful irony.

Mary Moon leaned forward, nearly toppling. "How very odd!" she exclaimed, looking from one glossy poster to the next. "In my merry condition they seem the dead-spit of photographs!"

The tramp nudged her aside.

"I find," he said, gathering up the posters as if offended, "that nature seldom needs to be altered *or* interpreted." He ogled her throat: *Except, of course, human nature.* "And now—" he reached for the candelabra, his fingers fairly twitching.

"Oh yes, of course! You will want to see the portrait!"

The woman tottered away more rapidly than the tramp expected.

*Ahhh, well.* He waited, with patience, as she rolled a lilac mirror back towards him.

"The portrait is here, where I found it."

The woman turned the mirror, then stood in front of it, her back to him.

The tramp sucked in his breath.

He raised the candelabra.

He advanced upon the woman, his black eye fixed on her papery skull, already hearing it crunch.

The woman stepped nimbly from the portrait.

The tramp stopped, dumbfounded. The light had fallen past her onto the canvas.

He stared. He shoved past the woman.

He examined the portrait so closely his nose scraped the canvas.

He drew back.

Mary Moon posed, flirtatiously, around the lilac frame, wearing the same dress she had worn for the portrait, forgetting her age in the girlish pleasure of the moment, unconsciously, and disastrously, inviting comparisons . . . *stinking of rose perfume.*

The tramp scrutinized the girl preserved in oil and the woman preserved in powder. Even now it was easy to see the portrait was intended as an elegant flattery—prettiness coaxed into beauty; the sort of forgivable fraud an artist of talent might dash off on a romantic whim or to support expensive habits. Except for the blankness of face. Without the face, the virgin banked in ice was at least a wistful satire. With it—art for a price.

The woman played suggestively with her wispy scarf, trailing the tail of it around the neck of the girl in the portrait. "It was rumoured to be the artist's habit to leave the face till last and then to double his price. I didn't believe such infamy until . . . I was forced to deal with the evidence of my own experience!"

The tramp looked from the prudish twist of the woman's mouth to the plump breasts displayed like day-old bread in a cut-rate bakery. *Stupid butter-wouldn't-melt-in-her-cunt! Re-*

*fused her· "treasure" to the finest talent of her time then peddles it to a tramp in the park!*

He set the candelabra before the portrait as if before an altar and asked, mockingly: "You mean you don't like this *fine* portrait?"

"Oh, yes!" exclaimed the woman. "But it has no face!"

"And since I am *another artist* you'd like *me* to fill that in for you?"

"It *must* have a face!" exclaimed the woman, drawing herself up with what she imagined to be dignity. "I have snapshots you can consult for a likeness. That is ... *if* we can come to terms on your talent and the price."

The tramp burst into raucous laughter. "What if my price and my talent are the same?"

"The same?"

"As the *other* artist's." The tramp prodded the woman with his black eye. "The same price you have been offering all evening on a platter of coyness and hypocrisy."

"Sir!" The woman, shocked, gathered up her skirts, the picture of Wronged Virtue.

The tramp laughed in her face.

The woman, losing conviction, fluttered like a frightened moth caught out in a storm.

The tramp pierced her with his black eye.

He cracked his hands, knuckle by knuckle.

He advanced on the woman, explaining casually, reasonably, "If you want to get your face from me you will have to accept my vision."

He ground his single barbed black eye into her gelatinous blue ones. "Do you know where I get my vision, eh? I get it from the *hate* in the eyes of corpses, covered in twitching blueflies, that I sold back to their relatives. I get it from the *greed* in the eyes of the rats who beat me to my profits."

The tramp reached for the woman's scarf.

He wadded the end, then drew it towards himself, slowly, sinuously, sugaring his voice as he shortened the distance between them.

"Do you know where I get my vision of you, eh? I get it from all the whores I've known, their legs spread thick with honey to catch gold coins!"

He put his hand on the woman's throat, *warm and squishy.* He wrapped his fingers around it, feeling a pulse leap and the quickening of her fear.

"Do you think *you* are any better than the other whores just because you haven't got your price yet?"

He shoved the woman against the back of a wing chair and began rubbing his body against hers, enjoying the gasp and quiver of her mounting terror, still speaking lightly persuasively, into the incredulous eyes.

"Listen, whore! When you have seen as many corpses as I, copulating in death—the good with the bad, the wise with the stupid—their rotting cocks in each other's ear, you know where a lusty man sticks his cock while he's waiting his turn to die doesn't much matter, eh?"

He brought his knee up between her legs, feeling silk stockings . . . rubber garter . . . sticky flesh.

"Where would you have *me* stick *mine*, eh? In a *pig's* backside? In a *nun's* cunt-of-Christ? In a *virgin's* silk purse tricked out in chiffon with a tight silver clasp?"

The tramp forced one of his hands down the woman's dress. He brought forth a pulpy breast and squeezed.

The woman, gasping, tried to wrench her shoulder free of his other hand.

The tramp, chortling, pressed his lower body more tightly against her, forcing the air up from her lungs, forcing her to stop struggling.

"I have had them all," he gloated, paddling the woman's breast with thumb and finger, playing with her pearls, rolling and pinching a nipple in roughened fingers and feeling his mouth go acrid with desire. "I take what is at hand and it is always the same . . . the crack between life and death, and the crack between one thigh and another, both the same. Death posing for a few moments as Life! False hope! So what does it matter, eh? The pleasure we take or the pain we give—*all the same! all the same.*"

The tramp was becoming excited, now, his hand working convulsively, now, his eye growing wild, now, his breath clotting in wheezy gasps, now, his voice rising sharply.

"Who screams, eh? Who prays? Who spouts poetry? Who laughs? It's just a fool's game, for a hole is a hole is a crack is a crack, and whether it's slippery crypt of a slimy cunt—both are the cunt of the Devil!"

The tramp felt the woman—sobbing, babbling, pleading—slump against him.

He opened his trousers, making a slow and busy job of it. He forced his cock between her thighs.

He stroked her with his cock, taunting her: "Pearls before swine, eh, *eh?*"

He pulled her head back by its silky hair so that her throat lay exposed across the edge of the chairback.

He put his mouth to her neck and bit through the pearls.

He spat out one, then yanked the rest from the string, spattering them over the floor, stamping on them and cackling: *"Pearls before swine!"*

He lay his mouth on the woman's throat.

He licked it, tasting salt.

He sucked up a piece of flesh, then sank his teeth in.

He nursed on blood.

The woman, clawing and kicking, yanked herself free.

She dashed across the room to the other side of the table.

She cowered behind the table.

The tramp confronted her between the table and the door.

Now the tramp unknotted the cord of his trousers.

The woman screamed.

She reached for a breadknife just as the tramp—one move ahead—yanked the cloth from the table. The bones of their feast clattered to the floor.

The tramp advanced upon the woman, holding the cord of his trousers, taut, before him, his cock sturdily erect, humming "Pagan Love Song."

The woman, her hands over her face, began to pray.

The tramp mocked her: "Thank you, O Lord for what we are about to receive." He sneered: *"Pah!* It's always the same! Those who do the least with their lives always make the biggest fuss about losing them."

The tramp kicked aside the table.

He lurched toward the woman, crushing cups like eggshells under his heels.

The woman darted past him, but slipped on a pearl.

He stepped on the end of her chiffon scarf, sending her sprawling.

He wrapped the cord around her neck, drawing it tight enough to make her choke.

He dragged her back to the bed.

He pushed her onto the bed with his spatted foot.

He picked up his umbrella and pressed the stiletto between her breasts, leaning upon it until she was forced to stop struggling or die.

She looked at him with terrified eyes, the vagueness torn from them . . . a deep and desperate blue.

The tramp, once again humming "Pagan Love Song," picked and prodded her with the spike of his umbrella, lifting a frill here and nudging an armpit there as if sorting through a heap of garbage for something of value.

He lifted her skirt and forced apart her legs.

He jammed the point of the umbrella between her legs, and pushed until she flinched.

He twirled the umbrella, asking politely, conversationally, "Tell me, when you were a romantic young girl and dreamt about such things, did you ever imagine that your *first* lover, and your *last*, might be an *umbrella?*"

The tramp, laughing, pressed upon the crook of the umbrella. "Well, what are you waiting for, *whore? Plead* with it. *Beg* it for mercy! Tell it your long record of Virtue Unrewarded. Maybe it understands appeasement *hee hee hee!*"

The woman opened her mouth as if to speak.

The tramp, suddenly angry, yanked the umbrella from between her thighs. Glowering, he forced it into her mouth. "Shut up, *whore!* My step-brother Anatole's first sexual experience was with a bayonet stuck up his rectum for spying. Why should *you* demand more consideration of life, for, let us say, *not* spying?"

The woman choked and gagged around the rusty spike.

"*Accommodate* it," urged the tramp. "*Suck* on it. Tell it it *tastes good*. Tell it you *love* it."

The woman's whole body convulsed.

The tramp, infuriated, yanked the umbrella from her mouth. He hurled it across the room. "Whore! *Hypocrite!*"

He grabbed the flimsy fabric of her dress and ripped it from neck to hem in a powdery cloud of rose sachet.

He took a blunt knife from his pocket and, panting through a lustful "Moonlight and Roses," cut away her garters, her silk stockings, her silk pants.

He posed over the naked woman, holding his cock in his hands, displaying it, caressing it.

"Plead with it," he repeated. "Beg it for mercy!" He forced his hands between the woman's legs. He probed, with persistent fingers, for the creamy opening . . . the pink-silk lining and, with a deeper thrust, the tight fleshy clasp. He played with the woman's silk purse, first with one finger, then another.

43

"Ahhhh," he mocked, "it is as I suspected. Even now, when you are still praying your virgin's prayers to—St. Uncumber, begging for a beard? to St. Palagia, insisting you'd prefer to be boiled in oil? Even now you can get up a little bit of juice for your seducer, eh? Even now your nether jaws slather a little for their feast, eh? Even now, there's hypocrisy in the virgin's stringy prayers, eh? Do you still think—*whore!*—there's any difference between you and any of your other *Sisters-Inside-the-Skin?*"

The tramp scowled down at the woman: "Well, I'm *talking* to you, whore!"

He slapped her face: "*Answer* me!"

He struck her again: "I *demand* an answer!"

The woman, sobbing, managed to gasp: "You have only one eye! You see only *ugliness!*"

The tramp choked with laughter. "You want to see my 'beautiful' eye, eh? You want to address yourself to that? Well, then—*here, look*—you shall have your chance."

The tramp tore away his eyepatch.

A red and yellow pulp fell like a rotten egg to his cheek.

Again the woman screamed.

The tramp roared.

"You want my vision, eh? Well, you shall have it! I shall stick my brush up your cunt and paint your silly face with your own juices!"

The tramp fell panting, voracious, upon the shuddering woman, feeling his cock, swollen and hot-headed like a boil pumped to bursting. He yanked apart the woman's blue-veined thighs and rammed himself between them, jerking and tearing upward through weeping layers of flesh and blood ... feeling her shrieking body break juicily against his batterings into a thousand separate convulsions and flapping against him like the broken bleeding wings of birds. Her hands, become claws, were tearing out fistfuls of hair and scoring the sagging flesh of his buttocks as he sank his teeth deep into her breasts and burrowed more fiercely with his cock, as it throbbed with its accumulations of hatred, thrashing with the woman in a sticky cloud of rose perfume that streamed from her pores to mingle powerfully with his own civet effusions so that he was having to fight his way up through that stench to consciousness as if through waves of ether, groping for the woman's neck, wanting to fix his thumbs to her windpipe, to time the launching of Mary Moon into outer space with the hot-pissings of pus and poison from his cock, the way he had launched the British Colonel *hee hee hee hee hee hee hee hee hee hee hee hee hee hee hee hee hee*.

The tramp climaxed in a spew of high-wire laughter . . . *but something wrong, something wrong.* No matter how zealously he squeezed his thumbs, this squishy fleshbag of unfulfilled hopes and dreams still clung to life, clawing, spitting, spuming, utterly refusing to give up the ghost, as if her whole life had been pointed to this moment, with her voice forcing its way up to him through a wheezy cloud of rose-scented ether, that shimmered round her, incandescent, like a silvery shroud gaining substance as, in some last resurgence of energy, she addressed his ruined eye, staring into the milky centre of it as if into a crystal ball, saying she had just had a vision! a vision of the future! saying she and the tramp were the perfect coupling, the one made out of the bowels of the earth, the other from the clouds in the loft! saying together—with her faith and his knowing cynicism—they could occupy the loft and save the Candy Factory!

*What? what? a challenge? a challenge?* The woman was crazy—hallucinating! Who, in her last moments on this earth, did she think she was? Who did she think *he* was? Was she trying to appeal to his sense of the absurd, or, worse, to his finer instincts? At least, *hee hee hee* she didn't pule about visiting leper colonies, the way of the British colonel!

The tramp afixed his hands more determinedly around the woman's throat and began to press.

"Look!" she gasped. "Look in my Special Accounts book! I have it all worked out—a program of modest miracles, *human* miracles, the very thing you have soured on!"

The tramp choked back a chestful of phlegmy laughter. The woman was a natural comedian, *but not good enough, not good enough!*

He felt his ruined eye twitch, as it hadn't done in a decade. For a moment, he was tempted . . .

# 3. Daphne & Danny

Daphne Foster darted about Danny's teakwood bedroom packing her beachbag for the Hunter picnic: suntan lotion, sunglasses, orange bikini, beach towel.

Daphne wasn't used to living in an apartment, cut off from the changes of season. Here it was the beginning of August and she hadn't had summer yet!

She thought wistfully of her parents' home on Vancouver Island—mountains instead of highrise, mist instead of smog, an ocean instead of a polluted lake, a breeze instead of air-conditioning. *Ahh, well.* She fingered the frayed Air Canada ticket in her sundress pocket and felt a bittersweet stirring ... *soon enough.*

Daphne could hear Danny singing "Coke—it's the *re-al* thing" at the top of his lungs in the shower—a careless bachelor taking the waters. Quarrels always turned him on. They depressed her. Daphne's parents had never quarrelled—at least, not unless they went down to the beachhouse and shouted in a thunderstorm. Maybe that was the trouble. They'd set too perfect an example. Anything less than cohabital bliss seemed a failure.

Daphne hooked her chestnut hair behind her ears and slapped Noxema on her face. Her eyes were puffy, her skin blotched. Hormone imbalance? an allergy? She felt the surfacing of a dangerous dread which she stifled. *Not yet, dear God ... too soon.*

A blast of jazz from the speaker over the bed jolted Daphne. Apparently Danny was out of the shower and in the den. Count Basie for breakfast again.

Daphne tried not to feel irritated by something she knew was meant to be irritating. She loved jazz, the blues, the classics, but Danny used music at the breakfast table the way some men used their newspapers: to shut out the person opposite. Daphne needed to talk these days, but their lives had

46

become one long jazz concert with conversation squeezed into intermission.

Daphne went into the living room to get her book for her beach bag. The black-white-yellow-red living room was a bachelor's showcase, the hard-gloss supercool kind often pictured in *Playboy* and cleverly sectioned off into areas of Danny's self-sufficiency: Danny's camera equipment, Danny's drums, Danny's telescope, and, laid out on the slate table, all the magazines covering all the expertise filed elsewhere: Danny's *Golf Life, Underwater Adventures, Yachting Today,* and yes, of course, *Playboy*.

The room was not just a showcase, it was a fortification.

Daphne had discovered that after she had framed a charcoal drawing she had done of Danny and presented it to him for his birthday. Danny had seemed pleased, even enthusiastic, and they had made a big thing of hanging it. A week later, the drawing had come down. When Daphne asked about it, Danny had replied, in a casual voice through which barbed wire had been strung, that he sort of liked the room just as it was.

Daphne picked up *The King Must Die*, lying face down on the polar bear rug by the fireplace. Hidden under it, like dust tucked under a carpet, she found her Matinees, a bookmark of wildflowers, a glass ashtray, and one cigarette burned to the cork. These were the only things of Daphne's in the room and, typically, the only things out of place. Danny and Exclusive Valet Service managed to wipe out every trace of her almost as she was happening. It was eerie, like walking on a beach and never leaving footprints. That messy little pile on the rug amounted, in context, to almost a cult of personality for Daphne. *A sandcastle waiting for the first lap of Tide to wash it out to sea.*

Daphne lit a cigarette, and slipped the pack into her pocket beside the plane ticket. At least when the time came, she could move around Danny's apartment in fifteen minutes with her eyes closed and pick up everything she owned. Most of her belongings were still in cartons in Danny's locker. That depressed Daphne. It was her nature to surround herself with her past and her present in a happy jumble. She thought, with homesickness, of her room in Victoria, filled with souvenirs from kindergarten to college. She thought, with a touch of the same, of the duplex she had shared in friendship with Beau Whitehead. *Their* place, even though they had never shared bedspace. The trouble was, Danny's apartment—and Danny himself—had seemed so resistant to anything he could construe as "invasion" that she had adapted herself like a cautious guest to fit in. That, she now believed, had been a mistake. She should have established herself from the start as a person with tastes and needs of her own, made an issue of what should have been obvious.

Daphne went into the kitchen—the only room in the apartment with more than a passing trace of herself. Danny, in his grail-like quest for the Perfect Souffle, the Perfect Boiled Egg, The Perfect Flan, had seen she was a good cook and had let her establish her beachhead here.

She measured coffee into his stainless steel pot—five level teaspoons, freshly ground, for The Perfect Pot of Coffee. She lost count, poured the coffee back and started over; lost count again, started to pour it back, then with a jangle, set The Imperfect Pot of Coffee on the burner, hating the feeling of martyrdom she found inside herself.

Daphne thought again, with a pang, of her comfortable relationship with Beau Whitehead. Beau, under his fusty scholar's ways, was a gentle person who had responded with gratitude to Daphne's spontaneity—the very thing Danny rejected. Danny had never understood her friendship with Beau, and she had not wanted to expose Beau to Danny's contempt by explaining. Poor Beau! ... Poor Danny! Under "Mr. Supercool!" he was a very old-fashioned guy.

Daphne opened the refrigerator, balancing four eggs, a jar of freshly squeezed orange juice, a half-pound of back bacon, and a quart of milk in her large competent hands.

The crazy part was she was pretty old-fashioned herself, about as radical as the girl in the Breck Creme Shampoo ads. In fact, ironically, that was why she had moved in with Beau in the first place. He had been her psychology instructor back home, and they had picked up the acquaintanceship when they had discovered each other working at Hunter's. Beau was looking for someone to share his duplex about the same time Daphne was becoming fed up with the competitive sex thing she'd fallen into by sharing an apartment with three girls she had met in Toronto. It was too much like the hassle she'd gotten into in college when—feeling sorry for the unattractive girls being shunted from room to room so their glamorous roommates could take advantage of the new male-sleep-in-rules—she had launched a petition for the reinstatement of *human* rights over *sex* rights that had so infuriated the "liberals" they had ransacked her room twice, put limburger cheese in her bed and obscene slogans over everything she owned—the same sort of "with it" gang-tactics the same liberals were cheering in the movie MASH that was "in" at the same time. Daphne smiled. Considering her notoriety as the Vestal Virgin of Waverley Hall, she was finding it hard to adjust to Danny's view of her as Good Time Daphne, Girl With A Liberal Past.

Daphne broke four eggs into a blue bowl, saw a blood spot on one, and, suppressing revulsion, discarded it. She added another egg, then beat them with a handbeater, adding water instead of milk to make them fluffier. She thought again about her mother and about the plane ticket. How could her mother have known? Was there some special intuition at work here? Daphne had been so surprised when the ticket had fallen from her mother's last letter. "P.S. Enclosed find a little gift from Daddy and myself, just in case you feel like coming home, dear." No explanation. No mention of Danny. Daphne would normally have sent it back, with a tactful thanks *but*. . . . Afterall, it was to be independent that she'd come east in the first place, though she missed her family like crazy. Instead—choking back tears that startled her—she had tucked the ticket into her trenchcoat and carried it everywhere with her, as if it were a talisman against some phantom dimly perceived. Then, the "phantom" had taken all-too-human shape.

Daphne turned the bacon, drawing back from a spatter of grease. Maybe she and Danny were just incompatible—or maybe she had gone into the whole affair backwards. They had met at one of Hunter's Image meetings, with Danny in the chair in place of Cy Hanover, and Daphne representing the P.R. department, in place of John Greenlaugh. She had been zonked out by Danny, right from the start—his boyish enthusiasm and his fantastic good looks had combined with his easy control of the meeting to turn her on, and being Daphne Foster, she had told him about it. He had been flattered, and pleased. Strangely, for such an all-round guy, he lapped up admiration like a starving puppy. They had had a few coffees together, then lunches, then actual dates, and if she was fattening Danny's selfishness by her obvious adoration, by playing it all his way, well, she had assumed that when he got to know and trust her more, things would naturally equalize between them.

Daphne now figured her big mistake was in moving in with Danny. She understood, now, that no matter what he said, he was the kind of guy who needed her to hold off on that one—probably even to insist on a commitment first. Daphne considered that sort of bargaining to be sexual blackmail. She was the kind of girl who had always had a steady boyfriend, and she had slept with two of them. Both relationships had been important to her, both had been pointed toward marriage; and although the first break-up had left the boy hurting, and the second had left her hurting, in both cases the person making the break had tried to see the other one through. That was Daphne's experience with men—friendship ripening into love, and love flowing back into friendship. And then, along came Danny. . . .

Daphne poured the scrambled eggs into a blue-enamel frypan, feeling a sad and ragged tenderness for Danny. She had had romances that had hurt *before* they got started, and others that had hurt *afterwards,* but she'd never had one, like this, that hurt all the time she was having it.

Danny was such a lovable guy—just like a kid, the way his face lit up when something touched him, and just as ornery when something hurt or displeased him. The hurts stayed with Danny. The joys slipped all-too-quickly away.

They were at an impasse.

Daphne had gone as far as she could, with dignity—maybe even too far. She had waited for him to catch up, but that hadn't happened. Either he didn't care enough, or he liked things the way they were, with him calling the shots. Or maybe he was afraid. *Fear.* That seemed to be it with Danny. He had this incredible vulnerability, but when you ran to comfort him, there was always that thud when your head hit glass and—the sickening sound Daphne thought she had heard lately—the sound of a malicious little boy laughing. Was there any way of reaching that kind of deep hurt? And was it still hurt, or had it hardened into a kind of showcase of vulnerability, a clever piece of false advertising?

Daphne understood a little of the source of Danny's aloneness: the betrayal he had felt when his mother had left and the long bout with polio that had cut him off from kids his own age. She had tried to help him find what barriers he could take down while respecting his need for privacy, but she had become lost in a maze of prickly hedges. There were too many conflicting hopes and fears there, cancelling each other out. Cries of "Help, here I am" through boobytrapped doors with pails of water overhead. Without her knowing how, or why, she had become the enemy, someone to be outfoxed and discredited. Now she had to think before she touched. To see what mood Danny was in, then to match or counter it. She had begun to feel as phoney with him as she had that summer she spent as a model for display ads: *Smile. Don't smile. Be sexy. Be the Girl Next Door. Look happy to see him. Remember, you're the little woman and he's just come home from a hard day at the office.*

Daphne was tired of being something she wasn't. She was tired of trying to understand Danny, of "psych majoring" him, as he put it. It all boiled down to feelings—either they were there or they weren't, and if they weren't, then better end things quickly.

Daphne buttered toast with short hard strokes, putting the lid on softer emotions. Her eye caught the blood-spotted egg, flopped over the drain. That, plus the smell of the food, hit her all at once. She sat on the chrome stool, her head in her hands, feeling the room go round. It was the same nausea that had caught her out twice last week escorting tours around the Production Sector. Then, she had blamed it on the noise, on the air-conditioning system that kept blasting hot air, on the all-pervasive smell of roasting chocolate. Now she would have to be . . . more realistic.

Daphne tried to stand. She was still too dizzy. Worse, she felt a crying jag coming on. She looked nervously at the door, afraid Danny might come in. She didn't dare let him catch her like this because she knew that—if he said certain things, looked at her in a certain way—she was bound to let it all come gushing out, and that would be a disaster. Though Danny never lost an opportunity to bad-mouth marriage, he was just the kind of guy who might now insist on it—a shotgun wedding, with *him* holding the shotgun to *her* head for the rest of her life.

Daphne fingered her plane ticket. Her parents would stick by her: no moralizing, no "my poor little baby." Just support, and honest concern for the very real problems she would be facing. Afterall, Victoria was not Hollywood. Or London. Or even Toronto. And she was not Mia Farrow, or Vanessa Redgrave. Her mother's friends—even her own—still expected a husband nine months before a baby's birth, and besides, morals everywhere had a habit of changing every ten years, catching out the next generation for the "sins" of the one before. . . . That was the stupefying part. To think of something as helpless as a baby, and to know you were responsible. *That* was what was hardening Daphne's heart against Danny these days—making her shore herself up against him with little grievances, like a housewife pinching pennies out of the housekeeping money till she had enough independence to get away. Because there was just the chance Danny would try to pressure her into an abortion, and then she would detest him for life.

Daphne put her hands, tentatively, to her stomach, prodding it, as if she might discover a head, or a foot, or an arm sticking out. She had not yet dared to allow herself to think of "it" as something with human personality, but just as an anonymous life with a right to be protected. Anything more was too dangerous . . . too painful.

She stood up. Breakfast was stone cold. She put it on a warmer, knowing Danny would notice, might even remark on it. To Danny, food that was imperfect was love withheld. Daphne felt a rush of tenderness for him. It was nasty to tote up his faults as she had been doing. She pictured him in the bedroom, still damp from his shower, his heavy blonde hair pressed in commas around his face, and she felt a deep yearning to go to him, to tell him about the baby and to trust him to see the situation through with her. She even started toward the door, but stopped herself, remembering last night, remembering their quarrel. It had been a stupid quarrel—the kind Danny loved, diversionary, a smokescreen, the kind they always ended up having lately when she tried to raise an issue.

Daphne turned back into the kitchen. No, she needed to get away from Danny and to sort things out. Afterwards, when she wasn't so weak, so bribable . . . when the baby was something to be cherished, instead of a chemical mistake to be quarrelled about . . . then, maybe, she would let Danny know, through a lawyer, of his bloodrights. Until then . . .

Daphne put the greasy frypan under the tap and swished a J-cloth around it, letting warm water run on her wrists, relaxing her. She loved the sea, the sand, the wind, the sun. Maybe today—at the lake—she could talk to Danny. Maybe, if he showed a little softness towards her, she could throw herself on his gentler instincts, let him know what had happened without making him feel more was expected of him than he wanted to give. Either that, or maybe she would find the courage to pack and leave, cleanly, like a roommate checking out. Without hysterics. The way Danny would respect.

Daphne heard Danny whistling down the hall, obviously in a good mood. She threw her J-cloth in the sink. *God damn him!*

Deepwater Lake was a rough piece of amber set in whitegold and piney-green shag. For seventeen years it had been the site of Hunter's annual picnic. In all those years Mary Moon had never missed attending. It was the only time she got out of the city.

At 9.15 A.M. the first chartered bus arrived from the Candy Factory, followed by three others and an assortment of cars.

Employees of the Candy Factory spilled onto the parking lot, then over the grassy lip of the cliff to the sand, self-conscious in their Saturday personalities. At least a dozen tested the water, each announcing with the surprise of someone challenging a Wet Paint sign: "It's *cold!*"

Bimbo Brown, an ex-football lineman now in Sales, organized the men in the setting up of picnic tables and sports equipment.

Eve Martin, Mr. Hunter's senior secretary, directed the other secretaries in the unpacking of picnic lunches.

Sam Ryan, also of Sales, laid out the bar, helping himself, with a loud and happy belch, to the first beer.

At eleven o'clock, President Charles X. Hunter, his wife Celeste, and Basil Fitch, vice-president and head of Computer Control, arrived by Chris-craft from the Hunter cottage on the far side of the lake.

Brigitte Young, Charles' junior sceretary, made the first sighting: a fleck of white of startling brilliance which grew, as more and more eyes were attracted to it, into the graceful V-front and foamy wings of *The Happy Hunter III.*

The yacht nudged into mooring at the end of the grey dock from which a gnarled old man with a peg leg was renting red canoes. He saluted Charles X., immaculate in white ducks and captain's hat, then secured the yacht.

Basil Fitch stepped ashore in creaseless grey slacks, the same shade as his computers, nursing a scotch. He helped Celeste Hunter onto the wharf, her strawberry hair swaddled in white scarves and a floppy Panama hat, her laughter breaking like a shattered crystal in the sunlight.

Cy Hanover, head of Promo, and Bill Fontana, Production Manager, met Hunter at the end of the wharf, commenting, as they did every year, on the power and the beauty of *The Happy Hunter III*—the closest good taste allowed them to come to paying Charles X. a personal compliment. Other department heads wandered down to the carpet of sand in approximately their order of seniority.

The official party took up residence in white wicker chairs under beach umbrellas near the bar.

Young men of ambition, galvanized by the sight of power made fluid by beauty and sunlight, found opportunity to present themselves and their wives to the Hunters, feeling a thrill of well-being as Charles gripped them familiarly by the hand, while their wives eyed Celeste's "little nothing" French frock as if looking at themselves in an expensive shop window.

The picnic moved into its "activities" stage.

Sam Ryan, dressed in a clownsuit from Display Ads, tried to whip up enthusiasm for games among the "young at heart," and acquired a Pied Piper's following of spinsters of retirement age for Pass-the-Orange and a shoe scramble.

Box lunches were distributed.

The young people took off their clothes and drifted down to the beach.

The Gold Star club, layered in scarves and sweaters, retired to a row of canvas chairs under the pines.

The politicians, drinks in hand, settled in loose orbit around the Hunter party, presenting lean profiles and firm opinions.

The hard-drinkers bellied up to the bar.

Sam Ryan, for whom self-destruction was an art form, did his infamous impersonations of the Hunter brass, not neglecting Cy Hanover's paunch, Basil Fitch's duck walk, and Charles X.'s twitching moustache.

Charles X. Hunter, who traced his sense of humour no further than Queen Victoria, found occasion, shortly thereafter, to go down to the beach to give Brigitte Young her first ride on waterskis. Basil Fitch, easing himself into Charles' still-warm chair with the silent, padding motions of a cat, paid unctuous court to Celeste, who laughed gaily through thin pink lips, her eyes focused like shards of green glass on Charles and Brigitte. Eve Martin, getting a little too drunk with Sam Ryan at the bar, kept watch in the same direction.

Beau Whitehead, a research psychologist working at Hunter's on a government grant, and Morgan Jones, the black youth from the Chocolate Department, sat on the edge of the cliff, playing gospel spirituals on piccolo and guitar. Beau, his mind dipping and gliding with the notes, the birds, the wind, watched Daphne Foster and Danny Steele rent a red canoe from Peg Leg Pete. He watched Daphne lean back against one of the wharf supports, her orange beachrobe luffing about her tawny body, her face tipped into the sunlight, pensive and withdrawn as she had been so often lately. He watched Daphne and Danny launch their canoe with swift graceful strokes, the red prow frothily folding back the amber water as they headed into the lake.

Beau picked his way down a clay path toward the water, still playing his piccolo.

He picked his way through the gaudy towels, twined with oily brown bodies like exotic flowers in a mat of vines.

He piped his way along the shore, parallel to the red canoe—an impressive figure, well over six feet, his blue kaftan rippling in puddles around his ankles, his flaxen hair gleaming like an aureole in the sunlight ... *ethereal,* as if he might walk on water.

He stepped over a plastic cord, delineating the end of the public beach, and flowed along a rougher shore, moving easily over changes from pebble to slate to sand, his eyes picking up the glint of blue-bottle licked into gem condition, or the whorl of a pink shell, or the sheen of a black pebble as his mind translated sensations of touch into words of sensuous power ... *foamy* ... *tingly* ... *squishy.*

He came upon a reedy bay.

A red canoe lay overturned in the water, abandoned, apparently, because of a broken seat and leaky canvas.

He righted it.

He climbed inside.

It was snagged on a log. He freed it with a split paddle, trailing his bony fingers through the syrupy water as the canoe nudged lilypads, enjoying the shimmer and shimmy of waterbeetles and the surprise of frogs, still translating sensations into words ... *quaggy* ... *slimy* ... *oozy* ... *gritty.*

Wind riffled the sun-glazed water.

Beau watched the light skip from pucker to pucker till it was as if the lights were flashing in his own head.

He lay down in the red canoe, smelling of rotted wood, frogs eggs, silt, and decay.

He closed his eyes.

He felt the gentle rock of the boat.

He heard the *lap lap lap* of water, like tongues, against the canvas as it drifted from shore. He thought of Daphne as he had seen her on the wharf, her body swollen against the orange folds of her beachrobe. She was pregnant, he knew. He could always tell. It was one of the few times when he felt a woman's sexuality, the tug of her incipient roundness like a waxing moon on the fluids of his own body, making him conscious of flesh as flesh. Beau loved Daphne. He wished he could help her, but he was afraid of causing trouble with Danny.

Beau angled his thin white arms over the side of the canoe, feeling a depressing sense of his own inadequacy. He dug handfuls of muck and smeared them up to his elbows, thinking now of Morgan Jones, as he had been a few minutes ago, sitting beside him on the cliff, his hair glistening like caviar, his hands—large, spatulate, powerful—caressing his brown guitar as if it were the body of a woman.

Beau lay back in the red canoe, playing his piccolo in a sad melancholy plaint, then making the notes higher and more piercing till he was wrapped in an envelope of strident air, full of sharp silver needles of sound, imagining himself safely back in the garden of the Jesuits where he had spent the happiest years of his life, tending the roses around his alabaster statue of the Virgin, dancing barefoot through petals and thorns, his feet shredded but unbleeding ... embracing the knees of the Virgin, then sliding between her alabaster thighs in the red canoe, like a fish through the legs of a statue ... catching his silver piccolo, now turned to a fishhook, in her flesh, and feeling a sudden hot spurt of blood, then the prick of the other barb through the jelly of his own eyes.

Beau, trembling, eased the red canoe back to shore, unaware that he was crying.

Brigitte Young, wrapped in a mended Indian blanket, straggly ashblonde hair in wet hanks down her shoulders, her freckles in bold relief, sat beside Morgan Jones on the clay cliff, exhilarated by her first ride on waterskis and needing to set herself, unequivocally, against the lures of the bourgeois capitalist system.

She was soon, as intended, into an ideological discussion.

"How can you *not* care, Morgan?"

"I said I had *no complaints.*"

"But you're *black!*"

"So? That's a colour, gal, not a grievance. Why should I go looking for complaints when they don't come looking for me?"

"Oh wow! It isn't a matter of *looking* for them. They're *there!*"

"So's that piece of broken glass, gal, but Morgan Jones is not about to pick it up unless what he wants in his hand is a piece of broken glass."

"You're impossible! You didn't see Watts! You didn't see what was happening down there!"

"Nope." Morgan ran his thumbs across the strings of his guitar. "I did not, and *you* did not see what was happening *up here,* back home in *Bart*onville."

Brigitte tore up a cat's-tail, then remembering ecology, tried to replant it. "What was happening?"

Morgan grinned. "Not a darn thing, gal. That's my point. Nothing except living."

He sifted sand through his fingers. "See this soil? That's chickenshit soil, fit for nothing except making *ce-ment,* but Morgan Jones was rooted in swamp soil so black, so rich, so *beautiful* that throw away an apple core and you'd get an orchard! Cabbages grew twice the size of a man's head. Tomatoes split their skins from *smiling* at the sun!

"Then there was the river, gal—the Jones River, named after my great grandpa down from slavery—a-boiling with little fishies, flashing in sport, like it was made of silver, with Morgan up to his waist, a-tickling those fishies into his frypan, as many as he had a mind to et and, when the spirit took him, scooping bushels for the whole town to have itself a fishfry, black and white sitting down together round the swamp, a-frying up those little fishies on sticks and laughing and joking, with Pa making everyone right welcome, and Morgan playing his guitar, and Mama, name of Big Nellie, making their hearts real joyful with her song, whilst Old Bones, our black hound-dog, a-howled up the moon. I tell you, gal, Morgan Jones knows where he has been, and Morgan Jones *knows* what he has seen."

"Oh wow! In Sudbury we just had snow and slagheaps. How could you *bear* to leave? How can you *stand* this *shitty* town?"

Morgan chuckled softly, "Now you sound like Big Nellie." He mimicked, in a voice unexpectedly strident: "*Where* you going, boy? *Why* you going? *Why* you g'win to Peacock Town and break your Mama's heart, just like you was a white boy?"

Morgan pulled a scrap of notepaper from his jeans and spread it over his guitar. "Look here, gal."

Brigitte read:

Dear Morgan,
Mama is very sick. Dr. say she is dying. Come quick. Mama won't eat. Mama is asking, where is Morgan, where is Morgan? Jud is off work. I think the cow is dying. Come quick.

Pearl

Morgan pocketed the note, his eyes crafty, his voice as taut as one of his guitar strings: "All the time she is calling for Morgan! Calling for Morgan to do for her in the dark, like he was sitting there waiting to be called! But Morgan is too smart! Morgan has got clean away to Peacock Town, and no power on this earth is gonna trick him back, and *not* Big Nellie playing possum, like old Bones with one eye open!"

Brigitte was startled, even frightened, by the sudden change in Morgan. He looked hunted and haunted. It was an expression she had seen in Watts. Shivering, she gathered the Indian robe around her: *Oh, wow!*

Danny Steele steered the red canoe into the island cove, enjoying the resistance of the river current against his paddle. The canoe nudged sand. Daphne turned and grinned. She held up two fingers in a V. It was a message from their early courtship days, meaning: *Hey, hon, remember, this is supposed to be fun!* Danny grinned back, easing the V of concentration between his brows, but stifling annoyance.

When it came to pleasure, he was strictly serious. He liked to look good and perform well. But—like the people in the beer commercials he used to write before joining Hunter's ad staff—he liked to think he also looked as if he were enjoying himself. He didn't appreciate being caught out on that.

Daphne stepped ashore, an orange scarf knotted around her chestnut hair, a yellow towel draped around her voluptuous body. She flopped on the hot sand, like an Aztec maid onto an altar: "Ahhh, that feels wonderful!"

It was such a spontaneous act of sunworship that Danny smiled, spontaneously, himself. *What the hell.* The day seemed to mean a lot to her. They'd both been under a lot of tension lately, with all the end-of-school tours through the plant and Hanover dropping his bombshell about retiring early as head of Promo.

Danny sprawled on the sand beside Daphne, again like a fun-lover from a beer ad, but gradually tensing up, drawing his knee to his chest, and frowning again. Probably he should be back at the picnic right now, bull-shitting Hanover and sucking up to Hunter the way John Greenlaugh was doing. He looked at Daphne, basking like a cat in the sun, and felt a twinge of resentment. Nothing to worry about. Nothing to knock herself out for. All she had to do was to get up each morning, and there was the world waiting for her, sunnyside up.

Danny lit himself a Rothman's, without thinking to offer Daphne one. He got restlessly to his feet and began exploring the small cove—the slatey cliff in back, the boulders strewn on either side. His explorations turned to pacing. He climbed a rock spine. The water was clear and deep, with no outcroppings.

"Think I'll take a quick one!" he called to Daphne, stubbing his cigarette, and turning his back before she could think of joining him.

Danny dove, snapping his hands to his ankles. It was cold. Icy. Metallic. The way he liked it. He stroked to the centre of the river, feeling his skin harden and pull taut, like armour. Danny Steele, the Man of Steel.

Danny swam against the current, co-ordinating the rhythm of his thoughts with the rhythm of his body—the Greek principle of inner and outer harmony. He found himself thinking again about the head Promo job and, embarrassed to find himself so tight about it, deflected his concern to something else, namely, Daphne. Something had been bugging her these last couple of weeks, that was for sure. You could feel the air snap-crackle-pop around her. Then there were the tears (*sob!*) in the eyes, and the catch (*sigh!*) in the throat. He'd had a hard time keeping the lid on.

Danny considered the two possibilities: (a) she wanted to force a commitment out of him, (b) she figured the best was over between them and was planning to cut out.

Danny considered (a) the hook up ... little wife and mother....Let's stop playing house and *really* play house. *Was that it?* If so, she was up against an expert. Danny had been that route with a dozen girls—never so serious as now, of course, but he figured the tricks were the same, just played closer.

Danny eased his pace, reflecting. It wasn't as if he'd ever specifically ruled out marriage. He'd even come close to popping the question a couple of times, which scared the bejesus out of him, because it always seemed to have everything to do with Moon and June vs the Lonely Blues, and little to do with the girl he happened to be with. The truth was ... he'd liked a lot of girls—this one's sense of humour, that one's smile, another one's temperature in bed—but when you came right down to doing a paste-up of the Perfect Girl, Daphne Foster didn't even come close. She wasn't his type. He liked cool brunettes or cuddly blondes, not brown-haired girls, practically his own height, who hasseled him for air space.

Danny stuck his head out of the water, orienting himself with the shore. He saw Daphne, building sandcastles ... engrossed, childlike ... and felt a sentimental twist in his gut ... because ... no matter what was wrong between them now ... there had been something special about her ... some shiny quality—a radiance, a natural generosity—that had got through to him. He'd thought, even hoped, it might lead to ... well ... some sort of Grand Passion—all or nothing, the works. As corny as hell, maybe, but he had to admit he had begun to feel jealous of the loves other men had. Or said they had. Danny had never been in love, just low-key stuff. He used to feel proud of that. Stainless Steele, they had called him back in college. But since then one girl had melted into the next to the point where he'd begun to forget who was sleeping beside him, even calling a girl by the wrong name once or twice. *Hell!* A guy didn't have to be particularly horny to have that happen. A bachelor of thirty with all the stuff there was around, ended up making the rounds eventually, till it was the sameness he began to notice instead of the differences. That's probably why he'd let his guard down with Daphne, pinned his hopes too high. He'd begun to think, fear even, that love couldn't happen to him, maybe even that he was incapable of it, a "cold fish." Some women had hinted at that. A few had come right out and said it. Of course—Danny raised his head for a cocky grin in Daphne's direction—it was always because they couldn't understand why Danny Steele hadn't fallen head-over-keester for *their* special brand of market-tested packaging.

Danny tread water, matching the tug of the current with the resistance of his body, enjoying the push-pull tension.

No woman—especially, Daphne Foster—had any kick against him. He was choosy, maybe even a bit of an operator at times, but unlike guys he could name he had rules. No tramps—he didn't need that hassle. No married women—he didn't cut in on another guy's territory. No virgins—he didn't like blood on his sheets or dads with shotguns at his door. No professional virgins—he didn't mind investing time but not wasting it. All his women were good kids who knew the score, and if he didn't turn to mush at the smell of a certain perfume, or tie himself up in knots when they played "Love Story," well, he wasn't like some of his old buddies either, crying into their beer one month, then cutting out for greener pastures the next. He was fair, and he'd been fairer with Daphne than with anyone else, so all that "psych major" bullshit she gave him about "holding back" was just that—bullshit!

Danny looked defiantly towards Daphne, daring her to contradict him. She was wading in shallow water now, so serenely oblivious to his hectoring that he had to laugh at himself, wondering if maybe he'd made up the whole problem. In fact, he thought about rejoining her, but held back. There was still point (b) to consider: was Daphne thinking of cutting out *on him?* It confused Danny not to know something that important. He'd always been such an expert at assessing all the little weaknesses in a relationship that he'd never been cut out on yet. Once or twice it had been close, but when the chips were down he always got in—pardon, out—first, with the superslick sign off. Usually he jumped the gun—got out with a wide margin of safety. *What the hell!* He didn't want to be left with egg on his face, mooning around in bars. It wasn't the DGS style.

Danny flipped over onto his back, drifting in folds of water, enjoying the play of the sun and shadow on his face as the clouds passed overhead and—*yes, why not?*—thinking about how great it had been when Daph had first moved into the apartment. That *had* been a really good time for him, maybe even the best in his life. No big issues, no push-pull tensions, just a gorgeous girl, *his* girl, propped up in bed beside him, for him to touch and hold whenever he wanted ... giggling together, eating when they felt like it, making love when they felt like it, sharing the same set of experiences from two different points-of-view ... the whole sentimental schmeer. He'd even enjoyed waking up in the middle of the night to see her beside him, her hair in a shiny mass on the pillow, her face cupped in her hands, feeling an unbearable tenderness clot in his chest so that he had no choice but to kiss her, and wake her up, and make love to her.

Danny, flipped over, face down in the water, seeing the shaggy outlines of boulders and tree roots, and the inevitable beer can, and thinking reluctantly about the rest ... later ... when he had begun to wake up from nightmares, afraid she wouldn't be there. Then he had lain in the shadows, smoking, refusing to wake her up, afraid to let her see the tremble of his hands and the sweat on his face ... afraid to let her see the power she had over him. That was when he'd begun getting out of bed in the middle of the night, reading, writing a bit of poetry, turning night into day, puttering around *his* apartment, taking possession of it again, asserting his independence of her, and enjoying the aloneness of his former existence as something she had stolen from him, moving more and more to the nightshift, resenting the daytime feel, smell, and sight of her. *Her* cigarettes in his ashtray, burned down to the cork. *Her* wildflower perfumes undercutting his Old Spice. *Her* big thumbprint in the middle of his Crest. *Her* goddamned hair twisted through his clothes brush. *Her* body taking up too much room in his bed—large, heavy, tumid, too warm, always smelling of sleep when he couldn't get any. He had begun to feel overwhelmed by her, squeezed out, forced to throw up barriers, find pockets of safety, close doors, take showers, smoke on the balcony, play his jazz records, go out for cigarettes. Couldn't she see she was driving him crazy? If she was so smart, with her psych major insights, why couldn't she lay off occasionally, cool it instead of moving in on him at all the wrong times with her middle-class expectations? Couldn't she see he didn't want that twenty-four-hour non-stop hands-hold jazz? She was like an amoeba, flowing under doors, through keyholes, suffocating him. He should never have let her inside the door of his apartment. That was too much like letting her under his skin, because . . . to be fair, it wasn't anything she *did*, exactly, but just her being there. As far as the apartment was concerned, he'd been on his guard, right from the start. He wasn't going to let anyone put cutesy frills on things or leave sentimental boobytraps all over the place so that afterwards just walking from the door to the bed was like a limp down Memory Lane. He'd seen all that with the old man when his mom had left. It wasn't until Lil had moved in and burned everything down to the wallpaper that the old man could get through a day without a bottle in his hand.

Danny drifted toward the whirlpool at the end of the is-land, getting close enough to feel the tug of danger, deliber-ately using the images of the past to barricade himself against the present . . . himself, a small boy, waiting in stuffy cars . . . waiting in strange restrooms . . . waiting in chilly parks . . . waiting while his mother went "visiting" or "shopping," with always the shadow of the dark stranger beside her . . . in a doorway, or behind a tree, or in another car, with his hat pulled over his eyes . . . himself waiting, hour after hour, till one day the stranger came out of the shadows into the sun-light to stand with his mother, their arms linked, with his hat off, but with the sun striking his glasses, so that he still had no eyes. Danny's mother was crying now . . . begging Danny to come to her, to kiss her goodbye, to forgive her, to give her some sign . . . his mother waiting, while Danny, impas-sive, rocked back and forth on the courthouse steps, watching his shadow slide across his mother's stricken face, like the pendulum of a clock . . . rocking in his new black suit, with his hands locked around his knees, till his father came and carried him off, at first back to the empty house, but then, when he started to shiver and his temperature wouldn't go down, to the doctor, who said Danny had polio, and although everyone claimed there was no connection, Danny only knew that the one loss had followed the other . . . and he never for-gave.

Now, Danny started swimming away from the whirlpool,

experiencing a touch of the limb-cramp that was all that was left of the polio. He shook out one leg, then the other, disciplining himself against the panic he always felt when the numbness hit. Then he began stroking against the current, with the speed and style that had made him Varsity freestyle champ . . . feeling invulnerable. Whatever Daphne was up to, he was ready for her. If she wanted to leave, okay. If she wanted to stay, okay, but strictly on his terms. No package deals. No insurance. No options on his future. No Retirement Savings Plan. What the hell! The whole marriage thing was foolish to the point of disbelief. He had read thousands of contracts—some real dogs, but never one a tenth as bad. How could *anyone* decide to spend the rest of his life with anyone else, all goods, all sex, on the line? No businessman would agree to anything like it, and if he did, it probably wouldn't be legal. It was probably the only contract you couldn't break by mutual consent. You had to go to court to prove your right to get out—it was crazy! He could really get exercised about it, if he thought about it. Danny had never knowingly sold a customer a bad package, and he made a point of knowing what there was to know. He was called the Smart Money man in the Hunter ad office. He made the most thorough surveys and collected the most relevant statistics—none of this jazz about dividing U.S. figures by ten. What were the statistics on "happy marriages? *Ha!* That was a laugh. Most he knew were either nastyville or deadsville. *Hell!* They insisted you be "of sound mind" when you wrote out your will, but when it came to deeding your life away, they didn't dare throw that one in because it contradicted all the other clauses!

Danny, feeling very sound of mind and pleasantly exhausted, waded ashore, running his hands through the matted hair on his thick torso, then through his blonde curls, shedding water like a sheepdog. Daphne was sitting in a complex of sandcastles, putting on suntan lotion.

Danny grinned. "Man, that's great! You should try it."

"I did," said Daphne. "See? I'm wet."

Danny towelled himself, then flopped beside her. He reached for the suntan lotion, feeling a little guilty for cutting out. "Here, turn over. I'll get your back."

Daphne handed him the lotion with surprise. Danny was

not one to offer services. She lay, face down, on her towel, unhitching her bra, scooping her hair over her head.

Danny poured syrup on his square hand. He grimaced. He hated guck. It reminded him of the stuff the nurses used to massage into him in O.P. when he had polio. Even now, he could never take out a nurse without smelling the hospital on her. He had no real complaints, it was just the bad association: the braces, the needles, the disinfectants. All that white starch bosom making motherly *now-I-see-your-little-dickie* assaults on his manhood. It had put him off boobs completely, which was too bad. A lot of guys got a lot of pleasure out of a good set, but he was strictly a leg and ass man.

Danny transferred the lotion from his hand to Daphne's back and, warming to his work, swept it down to her bikini-covered bottom, which he gave a proprietary pat. Daphne— he was pleased to report—had a lovely bottom, really classy. Same with the legs. She was, in fact, like that goddess the suntan people used to splash across two billboards, with the gawking plebes in their tin chariots cracking up at the intersection below. Danny sighed. If only beautiful women knew what power they had, they would just look beautiful and never ask for another thing. He felt the impulse to lay a butterfly kiss between Daphne's shoulderblades, then to flutter it down her oily spine, but held back. She would turn around and grin. Or want to make love. Galatea forcing her real self on Pygmalion. His suntan goddess climbing down from the billboard and demanding her modelling fee.

Danny poured oil in the small of Daphne's back and smoothed it in circles outward.

"Madame," he said, in a voice as syrupy as the oil, "it is my pleasure to inform you that—out of the many *millions* of applicants—*you* have been selected to try our new Aphrodisiac Elixir, made up of the ground balls of ten thousand gorillas, and seven other ingredients, so powerful each has been trusted to a different eunuch. Unfortunately, we have no available statistics on the results of our past tests, since not one of our market researchers has ever returned from the field, though subsequent investigation did—on one occasion—recover a large lustful smile spread in exhaustion upon the sand."

Daphne turned and giggled, her brown eyes full of darting yellow lights.

"Madame," chastised Danny, twisting her head back into

the towel, "do *not* force me to conclude, from your Flirtatious Manner, that you would be willing to Give Yourself to a Man *without* the Elixir. I had thought, when the terms of the contest were announced, that we had made it perfectly clear that we were only interested in dealing with Attested Virgins."

Danny had meant his voice to be light, amused, but at an inopportune moment he thought of Beau Whitehead and his mouth twisted like a tourniquet, cutting off the humour. How could a beautiful girl like Daphne get involved with a jerk like that? He supposed girls had the same needs as guys, and he had nothing against women's lib—well, come to think of it, he did! What did those ladies want anyway? But, Beau Whitehead! That *guru!*

Danny followed a trickle of lotion down between Daphne's thighs, noting two black hairs sticking like cat's-whiskers from the orange crotch—leftovers no doubt, from the Scariest Shave of All. He made his fingers into pincers, but stopped himself. Miss Psych-Me-Out Sergeant-Major would say he was hostile—and maybe she was right.

Danny slapped the cap on the lotion. He washed his hands carefully in the foamy water, then dried them on the yellow towel. He lay beside Daphne, two parallel lines, close but not touching.

Danny lit himself a cigarette, and offered one to Daphne.

He looked up at the sky.

He studied a bank of clouds, shaped like . . . a sailing ship, yes, with the Wind God, blowing with fat cheeks from behind.

He could feel Daphne's eyes upon him, prying into his privacy. He could hear her say (though she would never dare) *a penny for your thoughts.* Danny shifted, uncomfortably. He wished he'd lain down further away . . . out of her forcefield. He concentrated once more on the sky. He was a kingfisher circle three times, then dive, coming up—*ouch!*—with a silver fish pierced by his beak.

Danny hated predators. He hated—the hospital again— blood. He winced. He felt Daphne's fingers, cool, on his temples. They were touching a scar from a hockey puck. One that she knew, because he had told her, had produced great gouts of blood. He knew, too, with resentment in which was embedded a kernel of gratitude, that she had seen the kingfisher and was reading his mind. He turned to her, spreading a glossy smile over his sensitivities—the beer commercial again—so as not to allow her an excuse to dig through to his real feelings.

Daphne wasn't looking at him. She was staring up into the sky, her tiger eyes sad ... limpid ... very shiny.

Danny thrust his hands into Daphne's thick chestnut hair, drawing her to him with his fist, so that her bikini bra was left, like an orange rind, in the sand. She reached her arms out to him, but he held her at bay, requiring her to pose, head coyly to one side, with one skein of hair tossed over her shoulder and the other curled around a polished nipple, like the *Playboy* pinups, wet-dreamed upon by college boys and mechanics alike, rejecting her but pretending it was a game, still keeping it light, as they say. Daphne turned her head away. He felt her body tremble. She was crying, with the tears sliding down her cheeks, making no sound, just misery overflowed.

Oh God! Now Danny felt like a heel.

He hugged her, feeling her breasts squash against his chest, and experiencing, inside himself, a quite delicious melting.

Danny comforted Daphne, feeling her grow quiet beside him, feeling the prickly barriers of fear and resentment dissolve in the flow of flesh and sweat between them, and the anticipation of pent-up emotions about to break through.

They lay, in suspension, in the hot sand, joined at the chest and thighs ... conscious of the sand, the sun, the wind, and the sky as a hammock of silky textures, holding them close, with much darkness and softness between.

He kissed her on the nose, on the eyes, feeling the pulse of each warm globule skip under the tip of his tongue, and the flutter of salty eyelashes, now stuck with saliva ... still holding back, but out of tenderness now, wishing to prolong each step in the slippery walk down into intimacy ... enjoying the discipline of his cock.

They cuddled, and stroked—hair, arms, chests— memorizing textures, admiring classic shapes and contours, forgiving, even prizing, imperfections, as something more unique, floating fingertips over exposed patches of flesh in caresses, featherlight to probing ... alive to the smallest detail ... stroking and stoking.

He kissed her, drawing her fleshy upper-lip inside his own, nibbling and sucking, then thrusting his tongue deep, exploring the broken smoothness of palate, the sharp gloss of teeth, the sinewy strength of another tongue, now copulating in fierceness with his own, getting the first taste of her passion.

They clung, rocking in heart time, in the gritty sand, his body now pressed against every inch of hers, feeling the abrasions of clothing as both a barrier and a lure, with desire concentrated on each other's mouths, feeding greedily on each other juices, he wishing to disappear into her mouth or to draw her into his own, feeling—outside of this hot red kingdom—only the anchor of her hands, one locked tightly in the hair of his chest, the other curled round his neck with the nails dug inward.

She bit his lip, not sharply enough to draw blood, but enough to jar him, make him recoil . . . breaking the circuit.

They clung, giggling, but with his hands, roaming her body, each one independent of the other, scooping down the long brown back to the barrier of cloth, then moving upwards again, tantalizing, plundering, teasing, catching handfuls of flesh, fondling and squeezing, nuzzling her with his cock through a double layer of cloth, exchanging sighs and groans, some merely flattering, some wrenched free, still joined at the mouth, but with their thoughts plunging downward. . . .

Danny thrust his hand down Daphne's bikini. He grabbed the two plump pillows of flesh and squeezed, feeling the scrape of sand against his knuckles.

He withdrew his hand.

He slid it down the front of Daphne's bikini, his face buried in her neck hairs, feeling his own sweat bleed from the hair roots. He felt the sodden clot of her bikini as a mitt around his hand, and probed the plush mat of hair. He plunged one finger upward, into the heart and pith of Daphne, hearing her intake of breath, as she moved in quickening pleasure against him. . . .

He removed her bikini.

He removed his trunks.

His flesh stood out like a thick white root . . . blue-veined and red-eyed. He lay beside her, his cock against her thighs, leaving its first slimy kiss. She opened her thighs. He put his hand between them. She closed them, a fleshy envelope, sealing his hand in moss and liquid velvet. He felt her fingers close around his cock, and the sudden fierce, hot pump of his blood against the tight fleshy ring. He felt himself flow into his cock . . . a fierce concentration of power.

He kissed her on the mouth, then the throat—catching his lips in sticky criss-crossings of hair—then on the breasts, sucking one as he felt the shifting, ponderous weight of the other.

He plunged his face between her thighs.

He tasted her funky smells and eager drippings.

Danny felt Daphne twist under his mouth, responding, physically, to the probing of his tongue, and the greediness of his lips, and, in fantasy, to his desire to use the complications of her sex and his mouth to play all roles, simultaneously, alternately, fusing the functions of tongue-breast-cock-clitoris, mouth-vagina, lips-labia, in a lusty orgiastic banquet which she served, responded to, presided over, dined at, by grabbing his head with her hands, kneeding his skull with her knuckles, pulling on the sweaty curls now mixed with her own, groaning, sighing, alternately spreading her legs and wrapping him round, begging him to stop while making it impossible for him to do so, pressing his head down and inward so that it was difficult to tell whether he was being devoured or devouring, whether she was being worshipped or sacrificed, either, all, none. . . .

He lay beside her.

"Danny," she whispered, "I love you."

"I love you," he whispered, just loud enough to be heard, the first time he had said it and meant it, though he had said it and not meant it . . . and not said it.

He supported himself over the length of her body, looking deeply into her buttery brown eyes, which truly seemed to be spinning, feeling conquered, overwhelmed, busted open, zonked out . . . all those things. He kissed her with fierce tenderness, bringing to her lips the depth of his own vulnerability and the taste of her own body, feeling an almost unbearable tugging together of their fitting parts. Her legs were spread warm and viscous with her frank desire for him. He opened her with the tip of his cock. He slid inside. . . .

He began the rhythm of love, withdrawing a little only so he could plunge the more deeply, their bodies shifting over hot sand, crumpled towel, slatey rock, icy foam, with each new movement opening new windows of flesh to the air and the sun and the sand and the water so that it was as if the four elements of the earth made love to them as they made love to each other, inside a sticky cocoon of their own desire that bound them ever tighter, as they shortened the distance between pleasures, till his cock was thrust to the hilt in her sucking parts, drunkenly jamming itself into insensibility, embedded in deeper and deeper probings until nothing more could be stood and nothing more could be withheld. He pierced the center of her scream, and came in a single hot bursting. . . .

They clung, his cock still firm inside her, themselves misty, groping back from the deep purple side of their rapture . . . astonished to see the sunlight . . . blinking in the hard glitter of the day . . . laughing a little now, playing child's games— breath blown in puffs in the other's face, a finger thrust into a bellybutton—reclaiming for innocence what they earlier had made wise with passion . . . the best of both worlds.

Danny felt his cock grow small and weak inside Daphne. He began to feel his sweat, gritty with sand, as a prickly irritant. He began to smell the suntan grease on Daphne's body through her natural juices, and he recalled—by the non-chemical taste of her—that she couldn't have been wearing her diaphragm with its obligatory smear of greasy no-kid stuff.

Danny withdrew his penis, slimy with its adventures, from Daphne's grasping, clinging parts, hearing the suck of flesh as their chests separated, seeing his chesthairs sticking to Daphne's body—her breasts, her belly, her thighs—as if she were a sheet of adhesive from which he had just been ripped, raw. . . . Danny felt an almost unbearable returning of himself to himself, stripped down, now, peeled, naked. He experienced his vulnerability, now, as loss of power. His tenderness, now, as loss of control. The love he had received, now, only in the loneliness it had churned up from deep within himself. The completeness of the fusion, now, only in the pain of the withdrawal. The love given, as something lost, drained off, taken away. He lay in the sand, a clam with an open shell, exposed to the sun, waiting for something swift and sharp-beaked to scoop him up.

Daphne leaned over Danny, and kissed him on the cheek, still milky with her love for him. He felt her breasts, heavy on his chest, and experienced an almost irresistible yearning to kiss them, bury his face in them, suck them, eat them, bite them, cry into them. That yearning brought an equal resistance, an equal revulsion that cut to the marshmallow quick of Danny Steele, the Man of Steel.

Danny closed his eyes, feeling the familiar push-pull ten-

70

sions build up inside him, as he played—below the level of his own conscious thought—with a choice (a) to accept this humiliating new view of himself as a frightened and needy human being, very much in love or (b) to deny the experience that showed this side of himself to himself.

Danny scrambled to his feet, like Adam who has just had the Glory of God stripped from him. He sprinted into the frigid water, then dove. He took a short hard swim, feeling the sweat and grease and sand and semen slide from his body, feeling his flesh stretch and harden.

He came out of the water, grinning, shedding water droplets like a sleek-haired dog.

"That was a pretty good screw," he said, still grinning. He gave Daphne's behind a jaunty pat. "Beau said you were a good piece. I wondered when you'd stop holding out on me."

Danny flopped down on the sand.

He looked for the beach towel.

He remembered Daphne was wearing it.

He turned to Daphne.

She was staring at him, her eyes large and incredulous, her lips parted, her body so still the water droplets shimmered round her like a luminous casing.

She let out a choked wail.

Then her shoulders began to shake.

Then her eyes began to overflow.

*Oh Jesus!* Danny felt one part triumph and one part remorse. *Here we go again!*

And he was right.

The quarrel, when it came, was the same one they'd been having regularly, fought out with heightened intensity.

i.e.

"I can't take this any longer, Danny. Every time I get close you slap me back."

"Then don't crowd me. Get off my back."

"It's *you*, Danny. You keep changing. I don't know where it's at with us anymore."

"We share an apartment. We screw. That's where it's 'at.' Any attempt to make it anything else is just you pushing."

At approximately the point where Danny would have slammed out of the bedroom, or the living room, or the kitchen, he began to walk deliberately, compulsively across the cove, feeling each step, each gesture, as unreal because of its very familiarity, as if he were performing in one of those

71

schmaltzy slow-motion commercials, but with him moving away from the girl instead of towards her, passing Daphne now, and seeing her throw herself to the sand with what looked alarmingly like hysteria, but striding past to the spit of rocks, forcing himself to control the anger that ached through his body, even managing to make a little swagger of it as he felt his feet take the first step up the rock pile, his chest unbearably tight, his hands in fists, his jaw clenched till he thought he would explode, climbing faster and faster now, as the commercial speeded up, and disappearing over the brow of the cliff, seeing a pine tree, stiff and unyielding, and heading for that, leaning up against it, well out of sight of the cove, and enjoying the support, the rigidity, the abrasion of the bark against his body.

Danny lit himself a Rothman's.

He smoked it, sucking on the end, them smashed it, half-finished, against the tree.

He lit himself another, chain-smoking, letting his anxiety gush out in a diatribe against Daphne because this was no game anymore, their little Play House was *kaput, fini!* He'd taken about as much as he could stand. Forget everything else. This was it! He had to get things back to normal, *his* kind of normal, *his* apartment, *his* life. It was the end of the Grand Experiment. Never again. Get her out, as fast as he could. He'd tell her about the duplex on Roxborough, say he had planned to give her the first month's rent as a going-away present. Hell! He'd buy her a one-way ticket to Vancouver— *he'd give her the whole damned airplane if she'd clear out sooner.* She should know by now he didn't like to be hassled—wouldn't stand for it. He just wasn't the type. He liked his privacy, his own things, his own way. *God, what a mess!* He didn't want to hurt her, just to get rid of her. She wasn't such a bad kid, just stubborn, far too serious—a drag, real ball-and-chain material. He should know by now: keep it light or take the consequences.

Danny checked his SCUBA watch. He still felt a bit shaky, but he'd been gone over twenty minutes. He stubbed out his cigarette and ground it into the pile, remembering how often he'd done that to Daphne's half-smoked cigarettes with his hang-up about his aunt burning up in bed. He sauntered to the brow of the cliff, hoping to come upon her unawares and to check out the mental and physical landscape, maybe even—a thought way back in his mind—play it cool, pretend nothing had happened, and see if she'd go for the bait.

Danny took it all in at a glance—the abandoned cove, the missing canoe. He felt a queer emptiness in his gut that began as hurt but exploded in anger. *The little bitch!* She knew he was going to dump her and she'd bailed out first!

Danny looked along the shore, knowing he wouldn't see her, then out into the current, toward the end of the island.

He saw—or thought he saw—a flash of red through the trees where the lake and river converged. He squinted. Yes, there it was again. He felt a malicious grin spread over his face—Miss Camp Winnowawa, winner of three gold medals in watercraft, seemed to be having trouble with the currents around the whirlpool. In fact—Danny laughed outright—she seemed to have capsized!

Danny waited for two long brown arms to reach up, right the canoe, and collect the paddles, enjoying the thought of her having to tow the thing back to the picnic grounds, calculating the distance, and figuring he could finish his cigarette and still pass her en route.

No hand came up, though there seemed to be a lot of splashing. Danny felt a touch of apprehension. He scrambled down the cliff to the spit of boulders—just in case. He stood mesmerized, rocking on the balls of his feet. *Had she hit her head? Had she taken a cramp, or another one of those dizzy spells?*

Danny wanted to dive, but all he seemed able to do was to rock back and forth. His legs felt paralyzed. He sat down on the rock, and struck at his calves with his fists. He caught another glimpse of the red canoe, bobbing and foundering in the current near the whirlpool. *Oh Jesus!* Danny felt a clammy and familiar panic. He closed his eyes, feeling the sweat run into them. He saw Daphne's face, shimmering before him ... the skin white, the eyes pleading, the hair the colour of the water with his shadow rocking back and forth across her like a pendulum. *Oh Jesus Jesus Jesus!*

Danny rolled himself off the rock, not sure, even as he hit the water, that his legs would work for him. He felt himself plummet, like a stone, then slowly his body seemed to straighten out, and he felt himself surfacing. His arms were pumping even before his head broke sunlight. He still couldn't feel his legs, but the current helped a lot. He couldn't see the canoe. It was around the tip of the island. He wouldn't be able to see it until he was almost on top of it.

Danny began to feel the numbness drain from his legs and the beginning of a warm pulse. He could hear—or thought he could hear—a motorboat. *Charles X. moving in?* They could easily have seen the canoe from shore. It was only about half a mile away.

Danny rounded the island. Now he could see the red canoe, overturned in foam, and the motorboat, just cutting its engine on the other side. No one was clinging to the canoe. *Maybe she was holding to the thwarts underneath, breathing in an air pocket.*

Danny dove, hearing someone else strike the water at the same time. The current was churning the water so much it was hard to see. He reached the underside of the canoe. He felt . . . *no one.*

Danny dove again, this time going deep, down among the boulders and the broken trees. Visibility was only about one foot. He clawed at hair and felt it turn to seaweed. He dislodged what looked like a hand from between two slimy rocks, and felt it pull away as a rotted branch. He stayed down as long as he could, lungs bursting. Feeling lightheaded he started to surface, trailing blood from a broken vessel in his nose.

Danny saw a flash of orange. He shot towards it. He saw a tangle of thick hair. He grabbed. *Daphne!* She grabbed him at the same time. They seemed to be struggling. *She must be hysterical!* He applied a lifesaving hold. She broke it. They fought each other, hand to hand, to the surface.

Danny tried to drag Daphne to the motorboat.

"No," she protested. "It's *not me*, Danny. *It isn't our canoe.*"

She pointed to another red canoe beached nearby on the rocks. *"That's* our canoe. I headed back when I saw the motorboat coming!"

Danny, still holding onto Daphne, wanting to feel the reassurance of her body against his own, turned toward the second canoe. Charles X. Hunter had pulled it to the side of the Cris-craft. He, Basil Fitch, Sam Ryan, and the old guy who rented the canoes were examining it.

"It's the one I tossed out, first of the season," said Peg Leg Pete. "See? No. 10." He stuck his fist through the rotted canvas. "Nobody could have rid her out this far. Last I seen she was down to the swamp with mud in her. One of the kiddies must have loosed her, and the currents did the rest."

"I *know* I saw someone in the canoe," said Sam Ryan, sober under his clown makeup. "Somebody dressed in white, like an old woman."

Charles X. shrugged. "Possibly it was the foam, Ryan. The sun on the water plays odd tricks on the eyes."

Basil Fitch tapped Sam's beer glass with the back of his hand. "Yes, Ryan. I'd say the foam, definitely the foam, old chap. And too much sunlight."

"I was *sure* I saw someone," said Sam, stubbornly, but losing confidence.

"You *thought* you did, Ryan," corrected Fitch, "and in the difference between those two statements, old chap, lies the universe."

Charles X. Hunter hoisted anchor.

Daphne and Danny paddled back to the picnic grounds in their red canoe.

# 4. Sam Ryan

Sam Ryan of Sales always took a pee in the Executive Head on Fridays. Salesmen and other low life were allowed to use it on that day because the cleaning staff came in on the weekends. Sam did it for his good old mom. She always wanted Sam to get a head *ha ha!*

Sam set his feet on either side of the urinal where Charles X. Hunter himself unzipped every morning, and let it all hang out. He relieved himself in a golden stream, rich with the Vitamins from A to E which he popped, like candy, to save himself from having to sweat it out at Vic Tanny's. Sam hated exercise, except *ha ha* for the workouts he got in the sack!

Sam flicked off and tucked in, then washed up at a sunken marble bowl, noticing the creaminess of the monogrammed towels as he wadded his and tossed it into a corner.

Sam helped himself to some Yardley's aftershave, as he studied himself, appearance-wise, in the mirror: red hair, a little grey at the roots but still plenty thick; freckles, blended by a touch of Man Tan; Alan Ladd profile, loosening a little at the throat.

Sam checked his gums. The tooth battle moved from the crown to the gums after forty his orthodonist had warned him. He pumped Murine into his eyes and popped an Anacin for his ulcer. He pulled in his gut and clicked his oxblood loafers. *Not bad, Sammy. Oh, you kid!*

Sam started for the door, then spun round, catching himself in the mirror with a fast gun from the hip. *Bang, bang, gotcha. You're dead!* Sam slumped, not entirely as part of the act. It was the kind of gag that looked cute in a barroom can, but depressed him when framed in executive panelling.

Sam pulled at his plaid jacket. *Was it too loose?*

He fingered his red tie. *Too loud?*

He cocked his head, uncertainty reflected in his pale blue

eyes. He had been what was known in the forties as a "sharp" dresser, and his clothes hadn't changed much since then: jackets with broad shoulders that buttoned low; cuffed pants that slouched down into a fake drape; large baubly cufflinks that his ex-wife Matty still bought for him.

He frowned.

Truth to tell, he felt a bit dated, with some of the fancydans they were turning out these days, but what the H-for-Hairy was a normal, virile guy supposed to wear? He couldn't go around in blue jeans and cowboy boots, like the weirdos in the stockroom; he wasn't thin enough for the British gentry stuff Charles X. wore, even if he could afford it; and he was fucked if he was going to wear those fag outfits with the cutesy wraparound belts and the pants so tight they strangled the balls. *Jeez!* He'd read some place the friction made you sterile. Sam leered. Provided, of course, you *had* the wherewithall to cause friction!

Sam fiddled one of the buttons that were always falling off his jackets, yanked a stray thread from a cuff, and reclamped the loose ruby in his cufflink. *And now, Much Improved, as they say.*

He stuck his thumbs in his waistband, striking a pose like when he was one of the Old Jarvis Street Jets on the make under a lamppost.

He squinted sideways, trying to catch himself off guard, the way a stranger might see him, or say, a discerning chick like Laurie Temple of Quality Control.

The thought of Laurie gave Sam a twinge where it counted, at headquarters. He relaxed his eyes from squint to heavy-lidded. Laurie was about to crack. He was sure of it, and nine-times-out-of-ten, when those cool babies cracked, they split w-i-d-e open. Sam had set her up at the Hunter picnic, real nice and easy, playing her like a goldfish on a long silky line. They'd had lunch a half dozen times since, always casual stuff like in the cafeteria, as if Sam just happened to be passing by. It was time—Sam was convinced—to really move in, sweep her off her feet. The trouble was ... where was the action supposed to take place? Laurie lived with a maiden aunt, and taking a dame like that to his own room or to a hotel was strictly a waste of time. Sam's eyes narrowed. He had an errand to do in the Display Ad storeroom for some kids from Harbord Collegiate who wanted props for a Thanksgiving dance. That was right beside Quality Control.

Maybe he could get her to go next door to Display Ads, and help him *heh heh heh* pick a few ripe pumpkins?

Sam pictured the scene. Laurie Temple, with that sooty hair of hers pulled out of its pins, banging her tiny fists against his hairy chest: "Stop it, Sammy . . . *ooooh*, Sammy, Tiger, *stop* it, I *love* it!"

Sam grinned, drunk on his vision. That was the trick with those tight-pussy broads. If you asked them, they had to say no, but if you took the responsibility off their shoulders, they loved you for it. *Ooooh, Sammy, you great big hunk of man, you!*

Sam braked himself. The baby blue image of Laurie Temple kept freezing into that of another "cool" broad who hadn't cracked under the heat of Sammy's passion. Linda the Lady—ice cream clear through, that one, from the frosted strawberry smile right down to the frozen cherry at the bottom. Sam should know. He'd married the lady. They had met at a Red Cross dance on the first day of a one-week leave, when Sammy was a horny young army buck, and, by the last day of that leave, Sammy, the kid from Cabbagetown, was so crosslegged with *promises promises promises* from the highborn lady with the silver spoon up her ass that he would have cut off his balls and handed them to her if she's promise to fondle them occasionally. Instead, he'd married her. Then it was still *promises, promises,* but now with Sam making them. All told, he'd got it once on their honeymoon and about thirteen times in the next twelve years: once for new drapes for the den; once for a diswasher; once for broadloom in the kitchen; once more for broadloom in the bathroom, *my my my, that lady had a thing about wall-to-wall;* once for a freezer (*ha ha* Birdseye would have paid a fortune to patent the unit she carried in her twat!); seven times in the spirit of self-sacrifice, and the other time when Sam had come home drunk and more-or-less raped her. That last had resulted in Little Sammy (she called him Cyril), who created such a bulge of sympathy on behalf of the Plaintiff that the judge had awarded him, sight unseen, to his mother, adding the house, the car, all that broadloom, and Linda's weight each month in gold, after a jury trial in which two female jurors shed real tears while Linda—frequently revived with smelling salts—described, with a skill a pornographer would have envied, what she had endured at the paws of her hairy perverted mate, adding details Sam wished his mind had been agile enough to think of, which only proved he'd been fucking her in the wrong place all those years. He should have stuck it in her ear, and got her right between the legs of her dirty fantasies.

Sam noticed, with bitterness, that his hands were shaking. After all these years she could still do it to him.

He lit himself a weed with a match from The Jungle, letting it burn through the zebra stripes into his finger before throwing it into the urinal. Then, of course, he thought of Matty. Sam always thought of Matty when he thought of urinals, matches, *or* Linda. They went together, like black and white, fire and ice, or two ends of a match—one hot and the other dead. He'd married Matty on the re-bound. Good old Matty, with a heart as big as Maple Leaf Gardens and a space between her ears *and* legs to match! She'd screw anything that came up the front walk, from the deaf-and-dumb postie to the neighbour's police dog. Sam had caught her twice with her pants down. Once, on their first anniversary, with his brother in the closet—she said her squirrel coat was so hairy she thought Burt was Sam and—*who knows?* she was so stinko it could have been true. Next time, the dumb old whore was so proud to be making it with a college student that she took pictures which Sam passed around to another set of Twelve Honest Men, who granted him a divorce, no alimony, though one guy asked for Matty's phone number and offered to help set her up in trade.

Sam flipped his cigarette butt into a john and watched it blossom into little brown worms. *And so, ladies and gentlemen of the jury, when it comes to plumbing, old Sam Ryan has had it both ways, hot- and cold-running women, the Lady and the Tramp, and though Matty was a piece of bum-wipe I'll at least say this for her. When I flushed her, she had the decency to go down the drain, whereas Linda the Lady just sits up there with her lilywhite ass over my head and shits and shits and shits.*

Sam helped himself to a Montecristo cigar.

In fact, he helped himself to a dozen.

He was standing with his fist in the cooky jar, so to speak, when Basil Fitch paddled into the washroom.

Fitch gave him a slack smile and clapped an avuncular hand to his back. "Well, Ryan," he said, "I'm sorry to hear you'll be leaving us, but I'd like to wish you all the success in your new job."

Sam felt his stomach fall like an elevator from the tenth floor. He lurched forward: "Huh?"

Fitch inclined his polished black head in Sam's direction: "Have I spoken out of turn, old chap? I'm sorry, I just assumed when I saw you standing there with a fistful of *our* cigars that you had decided to take that job they were advertising down the street for a drugstore Indian."

Sam caught a glimpse of himself in the mirror with the cigars fanned in both hands and his Man Tan looking decidedly garish, given the pallor underneath. He felt his stomach reascend and the colour return to his cheeks. *A joke. Not an execution.* "Heh heh heh!" said Sam.

"Yes," affirmed Fitch. *"Heh heh heh. My little joke kemosavi,* old chap. Don't think another thing about it."

Sam returned half the cigars to the box. "About the *Indian* job, Fitch. I haven't got it yet, if *you're* interested. Just auditioning!"

It was, technically, one flight down from the Executive washroom to Sam's office, but, psychologically, it was the distance down from the boardroom to the very rank-and-file. Today, given his ominous little encounter with Fitch, the trip depressed Sam more than usual.

Company Status, as reflected in furnishings, was as follows:

A. Antique Originals (founding father stuff, very elite).

B. Wood Traditional (top execs, up-and-comers, heads of departments).

C. Plastic Modern (assistants to A and B—reflected status, but showing the company, though traditional, knew how to be "with it," too).

D. Metal Modern (just making it—maybe up, maybe down).

E. Junk Castoffs (for discarded employees, looking to the untutored eye exactly like Antique Original, though everyone at Hunter's could tell the difference between, say, one dented wastebasket and another dented wastebasket, the same way as they could tell the difference between Charles X. Hunter and, say, the daytime janitor).

Sam's office was Metal Modern, with every allowable insult in every sub-category, so that—even with or without the cute mobiles, the joke slogans, the pinups, and his own hand-watered lemon tree—it was clear to all that Sam Ryan was not on his way up to Wood Traditional, or even Plastic Modern, or anywhere else that was up, except—he gave Miss October the finger—you *ha ha!*

Sam slumped in his metal chair.

On his metal desk was the thing that had sent him up to Charles X.'s can to pee in splendour five hours earlier than usual in the first place. It was a business card he had found waiting for him that morning. It said: Armond Jesse Shultz, PANAMA INVESTMENT LTD.—but, ahh, the way it said it! In gold-leaf script on vellum so fine you could read through it. There was no note with it—here, a bitter laugh—Old Army couldn't do more than sign his name. But the message was clear. Another one of the old Cabbagetown gang had Made It Big. Sam dry-swallowed an Anacin, with Vitamin B and C chasers. He and Army had sold newspapers along Queen Street when Sammy was six. Or, rather, Sammy had sold the papers. It was Army's part of the deal to walk Sammy home for a percentage so he wouldn't get beaten up. Later they had belonged to the notorious Jarvis Street Jets, who had rolled drunks, stripped cars, and fought other gangs with chains and switchblades. The cops, after catching them red-handed breaking into the Lombard Street liquor store, had given them all a choice: either correctional farm or the army. Army and the rest, with a thumb to the nose, had chosen the correctional farm. Three had graduated to Kingston Pen. The rest had become postwar fast-buck promoters, with two making it as bona fide millionaires. Sam, alone, had chosen the army. He was the youngest in a depression family, which his father supported with three jobs and his mother by cooking potatoes eighty-seven different ways. They had skimped to keep Sam in school. He could even type, for God's sake! When the choice came, Sammy had been tainted by respectability. He had a little bit to lose, so he had to play it safe while the others played fast and loose.

"I got my highschool diploma," Sam announced to his pee-green walls, "so I was the one who got slapped with the life sentence. The others got off for *bad* behaviour."

Sam looked at Miss October, spread across a haystack, with the frost definitely off her pumpkins, then thought bitterly of the alimony that kept him poor. All any broad had to do was to trap one poor sucker and she had it made for life. In his own family, only his sister Enid, who had married a dentist, had got as far as the suburbs. A few minutes on her back, every couple of nights, while Dr. Lester filled her *ha ha* cavity, and *look, ma! colour TV!*—not to mention all the free bridgework she could use.

Sam fingered an Agatha Christie book on the corner of his desk, one of several hundred in his whodunit library. It was Sam's dream to parlay his ability to type into the writing of a crime-thriller that would make him rich and famous. He had a lot of ideas floating around in his head—really great stuff—but he just couldn't seem to get the right Twist of Fate to pull it all together.

Sam picked up Army's gold business card and dropped it into his Metal Modern wastebasket. Some day . . .

He checked his Mickey Mouse watch. He still had an hour before lunch to pull together his sales report, though no Twist of Fate was going to help much there, unless maybe he twisted his sales graphs upside down.

He took off his sports jacket, winding a thread around a button, rebending the claws of his ruby cufflink, and rolling up his no-iron sleeves in the meticulous manner of a man responsible for his own laundry.

He wadded a piece of paper and dabbed it over his sweaty brow, leaving—backward, indelibly—the exact amount of his September's drop in commissions, stamped on his forehead.

It had to be over ninety degrees in his Dinky-toy cubicle. The damned Heat/Cool System had gone crazy again! Last week it was freeze-the-balls-off-a-brass-monkey week, and now it was arab-jockstrap week.

Sam put his hand to the window, then remembered a memo he had received just that morning from Basil Fitch, on behalf of XKEM5S1R1, his chief computer, reminding all employees that the new super-deluxe Heat/Cool System, installed for their health and comfort, was so sensitive that the unauthorized opening of a window anywhere on the premises could cause malfunction for hours, and hence forbidding such an act as high treason.

Sam, moaning, pulled his hand back from the window, too demoralized to risk tangling with Fitch again today, even in absentia.

He looked wistfully at "Sweet Talk," the official company quarterly with its cover picture of Danny Steele and Daphne Foster in their bathing suits at the Hunter mid-summer picnic.

Sam opened the magazine to a writeup, by Eve Martin, on the "joke" rescue. He shook his head. *It sure was funny about that canoe business*. Even at this late date he could swear he had seen someone in the floundering canoe, and so had Laurie Temple, though she denied it afterwards.

Sam flipped pages.

He stopped.

He stared. Now he was looking at himself and Eve Martin, bleary-eyed at the bar, with a white smudge between—obviously a photographic flaw, but looking exactly like—

Sam snapped shut the magazine.

His imagination was galloping away with him. *Too much alcohol*. He oughta lay off. People were beginning to notice.

Sam looked once more, with envy, at the picture of Danny and Daphne—*her* juicy boobs pressed against *his* Charles Atlas chest—then shifted his longings to Laurie Temple, imagining her spread like Miss October across the Thanksgiving haystack in Display Ads. Maybe the heat would get to Laurie and she'd be a sport and slip off her pantyhose. Maybe it might even create emergency conditions like the Great Blackout in New York with everyone in *ha ha* heat.

Sam threw down his sales chart.

He picked up the Agatha Christie book he had promised to lend to Laurie: Old Sam Ryan was about to Make Hay Whilst the Sun Still Shone!

The Display Ad Storeroom had always been an offbeat favourite with employees of the Candy Factory.

Perhaps it was the magic of looking up and seeing an eight-foot rabbit, a ten-foot Valentine, a witch on her broom-stick, and a half-dozen Halloween cats with splayed hair and permanently startled eyes, but things happened in Display Ads that couldn't happen elsewhere.

At precisely 11.37 on the morning of October 31, the Valentine heart at the foot of the Thanksgiving haystack began to beat in the witchy darkness.

There was the sound of scuffling undercut by deep breathing.

The Valentine heart burst. Two people tumbled through—right under the eyes of the Halloween cats. They grappled with vigour on the Thanksgiving haystack.

"Get off me, you beast! Go a-*way!*"

"Aw c'mon, pussy. Don't play hard to get! You know you're loving it *ha ha!* You know you're drooling for your TI-GER!"

The two bodies tossed and pitched, straw flying, clothes askew in the *ha ha* haystack.

They rolled into the Dominion Day firework display.

The fire-alarm went off.

The couple sprang apart.

Each gasped, open-mouthed, hair standing on end like the hair of the electrified cats. Each leaped to his/her feet, buttoning and zipping. Each headed for a different exit.

The boys from Sales were converging on Display Ads for their Friday poker game when they heard the alarm.

Beau Whitehead, who had the office opposite, was first to the door, followed, in a bunch, by Harry Pulitzer, Bimbo Brown, Gordie Willis and Joe Duffy, of Sales.

They fanned out through Hunter's extensive inventory of props kept on hand for stores and public-service lending. They could not smell smoke though a couple of the boys remarked on the intense smell of crushed roses.

Beau Whitehead, satisfied all was now in order, and relieved not to have found Morgan Jones at the heart of the disturbance, disconnected the alarm.

Harry Pulitzer, noticing the fire-escape door was ajar, investigated, thought he saw someone running away in a lab coat, considered giving chase, but—*what the hell.*

He returned just as Bimbo Brown, kicking through the Thanksgiving haystack to see if anyone had been smoking, turned up a pocket book. It was a detective book, much thumbed: *The Mousetrap,* by Agatha Christie.

"Hey! Let's see!" said Harry.

A paper fluttered to the ground as the book changed hands.

Joe Duffy retrieved it. He burst into raucous laughter: *a prescription for tranquillizers made out to Sam Ryan!*

The boys from Sales passed the prescription around with much nudging and giggling. Sam's ribald claims re the Thanksgiving haystack were well known but not much documented.

Harry Pulitzer tapped the cover of the Agatha Christie book. "Exhibit A," he said.

He nudged the straw of the Thanksgiving haystack. "Exhibit B."

He tapped the ten-foot Valentine with its busted centre. "Exhibit C."

He jerked a thumb over his shoulder toward the fire escape. "Exhibit D, I just saw disappearing in a lab coat."

Harry took off his checked sportscoat and began methodically rolling his striped sleeves.

"What's your point, Har?" asked Bimbo Brown.

"My point," said Harry, his bushy brows concentrated in a V, "is that, speaking for myself, I did not much appreciate having Feen-a-Mints glued with coconut slipped into my sample case last week, especially—I will be honest—since they proved such a strong seller.

"My point," he said, putting a bearpaw on Bimbo's shoulder, "is that I don't think you appreciated having that fart pillow slipped under you at the last Image meeting when you had—otherwise—made such a favourable impression.

"My point," he said, putting another bearpaw around Gordie Willis, "is that you did not seem thrilled last spring when you left the church with your lovely bride only to find your honeymoon car stuffed with safes pumped up with helium and other indignities too coarse to mention.

"My point," he said, nudging Joe Duffy with his knee, "is that I do not think—unless I have seriously misjudged your general reaction—that you thought it was too hilarious when you woke up from Gordie's stag with your arm in a sling and did not discover until it was X-rayed two days of pain later that the splint was a gag and the arm unbroken.

"My point," continued Harry, guiding the boys to the Alice-in-Wonderland toadstool, "is that I believe we should make major effort to return this book in the spirit in which it was lost. While I would be the first to admit that the aforementioned gags were not always played without the cooperation of others, there was always that one devious mind working full time on what the rest of us took more ... *casually*.

"In short, gentlemen, I think it's about time Sam Ryan got *his* in the place where Sam is the most sensitive, namely, up his ass!"

The boys from Sales, boisterous in anticipation, took their places on crates and stools around the Alice-in-Wonderland toadstool, which they used as a cardtable.

Gordie Willis, as always, rubbed the left foot of the eight-foot rabbit. Joe Duffy positioned himself in front of the St. Pat's shamrock so it seemed to be smiling over his shoulder. Bimbo Brown tossed a penny into the Wishing Well. Harry Pulitzer dealt the cards.

There was much snickering around the toadstool, occasionally culminating in a lascivious roar. At the height of one such jest, the door of Display Ads opened.

Eve Martin, hand on hip, stood in the doorway looking both envious and annoyed. "What are you lunkheads up to? I could hear you all the way to the boardroom."

"Tsk tsk tsk," said Harry. "Surely not through all that density of broadloom and power unless, Evie, you had your ear to the ground and perhaps to the keyhole?"

"Yeah, g'way," said Gordie, "You sound just like my wife *and* my boss."

Harry looked up from his cards. In fact, he laid them on the toadstool. "Leave us not be hasty, boys!" He leaned back on his winekeg, his thumbs in his red braces, squinting at Eve with the shrewdness that would have made him Hunter's top salesman if he weren't also the laziest. "Evie may be just the talent we're looking for. C'mon in, and make yourself at home. *Five* dirty minds are better than four, but—" he pointed to the Halloween display "—kindly leave the broomstick at the door. We already have our token witch."

Eve hesitated, torn between her sense of corporate aloofness and her female-to-male curiosity.

Harry pushed Joe from his crate. "Get up, Joe and give the lady a chair."

He patted the crate. "Sit by me, Evie dear, take the load off your tongue and we'll deal you in, all ways."

The only female in a family of six, Eve Martin was a sucker for being considered "one of the boys."

Beau Whitehead went directly from Display Ads to the Chocolate Department, looking for Morgan, wanting to question him about the fire alarm. Morgan was not at his station, though Beau saw, from the work chart, that he was supposed to be. Where was he? Freaked out somewhere or hadn't he shown up today?

Beau tried the warehouse, where Morgan sometimes snuck to smoke pot.

He tried Hard Centres, where he often went to chat with Megan Mason.

He tried Soft Centres, where he occasionally spelled Irma Burbank on the Starch Machine.

He did not find Morgan, though Beau could tell from the word CHICKENSHIT scrawled in the starch dust that Morgan had passed that way.

Beau travelled swiftly, gracefully through the Production Sector, pulling on his wispy beard, his skin drawn into quotation marks under his mauve glasses. He was worried about Morgan. The always-dangerous spit in Morgan's happy-go-lucky facade widened alarmingly when he was under the influence of drugs, which seemed to be all the time lately—ever since his return from his mother's funeral. That experience seemed to have released in Morgan a deep inner disturbance that was clothing itself in racial resentment and revolutionary mumbojumbo. Beau knew that Morgan had secret access to the Candy Factory at night, and that he was engaging in acts of petty sabotage. More seriously, he had bragged to Beau that he intended to blow up the Candy Factory—the first thought that had come to Beau's mind when he had heard the fire alarm.

Beau slid open the door of the Enrobing Room. He was assailed by the clacketty-clack-clack of the machines that coated Hunter's soft and hard centres with Formula 581 chocolate. Beau liked the steady beat of the machines, which he found reassuring, like a mechanical heart. He tapped Matty Ryan on the shoulder: "Relief, Matty?"

She sighed: "Hell, yes! My varicose veins are killing me!"

Beau took Matty's place at the side of the Packer, where she had been plucking Turkish Delight and Coffee Creams from a metal-link conveyor-belt to pack in two-pound boxes. As Beau relieved one hand, then the other, he received broad smiles from Lila and Georgina, on either side.

Beau was a favourite on the line, not only because he spelled the girls as a way or researching industrial boredom, but also becuase he was a nice face to confide in. That last had frightened Beau until he understood that, since he did voluntarily what others were compelled to do, he was not a man but a God come to visit. That casting had reassured Beau, and since human compassion was not demanded of him, he found himself able to give it in generous measure.

"What's new?" asked Lila.

"Nothing with *me*," replied Beau. "How about you?"

It was the hoped-for invitation.

*"Hah*! Need you ask? Oh *bro*-ther! I could write a fucking book!" And she was off on the latest chapter of life with Simon, her fourflusher boyfriend, who sent her expensive gifts for which he also sent her the bill.

If Beau had spoken to Shirl, she would have told him about a new course she was planning to take on taxidermy, or fruittree grafting, in hopes of meeting a man.

Willy would have talked about her struggles with her priest, who insisted she renounce all but the rhythm method of birth control, and with her truckdriver husband, who threatened to kill her if she became pregnant again, with frequent cuts and bruises on account.

Jessie would ask him for jokes she could repeat to her husband in their anxious time of silence before the TV went on.

Agnes would cry over the illegitimate daughter she had placed in a foster home.

Beau was touched and fascinated by the combination of cynicism and naivety that marked the girls of the Line.

They were cynical, in a tough and foul-mouthed way, about all the jobs they had ever had and all the men they had ever met. They were optimistic about all the jobs they had never had and all the men they had yet to meet. Though each hated her job with a lyrical passion, each also clung to the belief that something or someone would rescue her, happily and forever.

The single ones believed the Right Man would solve all their problems, including that of money. The married ones believed money would solve all their problems, including that of having married the Wrong Man.

The single girls spent their pay on clothes to attract the Right Man. The married ones tried to save for a downpayment on the Right House.

It was as if the romantic dreams the rest of society had given up on had settled over them in a sticky pink cloud, so that each girl was blindly unable to read her fate in the fortunes of the girl one step further along the conveyor-belt. The single girls didn't hear the complaints of the married ones about "my old man." The ones without children didn't notice that the ones with children were not only still there but anxious for overtime. The ones who were engaged ignored the warnings of those who were divorced, and those who were divorced forgot everything they learned as they started out second time around.

"... and so I sez, okay, Simon, you jerk, but remember, *this is your last chance!*"

Beau felt Shirl nudge him. It was time to rotate. He shifted one place to the left on the conveyor-belt, his long white fingers now plucking Vanilla Fudge and Liquid Cherry, as he eased himself into the comfortable rhythm.

Shirl screamed.

Someone stopped the conveyor.

One of Beau's fingers was mangled between two links of metal. There was, of course, no blood. He hadn't, of course, noticed.

Sam Ryan holed up in his office, his coat collar pulled around his face, his eye on the door. *If only the fucking fire alarm hadn't gone off!* She was loving it, you could tell. She had *had* to fight him, that was part of the game, but she was so hot for him the friction from her panty hose nearly set off his safety matches!

Sam puffed on his executive stogey. He'd already had three triple scotches with Anacin chasers for lunch. The stogey was supposed to be part of his return to sobriety, but all he felt was queasy.

The *Playboy* cartoons plastered over Sam's walls mocked him. They made it look so easy. Sam fastened in moral indignation on an old geezer of the Colonel Blimp type with his head resting on two boobies that looked like they were blown up by a bicycle pump. He frowned, puffing on his cigar. *That was the trouble with the world*—guys like that, just leachers, out for what they could grab, whereas he, Sam Ryan, was a real romantic. He'd never learned to hold back. He just went in over his head, and women took advantage.

Sam looked at Miss October, winking indiscriminately at all comers over her pumpkins and deepened his frown into a glower. *That was the trouble with women*—they couldn't tell the difference. Like with Laurie Temple, today. He'd actually been performing a public service.

Sam's eyes slit like a man looking out a speakeasy. Would Laurie turn him in?

He puffed his cigar, feeling the smoke gush out of his ears. If she did, he'd be ready for her. Anyone could see, just by

89

the look of her, she'd be the sort to misconstrue things. Fall against her in an elevator and she'd think it was Carnal Knowledge! Charles X. was a man of the world, an aristocrat. He and Sam could talk things out, man-to-man. They hadn't called him the Golden Mouthpiece back at the corner of Jarvis and Church for nothing!

Sam saw Bimbo Brown strutting by with a full briefcase and he remembered. *Jesuz!* The stinking Sales meeting! His first reaction was to skip it, but then he knew that was the *last* thing he could afford. He had to be conspicuous, to make a real contribution so Hunter would remember he was there, as part of his alibi. Unless Laurie could pin him down to the *exact* time, he'd deny the whole thing. Just hint to Hunter that Laurie *thought* it was Sammy because *heh heh* she wanted it to be. *Oh, you had to get up early to put one over on Sammy the Beagle!*

Sam, humming in a tuneless tongue-clicking way, flipped through his basket for something flashy to make him look good at the meeting. He stopped. He looked at *it,* trying to look innocent, three down in his memo basket. A pink envelope with his name across it in red.

Sam reached for the envelope, then stopped, that sixth sense peculiar to all great detectives holding him back.

He sniffed it: *Ahhhhh, scented.*

He flipped it on to his desk with his hula-girl letter-opener then, holding it down with a paperclip so as to leave no fingerprints, used Miss Hula, as his glamorous assistant, to slit the envelope. He lifted out the note. He read:

TIGER!

The Haystack tonight at 9. I'll leave the truck entrance open.

PUSSYCAT

Sam snatched up the note. He planted a schmarmy kiss in the middle. Laurie! How could he have misjudged her so? She must have thought over what she'd missed, and now she was panting for it! Maybe she'd had lunch with one of his many satisfied customers. Maybe good old Matty had laid it on the line about the pleasures of making whoopee with Sammy. Maybe—

Sam's natural suspicion—call it paranoia—resurfaced.

He resniffed the note. It didn't smell like Quality Control. The most seductive perfume Laurie Temple had ever come up with was peppermint. This smelled like ... lilacs? geranium? *roses?*

Scowling, Sam reread the message, ransacking each syllable for hidden meaning, saying the words aloud to squeeze out hidden nuances. He shook his head, gravely. *No. Not Laurie Temple. Definitely not that little mouse. Even with it running down her legs she wouldn't have the guts.*

He scrutinized the signature. He'd read, once in a spy novel that a person's real identity always showed through their code name. They used the same initials or made a pun or something. In fact, he'd read that in a *real* spy story about a *real* double agent. They caught the guy because his code name was his dog's name spelled backwards and he always had his picture taken with his dog to defy danger.

He snapped his fingers. *Of course!* It was so obvious he'd missed it! *Irma Burbank, the Platinum Pussycat from Soft Centres!* Rumour had it Irma was trying to get into Promo the best way she knew how, so why not through the zipper, starting with Big Sam Ryan's own Greased Lightning?

Sam grinned. In fact, he salivated. Just thinking about Irma and he couldn't help making melon gestures. She'd give any of the dames in *Playboy* a run for their silicone. Sam leered, *eat-your-heart-out*, at Miss October spread in hope across his haystack.

*Whoops!* The haystack.

He'd almost forgotten that.

How did Miss Pussy Big Ones know about that?

He reread the note. TIGER? PUSSYCAT? More than likely it was one of the guys playing a joke on him. *Harry Pulitzer? Joe Duffy? Gordie Willis?* Sam chuckled in self-appreciation. Hell! When you came right down to it, *all* the guys were trying to get back at old Sam! He crumpled the note. *Imagine, him almost falling!* The folly of scotch and wishful thinking!

Sam started up from his desk, then—*Whooa back!* The haystack again. *Who knew besides Laurie?*

Sam uncrumpled the note.

He drummed his fingers beside it on his metal desk.

The fire alarm—*now that was real screwy!* Sam knew he was *hot*, but *heh heh*, enough to set off the fire alarm? How could that have happened? Could Laurie have deliberately lured him into indiscretion in the haystack? Had the fire alarm been set by an accomplice? Sam remembered, now, all through the assignation . . . the heady smell of crushed roses! *Could this be blackmail?*

Sam felt the Sinister Prickling he always felt when the Finger of Fate tampered too crudely with his life. Scowling, he checked his Mickey Mouse watch.

He was going to have to dash to catch the three o'clock Sales meeting. He manoeuvred the note between two clean sheets of paper, with his hula-girl slitter and a paperclip, wielded like Charlie Chan his chopsticks. Given the Forces of Evil that Sam felt operating about him, he had no choice but to take extra precautions. *Jeezus!* It could have been a letter bomb!

Panting, Sam reached the boardroom door at the same moment as Charles X. Hunter, meaning—*deduction, my dear Watson*—that it was 3.01 P.M. EST, and he was late.

Hunter, bending a pinstripe arm as cleanly as if it were a wire, ushered Sam in, a broad hint that he had expected Sam to be the first. Moreover, Hunter's nostrils were quivering like a fox terrier's that has just got the scent, and Sam knew pretty well what that scent was: cheap scotch, 80 proof.

The boardroom was already heavy with cigar smoke and male aggression. Charles X. walked coolly—in the seamless way he had of moving as if through a series of well-oiled gears and pulleys—to the Throne Chair at the head of the Antique Original table. There was one chair left, beside Bimbo Brown, stuffing his piggy face with chocolate nuts. Bimbo had been hired as a football star for his image-making potential. Off the field, he had quickly run to blubber, retaining from his athletic career only his athlete's feet and the smell of the locker room. Sweat rivuletted his face and clotted his grey-serge armpits. He grinned at Sam, *palsy-walsy*, through masticated chocolate. Sam—nostrils quivering like a fox terrier that has just got the scent and knows that it isn't Right Guard—took the seat beside Bimbo, shooting his pink cuffs to demonstrate the vast social distance he felt between them. He heard a loud clunk. The ruby bauble from Sam's cufflink fell, like a drop of blood, to the table, rolled to the centre, pirouetted, then settled noisily, paste side up. Charles X. Hunter, standing erect at the head of the table, the sun glinting from his own gold monogrammed cufflinks, waited for Sam to retrieve his merchandise. "And now, gentlemen, if we are *all* ready—"

Sam looked, in resentment, from Charles X., standing lushly in ferns watered daily by Tidy's Florists, to the portrait of Xavier X. Hunter, founding grandfather, in oiled ferns, behind him. The two men, though separated by two generations, looked exactly alike: The same blue-chip eyes. The same pinstriped tailoring. The same rep tie. The same gold thumb in the same vest, displaying the same gold watchchain. The same half-moon glasses, lying before each, on the same walnut table, and the same unsmoked Montecristo cigar. The same frosted black hair, full to the collar, with the same cavalry officer's moustache, so right for both times ... Sam thought of the anguish he had experienced in merely allowing his sideburns to grow. Clearly, the Hunter family model, unlike the Ryan one, was designed For All Seasons.

Sam butted his cigar in the Antique Original ashtray.

He looked down the table at the other salesmen, nodding their heads at everything Hunter said, while their butts squirmed in the heat of the gone-crazy Heat/Cool System, not one of them daring to take off his jacket until Hunter did, which he never would. *That is not a jacket, you are looking at, gentlemen, that is pinstriped paint!*

Sam reached for an Anacin.

He stopped, in mid-pop.

He just had a brilliant idea!

In fact, it was so brilliant it knocked the headache out of his head: Charles X. Hunter was not human! He was humanoid! *a robot!* He had been sent from another planet to take over earth! That's what the X in his name stood for— Planet X, meaning Xerox! That's why Hunter's needed a super-sensitive air-conditioning system instead of the ordinary kind—for when the machines moved in! The takeover had already begun, but someone in the plant—someone *human*— knew Charles X. was a robot and was opening windows to bugger up the system and thus keep the place fit for humans!

Sam felt jubilant.

He was *sure* he was right!

It was clear in everything Charles X. did that he was not real—from the eerie way he glided over the floor, to the way his clothes never creased, or his cigars never burned, to his total lack of sweat. He was controlled through invisible wires by the real brains of the operation. Sam looked about the room, eyes slit, forehead puckered. His face broke: *Ah ha! The picture of Xavier X Hunter.* Old Xavier was the real brains of the operation! Charles X. was just his puppet. Sam knew for sure because—here was where his brilliant detective's eye set him above the *zombies* in the room—CXH parted his hair on the *right*, whereas XXH parted his hair on the *left*. That mean Charles X. used Xavier X. as a mirror. When CX stood in front of the painting, every morning, to get his instructions, *both thought they parted their hair on the same side!!*

It was all Sam could do not to stand up in the middle of the meeting and make his accusations, but he calmed himself, considering. Here was the sort of Secret Knowledge you could use against a man at any time. It was also the sort of meticulous detail, the Twist of Fate, so to speak, on which all great detective stories turned. Now, if only he had about two hundred more pages of plot.

Sam watched a fly, groggy from interrupted hibernation, bumble between the *real* ferns and the *oil* ones, then settle on the nose of Xavier X. Hunter. He thought: *If that bastard sneezes, I'll have him! I'll know he's The Brain!*

Sam corrected himself: *No, if he sneezes, that means he's human which means he's one of us being used by one of them! If Charles X. sneezes, that means he's off-balance as a robot because of the mistake with the hair-part, and could rebel against the machines and become human!*

Sam's head began to throb.

That last part about Charles X. becoming human was too much even for *him* to swallow.

He seemed to have lost the thread of his narrative.

Sam watched the fly fall asleep on a fake fern—proving nothing. Or everything. *Hell!* Maybe it was *the fly* that was running things. Sam popped an Anacin. He looked around him, at the mouths sucking on cigars and smiling through their teeth. He also seemed to have lost the thread of the meeting.

Sam forced himself to concentrate.

Charles X., man or defective robot, seemed to be on the warpath about a drop in sales since the good old Canadian Department of Health announced that sugar was a "poison" to be controlled, right along with alcohol and nicotine.

Sam took a nervous look at his sales graph.

Half of his outlets were in the rich-bitch suburbs where the housewives, with their festering B.A.s, had nothing better to do over their second cup of coffee-with-saccharine than to needle their kids about their teeth and their husbands about their paunches. Sam's chart showed a nosedive that couldn't be seasonally adjusted. He looked at Bimbo Brown-nose's chart, with the black line soaring up through chocolate smears, like Everest poking through the clouds. As public relation's material, Bimbo had proved a disaster. To everyone's surprise, he'd turned out to be a first-rate salesman.

Sam popped another Anacin.

He allowed his mind to drift, like the fly on the wall, so to speak, from one to the other of the women flanking Charles X.

Eve Martin, executive secretary, was old-style career woman, thin as a razor turned sideways, blood-red lips and nails, hair coiled like a licorice whip, probably no looker till the bones came out, but now quite a broad under the lacquer.

Brigitte Young, junior secretary, was strictly "now," as they say, stringy lightbrown hair, big mouth with lots of teeth, mini-skirt the size of a Band-Aid, no-bra nipples like Sultana raisins.

Sam looked from Charles X. to Brigitte to Eve. Rumour had it Hunter was getting into Brigitte's pants and faithful retainer Eve wasn't liking it much.

Sam studied Hunter's face. He looked entirely too smug for a man discussing the profit potential of cinnamon lollypops. He was probably getting a little "lolly" for himself, right now, on the wrong side of the table. The horny old coot was probably finger-fucking Brigitte with Eve massaging his nuts!

Sam felt his own cock prickle, rise, and declare itself: *Old Peter T. Reliable*, now that he couldn't take advantage of it. He looked at Brigitte's left hand, curled around her pencil as she wrote, awkwardly, in longhand in her shorthand book. He imagined it, claws extended, slashing at the page, as he threw her, by her hair, onto the walnut table, and fucked her, tom-cat style, till her eyes popped, with maybe Eve, in back, on dildo. *Yeah*, he bet Eve could work a mean dildo, with her talons and teeth dug into his back, sucking *real* blood. Sam had never had two broads together—he never could trust one in back and one in front, in case they decided to grind up his balls between them, like Matty and Linda, and

95

just have it off with each other. He imagined how Brigitte and Eve might do each other—probably mouth to whisker, with lots of lapping and sucking and groaning, really digging into each other, humping and rolling over the walnut table, not giving a good goddamn who was watching, with maybe a Vaseline finger stuck up in back for good measure. . . . Sam had seen something like that a couple of times in the army, and he had to admit it was pretty exciting. What the hell, you'd wait in line just so long while a couple of old pros worked their way up the barracks, and then it just seemed better—more *humane*, somehow—to let them do each other, with everybody jacking-off—them really loving it too, putting on a real show, not like the tired stuff they fobbed off on paying customers—and then into the showers, everybody, with the stalls as slippery as the ramp in a stud farm. Well, what did they expect? You couldn't put a couple dozen of the nation's horniest together, cancel all leaves, and not expect a *little* trouble for the taxpayers' money. Afterall, they hadn't done anything but answer their country's call to duty, had they? It wasn't supposed to be a prison farm!

Sam remembered the only other time he'd been at camp— the summer he was ten, when a bunch of social workers had descended on Cabbagetown and packed every seventh kid, head shaved for kooties, off to fresh-air camp. There'd been this fat guy, named Elmo, who cried every night, especially in thunderstorms, wanting to crawl into bed with the other guys, said his mother used to hold his "teddy bear" till he got to sleep. Well, the boys in Elmo's tent did the best they could for Elmo all that summer, with one of them sitting on his head with a pillow, while he hollered for his mama, and the others working him over real good, till one night the tentmaster came in with his flashlight, and turned out to be the biggest fag of all! *Hot dog! The badges Sammy collected that summer!* Sam looked over at Bimbo and grinned. He just remembered that Bimbo was a Boy Scout leader, even saw him once on parade in short pants with his legs so fat the flesh hung down between them like an extra set. As a matter of fact, Bimbo even looked like Elmo. Probably a bedwetter too. Sam had heard the jocks were the worst when it came to that sort of thing. Real babies, trying too hard to get away from their mommies. Lots of getting it up for the game and not being able to get it down again without a little showerplay. *Boys will be boys, and all that.*

96

Sam felt his cock throb.

In fact, he was expecting it to poke its head through the table and introduce itself. "Hi, girls, we haven't met yet, but I'm Big Red. You saw me last in *The French Connection.* Put her there, pardner *heh heh heh.*"

Should he go to the can and take a little pleasure for himself? It was a shame to waste it now that—truth to tell—he was Having a Little Trouble in That Department. *Nothing serious, you understand, Mesdames. Do not re-adjust your pantyhose or your receiving sets, ha ha!*

Sam felt a wave of hopelessness, dangerously close to self-disgust ... the look of his sales graph, like Bottomless Canyon, next to Bimbo's ... the aftermath of cheap scotch and expensive cigars ... the fuckup with Laurie. Could it be, as Linda the Lady had always said, that Sam Ryan was a loser?

Sam thought of the line she used to taunt him. *You can take Sam Ryan out of Cabbagetown, but you can't take Cabbagetown out of Sam Ryan!*

Sam felt a poignant need to believe something good about the day.

He nudged the note from PUSSYCAT from its plain wrapper and smoothed it. Why *not* Irma Burbank? Why *not* the Platinum Pussycat? Sam distinctly recalled her rubbing that juicy set of hers up against him once last year on the elevator, full frontal displacement. It couldn't have been an accident, is wasn't *that* crowded. She sure was hot for her share, so why not Old Sammy? Afterall, he could fuck the feathers off a goose when he was In the Mood, as plenty of chicks could testify. Sam imagined Miss Big Ones with her blouse pulled way *way* down, and her skirt pulled way *way* up, like Jane Russell in The Outlaw, her haystack spread over the Display Ad haystack, running like molasses for Sammy.

The trouble was ... Sam's detective nose began to twitch ... the trouble was, he didn't figure the P.P. for the premeditated stuff. The way he figured her, it was off into the broomcloset, and *bang bang bang you're dead*—no need to set something up for Display Ads. No need to steal a key for the truck entrance.

*The key to the truck entrance.* Sam pondered that angle. Who could easily get one?

He looked, wistfully, at Brigitte. She was gazing at Charles X. as he unfolded his plan to market no-nut, cream-centred Granny Gumballs for pensioners without teeth, as if she thought he was one of the world's great humanitarians. Sam felt the bitter despair he always felt when he heard such things as how a guy over forty loses a few million testicle cells to scar tissue every day. Definitely not Brigitte, and probably not the P.P.

Sam felt his cock roll over, like Fido, and die.

Poor Big Red, not a sniff of snatch for over two weeks and that geriatric bastard, with his no-nut cream-centred prick is sitting there, with alleycat on one side, Siamese on the other, and at home, purring for him between silk sheets, the fluffiest piece of ginger-persian pussy that—Sam had a stunning revelation. *Celeste Hunter! Mrs. Charles X.! Of course! She was the one who had sent the note!* Sam nearly laughed outright with the clarity of it. *Of course!* That was how she could get the key! All she had to do was to pry it through the pinstripe bars of Charles X.'s pocket along with his credit cards. She knew about the alleycat working the day shift, and she was planning to rub out Charles X. and make Sam president! She'd already started to do in the old bastard with poison! All of history's great poisoners were women, from Lucrezia Borgia right down to his second wife, Matty, for whom actually adding the poison to her cooking was an unnecessary expense! Celeste Hunger was feeding Charles X. arsenic— inheritance powder, as they called it before crime detection became a science—mixed in the whipped cream on her snatch. *Lead* arsenic, so that it would collect in Charles X.'s balls. Any second now, they would drop from the sheer weight! It was Sam's job to catch them, as they rolled down the table and to smuggle them out the truck entrances in a bag of Granny Gumballs. He and Celeste would be tried for the crime, but the coroner would testify under oath that nine-tenths of all married male corpses were ball-less. It would be The Perfect Crime! Sam could even write a bestseller about it, because *double jeopardy, ha ha!* he couldn't be tried twice for the same crime. Then he, President Samuel X. Ryan, would stand in this very room, at this very table, where Charles X. now stood, playing, like Captain Queeg, with Charles X.'s lead balls, dipped in gold, and monogrammed.

Sam let loose a rattle of mirthless laughter, mercifully blotted out by the scraping of chairs.

The meeting seemed to be over.

Everyone was shoving, with Friday afternoon haste, to the door, with the exception of Bimbo Brown, who had polished off three bags of chocolate nuts and was waddling over to give Charles X.'s own personal supply another good lick. Sam jostled to the door behind Brigitte Young, letting his portfolio slide—by way of compensation for a rough afternoon—down her bumcrack, in a casual way no lady could pin on him.

He had forgotten. Brigitte was no lady.

She turned on Sam, eyes shooting thumbtacks: "Keep your pea-picking self to yourself, you motherfugger!"

Sam drew back, offended. These kids today. Where were their mothers? Where were their manners? Their language was atrocious and you knew from the statistics that they all had v.d.! He'd even heard Brigitte was Women's Lib, which probably meant she didn't wash. *Ugh!* If Sam had *his* way, he'd scrub out the mouths *and* the cunts of every female under thirty with lye soap!

Sam went down to his Metal Modern cubicle, humming tunelessly, "Gonorrhea went to Korea, To give the boys a ball. . . ."

At least, he could be grateful to a conservative management that Hunter's did *not* have co-educational toilet seats.


Sam's phone was ringing when he reached his office.

It was the guy from Oshawa Sam was supposed to meet for dinner to discuss new Hunter outlets.

He'd forgotten, when he made the appointment, that it was Halloween, and his kids wanted him to drive them to grandma's farm to show off their costumes. Would Sam mind if they put off their meeting till next week? He was sorry, but he sure hated to disappoint the kids.

"Yeah yeah yeah. Fine fine fine. Sure sure sure," mumbled Sam into the phone.

"Halloween's one of our best times in the candy biz. We gotta be nice to the hobgoblins."

Sam threw his lousy appointment book into the garbage. *Halloween! The kids' costumes! What an insulting excuse!* He felt overwhelmed with the bittersweet mixture of envy and contempt he had always felt when confronted by family men. *Henpecked! Kidmauled!* He suppressed an image of Young Sammy. Hell, the kid was too old for Halloween costumes anyway, unless you counted the freak stuff his mother did him up in! Sam sat down at his desk. *Now* what was he going to do with the evening?

He experienced a Moment of Truth in that raw and defenceless zone between drunkenness and sobriety. He had counted on this guy from Oshawa—this prick he'd never laid eyes on—to fill in his evening for him, to flow with him, from bar to bar, becoming more palsy-walsy, till Friday was over and Saturday taken care of with a hangover.

That humiliating view of himself panicked Sam.

He blacked it out with a wink at Miss October.

He put on his new mirror "shades". . . . Sam liked his mirror shades. They had been "big" when he was big, in the forties, and now they were big on the ski slopes. They made Sam feel he was covering a lot of bases.

Sam strutted through the Sales office, his thumbs in his waistband as if packing sixshooters; his dyed red hair a stiff coxcomb; his pelvis thrust forward like a Friday night bachelor who was already halfway *there!* He laughed aloud, and waved to the other inhabitants of Metal Modern desks, leaving a trail of broken wisecracks, while his mirror glasses hurled back the office into everyone's face . . . giving as good *ha ha* as Sam Ryan had always gotten.

Sam's favourite bar on the Yonge Street strip was called The Jungle. It was dusky, like a cavern, with lots of fake palms, fake bamboo, and fake overhead fans—a blend of the veldt, Waikiki, the Punjab, the bundah, and good old American knowhow, with the only wild things you had to watch out for being the animals that crawled out of their dens at night to scotch-and-HA HA-water there.

Sam's favourite drink was a triple scotch, no ice or—as they called it in The Jungle—a Triple Tiger, no stripes.

Sam's favourite bartender was a long-armed, nimble-tongued cockney named Ralph, who wisecracked from drum-stool to drum-stool as he poured drinks like a monkey swinging on vines and splitting coconuts.

Unfortunately, Ralph had gone "over home" for a holiday. In his place was a beefy ape with a light voice and a battered pink face.

He was watching Lawrence Welk on the TV set over the bar.

Sam told him—just to be friendly—about the jerk from Oshawa who had cancelled a $500,000 business deal (give or take a few zeros) to drive his kids out to their grandma's to show-off their Halloween costumes.

"Yeah, I'd take my kid to Granny's too, if she were still

alive," said the bartender, completely missing the point. "My little guy's going as Phyllis Diller. The wife's bringing him down this evening, and I can tell you I'd feel a lot better if I was sure she'd take a cab. The fags in this neck-of-the-woods are really something, and Halloween's their night to howl."

The bartender, turning his back, watched the rest of Lawrence Welk.

Sam drank and brooded. About tight-assed chicks, in Quality Control, who didn't know quality when they saw it. About sales meetings conducted by robots. About guys who broke dates because of Halloween. About bartenders who watched—Sam wouldn't believe this, if he weren't actually seeing it—re-runs of Sesame Street. What was happening to the raunchy old world Sam the Pecker knew and loved? Where was Sophia Loren tonight? Was she still with that fat Italian director? Where was Liz without her *ha ha* Dick? What about Jackie O and her Adenoidal Adonis?

Sam took out his note from PUSSYCAT—now gummy with fingerprints, the way some stupid flatfoot would bugger the evidence—and smoothed it on the counter, watching it greedily lap up a spill of Triple Tiger.

He showed the note to the bartender, deciding to give him another chance: "Look what one of the guys at the office sent me. Imagine! Thinking I'd fall for a trick like this!"

"Yeah, the fags sure are getting pushy, they just can't believe a guy could be straight," replied the bartender, as usual missing the point. "Ever since that guy Trudeau got the nation out of their bedrooms, they've been trying to get us all back in. If you want *my* advice, I'd take it right back to the guy and threaten him with the cops."

"No, you've got it wrong," explained Sam, patiently. "A *guy* wrote it, pretending to be a *girl*, but it's a *gag*. The boys are trying to get back at me."

"You wouldn't think it was no gag if you worked in here!" exclaimed the pink-faced bartender, getting more pink-faced. "I get them in here in drag, and the first place they head is the woman's can. *I'm* the guy who's gotta go in and get them out. Do you know what I could get for false arrest?"

"No. You're misunderstanding me. When I say it's a *gag*, I mean it's a *trick*. Like one guy plays on another!"

"I don't want to know *how* they do it," exclaimed the bartender. "I just don't want them doing it in here! The nerve! They come in with padding stuck out like a shelf, and some poor straight boob slobbering all over them thinking, *wow!* he's gonna get his hands on all that, buying them drink after drink, and then an expensive dinner! I tell ya, it gives me goosebumps to think of my only kid wandering these streets dressed up like Phyllis Diller!"

Sam, disgusted, turned his back. He stared into the face of his Triple Tiger, then around him in The Jungle. The bar was filling up with the tough night-time crowd. There were a dozen guys and a half-dozen broads down the counter, clearly on the make. At least Sam *thought* they were broads. The peanut-brained pink-elephant behind the bar had begun to undermine his confidence.

Sam caught the eye of a rhinestone blonde, with big yellow-silk boobies resting on the counter. Sam rolled her with a practised eye, started towards her, then swerved past, into a phonebooth disguised with bamboo as a hunter's break. If he was going to squeeze the grapefruit, he had the sudden desire to do it at a place where he'd bought before.

Sam fished his famed black book from his pocket, and began dialing, alphabetically. A said no, without giving a reason. B didn't answer. C claimed she was going steady, whatever that jackoff phrase meant anymore. D hung up as soon as she heard old Sammy's name. E replied to Sam's airy "What's new?" with a string of adjectives so obscene that Sam hung up on her.

He returned to the counter, feeling sorry for himself. The bartender—this guy sure had funny tastes—was fine-tuning Sir Kenneth Clark's seventh installment of "Civilisation," instead of the Toronto-Montreal football game!

Sam stood the toney British accent—sounding altogether too much like Charles X. Hunter's Harvard—as long as he could, before turning the full light of his brash Canuck charm on a redhead with a three-inch firebreak along her part. She listened, blank-faced, while he told her his best Newfie joke, getting the accent just right, then waited modestly for laughter. Sam repeated the punchline. The girl yawned: "Don't knock yourself out for me, buster. This is my night off. I got my monthlies."

Sam moved on down the bar.

He struck up a conversation with a slutty Chinese chick with a face like a mashed pekinese and was kidding her along pretty good—the how-come-a-beauty-like-you routine—when he began to think there was something wrong with her voice.

A little too throaty? A little too much whisker in it? *Damn that bartender!* Sam began to feel a definite buildup of hostility towards the world. He'd already bought the dame a drink. Was he one of the suckers Bulldog Welk had been jawing about?

That possibility upset Sam very much.

He didn't like to think he was the kind of schnook who could be fooled by a fag.

*Well.* . . . Sam peered at his companion through his empty glass like a zoologist examining a rare sort of tropical *ha ha* barfly. *Was she or wasn't she?*

Sam wanted to know!

A dropped olive gave him his excuse.

He was down there, groping in the long grass and angling for a quick peek up Susie Wong's *ha ha* slit, when a cowboy boot pinned his hand. Sam traced the boot up past a bulging bluejean crotch. No doubt about this one. *Fake Marlon Brando, but otherwise real.*

The foot ground Sam's hand. "Next time, it'll be the *balls*." He looked at Sam with the same honest doubt Sam had felt about Susie Wong before adding: "If you *have* any!"

Sam shook his hand, feeling pain through feeling-no-pain: *Paranoia . . . It was catching.* He crawled up an empty barstool, shaped like a drum, and beat upon it with his good hand, looking for sympathy, or humour, in the eyes of the other animals at the waterhole, but finding none.

He climbed the rest of the way and spread his bruised hand on the fake zebra counter. The same hand that had brassknuckled Ace of the Spadina Street Shivs. The same hand that had K.O.'d (with the help of a baseball bat) Boris, the Ballbreaker cop from Precinct 29.

He looked at his reflection in the mirror: the hanging jowls, beginning to do a Bimbo on him; the dyed red hair, looking a little greenish in the fake moonlight; the freckles, standing out like leopard's spots. The bar's Ernest Hemingway backdrop with its plastic virility mocked Sam. He stuck his head through a paper thicket and mouthed to his reflection: "Ti-ger!"

Sam put on his mirror shades.

That was worse.

The two mirrors threw his face back and forth like a shrinking shrunken head till he had to snatch them off before he disappeared completely.

Sam—horrified—felt tears trickle down his cheeks. He saw the bartender looking at him suspiciously, from under his beetle brows, started to tell him to mind his own business, and ended up blubbering—about what a bum rap life was . . . about how lonely he felt . . . about how *scared* . . . yes, me Sam Ryan, *terrified.*

The bartender shrugged inside his oversized shoulders like a monkey in a gorilla suit. "Look, buddy," he said, not unkindly. "I don't mind myself what people do, so long as they don't hurt other people, you know? It takes all kinds, I always say, so if this guy from Oshawa stood you up for some other guy, then why don't you take the date you got—the guy who sent you the nice note. Halloween's kind of important for you guys, isn't it? It's sort of like your New Year's." The bartender patted Sam's paw. "Live and let live, I always say."

Sam stopped, in mid-blubber. He fixed the bartender with eyes like poison spears and, removing his PUSSYCAT note from his breast pocket, smoothed it on the counter.

"See, *see?* Take a good look, my good fellow," he said, with the precise nasal inflections of Sir Kenneth Clark pointing out Civilisation to those who otherwise would miss it. "Does *that* look to you like the handwriting of a *male* person? *That,* my dear chap, is the handwriting of a *female* person. I even know *what* female person. That, my dear chap, is the handwriting of Irma, the Platinum Pussycat, who—" Sam's aristocratic accent foundered on the vernacular "—has a pair of knockers down to her dimpled knees! Irma! The Platinum Pussycat from Soft Centres. This is no joke! It's just that the guys want me to think it's a joke because they don't want old Sammy to get what's coming to him! They've all got these old hags at home—*hag-ridden!*—and they can't stand the Sweet Stuff that sends it to Sammy, Special Delivery, from all over the goddamned Candy Factory! This chick, *this Irma Burbank, by name,* she's so hot for her Sammy that just the look in her eyes, through concrete walls, melts my zipper! And do you know where she is right now? She, my dear chap—" here, a brief return to Sir Kenneth's England "—right at this very second of Greenwich time, is lying in a thatch, with her snatch spread like the Suez Canal, just waiting for Admiral Sir Sammy to launch his flag ship! And do you know why I'm *here* instead of *there?* Because of jealous pricks like you trying to make me think it's a joke, and do you know why? *Because you're just a bunch of fags, who couldn't get it up for Venus with balls!"*

Now that Sam had explained it to himself—uncovered the dastardly plot, so to speak—it all seemed clear. Of course! Irma the Platinum Pussycat! How could he have doubted? How could he have been so callous as to keep her waiting?

Sam let his hand fall, ever so debonairly, to the crotch of his Abercrombie & Fitch safari suit. *Eureka!* He was like an elephant gun down there. Big Red said GO! Taking an arrogant glance around the *bundah,* he swung from his barstool, and swept out the back door of The Jungle, feeling like a litter-borne *bwana* whose feet—thanks to cheap native labour—need never touch the ground. In fact, thanks to the beefy fist of the bartender, his feet did *not* touch ground. The same fist stuffed him—litter-born—into a garbage can, while the pink face, thrust into his warned: "The next time you expose yourself in *my* bar, buddy boy, *I'll break every bone in your fag body!"*

The raw autumn air, tangy with refuse, came as something of a cultural shock to Sam, so recently of the tropics.

Moreover, he could not seem to get out of the garbage can, which he now tended to think of as an Air Can economy seat with a faulty belt. Managing to shake himself loose, he staggered down the alley, carrying the garbage lid, full of fishheads and rotten potato peels, in front of him as his meal tray, complaining about the lousy service, but glad to see they had at least done something to improve the food at Air Can. . . . Sam found the washroom—a mere hole in the wall—and was relieved *ha ha* to see the lights of the landing field but a few yards off. He touched down, on concrete, having made the trip, from Jungle to Civilization, in only—Sam scowled into the luminous face of his Mickey Mouse watch—a few minutes.

Sam's first impressions of Civilization were enough to make him doubt his sobriety. *Witches! ghosts! tramps! clowns!* Sam rubbed his eyes, promising himself: *If I see a pink elephant, like the one I just left in The Jungle, I will go straight home, wherever that is.*

He saw, instead, a jack-o-lantern.

*Aha!* Sam's trained detective's mind seized on that as a vital clue. *Halloween!* He'd almost forgotten.

Sam felt pretty good about figuring that out. It proved, despite the wobbliness of his legs and a little bit of air sickness, that he was still thinking pretty clearly. That he had not, like so many good men, Gone Bad In The Tropics.

Sam decided to throw himself into the primitive celebration.

He stole a hubcap and, using it as a shield, leapt out at a guy in a hula skirt, shouting: *"Me* head-hunter!"

He found three clowns, putting ancient soap writing on glass pyramids, and joined them!

He swung, ape-like, down from an awning, on a guy dressed as a policeman, and thwacked him on the head with a taffy apple like it was a coconut!

He chased a skinny kid in a blonde-wig—the deadspit of Phyllis Diller—along with what he tried not to notice was a female pink elephant.

*What a ball!*

In fact, Sam might have forgotten why he had returned to Civilization if he had not at that crucial moment seen a kid wearing an old Esso promo-mask that reminded him of his True Mission and his True Nature. Sam thumped his chest, like Tarzan, and gave the mighty roar of Imperial Oil. *"Gggggrrrrrrrrrrraaaahhhhhhhhh!"* Adding, for any who should doubt it, "I've got a Tiger in my Tank!"

Sam fell, giggling, against a Volkswagen. *"Gggggggggrrrr-ahhhhhh!"* he roared. *Oh, you could take Sammy out of The Jungle, but you couldn't take The Jungle out of Sammy!*

It was then Sam had another great idea. He would combine Halloween high jinx *and* animal action. He'd go to the Candy Factory in disguise, like Romeo to his Juliet. A masked Balling *ha ha!* He bet it would give PUSSTCAT the thrill of a lifetime to be humped by a real TI-GER! Besides— *oh, Sammy was a crafty one!*—a disguise would be protection on the off-chance someone was trying to play a fast one on him!

Sam waited, behind the Volkswagen, till he saw a kid with what he wanted, then leapt out roaring: *"Ggggggrrrrrhhhhh."*

The kid started to cry.

Sam stuck a sawbuck under his fuzzy nose and reached for his fuzzy ears. "Trade, kid?"

The kid stopped crying. He gave Sam the mask. Sam put it on "TI-GER!" He leapt over a hydrant, like it were an anthill. He leapt over an MG, not noticing it had the top down, and he nearly castrated himself on the gearshift—*Egad, Stanley! A spear pit!*

Sam was almost forgetting again. *The Candy Factory!* He stood, with one foot on the metal carcass of the convertible like it were fallen prey, shouting, "I've got a Tiger in my Tank!"

Sam wiped the tears of laughter from his eyes. That was the trouble with him. When he got nervous or a bit drunk, he really got funny. He repeated his Tiger joke, roaring and pawing the air. It was so hilarious, he thought of going back to The Jungle and telling it to all his friends there, but then he remembered something about Phyllis Diller and a matched set of pink King Kongs and, seizing his elephant gun, decided, *ha ha ha,* it was Onward and Upward to the Candy Factory. . . .

It was nine (or ten, or eleven) according to Sam's Mickey Mouse watch, when he reached the truck entrance. He kicked the vast steel door with his oxblood toe for a quite a few minutes before he remembered it was supposed to be open. He reached down, gripped the edge, and flung it upward. *Open, Sesame Street ha ha!*

It took fifteen minutes for Sam to find the Display Ad storeroom—what with having to avoid the coon from the Chocolate Department who seemed to be in there writing CHICKENSHIT on the walls. Sam adjusted his tie and his fuzzy ears outside Display Ads, feeling the sudden self-consciousness of all blind dates. *Would she like him?* He puffed up his chest, explosive with Triple Tigers, and rapped out: *Shave and a haircut, two bits!* He rammed his shoulder against the door and pushed: *"Gggggggggrrrrrrrrraaaaaaaaaaahhhhhhhhhh!"*

Sam's natural suspicion made a brief farewell appearance. He paused on the threshold like a man who has learned early in his sales career to Beware the Dog, and sniffed. He caught a whiff of perfume—roses! He growled, pawing the air, and calling gently through his hot Triple Tiger breath: *"Pooooo-sy-Cat!"*

Sam heard a soft curling mew from the haystack/thatch-hut/grass-thicket, whatever. For the second time that long day, he took a flying leap through the Display Ad Valentine, which he now saw as the throbbing heart of the jungle/Punjab/veldt/bundah/savannah. It was too dark to see much, but the haystack was twitching and groaning, definitely inhabited. Sam—half-man, half-beast—ripped off his

107

clothes along with the last of his inhibitions: the plaid jacket, the wine pants, the pink shirt, the red tie, the fishnet jockey shorts with built-in tummy-support. No need to check Action Central. *Hard as a bone!*

The haystack was positively pulsating. Groping, Sam found ... a heart-shaped ass ... a wasp waist ... a set of the world's most unbelievable knockers! *Oh, it was Miss Big Ones, all right!*

Miss Big One's thrashing thighs were already slippery with ooze. Sam was used to fast *ha ha* trigger work. Holding his cock *ha ha* cocked, and feeling it start to smoke, he fumbled for the haystack, then the target, then—*bang bang bang!*—he exploded....Sam sank, euphorically, into layers of quaking flesh. *Egad, Stanley ... Do you hear drums?!*

Sam came to very slowly, very reluctantly, and even then, what he saw over his shoulder was not encouraging: An eight-foot white rabbit? Santa Claus and his reindeers? A busted Valentine?

Sam's head, face down in the straw, ached.

In fact, it felt like a balloon into which someone was pumping poison gas.

His tongue was so furry he figured a small animal must have crawled inside to die.

He had straw sticking to his mouth like cat's whiskers. He tried to pull off a few pieces. They stuck. *Real* whiskers?

Sam groped in the haystack under him. He felt something fleshy pressed against his chest. *Ahh, yes ... Me Tiger. You Pussycat.*

Sam's first clear desire was to slip into his clothes and off into the night. He hated pussycat for breakfast. It upset his ulcer. He pawed through straw on the right side of Miss Pussycat, feeling for his jacket. He needed an Anacin. His hand closed on ass. He squeezed it. He felt an answering twang in his dick. That surprised Sam. He was no repeater, which was one reason he liked to slink off early. He sighed, nostalgically: *Whatever Miss Big Ones had, she sure had a lot of it and in all the right places. Oh, you great big beautiful doll, you!*

Sam snuggled down into Miss Big Ones, his throbbing head between her two tits, as soft as water-pillows, just like that other romantic had done—the nice old duffer in the cartoon on his office wall, for whom he was beginning to develop an affection. Sam began to pat thigh, experimentally, imagining telling the boys in Sales about it, with appropriate gestures, next Monday at the watercooler. Male envy did as much for Sam's lusts as female flesh; he was a very competitive guy. The day Bannister broke the four-minute mile, Sam had invented the four-minute orgasm. The boys in Sales counted on him. He counted on the boys. Now, Sam felt his Dick *ha ha* Tracy harden.

Sam had a great idea! Why not let Big Red take the P.P. all over again, doggie-style, in her sleep. Then, when Bimbo Brown, sweating like Porky Pig, asked as he always did, "Did you give her an extra one for me, eh, Sammy?" Sam could, with the authority of truth, reply, "You bet your sweet ass, Bimbo! I entered her the way you do all your house calls—by the rear door!"

Sam burst into giggles, which he stifled in Miss Big Ones boobies. He listened apprehensively. Had he awakened her? . . . *Jeez-us!* She was sleeping like a tub of lard! He tried to roll off her but felt—*oh oh*— a sharp twang in his *wham-bam* that was more than just a *thank-you-mam*. He shoved himself up on his elbows feeling an actual stab of pain.

Sam gasped. He seemed to be caught!

He remembered, with terrible premonition, a joke he used to tell to great acclaim about the thread salesman who lost his *ha ha* needle in the farmer's daughter's *ha ha* haystack.

He felt his mouth go dry.

He began punching Miss Who's It in the Big fat tits. "All right, *bitch!* Let go!"

Sam's fists disappeared into Miss Big Ones, right up to his wrists. She didn't wake up *and she wouldn't let go!*

Sam stopped punching. *My God, she's dead!*

Through his mind whirred film clips of the various ways of disposing of a body—acidbaths, limepits, cement blocks, giant kilns. Who the hell did he know in the Mafia?

Sam got a grip on himself.

Sobriety hardened around a tough knot of suspicion in his head. He reached down, ever so coolly—like James Bond, like Mike Hammer, like Sam Spade—and pinched Miss Big Ones' right nipple. He rolled it scientifically, between thumb and finger. He concluded: *India rubber*. He spread his hand over her breast: more rubber, of an incredibly flesh-like texture. Sam felt it take on the warmth, sweat, and pulse of his own hand so quickly it was as if it possessed these qualities of its own.

Sam remembered the doll's thrashings. He slipped his hand under her hair: *wiring*. He ran his hands over her face. She seemed to be wearing a pussycat mask. He removed it. There was no face underneath—just like a balloon. The manufacturer, so precise in all other details, hadn't bothered to give her one. Sam laughed cynically. Of course! *I should have known! She didn't ask for money and she didn't make me tell her I loved her.*

Sam began clearing away the straw like a dog after his *ha ha* bone. He was caught, but good. *Right inside her goddamned twat!* He grimaced. *As usual, some dame had Sam Ryan by the balls!* He burst into derisive laughter: *the sound of one tonsil laughing!*

The doll's thighs were covered with goo. Sam reached down, under himself, and pried them apart. He tried to pull out Formerly-Big Red, using the stuff as a lubricant. *No dice.*

He stuck two fingers up the doll and pulled, like a fastidious man cleaning a chicken. He found something hard—not *ha ha* exactly him. He eased it out of the opening, himself with it. *Jeezuz H. Christ! A mousetrap! With Sam caught inside it like a furless mouse.*

Sam felt hysteria bubble in song to his lips: *"I'm just a prisoner of love, ha ha!"*

Sam rolled off Dollface. He counted to ten, calming himself. He examined Poor Red, as impersonally as he could. The circulation wasn't cut off, and he wasn't in pain, but the hard plastic contraption was set in place with all the assurances of a chastity belt. *Build a better mousetrap* HA HA *and the world will beat its meat to your door!*

Sam looked around him for something to pry himself loose, but it was too dark and cluttered to see much. He started to his feet, then fell back into the haystack. *Whoooa, steady boy. What now?* He brushed leaves from his feet. One of his ankles was manacled! His eyes followed the slim chain to a steel girder. *Good God, what was he dealing with here? The White Slave Trade?*

Sam lay back, quietly, in the haystack, his twitching hands clutching *ha ha* at straws.

The utter silence recalled something to his mind: *a vital clue.* Sam slipped his hand behind the doll's head: *wiring, but no soundbox.* Sam recalled now—with a Sinister Prickling—how the doll had both pitched *and* groaned.

Sam spoke calmly, putting into it as much toughness as could be expected from a man with his *ha ha* dickie bird locked in a cage: "Okay....Whoever you are ... what's your name, and what's your game?" *Come out with your hands up,* so to speak.

The silence lengthened. Sam sweating it out, was about to repeat his question, when a voice interrupted him ... slowly ... with a sharp edge of menace.

"My name is not important. As for my *game,* that depends on what we both choose to make it."

Sam felt a prick *ha ha* of relief. *A woman! Someone hiding behind the busted Valentine heart! Someone trying to disguise her voice! Was it a joke?* He thought of Rosa Grebb in *From Russia With Love* with razors in her shoes and again felt that all-too-familiar Sinister Prickling. *The kind of twisted mind that would do such a thing! Jeezus! She must be bonkers!*

"I'm not crazy, this is no joke, and I'd advise you not to try any funny stuff," said the voice anticipating his every thought. It paused, then added, "This may seem a little *strange* to you, Ryan, but you'll get used to it."

*A little strange!* Sam was about to make a smartass remark with the compulsive part of his mind that did such things, but the detective part seized on another vital clue: "You know my name?"

"You bet I do, Ryan, though when we first met, twenty-five years ago, you were using the name Hancock."

Sam spoke very flatly, very positively. "I don't know anyone by the name of Hancock. Besides, twenty-five years ago I was still selling papers." He added amost plaintively: "I'm only forty-two!"

"Forty-*eight*," corrected the voice, with awesome authority. "I checked out your personal references, and very tacky they were too. As for you and Hancock—I didn't mean you were the same person, just the same type. You're both thieves!"

"Thieves?! I've been clean since I came out of the army!" exclaimed Sam, indignantly. He remembered this person seemed to have a direct line to the files and added grudgingly: "If you've been nosing through Expense Accounts

111

that's expected as part of income. It's the Hunter way *heh heh*—non-taxable!"

"No, Ryan, I'm not talking about Expense Accounts, though if you want some off-the-cuff advice, I'd suggest you lop a few zeros off your last creative effort. Hancock was an old buddy of my father's who kept turning up when Dad was out of town to try to sell me on what turned out to be a pretty rotten bill of goods. To make a long story short, he got what he wanted then bragged about it to my father—rather a dirty deal, wouldn't you say, for a cheap thrill and a bad anecdote?"

Sam felt a chill slide like an ice-cube down his spine. There was something about the deep-rooted bitterness in the woman's voice that was more frightening than any direct threat she might make. He looked at his cock, trapped in its cage, and thought about James Bond in *Goldfinger* awaiting castration by laser beam. He forced himself to ask, defiantly: "But what does *that* have to do with *me?*"

The woman laughed, harshly. "I think you've guessed Ryan. I want to do now what I should have done then and since I can't get my hands on Hancock, I'll have to settle for you!"

"But that's insane!" exclaimed Sam, trying to keep the tremor from his voice. "Whoever that bastard Hancock was, he has nothing to do with me! You can't go around substituting one person for another. It's inhuman."

"Right on!" exclaimed the voice, edged with Rosa Grebb's slipper-steel. "It is inhuman. But you jokers do it all the time, Ryan! The dame you screw one night is the same as the one you screw the next. *Hell!* You can actually screw a rubber doll and not notice the difference! How can you, of all people, complain about me substituting one double-dealer for another!"

Sam felt his breath exhale in a long sour stream. "I see." He couldn't take his eyes from Poor Big Red: *Was the cage electrified?* "You want revenge!"

"Yes, Ryan," agreed the voice, dripping with contempt. "But you have a *rotten* imagination and a dangerous habit of making love to your own doom. I got over the sort of revenge you're suggesting a long time ago. What I want revenge on now is stupidity!"

Sam laughed sarcastically. "Is that why you put this rattrap on my tail? Is this my rotten imagination?"

"As a matter of fact, it is," said the voice, tasting satisfaction. "Or at least, an extension of it."

"Come again?"

"Paranoia about the female 'trap' is common with you guys, Ryan. For you and the Hancocks of the world, love is a thieves' game. You like to snatch your thrills, fast, and cheap, like a piece of cheese, then get out, fast, before the trap shuts. For you, the whole game is in escaping the trap so you can brag about it afterwards, and not the mutual enjoyment of the cheese."

Sam, on a hunch, stuck his finger into the gooey stuff on the doll's thighs. He sniffed. *Cheeze Whiz!* He quipped: "Caught like a rat in a trap!"

The voice laughed, mockingly. "No, Ryan. I said you were a *thief*. I didn't say you were a *rat*. I might have said so a few hours ago, but that was before I saw how right you looked in the mask you've got on now."

Sam remembered the Halloween mask he bought from the kid for a sawbuck. He had—in his considerable excitement—forgotten to take it off. He fondled the fuzzy ears, deriving a certain tigerish reassurance. *Ahhhh, yes!* He rattled his cage in bravado: "You've got a Tiger by the tail *ha ha!*"

The voice corrected him, still with that ironic edge: "No, Ryan. 'Tiger' might have been invited, but judging by your mask, that's not who came."

Sam was puzzled. "Not Tiger?"

"Definitely not Tiger."

Sam, wary, put his hands to his face. He felt ... *large round eyes ... a little turned-up nose.* He remembered, very clearly now, the kid *and* the mask. Definitely not Tiger. With a sinking feeling he felt the wide idiotic grin: *Mickey Mouse!* He remembered something else: in luminous paint, yet!

Sam felt his stomach churn. "It was a mistake!" he blurted. "I was dead drunk! I just paid the kid a sawbuck and grabbed for the ears!"

The voice cut softly through the dark: "No, Ryan. No mistake. Out of a whole streetful of masks you *chose* Mickey Mouse. Given your talents for self-satire, you, more than anyone else, are the type inclined to wear your real feelings about yourself on your sleeve."

*Sleeve?* Again Sam felt a digestive lurch. He looked down at his wrist: Again, Mickey Mouse grinned back ... luminously! Sam tore out a curse that ended in a groan. He ripped the watch from his arm and threw it through the broken heart. "It's a *joke,* you idiot!" He remembered having trouble over just that point with the bartender and shouted: *"Doesn't anyone have a sense of humour any more?!"*

The voice continued relentlessly: "No, Ryan. No joke. We all 'rat' on ourselves one way or another. You like to think of yourself as a hotshot detective, eh? Well, old fellow, even Dr. Watson could look at all the clues you leave around and see you're no tiger as you like to think or even a rat as you fear. You only pretend to be tough while you snatch the cheese, but when the trap shuts you become what you are—a mouse who enjoys the trap . . . a mouse who likes to roar!"

The voice turned unexpectedly soft, even gentle. "I called you a thief, Ryan, a love thief. But no one steals anything he has a right to. Why do you think you have to steal love, Ryan? Why a rat or a mouse? Why a tiger or a pussy cat? Why not just a man who's sometimes mean, sometimes meek and often lonely? It's my experience, Ryan, that while most guys pretend to be out for what they can get, most settle for what they think they deserve."

Sam put his Mickey Mouse head between his knees and, in a petulant child's voice, wailed: "It's all very well for *you* to talk so smug, so knowing in the dark, where no one can see you. What about me, sitting here with my cock in a goddamned cage!? If I weren't trapped, you wouldn't be so smart!"

"Ahhh, yes," sighed the voice. "I had forgotten the 'trap,' Ryan, because . . . you see, the cage isn't really a cage. It's just a device made by the Japanese to aid them with 'problems' to a lustier love life. If you had looked for the catch instead of rattling the cage, it would have fallen off. The same goes for your 'manacles.' They're from a kid's detective set. You're free to go, now, Ryan, as you always were . . . if you hadn't deen so damned eager to prove your fantasies about the treachery of women."

Sam, tight with fury, yanked the cage from Big *ha ha* Red Herring. He wrenched the chain from his ankle. He snarled, *"Gggggggggggrrrraaaaaaaaa!"* feeling the sound catch on his Mickey Mouse mask.

Sam started to laugh. He laughed until he choked. He tore off the mask and fell into the haystack. He vomited into the haystack. He retched into the straw, remembering what it had been like to sleep with three brothers, face down in a tick full of cockroaches, masturbating while they told each other what they were going to do when they got to be Big Shots. He remembered that day at camp when the boys had stopped laughing at Elmo and had started laughing at him because he picked the brown seeds out of the Red River cereal, thinking they were bugs, then had eaten the rest!

"I'm sorry, Ryan. I didn't know things would go so far. That's the trouble with jokes—we all know a hell of a lot more about ourselves and each other than we dare let on except when we're 'kidding'. . . . You're right about the courage of the dark—I had that all right, but it still doesn't change the fact that *you're a fool!* All you were supposed to do tonight was to come here, see the doll, know you'd been had, and, maybe get your finger caught. It was *your* idea to turn up dead drunk. It was *your* idea to wear the Mickey Mouse mask. It was *your* idea to accept the goddamned invitation in the first place when you knew all the guys were out to get you. As for myself, Ryan, I'll just say this—maybe I was part of the joke from the beginning, or maybe I got curious and came along on my own hook. Maybe the others got tired of waiting when you didn't show and buggered off to get drunk, or maybe they didn't come in the first place. The only thing I'll tell you for sure is that this place is spooked—can't you feel it? Can't you smell it. There's something in here—something that gets to you after a couple of hours. I'm leaving, Ryan, bailing out, and if you're smart, you'll sober up and do the same. Why don't we just say I was a figment of your imagination and put the whole thing down to an interesting evening?"

*Interesting? Interesting!* Again Sam felt a Sinister Prickling, only now it was more of a tickle. He started to laugh, this time in a great belly boom tippling up through his torso, in waves so powerful they nearly capsized the ship he had tattooed on his chest one never-to-be-forgotten night in Halifax. He was drunk, of course. He was hallucinating! That's why he felt so relaxed, so free, so happy. Sam rolled over and over in the Thanksgiving haystack, imagining he was caressing a dainty female foot, smelling sweetly of powdered roses. Rosa Grebb, smelling of *ha ha* roses! *Of course! A figment of my imagination!* Only Sam Ryan could have thought of something so clever. *Oh, me and my sense of humour! If only I could get some of this good stuff down!*

# 5. Beau & Morgan

Beau Whitehead sat on a stool in his office in the basement of the Candy Factory, his long legs wrapped around the stool's long legs, his thin shoulders hunched in his white kaftan as he wrote in an onionskin notebook.

Beau's work was, as usual, interspersed with much fussy detail. He would rub his palms, or catch a dry cough, or mop us leakage from his pen, or play with his mauve glasses, or pass his fringed white scarf over his skull that glowed through flaxen hair like a lightbulb.

The office and everything in it had been compulsively painted white, and furnished by Beau with items of religious significance.

His desk was once a cathedral altar. His seats were formerly church pews. On his walls were brass-rubbings of saints which he himself had done on a tour of European churches. Dominating his office was an alabaster replica of Michelangelo's Pieta.

Around Beau's desk were columns of notebooks, taken from drawers and filing cabinets. The research project, for which he had been government-funded, was nearing completion. Though Charles X. had mentioned vaguely he might like Beau to stay on as a Personnel Consultant, Beau did not think Basil Fitch would tolerate him on the premises one semi-colon past the time it took him to finish. Basil Fitch had his heart set on replacing Beau with a Time-and-Motion man.

Beau was relaxing now, day's end, with work on a psycho-analytic paper on which he liked to lavish his passions.

Sucking on his white pen, he reread what he had just written:

HYPOTHESIS
It is my belief that much seemingly erratic, bizarre, and "illogical" human behaviour can be attributed to the

117

workings of the Death Wish in opposition to the Life Wish.

## DEATH WISH IN THE HUMAN PSYCHE

Though the Death Wish is found "pure" in humans only during the act of suicide, at other times it can be found in admixtures throughout the personality, such as in dangerous "thrill" activity, excessive smoking or drinking, in drug-taking, in "killing" workloads and in other masochistic behaviour.

Danger mobilizes the wish to live, but what isn't properly understood is that it also mobilizes the wish to die.

Imagine the human head to be full of magnetic bars with positive charge (Life Wish) on one end and negative charge (Death Wish) on the other. In "normal" situation, these charges lie about haphazardly in the head, more or less neutralizing each other so that a person survives day to day with the Death Wish visible to others only in what appears to be a wasteful, stupid, or masochistic deposition of his energy.

Now, imagine danger to be a magnet outside the person's head.

Immediately, the electrical charges line up so that all the positive charges face to attack the enemy. That means the negative charges, too, will be lined up, but *in the opposite direction.* If the danger is shortlived—as when a man is attacked in a barroom fight by another man—afterwards the magnetic charges revert to normal (to neutralization) before much damage is done. However, if danger is prolonged—as in modern warfare—the effects of the polarization of negative power must inevitably be felt so that while the will to live controls, say, the right hand, the will to die begins to control the left. Therefore, an organism too long involved in the fight for survival becomes, inevitably and secretly, a schizophrenic organism as bent on destroying itself as its enemies; and the longer the Death Wish is suppressed, the more dangerously it builds up as a Destroyer inside the self.

I will illustrate this from an analysis of nations.

## DEATH WISH IN NATIONS

Consider Canada, a country with little history of war

and, hence, one with a "normal" personality in which the Life and Death Wishes are neutralized internally.

In this country the psychic balance is struck, and held, by the largest population bloc (the English-speaking bloc). This bloc balances its Life and Death urges by dominating (Life Wish) the French-Canadian bloc while allowing, even enjoying, domination (Death Wish) first by Britain and then by the United States, rather like a man who bullies his wife while toadying to his mistress. When the French wife rebels, upsetting the balance, he must look for better terms from the mistress, since the *balance* is more important to his personality than either the wife or the mistress.

Now consider Germany, a polarized nation with a history of war. Today, Germany is popularly seen as a "winning" nation that "just happened" to lose two World Wars. The importance of military aggression (Life Wish) to the German personality has often been analyzed, but what has *not* been properly assessed is that nation's masochistic need for self-destruction or—to put it in metaphorical terms—the German nation's need to play, like a compulsive gambler, through victory after victory to defeat.

Hitler has been fashionably seen as the personification of Germany's aggressive needs during the Second World War, but historians shrink from also seeing him as the personification of Germany's masochistic needs, although a polarized Life Wish *and* a polarized Death Wish *always* go together, so that when you see an exaggerated need, in any nation or in any individual, for domination or success or pleasure or sexual gratification or material possession or territorial expansion, you will always find the opposite and equal need in that same organism for subservience or failure or pain or sexual denial or poverty or dispossession. This opposite masochistic need may be played out simultaneously with the Life Wish, or alternately, or in competing spheres, as seen, for example, in the tycoon who balances spectacular professional achievement with spectacular personal unhappiness.

Consider, again, the tyrant Hitler. Here was a man who, while presiding over the slaughter of millions, reportedly chose as his sexual "pleasure" to have his mistress defecate on his face. To put it another way:

while raining destruction upon his enemies, he acted out his own Death Wish by having destruction pour down on his face in identification with his victims.

He was also, not surprisingly, a man with a history of attempted suicide, once actually having to have a gun wrestled from his temples. Is it not possible that Germany merely became the revolver that he chose to shoot off, sometimes wildly, sometimes devastatingly, into the crowd, acting out a fluctuating Life-Death wish as lunatics often do before turning it, as he always intended, on himself? Is it not possible that, in allowing herself to be such a revolver in such a hand, Germany might have had the same conflicting Life-Death urges and, in the end, shot herself?

In speaking of Germany and Hitler in the last days of the Second World War, I am illustrating how sometimes the Death Wish in a schizophrenic organism will break out even while the fight for survival is at its fiercest. Thus, the last days of the Third Reich were characterized by military blunders that can be understood only when that country's secret connivance against itself is taken into account. Similarly, the atrocities that characterized the German struggle, and the selection of the Jews as official victims, were the ways in which that country acted out its secret Death Wish in a desperate attempt to control it, for a tyrant is always joined to his victim by his own need to suffer, and any victim, too long a victim, acquires the same polarized need both to suffer and to dominate.

More usually, during an actual battle, the countries involved store up their Death Wish until the end, then play it out masochistically over a period of years.

This accounts for some of the strange aftermaths of war: e.g., the frequency with which "victor" nations destroy themselves politically or economically after their victories, or are seduced by the culture of their "defeated" enemy, while the enemy that has satiated its Death Wish in defeat arises like the proverbial phoenix from the ashes.

Consider the stunning economic recovery of both Germany and Japan after the Second World War in contrast to the way in which Britain has *wilfully* plucked ruination from the jaws of victory with an air of stiff-upper-lip enjoyment. Consider the predictable military emergence of Israel (Life Wish) after the years spent as Europe's conspicuous victims (Death Wish). Consider the purges of Stalin, which satisfied his own and Russia's need to act out a Death Wish against itself after victory. Consider the Cold War which, by extending hostilities through international intrigue, provided a wartime denouement that probably saved both Russia and the United States the psychological need for economic disaster.

The last country I will mention in any detail is the United States. Here is a young country settled by polarized people fleeing religious, economic and political oppression, who further polarized themselves through struggles with the land and with the Indians. As a nation, the United States has fulfilled its aggressive needs (Life Wish) through economic imperialism and its destructive needs through civil war, clinging to the frontier tradition, and latterly, in crime and civil disorder.

The tragic problem for this country is that it became mobilized for war at the same time modern warfare became too dangerous. Since it could not *dare* to fight a large country to win, it had no choice but to fight a small country to lose. Consider how vaingloriously that country strove for defeat in Viet Nam, like an elephant casting itself on bamboo sticks in hopes some were poisoned. Even then its wounds were not sufficient for its self-destructive needs, and its citizens have had to take to the streets with guns and clubs to destroy it from within. *I pity that tormented Goliath!* When you must destroy yourself as Rome did, the terms of defeat are not nearly as generous as when you throw yourself on the mercy of a grateful conqueror who knows, in his secret soul, he must nourish your resentment against the time when he himself is in masochistic need of crushing defeat.

Beau put down the report.

He pressed his fingertips to his temples, then, gripping his white pen, wrote in a rapidly flowing script:

PERSONAL APPLICATION

I write of countries only by way of illustration, since

121

their battles are external, and hence there to be studied. My main concern is the personal application of this theory to myself and to my troubling relationship with—

"Hi, man!"

Beau looked up.

Morgan Jones filled his white door frame to overflowing, his shadow more than doubling his bulk.

Beau started guiltily. He turned out his light—a gesture of welcome, since Morgan didn't like the whitewash glare of the room, which he said reminded him of the Jones' chickencoop back in Nova Scotia.

Morgan grinned: "You going to the Daphne leavetake?"

"I thought I would, but there's no hurry," said Beau. "Come and sit if you like."

Morgan strolled into the room, carrying his battered guitar. "Sit? You mean *set*." He flapped his arms and clucked as he settled like a chicken come to roost, then, breaking that pose, *sp-r-aw-led* over Beau's church pew with such confident control that he seemed to bend the starchy boards to the looseness of his own body. He was wearing faded cherry-velvet pants, a mended turquoise satin shirt open to a silver buckle, and a string of lovebeads given to him by one or another of the "chicks" with whom he smoked pot, freaked out, watched horror films, mated. "Don't let me distract you none," he said, plucking his guitar strings. "My head didn't get up with me this morning. It's just a *hole* in the air."

Beau tried to continue writing, as instructed, but conscious now of the nearness of Morgan as if Morgan were his own shadow, blotting him out the way the shadow of his hand tracked itself across the page, blotting each word as it was written. Six months ago the two of them had often sat like this, with Morgan strumming his guitar and humming in a honied bass while Beau poured words from his white pen onto the page, occasionally intoning them in a sing-song falsetto, making a liturgy of it, each seeming to derive humour and comfort and stability from the presence of the other. Now, however, that balance had been broken, tipped in Morgan's favour so that those things that had once complemented seemed to be gathering to challenge. Beau felt that challenge as one of a crouched and watchful sexuality between them. He looked covertly at Morgan's turquoise shirt, framing a glossy black arrowhead of flesh that pointed to the

122

guitar he held like a woman between his legs, with his cherry-velvet thighs shifting round it, embracing it. Was Morgan tempting him? *Consciously? Unconsciously?*

Beau toyed sweatily with his white pen, accidentally ejecting a squirt of ink onto his notebook. He nervously dabbed up the spill with Kleenex, feeling Morgan's chocolate eyes nudge round him. Beau disciplined himself. He stroked his pen slowly, methodically, wiping off the last traces of its effusions, then, clasing it against a permanent finger callous, inscribed in bold block letters:

## PHYSICIAN HEAL THYSELF

Beau capped his pen. He folded his hands on his desk-altar. He peered down at Morgan through mauve glasses. He asked solemnly as a preacher announcing his text: "Morgan, do you understand the source of the attraction between us?"

Morgan looked up in exaggerated surprise. He lay his hand, flat, against his guitar strings. He grinned flatteringly: "We *commune*, man."

Beau persisted: "Do you know why we commune?"

Morgan laughed, a mellowy gut-sound ending in a lot of pink tongue and white teeth: "What sort of chickenshit question is that, *friend?* You want something in writing? Some personal *tes-ti-mony* saying what a *f-iiii-ne* boy Beau Whitehead is? Because if *that's* what you want, man, you better ask a white boy with *ed-u-cay-shun!*"

It was the sort of response Beau expected—a plea of ignorance wrapped in nuances that mockingly indicated the opposite.

Beau leaned back on his stool, pretending more casualness than he felt. "I know you like to play 'little Black Sambo who ain't got the sense he was born wif,' but I also know that you have a lively, intuitive intelligence, when you care to use it. I've talked *at* you, many times, about my theory of opposites—that whenever you have apparent opposites you should always look for the connection between them. We're opposite, you and I. We're every cliche about black boy and white boy, sensualist and rationalist, man-of-action vs. man-of-words. What would *you* say is the connection between us?"

Morgan shook his head. "I *wouldn't* say, man. That's *your* bag, but if I *had* to say, I'd say the connection between us is

123

*craziness.* You *talk* crazy, and I'm sometimes crazy enough to listen, but you're crazier than I am, *white boy,* because you're a wet white hen flapping your chickenwhite tongue while the sun goes down, whilst I am big black jim-crow sitting here a-hatching my nice nest of *ex-ploding* black eggs whilst the moon is rising."

Morgan began flapping his arms and cawing as he had before, making a comic act out of a speech laced with menace. He moved easily into a chorus of "Old MacDonald Had A Farm," expecting Beau to join in.

Beau did not. Instead, he sat, soberly, his alabaster fingers laced on his desk, studying Morgan under brows like twin gothic arches.

Morgan stopped singing.

He wrapped his arms around his guitar, hugging it to him. "All right, *pro-fes-sor.* You have my attention, but don't be surprised none if it wriggles a little whilst you are holding its tail." He laughed. "Don't be surprised if it curls its head, right around, and sticks its black tongue into your mouth."

Beau broke his stiff pose, scattering his power in a clutch of fussy gestures—wiping his forehead with his scarf, coughing into his hand, readjusting his mauve glasses.

He began to pace, his mind rushing ahead with his thoughts, his kaftan whipping about his ankles, not daring to look at Morgan, speaking rapidly, earnestly, matching compulsive action with a reckless gush of words. "You know very little about me, Morgan—much less than I know about you. Though you were poor and I rich, I, too, was the spoils of a bad marriage. From the instant of my birth, my parents fought for possession of me. My father tried to seduce me with external success. My mother with a loveless love that enslaved. I had no choice but to deny both the material world and the sexual feelings my mother aroused in my body. It escaped into my mind, leaving my body to smile and nod politely at all the appropriate intervals. I escaped—"

"Whooa back!" interrupted Morgan. "Whooooooa back, man! You are like Dirty Nick on a bad road with a hot coal stuck under his tail. I *told* you, pro-fes-sor, that you have my attention."

Beau stopped pacing. He ran his scarf over his dewy forehead, still not looking at Morgan. When he began to pace again, it was with a slow, cautious tread, picking up the words where he left off, and laying them down along with his feet.

"One day . . . when I could stand the battles no longer . . . I ran away from home—as you, Morgan, ran away. Whereas you fled to the Temples of the Flesh, I chose the Temples of the Spirit.

"I hid out in a Jesuit Order in Quebec.

"I was a great success in that Order.

"I had fought so long for survival that my Life-Death urges had polarized, creating large caches of aspiration balanced by self-destruction in my personality, corresponding to the strivings and denials of Christianity, a faith which itself is founded by martyrs who were polarized from fighting too hard for survival.

"I developed a wondrous taste for flogging and self-torture. Pain had become my only allowable physical pleasure and though such practices were officially frowned upon, 'stripes' had a secret prestige equivalent to, say, duelling scars among German youth. The whip, slicing into my flesh, was like a deliciously cruel phallus. Add to that a hairshirt and you will see I was well into sexual perversion."

Beau stole a look at Morgan. He was outwardly relaxed, though he had drawn himself into a tighter, more protected entity on the white pew, his eyes watchful. Beau continued, soothed by the familiar flow of his own words, gaining confidence.

"At the same time I was being encouraged to eat and drink another man's body and blood, snatched from the grave for me. How comforting this was, now that I was beginning to believe I didn't properly have a body of my own! Of course I did not express these things to the others, or even to myself. The way it was put in the Order was that we were not so much denying feelings as developing *higher* feelings. We were not grave-robbing but putting on the spiritual body of Christ."

Beau picked up a dagger from his desk-altar. He held it like a crucifix and, unsheathing it, ran his thumb along the blade.

"I was happy for about a year in the Order, learning the Latin names for all the flowers in the Garden of Eden, planting beads in rows, growing vines from staffs and adoring the scarecrow that was all that was left of the body I and the other crows were picking clean. But, you know, I was like Eve, all the time shaking that Tree of Knowledge, and sneaking apples between the ritual meals of bread and wine, so that my head got too fat for my soul, and the others began to notice. Oh, they gave me Thomas Aquinas to help trace my trail of apple cores back to the Garden, but anyone that far out on the forked tongue of disbelief can never do anything but hiss and quibble on his belly through the tares and thistles of sincere regrets.

"The religious game was over for me, in any formal sense. I left the Order but—" Beau gave a philosophical shrug "—the damage begun by my parents had been completed. The physical had become so fused with guilt that all thought of bodily intimacy made me throw up—the most infantile celebration of the Death Wish."

Beau sighed, feeling the effects of his mental exertions, like an athlete relaxing after a workout: "Since then, I have devoted myself to theoretic research." He gestured to the notebooks, in white columns of varying height, forming a cage around his alter-desk. "Do you know what happened to those aspirers God struck from the Tower of Babel? They are all down in the bedrock of logic, worrying at the foundations of that ruined Tower, throwing up bricks of syllogisms, mortared by dictionaries on their search downward to the First Premise, but all they are going to find is the Devil's split tongue, pointed to Hell in two more directions!"

Beau took off his mauve glasses. He fixed Morgan with his gaze, unscreened, directly challenging him for the first time, his eyes of a startling blueness and intensity.

"Do you see, now, what I have been getting at? Do you see, now, the connection between us?"

Morgan yawned—elaborately. "*She-it*, man. You have been getting at shit. *White* shit. *Chicken*shit. I never knew anyone could pile the *shit* on like you, and I have seen *shit*-pilers in my time. Only one to come close was a teacher I had once. Scrawny, she was, with her head stuck on the cords of her neck like a potato on a fork, keeping Morgan after school whilst she ran her yellow claws up and down her *con-cave* chest like it was a scrub-board, the words cackling and crackling, dry as dust, in her throat, spraying all over Morgan like ce-ment dust."

Beau pursued: "The difference and the connection between us, Morgan, is that we both fought our parents in the same hopeless battle against takeover, but whereas I abandoned my body and escaped into my mind, exaggerating its function, you abandoned your mind and escaped into your body, exaggerating its function.

"Both victories were pyrrhic. What began as a defence became, through the release of our Death Wish, the route of our destruction.

"*I* have taken the flight from the body so far into the mind that it has become the strangulation of the body in the words and thoughts of the mind.

"*You* have taken the escape from the mind so far into the pleasures of the body that it has become the destruction of the mind through abuse of the body. You are grooming yourself to be a revolutionary who lusts to blow up himself while pretending to blow up the world."

Beau confronted Morgan, now tensed on his pew, his defences in a prickly forcefield around him. "Oh, I know you have legitimate racial grievances, but that isn't what's motivating your silly acts of sabotage against the Candy Factory. *All* acts of violence which are misdirected, or symbolic, or exceed their rational motive, or are sadistic, or exhibitionistic, or needlessly reckless, or martyrish are acts of self-hate projected as hatred of others, and it makes no difference whether the actor claims to be an assassin acting out of high political concern, or an activist righting a social wrong, or a hijacker robbing the rich for the poor, or a cult-leader blood-sacrificing to a new religion, or a tyrant correcting history, or even if the person succeeds in accomplishing a desirable purpose. The clue to the *real* motivation lies in the element of the irrational . . . of excess."

Beau pierced Morgan with his hypnotic blue eyes. "To sum up: I am becoming a man without a body, incapable of *rational action*, while you are becoming a man without a mind, incapable of *rational thought*."

Morgan struck a derisive chord on his guitar. "That is the craziest thing I ever heard!" He shifted on his seat, fusing the swishy sound with a low growl: "It is *you*, man, who has lost your head—clean vacated! You are *crazy*, man!"

Beau gave a small vinegary smile. "Craziness is a matter of degree, and how many others one can seduce into sharing one's own brand of delusions."

Again he picked up the dagger from his desk. He tested the point against his palm. Turning toward the wall, he spread the palm of his left hand against the flat surface, drew the knife back to his shoulder and, with a powerful lunge, stabbed through his hand into the wall behind.

Morgan pitched forward, as if struck. "Hey man, stop!"

Beau wriggled the fingers of his grotesquely impaled hand. "I didn't feel that and my hand is undamaged."

He wrenched the dagger out and displayed his hand, back and front. "See? The skin is broken but there is no blood. Bodily function without feeling."

Morgan let out a low whistle. "A *car-ni-val* man I knew used to do that back in Hal-i-fax. Put knives right through his skin and walked on fire. Name of Old Elephant Skin. What's the trick, man?"

Beau shook his head. "No trick. At least, not in the sense of fakery." He sheathed the dagger, again holding it like a cross. "Eastern mystics have long known the secret of withdrawing blood supply from chosen parts of the body and controlling 'involuntary' action such as heatbeat, though western doctors are just now studying it scientifically under the name of biofeedback."

"C'mon, man!" cajoled Morgan. "What's the trick. Or do you belong in that *other* tent, the *freak* tent?"

"No trick," affirmed Beau. "As for my *freakiness* that doesn't lie in my ability to withdraw feeling but in my having lost the knack of returning it. I'm a man without the sense of touch or any sensitivity to physical pleasure or pain. I am a man without a body . . . except for the eyes."

Beau tossed the dagger to Morgan. It landed on the church pew with a terrible clatter. "See for yourself." He stretched his hand against the wall, his voice rising excitedly: "Stab me. Plunge the dagger into me. Pierce me through."

Morgan scooped up the dagger, with unexpected energy. "*Stab* me!" he mocked, in a strident falsetto. "*Plunge* the dagger into me! *Oh, Morgan, baby—pierce me through!*"

Beau flushed—a crimson glow beginning at his chin and moving up through his cheeks and ears like a chalice filling with wine.

Morgan laughed in a high-pitched whine, accompanying himself with dark chords on his guitar. "What *you* need, man, is now plain! *Now* I see where all this *shit* has been leading! What *you* need is a *woman*!" He began to sing:

"A *fat* woman!

"A *car-ni-val* woman!

"A few hundred pounds of Mrs. Jones

"A-jiggling and a-jiving over your bones!

"A *car-niv-orous* woman

"To flatten Beau out!

"As flat as a pancake!
"A Aunt Jemima pancake!
"As flat as a wa-fer!
"A Je-sus wafer!
"To *squeeze* a little syrup out his spout!"

Beau got down from his stool so awkwardly he upset it. He fled across his office to his statue of the alabaster Virgin holding the crucified Christ in her arms. He composed himself, his back to Morgan, his body as stiff and white as the statue, his hands knotted.

"This is my Pieta," he said in a tight voice. "I bought her from the Jesuits, with a small legacy from my grandfather. See how radiantly her skin glows! See how real she is! How human!

"Tell me, Morgan, does a statue have feelings? Can a statue, that is treated as if it were human, become human, in the same way a person who is treated as a statue, becomes a statue?

"The Indians believed there were spirits in stones, in clouds, in corn, in water. Were they wrong? Did they anthromorphosize nature by projecting their own humanity on it? Or did we mechanize nature as an extension of the way we have dehumanized ourselves?

"For my part, I have read every story, every legend in which statues are said to have come to life, and I have studied every historical incident in which statues have been said to weep, or shed blood, or to express other signs of humanness. Except where there is deliberate fraud, I am inclined to see all such incidents as authentic, and it doesn't matter that the season was more humid than usual, or the statue exceptionally porous, or that a leak was discovered in old plumbing. When one thing wishes to speak to another in a language that is not its own, it must do the best it can with what is at hand."

Beau put out his hand to the face of the Virgin, then floated his fingers down to the face of the crucified Christ, fondling its features as he sometimes fondled his own.

"I am a man of great limitations, but also of great hope, for I believe that if this statue, being stone, could bleed and cry, then maybe I can someday unlock my own passions and looking into her merciful beauty, it is impossible for me not to have faith.

"You, too, must keep alive such a hope, Morgan.

"You, too, must struggle against your Destroyer. You must

track him back through the pitchy maze of hatred and guilt that gave him birth. You must make peace with your past, as I am struggling to do. You must strangle your Destroyer with understanding. You must leave room in your heart for a miracle."

Beau turned.

He took two steps toward Morgan, his arm extended, like the statue's, a look of intense sweetness on his face.

He recoiled.

Morgan had drawn into the corner of the pew like an animal into a hole, his body drenched in sweat, his eyes rolled back into his head. He was masturbating, his penis pointed toward Beau.

Beau put his hand to his mouth.

He turned.

He fled.


Morgan Jones rocked back and forth on the white pew, holding onto his cock for dear life.

He could feel sweat in a hot white band around his forehead.

He could feel it a-boiling in his armpits and a-trickling through the swampy hair of his chest.

He felt his cock burn—a hot, hard stick of dynamite as he held it in his hands and rocked on his heels, his eyes rolled clear round in their sockets, shutting out the white chickenshit room, shutting out the whole chickenshit world ... going back into his own self, into the dark of his head like it was the dark side of the moon, riding his cock as a firecracker through the night sky, like he should have done when she first called him, going back home *I'm coming I'm coming I'm coming* to Big Mama. . . .

Pearl and Tillie were already sponging off the clammy mound of *flesh of my flesh of my flesh* when Morgan opened the tarpaper door, with Mama *inside* her scrub tub instead of *at* it, and the steam rising and the soap suds flying as they scrubbed the pink soles of her feet, with Pearl singing the high notes and Tillie the low, instead of taking them both together, like Mama would do, crying and carrying on as if they both thought Mama was really dead.

They stuffed her into her pink corsets that were hanging around her like the broken staves of a pink barrel, lacing them tight, like Mama always did for an occasion, squeezing her like two purple eggplants into the neck of the black silk dress, paid for from the catalogue, but never worn, still creased from the package, with seams filled up out of pieces from another dress, almost matching—Mama was too big for a store-bought dress, the brown flesh a-bubbling and a-boiling, sweet and funky, right through the seams, like chocolate poured too hot into its wrapper. *Oh mama mama mama mama. . . .*

Jud and Lionel made the box out of pineboards bought for a pig pen to replace the one burnt down three times by the town toughs, with Morgan wanting more nails, more and more nails stuck in. Even then he could feel Mama restless, threatening to come *oozing* through the seams—too big for a store-bought box.

The twins fought over the shoes.

Which to put on? Would Mama want the old ones, with the places cut for the bunions, because of the journey, or would she want the new ones, because of the occasion—*Devil's hooves*, she called them, sent to try her.

Pearl decided on the new ones—but, to please Aggie—without the laces. Then they had to roll Mama into her box, 357 pounds, last time she got weighed at the *car-ni-val*, with the man with the spangle-headed cane running his hands over her haunches and guessing 326, and Mama *a-hee-hawing* while they dragged the scale from the cattle tent, stepping on it like she was a queen, proud of her honest weight, and the man paying her with the spangle-headed cane, and then, when the crowd clapped, adding a celluloid doll, and then, when Mama curtseyed and the crowd cheered, asking her *psst* private, to come back the next day, and the next, giving her a horse with a clock in its belly, the once't and a velvet pillow with a palm tree on it t'other, then telling her—*say, lissen, Nellie*—next time to tie leg-irons up her skirts, with Mama hitting him *swoosh* with the spangle-headed cane, leaving the spangles on his forehead: "I ain't wearing no leg-irons, *mistah*. You get yourself a *nig-gah!*"

They started the funeral at the crack of dawn the way Mama always started her day, first needing to hoist the pinebox onto the wagon. Why weren't Lionel and Jud lifting? Mama would give them mouth, if her tongue weren't curled tight round her lucky silverpiece that Little Pa found stuck in the tar under the steamroller, before he got stuck there hisself

131

and then rolled flat, busting every bone in his body. *Oh mama mama mama mama. . . .*

Morgan wiped his forehead with his fist, then struck it against the pinebox. He shouted at Jud and Lionel in Mama's voice: "Lazy no-counts! Where is your *brawn*, boys? Where is your *brains*?"

He called Pearl and Tillie and the twins to the side of the box, all breathing together and hoisting, so, in the end, it was like their breath pumped up Mama from the ground and floated her, light as a feather, onto the wagon, the way Mama used to start out, real low and easy, when she "caught the spirit" in church, with the notes a-growling in her belly, then rumbling up through her chest, so full and deep she drowned out Benny Bowles on the organ, even with his son under his white gown, pumping the pedals, then pitching her notes to the top of her skull, so high and shrill she could a-set the churchbells ringing by themselves, with the white chicken-folk, sitting bolt upright on their roosts, their fillings rattling in their teeth, and even deaf-as-a-post Mr. Mote, a-yanking at his hearing-aid, spinning the dials, till Rev. Gaul set her to sleep, too often, praying too long with his flabby white-coat tongue, and Mama decided to stay home, of a Sunday, for to sing to the pigs and the real chickens, not nailed down to the notes aforehand, just pitching them out as they came of themselves to her throat. . . . *Oh mama mama mama mama.*

Morgan hitched Dirty Nick to the wagon, his bones sticking through his hide like they was a silver saddle, his brasses polished till they glinted like gold in the risen sun, the wagon whitewashed by the twins, and twisted with black-crepe streamers and roses from Mama's brier patch.

Morgan climbed onto the seat, flicking the dust from his shiny silver-cleat shoes and his velvet pants, as red as cherries, sitting where Mama used to sit holding hands with Pa, for as long as he had lasted, feeling the reins rough in his hands, gone soft as white-flour since he went to Peacock Town. He waited for Jud and Lionel and Pearl and Tillie and the twins to climb aboard, and then he started Dirty Nick, *gee-up*, down the dusty road, holding his turquoise satin arms out from his body, for to keep them from sweating, and feeling the cart swaying from rut to rut, like it was Mama herself taking a lame road, and remembering her telling him when he was little, with the tears rolling down her cheeks, half singing the words, the story of Old Sheena, Queen of the Elephants, taking herself across the golden desert for to die, with the sun like cup of blood a-boiling in the sky, and the rest of her family strung out for a mile behind . . . first Shula, the crown prince, and then the elders joined one to t'other by trunk to tail, with their ears billowed out to the sides, like they was big black sails, and their tusks held high like golden scythes, one foot and then t'other, with the sand a-shimmering as hot as if it was a-fire, holding each other up, when they fell to a knee . . . taking Old Sheena to the Elephants' Graveyard for to die.

They come upon it just as the sun was setting, and it was right cool, and black, and wet, and green, with the palms waving like they was fans, making them right to welcome, and they started dancing around it, slow at first, like they was scarcely moving, just setting the ground a-gently to rumble, with Sheena in the centre of the black bog, and them going round and round, the one still joined to t'other, then faster, now, pounding their feet, first one and then t'other, round and round in that thick black bog, folding back the palms now, like they was blades of grass, their corrugated trunks a-tonguing that black earth, and throwing it over Old Sheena in a swooshy stream, then tossing back and trumpeting to the reddening sky, with old Sheena, up to her knees now, gleaming wetly like she was oil, turning to pink in the setting sun, and the others going round and round, like they was a single ring of heaving flesh, a-rippling and a-heaving in a squishy circle, with those little kid elephants a-sliding in and out, under their mamas' bellies, in and out, with the mist rolling up from the bog, and Old Sheena up to her hams now, head held high, till—*sudden!*—the tops of them gum trees EXPLODES!!!

Then comes a *bar-rage* of bullets, from every which way! and now the elephants are falling to their knees, one and then t'other trying to hold each other up, with this and that one, flopping on his'n'her side! and the little kids diving under their mamas' bellies, for to hide! and this and that mama falling over, and crushing her own! and the trunks going up, a-trumpeting to the skies! and the bullets pumping, one and then t'other into them shuddering hides! each one flopping over, up to their knees in gore and slime! and Old Sheena is strung to the trees, by her golden tusks, with the blood of her family up to her eye! and they is onto them elephants, not yet dead! and they is hacking them tusks, right out of their heads! and Old Sheena is seeing her family with blood spurting up to the blackening sky! and they is hacking her tusks, first one and then t'other, without the mercy of a bullet to the eye! and now she is sinking below her eye, and it is dark across the sky, and the tusks is piled in a gory heap, and all of them Big White Hunters is fast to sleep, and now it is black as it can be, and there is a bit of twitching in the elephant heap, and out of Sheena's belly Prince Shula creeps, while rising beside him, into the sky, right full and bright *is Sheena's eye!* She shines and shines for the prince to see ... one white face, my son, and then t'other ...

Prince Shula throws back his trunk and screams to the sky: "A ELEPHANT NEVER FORGETS—OR DIES!!!!!!!!!!!"


Morgan slowed Dirty Nick.

They were at the "Welcome to Bartonville" sign, with a pothole the size of the road to make it official. He eased the creaky wagon over the hole, with Mama jiggling in her box, and the village stretched for two miles down the road, strung gap-toothed, with a store, a poolhouse, and a church at either end.

Morgan stopped the wagon.

He looked up the double row of unpainted houses, and tasted bile: Big Mama should have waited to die. Then he could've bought a car and driven her in style. Then everyone would've known that Morgan Jones had been to a place where Black was Beautiful, and even the white chicks had lined up to play with his hair and to ask to lick his big black cock like it was a popsicle, instead, here he was, back on the wagon, with Jud and Lionel and Pearl and Tillie and the twins, in their mended best, like when they used to ride through town on Sat'day night, with Mama's box a-jiggling where the can used to rattle for to catch the slops as Morgan and Pa threw them up from the town privies, with the saloon toughs a-running after them like they was flies, a-holding their noses and shouting: "Here comes the honeywagon!" and pointing to Dirty Nick every time he had to lift his tail, "Watch out, yer leaking!" and dropping their pants, offering to do it, bums out, right in the can, and tossing toilet rolls so they strung out all over the shitcart, over Dirty Nick and Ma and Pa and Morgan and the rest, like they was streamers, never a-tiring of the game, something to do, something to do, on a Sat'day night, till the guv'ment put in a bit of money in time for an election, and most of the plumbing moved indoors.

Morgan felt his satin shirt, sticking like sheet metal to his back, and the sweat trickling down his lovebeads. *She'd done it on purpose! She hadn't wanted him to leave! She'd cursed him! She'd tricked him to come back!* He could hear her guts, a-jiggling and a-laughing back there in her pinebox. *Laughing at him!* At the men's *co-logne*, and the *gir-lee* beads, and the *dan-di-fied* clothes, *like any white nig-gah gone to Pea-cock Town.*

Morgan could feel the shirt clot under his arms, and the white dust seep up from the road, over his velvet pants and shiny silver-cleat shoes. He could smell the shit through the whitewash and roses with his *ci-ti-fied* nose.

Morgan felt his cock burn, like it always used to when he saw the toughs run toward him with the toilet rolls, shouting, "Morgan! Mor-gan! Let's see your or-gan!" He had to pee something awful, the way he always used to, with Mama slapping him across the knees with her carnival cane, with the spangles wore off, making him to sit straight, with his legs crossed, feeling the pee burn through his guts like they was a-fire, waiting for the toilet rolls to hit, only now the toughs just stand there, outside of the poolhall, not moving, except maybe for to shift their eyes, and Tom Court, raising his battered fedora from his cabbage patch, and the Benoit sisters, home from Mass, ducking their heads and crossing themselves as Dirty Nick stumbled by, with black-crepe streamers replacing the white, bearing the last remains of Big Black Nellie Jones to her final resting place, by the Baptist church, at the far end of town.... Maybe Morgan would ask for the spot right beside the church, so Mama could be sure to hear the organ, with maybe a white marble angel over her, paid for by the money in Pa's silver tobacco tin, like the angel for Rev. Gaul's own wife, smiling down with big wings stretched wide for to shade her. . . . *oh mamamamamamamama.* . . .

Morgan stopped Dirty Nick.

The Baptists of Bartonville were spilling out of the church like skimmed milk from a jug, leaking across the wilty grass, with the whitewashed cart blocking the steps, and Dirty Nick not thinking about budging.

Rev. Gaul came towards them in his black robes, looking as if he'd just as soon not, his face a sickly yellow like it was a parsnip yanked up by the green hair.

135

Morgan stood up, in his velvet pants and satin shirt—still grander than anything else to be seen—and showed him the money in the tin box: $257.35, with $53.32 of it brought back from the land where Black is Beautiful, and the rest from a paper Pa had when he worked for the city—*stip-ifying* to Rev. Gaul his family's preference for a spot near the church and the organ, but not mentioning, out of politeness, how Mama had felt about their singing.

Rev. Gaul was not taking the tin box, glinty in the sun.

His hands were up to his gold-rimmed eyes, shading them, with the box dangling at the end of Morgan's arm. "Sorry, sorry. Impossible, sorry. Not enough room. Just families who are in already. You can't split the families, but nobody new, the same rule for everybody. Sorry, it's the county. They won't give us more land. . . . Where's your father? *Ahhhh*, yes, the accident. Why not try the Methodists?"

Morgan, a-sweating and a-burning drove the wagon back through town, this time with the Baptists stretched out in their cars behind him, and Dirty Nick, a-hogging the road, and taking it into his head to stop, like he hadn't done for a half-dozen years, at every shithouse, now a garden shed, and waiting a good thirty seconds each, ears back, paying Morgan no heed, swaying up the pitted road as far as the Methodist church, with the Baptists strung out behind.

The Methodists didn't have any room for Mama either, why not try the Catholics over to Port Doiron way?

Now Morgan was seething inside, feeling it a-boiling up through his cock, and leaking through the hair of his chest, with the poolhall toughs a-nudging each other now, and standing in a row, with their caps held over their hearts, and Dirty Nick still taking it into his head to stop at shithouses, and Morgan was whipping him now, whipping and whipping him across his bony silver back, first with the reins, and then with Mama's formerly spangled cane, till Dirty Nick recalled, of a sudden, why he was called Dirty Nick, and heaving hisself up like he hadn't done for at least a dozen years, bolted through Tom Court's sideyard, snagging the fishnet, hung up to dry, across the front of the shitcart, with Morgan wrapped inside, then through the cabbage patch and across the woodlot, ears flat, mouth foaming, with everyone holding onto everything for dear life, and the reins cutting through Morgan's *Peacock* hands, and the sweat drenching his turquoise shirt, so he can smell hisself through the cologne, and he has to pee something awful, still caught in the fishnet, with Mama jiggling in back, *a haw-hee-hawing* like she was fit to be tied, till they came to the black swamp where they used to bring forth plenty before someone strung up a barbedwire fence, and then shot Old Bones in the mouth, with Pearl only ten feet away (though on the report they said it was thirty-two feet, explaining how dogs were supposed to have licences off their own land, but to Old Bones, it *was* his land), and right then and there, by the swamp she loved. Mama took things into her own hands, and picking up her pinebox, like it was a wooden skirt, she stepped right off the wagon, planting herself on a rock, the way she used to sit down on a nailkeg, before announcing to the world: "Bless my soul, and fry me for the Devil, if this old tub of black butter is g'win to churn one more step before it takes its rest."

As soon as Dirty Nick felt Mama leaving, he stopped too. What Morgan wanted was one thing. What Big Mama wanted was another.

Jud and Lionel and Pearl and Tillie and the twins looked at Morgan, and Morgan looked at the swamp. He unhitched Dirty Nick. Mama had opined.

They took the whiskey, in jugs, off the wagon, and something good for snipping barbedwire, and they snipped their way through to the black waters and they pushed Big Mama through to the swamp on them jugs of whiskey, like they was wheels, and they prayed whatever anyone could remember— *Now I lay me. Yeh, brothers, hallelujah!*—watching the pinebox sink *sl-ow-ly* into the black bog, and dancing round it, first shuffling real slow, then faster and faster, like Morgan had once see on TV, throwing their heads back real far and flinging up their arms real high, carrying a scarecrow they got, along with the nets from Tom Court's sideyard, making yips way back in their throats, with the tears rolling down their cheeks, feeling the urge, the need, now that the sun was setting, to get it all out, and knowing this was how it should be done, up to their knees, now, in the black bog, with Black Nellie, in her black crepe streamers, sinking *s-l-ow-l-y* into black muck in a long low sucking sound, like she used to make herself, before pitching high, till there was nothing left to be seen at all, except for the rings of oily water, like they was black blood oozing out, with Morgan and Jud and Lionel and Pearl and Tillie and the twins, still dancing round and round, one foot and then t'other, chanting and a-swigging, till the sun had set and the mists had risen, a-boiling over the swamp, wrapping them round, with the moon riding high and full, like Old Sheena's eye, when—*sudden!*—the trees EX-PLODE! *sirens! lights!* the whole town moving in on them! blasting their flashlights in their faces.

Nobody interested before, but now: "Where's Nellie Jones? Where's Black Nellie? Foul play! contamination! typhoid! VD! Imagine! imagine! Puts their mothers in the swamp! Voodoo! black magic! witchcraft! the Devil's work! I seen their doll myself, up on stakes they had it, carrying it around! Couldn't believe my eyes—there they were, drunk as skunks, shuffling and singing, making sounds in the back of their throats like you'd never believe, not human! . . . Two calves sick, already, on the Thibodeau farm, just downstream. Oh, the Devil's work, the Devil! If not foul play, at least foul odour!"

They came with their ropes and their hooks and their pul-lies and their winches, and they blasted the swamp with their floodlights, poking holes into Big Nellie's grave, dredging up tires and rubber boots and half a car till they was bleeding up to their hips, in Mama's black blood, and, finally, bringing up the pinebox trimmed with black roses and—*ha-hee-hoohoo*—the back door *w-i-d-e* open, and Old Bones howling, and Big Nellie's silver eye riding high, blinking through black clouds.

A ELEPHANT NEVER FORGETS—OR DIES!!!!!!!!!

Morgan hurled himself around the white chickenshit room.

He flung himself to the floor. He twitched. He contorted, recalling the time everyone excepting the Jones family was in-vited to the Centennial fish fry, down to the Jones river, once't their own, with Morgan and Lionel and Jud, dead drunk, rav-aging every chickencoop in town, wringing the squishy white necks, throwing the corpses against the walls, trampling eggs and plucking white feathers by the handful from the shivering squawking white bodies, and slicing off heads, and watching those silly white stumps running round and round and round, bumping into each other with the blood spirting out in foun-tains and pinwheels till the air in those little white houses was drenched with it, raining blood. . . .

Morgan clutched his head, howling, moaning, tearing his hair. He shuffled round and round Beau's chickencoop, tossing back his head and his arms, making high-pitched yips and yelps in the back of his throat. He kicked over one white column of notebooks, then another, enjoying the spatter. He toppled Beau's altar.

Morgan tore pictures of saints from Beau's wall. He smashed them over his knee. He trampled glass. He broke the long legs of Beau's stool, as if they were bones.

Morgan looked at the statue of the lilywhite lady, smiling slyly at him. *"Mor-gan! Mor-gan! Let's see your or-gan!"*

Morgan's cock burned.

Taking it in his two hands, he waved it, like a black tongue, at the white lady. He spit in a thick yellow spatter into her alabaster eye.

Morgan urinated around the ruins of the white chickenshit room, feeling relief from the burning between his legs for the first time.

He turned.

He saw Beau standing in the doorway, in flowing white robes, like the white angel in the cemetery.

Beau took two steps forward, arms outstretched, staring in rapture at the tears spouting from the eyes of the Virgin. He put up his hand to touch her cheek. His hand spouted blood, from where he had stabbed it!

Beau gave a gasp of joy. He put out his bloody hand to Morgan. Morgan smashed him over the head with his guitar. The tall white figure crumpled.

Morgan hurtled himself headfirst out the door of the ruined chickenshit room. He shuffled down the dark basement corridor of Old Factory, tossing back his head and his arms, on his way to the Chocolate Department, on his way to Big Nellie, feeling her need of him, hearing her call to him, planning to do for her as he always had done since the death of Little Pa . . . not being able to hold back any longer.

Morgan shimmied through a ventilator shaft from Old Factory to the new Production Sector. He shuffled down concrete corridors through the clotted smell of roasting chocolate, sweet and funky like the flesh of Big Mama . . . *I'm coming, I'm coming.*

Now he could see the door of the Chocolate Department.

Now he was at the door of the Chocolate Department.

Now he was letting himself in with a stolen pass key.

Now he could see the vats, belts, and pulverizers that liquefied chocolate, gleaming in a patch of moonlight.

Morgan burrowed deep into a mound of cocoa beans, throwing sacks over his shoulder.

He brought forth grenades, plump as eggplants.

He brought forth black rope, thick as intestines.

He brought forth sticks of dynamite, dry as bones.

He brought forth a clock, beating like a black heart.

Now Morgan was stringing the ropes and the dynamite and the clock around the vats of liquefied chocolate, taking his time, humming to himself.

Now he was mounting the steel stair.

Now he was on the steel ladder by No. 1 chocolate vat.

Now he was leaning over the bubbling cauldron, talking into the vat—*talking, talking* fast and sweet, with the veins jagged across his forehead, and the sweat dribbling down from his own body into the sludgy liquid ... talking into the gently heaving body, *li-que-fied*, telling Big Mama how he was sorry he'd taken so long, he'd been stubborn, that was true, like she always said when she called him to do for her in the dark, but they'd gone and strung concrete walls around the swamp, instead of just the barbedwire, and they were watching the place with guns, ready to shoot him like they got Old Bones, but he was too smart for them, he'd found a secret way in through a window by a drainpipe, right in the bossman's own office, so he could get in any time he wanted and, besides, the time hadn't been wasted, he'd already been back at the ones who had denied her—boasting now, puffing out his turquoise chest and letting her see the pride in him—telling her how he'd busted down the cemetery and the church they'd kept her out of, toppling their statues and letting them taste a black man's pee for all the times they'd mocked him on the wagon.

Now he was ready for the rest.

Now he was going to get back at those who had defiled her grave, who strung the barbedwire and concrete walls, and had shot Old Bones, and stuck their poles into her spilt blood. ...

Now he, her son Morgan, was going to blow up these other walls that were choking her in, confining her. He was going to blow up this *mau-so-leum* where she was kept. He'd stole all the dynamite sticks he needed. Pa had once showed him where they kept them in the sheds of the Public Works department, and how to set them, and that's why he'd been so long. He'd already set them. As soon as he wanted, he'd start them going off, the one setting off the other, and the whole building crumbling, but she wasn't to mind the noise none because as soon as it started, he was going to jump into the swamp with her and do for her as he used to after Pa died, as Pa used to do, just letting her flesh roll over him, sucking him up into the pit he had sprung from, not fighting her any more, knowing it was no use, knowing she was too strong for him, had always been too strong for him like she'd been too strong for Pa, and even though he'd run away with his body, stolen it from her, riding his cock to Peacock Town, he'd never gotten away with his mind, she was always in his head, laughing, and *hee ha hooing*, and saying, "Devil take your brains, you crazy boy!" till now he was going to give her what she wanted, the rest of him, and do for her like she wanted without holding back, because it wasn't no good the other way, with her having his head and not the rest as she was used to, and so he was going to jump into the vat, letting her flesh swallow him up, eat him *gobble gobble gobble* like she wanted, taking him back home where he belonged, never running no more to Peacock Town.

Morgan took off his ragged satin shirt.

He leaned over the edge of the steel vat.

He felt chocolate bubble up into his face, spattering in warm kisses against his cheek. Morgan tensed. He opened his eyes. He listened, still keeping his head low in the chocolate. Was someone calling him? *Morgan! Morgan!* He peeked up over the edge of the chocolate vat. He sifted the darkness, suspiciously, with his eyes. *Morgan! Morgan!*

The voice seemed to be coming from over his head. He looked up into the pitchy dark ... up into the pipes ... up into the catwalk. He saw ... over the furthest chocolate cauldron ... a single eye of light, in-can-descent, riding the dark like it was the full moon, with maybe a flutter of white robes, like they was wings spread wide, and the drip of mud like from a brown angel newly risen.

*Morgan! ... Morgan!*

Now the voice began talking *softly, gently* at first with one word sliding into another ... chanty, in a hum, like he heard passing the door of the church in summer, then more so he could understand, with the words separate ... calm and easy, telling him things ... talking like Big Mama used to talk a long time ago when Pa was still alive to do for her, and they all spoke to each other more than for to quarrel ... speaking right nice and kind, like warm bubbles breaking against his ear ... telling him, no, it was not Big Mama, but that now it knew all about Big Mama ... that it had been listening to

141

him, talking to Big Mama for a long time, in the dark . . . telling him that it had a message for him from Big Mama . . . telling him it knew the words were what Big Mama would say if only she could get back to say them . . . telling him that Big Mama was gone for good now, and that she was sorry they had missed each other there at the end, but that she understood that he'd had to get off on his own . . . telling him that it was right that he had gone away, that he was old enough now to do things for himself as he saw fit . . . telling him that it didn't matter about the place in the cemetery, that she had her own place now . . . telling him that she didn't need the swamp either, this one or any other . . . that he didn't have to blow up the concrete walls or the barbedwire, that she didn't want him to bother doing that . . . telling him from now on, if he wanted to show others how they had hurt him that he should find a better way . . . think about it some first and get the thing right . . . not to lose his head again, or act foolish like he was inclined . . . telling him he was free . . . telling him he was forgiven . . . telling him she loved him . . . *telling him . . . telling him . . . telling him . . .*

Morgan lay his head against the edge of the chocolate vat, feeling the bite of steel into his forehead, smelling the sweetness of the chocolate, feeling its gentle warmth as it bubbled up out of the earth, hearing the kind voice telling him to be still.

Morgan called up into the bright eye of light. "Beau? Beau? Is that you, Beau?"

Sometimes he thought it was. Sometimes he thought it wasn't.

Morgan wept, smelling roses like in Mama's brier patch, feeling an easing of the black ache, like a fist round his heart.

# 6. Eve & Brigitte

Eve Martin, Executive Secretary to the President, sat at her wraparound desk, eating lunch with her door ajar. That casually askew door irritated her. Eve liked things one way or another, but the slit door was the easiest way to keep track of Brigitte Young, Junior Secretary, who had the outer office.

Brigitte's desk guarded the only other door—recently blasted through a wall—into Charles X. Hunter's office. They were in there now, having lunch and going over the sales reports. Lunch, behind closed doors, had become a cosy habit.

Eve felt the tic in her left eye. Until Brigitte, she had been the one-and-only sphinx-like extension of Charles X.'s power. Now some of the sharper lobbyists were beginning to suck up to Brigitte at Eve's expense. She had even heard Bimbo Brown, the slobbery lunk from Sales, go out of his way to praise Brigitte's ability and charm to Charles—a task of some ingenuity given Brigitte's total lack of both. *Male chauvinist pigs? Hell, no!* It was the *ladies* who couldn't get along, you understand! Too petty. Too concerned with personalities. Not like the camaraderie of males, fierce but aboveboard, *ho ho ho!* Fused with a desire to get the job done.

Eve landed an uneaten apple, in a set-shot, into the basket. Okay, let the s.o.b.s have their fun. She hadn't worked her way up from Invoices to be out-manoeuvred by a bunch of jerks with dandruff on their collars. She picked up crumbs from her desk with the wet end of a scarlet talon, enjoying the dangerous look of it as it travelled over the white plastic surface. She had her proscribed list, with Bimbo Brown at the top. Just let anyone on it stick a face into *this* office looking for favours and she'd show them what it was like to play funny with Eve Martin!

Eve heard a smattering of giggles from the Inner Sanctum. She lifted a hairpin brow. Laughter? Over the sales reports?

*My my*, how their style must have changed since the days when she used to do them, alone.

She X-rayed the closed walnut door, developing in acid the scene on the other side. Brigitte, asprawl on the horsehair sofa, with Sexy cx'y dictating to the crotch of her dirty pants. "Take a French letter, Miss Young . . ."

Eve's phone rang.

She answered it, with professional good cheer: "Mr. Hunter's office."

"Hel-lo . . . *Eve?*"

The sound of two champagne glasses clinking. No need to sat the rest.

"This is *Celeste* Hunter, I'm sorry to bother you, *Eve—*" another lovestroke on the name "—I was planning my luncheon for *Charles' girls,* and I was wondering. Do you think Valentine's day would be a satisfactory choice again this year?"

*Ahhh, yes.* Mrs. H.'s annual slumming-it tea for female employees, planned months in advance to accommodate her bsuy busy schedule.

Eve checked the master timetable. Blank, of course. *Charles' girls* did not have the same pressures from Palm Beach and New York as *Charles' wife.*

"That date seems clear, Mrs. Hunter," said Eve. She added, impulsively, tongue-in-cheek, "As far as I know. I do have a strange feeling about it, though . . . as if Mr. Hunter might have mentioned saving it for something." She smiled at the closed door: "Would you like me to ring you through so you can ask?"

Celeste, hesitantly, The Perfect Wife: "Well, I wouldn't want to bother *poor Charles* with one of *my* little projects!"

Eve, The Perfect Secretary: "Oooh, I'm sure it wouldn't be a bother, Mrs. Hunter. He's just having lunch *with Miss Young.*"

Celeste: "I see . . ."

Eve laid down the phone.

She picked up her nailfile.

She delayed a full two minutes, allowing Xerox copies of the lewd pictures in her own mind to be delivered to Celeste Hunter's gilded "in" basket.

She jabbed Charles X.'s buzzer, imagining she was sending an electrical shock through the lovers on the sofa, seeing them leap apart, fuses blown, sticky flesh coming unglued, commas and exclamation points tumbling from Brigitte's shorthand book. *End of insert. Close bracket. Period. That's all for now, Miss Young. Yours sincerely, etc.*

Charles X.'s response was immediate and irritated: "Yes!"

"Your *wife* is on the phone," said Eve, emphasizing the relationship, like a tactful secretary giving warning. "She's arranging her Valentine tea. She seems to want to check with you, though I told her that date was clear on the master."

"Oh?" The innuendo in Eve's voice easily seeded suspicion in Charles X.'s voice. Suspicion, intrigue, guile were the Hunters' favourite forms of communication. "Put her on," he said warily.

Eve announced into the phone: "He's ready *now*, Mrs. Hunter."

She hung up the phone, and relaxed into the contours of her black-leather chair, contemplating her little manoeuvre, petty but satisfying. Since normally Eve would have told Celeste that her husband was "in conference," Charles would think Celeste must have insisted on speaking to him. When Celeste told him *Eve* had insisted on putting the call through—as Eve knew she would, losing no opportunity to play the self-deprecating wife—Charles would think she was lying or, in the euphemistic terms the Hunters preferred, "not telling the truth." Celeste might even—in a lighthearted way—drop the information that she knew he and Brigitte were having lunch together. Charles X. would return to Brigitte convinced that Celeste was "up to something," meaning, again in the Hunters' convoluted terms, that *Celeste* knew *he* was "up to something."

Eve looked at the keyhole of the closed door. If she had not been able to smuggle a snake into Paradise, she had at least managed to slip a green worm in. She grinned. Just think what she would be able to arrange when Ma Bell brought the new picture phones in!

Eve swivelled so she was looking out the window, unconsciously twisting the wedding ring she had worn since her mother's accident, thirty years ago, contemplating the enigma of Celeste Hunter.

Celeste was one of the shrewdest people Eve knew—at least in her area of specialty, which was the maintenance and patrol of Charles X. Hunter.

In this, she was both professionally blind and paranoid, a neat piece of hypocrisy for those who can handle it. She seemed to have the knack, as Charles X. himself did, of vacuuming up, through eyes and ears and especially the nose, all suspicious bits of information and acting "instinctively" upon them, often in the most vindictive way, but without ever letting any knowledge of this pass through her own brain or other vital organs, so never having to take responsibility for anything . . . unpleasant.

Eve and Celeste had, from the start, regarded each other with respectful distaste.

When Eve had been hired, Celeste had come on all sweetness and bristled strength. The two women had exchanged signals, and Celeste had retired, satisfied but ever-alert.

In this, she proved herself superior to ordinary office intelligence, which had always assumed there was something going on between Eve and Charles—an idea vaguely encouraged by him for reasons of ego and by Eve for reasons of power.

Not that an affair hadn't been considered. It was just that when it came to the crunch Charles X. was too selfish to risk anyone as useful to him as Eve, and Eve had been surer of her shorthand than of her femininity. They had flirted, teased, skirmished, then let "unrequited" feelings flow underground into What Might Have Been, a flattering pool to dip into during almost-business lunches and otherwise draggy overtime.

All in all, a convenient relationship—until Brigitte.

Eve glanced at her watch, a slim twist of silver with a numberless face. She felt restless. She wasn't used to sitting around doing nothing, but she was damned if she was going to start back to work before the lovebirds.

She noticed the red light was out on her phone, meaning Celeste and Charles had finished their Valentine chat.

She took the phone off the hook.

She walked to the window, exaggerating the Voguish slither of her thin body inside its tweed armour.

She plugged in the coffeemaker.

She stared across at Hunter park. It was beginning to snow. *A white Christmas?*

Eve shivered, though it wasn't cold. It seemed odd to be around for Christmas this year. She usually took her vacation so as to miss it—some place hot and handy, now that she had run through such exotica as Kali Lampur and Yucatan. She needed a vacation, but it all came back to Brigitte. She had been hired ostensibly so Eve could get away. Now she didn't dare.

Eve poured herself black coffee in a red mug, and nursed it back to her desk. She sat down, scissor legs flung wide, and inserted a Cameo into her silver holder. She fished a flask, also silver, from her snakeskin purse, and poured a little "Irish" into her coffee. *What the hell!* The Big Boys were all out there lapping it up. They might as well start even after lunch.

Eve took her social calendar from her desk and began the countdown to Christmas:

TUESDAY, DINNER, WARREN'S 6:30. Eve frowned: That meant Sally's overcooked roastbeef if Brother Warren was going to touch her for more dough, or Sally's dry meatloaf to demonstrate resentful poverty if Warren was going to choke up a little of what he owed. Eve was betting on the roastbeef. Warren had sounded so glad to talk to her, with Sally's gay rejoinders from the background. *The buggers!* She'd tell them where to go, if she didn't feel so sorry for the kids, especially the youngest, Kimberley.

Eve mouthed that name, with disapproval: *Kim-ber-ley,* then added Can-dace and Bam-bi. Child-centred names, indulgent in the worst way. In *her* day, all the spoiled brats were Somebody-Anne or Somebodyelse-Jo. Hyphenated children in tap-dance shoes, carrying around their extra name, like a loaded teddybear, stuffed full of Mummy and Daddy's love. After that—judging by her file of baby announcements—the finger of lovesick expectations had fallen upon the diminutives: the Tammy's and the Terri's. Then came the cutesy made-up children with made-up names. *Could a girl named Darlene find happiness in the real world? Could a boy named Brick ever get through life without worrying about his virility?* Then came the children pressed into Victorian lockets: the long-haired Millicents and Penelopes, with the never-to-be-shortened names in velvet dresses.

Kimberley came from the Hollywood cutesy-vogue, though—give discredit where discredit is due—there was a chance old Sally *The Lush* Anne found it on the Kimberley-Clarke toilet paper while barfing down a barroom john. Sally of Our Alley.

*Ahhh, well.* Eve lit her cigarette and exhaled a polluted stream toward the gold-plated Charles X. Hunter door. At least the kids with the trendy names belonged to their own time and place. The really tight-swaddled kids were the ones delivered back to God gift-wrapped in their daddy's names. That's when the kid gloves came off the dead hands.

She added a little more Irish to her Irish.

She turned to the next entry in her diary:

WEDNESDAY, 8 P.M., LICHEE GARDENS—HUMBERSIDE COLLEGIATE "OLD GIRLS." BRING JOE XMAS GIFT UNDER $1—*ho ho ho, and a merry merry to you! How the class of '48 still clung together!* Eve could hardly wait to see how the "gals"—their name for themselves—were coping with women's lib and zero population growth. But a joke prize? Surely that was excessive! Surely they were all their own best entries!

Eve drummed her red nails, reflecting: Reunions '53 and '58 had been hell for her, full of patronization for the tragedy of her spinsterhood. By '63 the perfume was coming off all those forties and fifties Doris Day love-matches, and by '68 she was emerging—in the absence of flashier candidates—as The Lucky One Who Had Made It. How *betrayed* some of the gals of '48 felt! How *surprised* they were to discover there might have been a life other than the one of Marital Bliss for which they had bartered their virginity! How the self-pity flowed as the statistics rolled in and they found themselves included—on divorce! on philandering husbands! on mediocrity! on failure!

"Dear Ann Landers, I keep myself nice and clean. I run a nice house, have 2.7 nice children, and I can still fit into my wedding dress. I just wanted to ask you: Why am I sitting here, in my suburban bathtub, slashing my wrists with a razor and watching my blood seep down the drain?"

Eve rejabbed a tortoise-shell comb through her french twist. Well, she didn't feel sorry for them. They'd been smug enough as long as their girlish charms had held out. And she sure didn't envy them their little homes and families. After bringing up five brothers (plus Dad, make that six), Eve hadn't wanted to start all over again, with sticky hands and the ABC's. She'd wanted to bust right on through M for Marriage, to see what was at the other end of the alphabet, and if sometimes she got to feeling a little lonely, down around the XYZ's as a single guest at other people's tables, well, she had only to look at the casualties on the other side to feel damned lucky. Who wanted to spend the best years of your life bringing up a couple of kids so they could blame you for their drug problems? Who wanted to ride, double-harness, just to have someone else to blame for the stodgy pace? Resentment hung in the air, these days, like unpaid bills. It wasn't anyone's fault. Just the general fuckup, and everyone looking for a scapegoat. Best to travel light, on the fringes of things. Best to be some kid's generous old aunt than his poor martyred mom! Best to be some man's thin mistress than his fat wife!

Eve set down her mug with a clunk, prepared to admit that part of the proceding had been a commercial to prepare her for the following item in her datebook:

HUNTER XMAS BASH, DINNER AND DANCE, 7 P.M., THE ROYAL YORK BALLROOM—WIVES AND ESCORTS. Because, there it was facing her: The Single Girl's Dilemma. Eve shot a sour look at the Charles X. Hunter door. She especially needed to turn up with someone decent this year, now that her pride was being publicly worked over by Miss No-Bra No-Brain.

Eve trotted out her list of small possibilities.

*Derek Smythe?* Good company but too dangerous. A limp wrist here, a smirk there, and the office would nail her. Same with any blind date or arranged escort. *Better a gay blade you knew than one you had to pay for.*

*Peter Thorpe?* That meant dinner for three—he and his shadow, meaning the gumshoe his wife had sicked on him, who slid under doors like a telegram full of bad news. Besides, wasn't Peter in Mexico?

*Percy Borden?* Presentable, but he'd have to ask his mother. He'd keep Eve toe-tapping till the last minute, then complain about the taxi fare.

*John Wilmington?* Hmmmmm. Eve got as far as to write that one down. Man-about-town. Urbane, Distinguished, but . . . they hadn't had a date since April. Eve had been John's official date for concerts. She had jumped categories by inviting him to dinner a couple of times, and it had offended his rigid system of controls. *Well? Why Not?* Eve dialed nine, dangled the receiver from one scarlet finger, then tossed it into the cradle. Screw the dating system! She'd go by herself or forget it.

Eve drained her mug, beginning to feel her Irish, and, under that, something very vile, very bitter. Because—let's face it—that's what got career women in the end. Not the loneliness. Not career problems. The goddamned dating system!

Eve swivelled in her chair, twisting her mother's wedding band, feeding her fury with the nastier snapshots from her scrapbook: Herself, waiting by the phone in saddleshoes and crinolines, while her brothers horsed around making and breaking dates. Herself, in pearls and twin-sweater set, dancing scrunched over some jerk at Teens Canteen who just made it, panting, up to her bellybutton in his elevator shoes. Herself, smiling through her teeth, while a slob in rented tuxedo puked over her net graduation dress, purchased with babysitting money. Herself, in a split-to-there designer's dress, reeking of Shalimar, watching some geek pick his teeth over her *cordon bleu* dinner, only to have him remember he was due at a cocktail party in fifteen minutes, or had an appointment with his chiropractor first thing in the morning.

Eve heaved herself up from her chair and strode to the coffeemaker. No wonder the gals, clas of '48, married gratefully and early to the first decent lunk who asked them, and then led rich fantasy lives! Who could blame them for panicking? Who, with any brains, could stand a lifetime of this shit?

Eve filled her cup, spilling half of it.

She flounced back to her desk.

She threw herself down into her chair and yanked a green sheet at random from her "in" basket. She scrawled across the back: "ATTENTION! ATTENTION! . . . WHAT THIS COUNTRY NEEDS ARE BROTHELS FOR WOMEN!!!!!"

Eve circled that, then underlined it, because—forget the niceties—that's what it all boiled down to: sex! After she had busted out of the chastity belt society had clamped on her (one man, one key), Eve had discovered she was a passionate woman and, given the choice specimens left on the market, the solution was inevitable: married men, the less "kidding ourselves" the better. Now, however, quite a few of the sex-machines she had counted on were breaking down and just couldn't seem to get the right parts for their particular year, make, and model. She had had quite enough, this last year, of lovers with burnt-out fuses, crawling to her in their tattered Superman suits, with their testicles in one hand and their broken mechano sets in the other, wanting her to kiss it and make it better! To give them back their youth and immortality! To flatter them into thinking they could leap tall buildings at a single bound, when they could barely make the front steps!

Eve chuggalugged her Irish. Where were the real men? The survivors? She had begun to identify with that cartoon of the animals filing, two-by-two, into the ark . . . with *one* unicorn, head-swivelling. . . .

Eve toasted the closed door. Well, give credit. . . . *Maybe Sexy CX'y was still in there, pitching!*

Eve set her coffee on her Green BROTHEL memo.
In curiosity, she turned it over.
She had to laugh.

Here was her weekly circular for the Women's Movement, courtesy of Ms. Brigitte Burning Bra, complete with misspellings and typos as good as a signature.

Eve read:

> DEAR SISTER:
> It has been our sad absurdation that all too often it is WOMEN who impeed the forward serge of their sisters, more than men.
> ARE YOU AN AUNT JENNY?
> Do YOU prefer MEN against your SISTERS?
> Do YOU misabuse your position TO KEEP OTHER WOMEN OF ABILITY DOWN?
> Do YOU collarbait with the MALE CAPITALIST SYSTEM?
> Do YOU treat the women who work for you as SURFS or as POTENTIAL EXEC-UTIVES?
> Do YOU—

Eve flipped the paper to the BROTHEL side, eyes congealed: enough was enough. She shoved aside the green paper, still tapping it with a scarlet finger. She would have to deal with that ... *and soon*.

Eve checked her watch: 12.40. She swivelled toward the window. The snow was coming faster and thicker now, with fluffy drifts collecting at curbs and around trees. She watched people, bundled against the wind, most of them in a hurry, most carrying Christmas parcels. She saw Morgan Jones, Bimbo, and a couple of boys from the stockroom fooling around with hockey sticks, and remembered she used to play a pretty good rinkrat game herself.

Eve saw the office boy, Zeve Ross, pedalling up the street, his poor-boy cap pulled low over his ears, his thigh muscles pumping against the wind, his cheeks red as apples, snow seaming his jacket.

Eve had fantasized a good deal about young boys, lately.

She leaned back in her chair—*way back*—almost reclining. She closed her eyes. She folded her long fingers across her stomach. She treated herself ... *yes ... yes ... yes ...* to a nice lusty fantasy about the office boy. *Technicolor. Hail, Columbia Production! X-rated but suitable for daytime viewing* ... beginning with the moment he stepped into the hallway of her Avenue Road apartment, stamping snow from his cowboy boots, and she rushed, in a matronly fluster, to offer him Tea and Sympathy, à la Deborah Kerr ... progressing through An Older Woman's Unselfish Understanding to the point where she herself might shed a few *Life Is Hell* tears, à la Cloris Leachman ... then, taking him gently by the hand ... yes ... yes ... it is time now ... she would strip him of his tie, his belt, his shoes and socks—the more awkward outposts of love—and lead him ... did she already say, gently? ... to the bedroom. ... There, feeling The Rise Of His Youthful Lusts, she would Grow Tender, with the fresh maturity and radiance of the newly widowed Jennifer O'Neil—Not Stealing His Youth, you understand, But Giving Him The Gift Of Her Experience. And then ... and then ... becoming Frankly Sensual, she and Mrs. Robinson would teach his vibrant body The Ways To Please A Woman And Thus To Please Himself, until ... until ...

The phone rang ... *Ho ho ho! It was the Harper Valley PTA!*

Eve answered briskly, professionally: "Mr. Hunter's office."

It was Sven Jenson, foreman of the Chocolate Department, wanting to report—immediately, directly—to Mr. Hunter on the odd happenings last month in the Chocolate Department.

Eve nodded into the phone: "Yes yes yes. I know Mr. Hunter is aware of the importance of the report, Mr. Jenson, but—" She smiled at the closed door, as she assiduously trotted out her best Oxford usage: "He's having *intercourse*, right now, with his junior secretary, and cannot be disturbed. I shall have him call you as soon as—wait a minute, please." Eve caught sight of Brigitte returning to her own office. "I think he might be free now, Mr. Jenson. Yes ... I'll connect you."

Eve pressed Charles X.'s buzzer, her eyes fastened on Brigitte through the slit in the door, assessing. The girl looked more dishevelled than usual, her face red, her eyes puffy, as if she had been crying. *Yes!* She seemed to be having definite trouble keeping her rabbitty upper-lip pulled down stiffly over her orthodontal problems. *Trouble in Paradise? Wouldn't that be a nifty Christmas gift!* Eve's eyes narrowed: Christmas was a difficult time for lovers. She felt a touch of woman-to-woman sympathy, which—seeing the Aunt Jenny memo on her desk—she easily squelched.

Eve settled down, with a will, to work, attacking her "in" basket like a woman eager to make it up to a neglected lover. *Let me see. Where to begin?*

She emptied her basket on her desk, and started from the bottom up, turning and sorting:

A sheaf of complaints, in pious longhand from the General Public, to be answered routinely from Charles X.'s jottings.

A memo to cx from Cy Hanover, head of Promo, setting his retirement date for the following month, and recommending Danny Steele for the job.

The usual sheaf of complaints about the Heat/Cool System.

The usual application from Irma Burbank of Soft Centres requesting work in the Promo Department. "See photos attached." Eve had to laugh. What-the-hell did Irma think they promoted in Promo? Certainly not chocolates!

A request from Basil Fitch of Computer Control—a demand, actually—for authority to annex Special Accounts and the Hunter Museum as part of Computer Control.

A warning from Bill Fontana, Production Manager, of an impending increase in price of cocoa beans.

A report from Ches Lukas, head of the stockroom, on wholesale theft of the Santa Claus sucker line.

A personal report from Sam Ryan—first of a series—telling of his progress in therapy. Eve smiled wryly, recalling the whole Sam Ryan fiasco, including the denouement in which Charles X. himself found Sam, still naked and sleeping it off, in the Display Ad haystack. Instead of firing Sam, as he had intended for some time, Charles had given him the option of quitting or drying out, explaining to Eve later, with unaccustomed frankness, that Sam had reminded him of a pilot he had once seen, strangled in his own parachute cord, and that he had rather envied the both of them, since they had obviously been flying pretty high before they crashed, whereas he himself sometimes felt he had never gotten off the ground. Eve, glancing through the report now, noted that Sam's style was all wrong for Charles X., full of bombast and over-optimism. Shrugging, she tossed it onto the delivery pile, then,

153

feeling a sense of responsibility, put it aside to give Sam some off-the-cuff advice on it.

The next folder was directed to Eve with Charles X.'s priority card on it.

Eve took this one out—a fat file bristling with paperclips—and spread it over her desk.

The original memo was from Bimbo Brown of Sales to Cy Hanover, head of Promo, suggesting an outdoor Beauty Contest, in mid-January, to select a Miss Bon-Bon as the kickoff for an ad campaign to establish Hunter's new Sweetheart Bon-Bons as The Warmhearted Gift To Give Your Best Girl For Valentine's day. The Ad department had vetoed the idea, with Danny Steele in particular denouncing it as "corny, tasteless, and something from the Dark Ages." Charles X.'s memo to Eve said, simply: "What think? Soonest!"

Eve rolled a memo sheet into her typewriter, preparing to clobber Bimbo Brown's idea *soonest* with her *what think*.

Her buzzer sounded.

She answered it, still skimming through the file.

Charles X.'s voice sounded weary and a little distant. "I was wondering, Eve. Have you come across my note on the Bon-Bon thing? It was in the last pile I sent out, but I'm on my way down to Promo, and I'd like to give them an answer on it now."

"I was just looking through the file, Mr. Hunter."

"Oh, good." He prompted: "Frankly I'd like to toss the bloody thing out, but since I'm trying to phase myself out of Promo, I don't like to stamp on the first thing they come up with. Any strong opinions?" He chuckled: "Miss Young seemed bitterly opposed, but then she's pretty deeply into the women's lib business and"—his voice softened flatteringly—"I need a *more balanced* opinion."

Eve bristled far more than she purred.

She could see Brigitte through the slit of the door, flirting with Morgan Jones *and* the office boy, her chest straining against the sleazy fabric of her sweater as she leaned way up over her typewriter, typing another goddamned green paper with her boobs!

"I think the contest is a real cute idea," Eve heard herself say, quite jauntily, into the intercom. "A real attention-getter."

Charles X. in surprise: "You do? Mmmmm, well . . ."

"After all," continued Eve, persuasively, "it isn't the women's libbers who are likely to be buying chocolates!" She chuckled, as Charles X. had done: "You can't liberate Valentine's day. It's *supposed* to be corny and old-fashioned."

Charles X. doubtfully: "Well, I guess. The whole thing sounds stagey to me. I can't imagine any woman, no matter what her politics, wanting to stand around, half-naked, in January."

"They're paid professionals," said Eve, airily. "If they want the work, they'll jump at the chance."

"Hmmm ... well ... I guess so. If you say so—" Charles X. paused, considering: "I wonder, do you think any of our girls might be interested in participating at the regular model rates? It might look a bit more like a real contest, with the different body types."

"I'll put up a notice in the lounge, if you like. And on the rec board."

"*Would* you? Actually, Eve, I'd feel a lot better if you'd keep your hand in on this one. There's already so much friction between Ads and Sales the way this has ping-ponged. Somebody's likely to go off half-cocked if they're not sensibly watched."

Eve smiled into her red nails. "I'd be delighted to, Mr. Hunter. Anything to help."

"Good girl, Eve!"

Charles signed off.

Eve, grinning, reclined. *Well!*

She lit herself a Cameo, squinting through the smoke at Brigitte. She ran her fingertips over her typewriter keys, planning.

Eve stubbed her cigarette.

She typed, "ATTENTION, MS. YOUNG," and then, fingers flying composed the most insulting memo she could, requesting Brigitte to order up models for the contest in "a variety of body shapes and types, to reflect the variety of candies available in the Bon-Bon Sweetheart pack, and the chest banners they will be wearing—Miss Liquid Cherry, Miss Coffee au Lait, and so on."

Eve waltzed the memo out to Brigitte's desk, and floated it down to her: "Soonest," she said. "Mr. Hunter is anxious for us *both* to get working on this."

Eve sauntered back to her door.

She placed her hand on the knob, then turned. "And by the way, if you're going to keep typing that women's lib junk, on capitalist time, at least learn to spell. I've worked too hard to be Aunt Jenny'd by a piece of trash who doesn't know the *o* in *stoopid* from the hole in her head."

Eve had the satisfaction of seeing Brigitte's jaw drop before she slammed her frosted door.

Her legs felt rubbery. Her tic was skipping out of control.

Eve sat down at her desk. *Well, there it was ... the challenge laid!* She toasted Charles' closed door, straight from her silver flask. *A merry merry to you! God Blast Us Every One. . . .*

Christmas brought the usual measure of misery and good cheer to the employees of the Candy Factory.

Morgan Jones and Brigitte Young organized a Hunter's Christmas Carol Sing at several old peoples' homes, after which Morgan took Beau home to Bartonville and Brigitte took Megan home to Sudbury to plot women's lib strategy.

Bimbo Brown returned home to Moose Jaw, proud of having lost five pounds, and was stuffed fuller than the Brown's Christmas turkey by his mom and three sisters, who thought he looked thin for his frame.

Danny and Daphne Steele went to Victoria to be with Daphne's folks, and were interrupted, during a traditional turkey dinner, by the pending arrival of Sara Daphne Steele, seven pounds three ounces.

Basil Fitch took his wife and three children, expensively outfitted in the latest in ski equipment, on a winter safari to Switzerland, and broke his ankle the first day.

Celeste and Charles Hunter, unable to stand their Deepwater Lake cottage without the children, flew to Palm Beach and bickered for a week about the terrible terrible weather.

Sam Ryan, in his fifty-fifth day of sobriety, called on his ex-wife Linda, early Christmas morning, bearing a large bottle of cologne for her and an armload of stuff for young Sammy, only to be told by his ex-mother-in-law that if he showed his face once more unannounced, the police would be called. Back in his Cabbagetown room, lying on his unmade bed, looking at the greasy wallpaper with shadows where his pinups used to hang, he unwrapped, and uncapped, the cologne ... tempted.

At 11.05, Sam called his therapist, knowing he had gone to Barbados. He let the phone ring eighty-one times, taking perverse pleasure from the hollow ring.

He called up a couple of the boys from Sales that he knew were out of town, and then Harry Pulitzer who said, as could be expected. "What-the-hell, Sammy, have a little snort for Christmas."

As a final gesture to sobriety, Sam called Eve Martin, remembering she had told him at the Christmas party, her voice larded with sarcasm, that Christmas this year would be *family* time, in gay reunion with her brothers.

Sam was counting the rings, *five, six*, already tasting rejection, when Eve barked "yes!" into the phone so fiercely he nearly hung up.

Recovering, Sam poured out his sad story, even adding an anecdote about finding a rummy passed-out in the john of his rooming house, which had happened last week, as a matter of fact, but had the right mood and flavour.

Sam waited, confidently, for sympathy.

Eve gave a loud horse-laugh into the phone—"Ha ha ha, you ASS!"—before telling Sammy, in precisely enunciated syllables that indicated she herself was already into the glog, that having been out with every divorced man in Toronto, she could guarantee what he should have figured out himself by now—namely, that in any divorce the kids were the weapon, female, ready to be fired off in any direction, and that if he *demanded* to see his kid, the kid would almost certainly be kept from him, but that if he acted like he didn't care, maybe even had a little action going on the side, the kid would be on his doorstep every weekend with a tape-recorder sewn into his shirtpocket, and his mom crying the blues all over town about what a rotten father he was, heartless, cruel, a monster, why he didn't even send over a Christmas gift for Little X who sobbed all night on a packet of Christmas cake he had saved for his daddy, and while she didn't care for *herself*, being well rid of the bum, she didn't see how *any parent* could punish *helpless children* from what was *their tragedy* and certainly *not their fault*.

Of course!

As soon as Eve explained it, Sam could have shot himself for the schnook he was. It was the oldest sales rule in the book: turn a cool profile and hold back the thing you have a warehouse full of!

He wondered, aloud, how he could have failed to see something so obvious, whereupon Eve let him have it, once again: "Because you're a *fool*, Ryan! And what's more, you love it that way! That's why you live in that stinking rooming house—as an excuse for failure!"

Sammy hung up the phone, feeling much much better. He rewrapped the rosewater cologne, and put Eve's name on it.

Eve hung up the phone and headed back to her liquor cabinet. She continued on the toot which, before New Year's Eve was over, had seen her tell all her brothers, individually and collectively, exactly what she thought of them, saving her best effort for God Old Dad. *You're a fool, Eve Martin, you're a fool, you're a fool!*

The Nellie McClung Cell of the Women's Movement marched ten abreast down Bloor Street in bluejeans lined with flannel, ski masks, and sheepskin jackets, their boots crunching, in unison, through the crusty snow that covered Toronto like fresh meringue.

Bloor Street seemed in a zestful mood.

Scarves pulled up over mouths, toques pulled down over the ears, runny noses and steamed glasses all but wiped out summer's social distinctions.

Boutique windows were a jumble of froufrou at January sale prices.

Cars, made cautious by the slither of wheels, were easily overwhelmed by pedestrians, who ignored both traffic lights and honking horns.

Workmen were dismantling the last of the electrical displays that had joined the east and the west side of the broad avenue in convenient good cheer.

A line of Hare Krishna—their shaved heads and peach-robes husked in grey parkas—were shuffling and chanting as much to keep warm as out of religious fervor.

The Nellie McClungers made grim and forceful progress through the shoppers, trying to maintain their line. In their mitts they carried green pamphlets, grey blankets, and snowballs that had spent the night in Megan Mason's freezer.

They stopped, abruptly, to one side of the Colonnade Drug Store.

Brigitte proceeded ahead, as scout. She peeked around the glass corner of the Colonade bookstore.

There it was, as advertised, in front of the Colonnade boutique-complex: a red platform holding the Giant Valentine Brigitte herself had been commanded by Eve Martin to order up from Display Ads and to mend with her own capitalist-hired hands!

Draped all over the heart were a dozen girls, in red-satin costumes, with bitsy fur trim, including Irma Burbank, the platinum blonde from Soft Centres, arch-enemy of the Movement, waving to the crowd like a goddamned Queen of the Rosebowl Parade, from behind her chest banner: MISS MARSHMALLOW MOUNDS. The other serfs were shivering so hard you couldn't read what their ribbons said. Their smiles had frozen, in little red rings, around their icecube teeth. Their kneecaps were the color of old snow.

The red platform had *his* name on it in gold, like he thought he had something to be proud of: HUNTER'S CONFECTIONERY, SINCE 1896. Behind that, looking very warm, in a snazzy redfox coat and hat that must have cost a few thou, was Eve *Dragon Lady* Martin, beside a slagheap of Sweetheart Bon-Bons she was passing out to the crowd. On the platform was Bimbo Brown of Sales, bundled up to his piggy nose in a Hudson's Bay parka, telling everyone to stop for a taste of Hunter's finest. "And, while you're at it, feast your eyes on the luscious ladies parading before you, each piece different, one of whom will be chosen Miss Bon-Bon, this very afternoon."

Brigitte, triumphant with scorn, signalled the other Nellie McClungers into position: Tina and Jo-Jo from Hunter's Shipping; Lucy and Carol from Steno; Phoebe, Ann, Georgina and Shirl from the Line and, of course, Megan Mason, the foreperson of Hard Centres. Their eyes steely upon the platform, their mitts twiddling iceballs, they bore sober witness as ex-football star Bimbo Brown—enjoying another turn in the spotlight—pushed his product and his luck: "Who will she be, ladies and gents? Will she be Sweet Miss Peaches 'n' Cream? Will she be *ex-o-tic* Miss Turkish Delight? Look them over, folks, but *please*, don't *squeeze!*"

Brigitte saw the Dragon Lady gesture to Bimbo, then point indoors, as if she were splitting for a coffee. Brigitte and Megan exchanged a smirk. They watched the D.L. saunter off.

"Okay, now?" whispered Brigitte.

Megan snapped her chin. "Yeah. Let's go get the mother-fugger!"

Brigitte, Megan, and the rest stormed the dais.

Megan, leaping on the stage, grabbed the mike. Tina, Shirl, Jo-Jo, and Carol grabbed Bimbo. Brigitte, holding her nose by way of political comment, cannonballed the chocolate pyramid, feeling it squish—*oh wow!*—underneath her.

Tina, Jo-Jo, Shirl, and Carol had the stammering Bimbo pinned to the mat, and were wrestling off his parka.

Megan had his mike, and was really shouting it out. "Friends! We, as human beings, will not stand idly by while our sisters are exploited. We, as women, will not endure these insults to our minds and bodies. Why should one half of the human race be subjected to the piggery of the other half? Why should the bodies of women be stripped of their dignity while men snigger from behind the rotten figleaf of male chauvinism?"

Bimbo—hampered by a belief that he must be gallant to women in public, whatever else he might say about them in the locker room—was about to lose his trousers. Brigitte and Georgina were handing out grey blankets to the beauty contestants with CLOTHE YOURSELF IN THE DIGNITY OF THE MOVEMENT whitewashed across them. All the girls but Irma accepted them gratefully. Irma, hands on hips, her platinum head thrust forward, tried to shove Brigitte from the platform. "What are you *dykes* doing here? Get lost, eh? Pedal your envy somewhere else! What do you babes think you're doing?!"

Now there was a large, curious crowd jostling for position around the dais.

Megan, holding up the hand of the cell-shocked Bimbo Brown, peeled to his red Stanfields, hit them with The Message: "We of the Nellie McClung cell of the Toronto Women's Movement officially declare this *sexist* contest to be a *liberated* contest, open to both sexes! Feast your eyes, sisters, on this specimen of male beauty, and vote for Mr. Nut-Clusters as a write-in candidate!"

"Smear 'em, Bimbo!" shouted someone from the crowd, recognizing a vanquished hero. "Smash her in the tits, if she has any!"

Fists began to fly about the dais, with opposing philosophies almost certain to break into open riot if Irma Burbank had not, at that moment, emerged as a gladiator for the not-so-silent majority. Tackling Megan just below the knees (as Bimbo would have done if Megan were only Joe Theisman) Irma brought the six-foot amazon to the carpet with a reverberating crunch.

The crowd—appeased—clapped and thumped.

Bimbo, snatching Irma's blanket, leapt, cape-flying like Superman, through the mended Valentine.

Irma stood over Megan, spike heels astride, in a pose from *Justice Weekly*. Bending, she grabbed Megan's braid and snapped it like a whip. The crowd cheered. She turned to grin, as Megan scrambled up behind her. Irma turned back. *Too late!* Megan gave Irma the clenched-fist salute of the Movement—right on Irma's jaw. Irma staggered backward. Recovering quickly, she got back at Megan with five in the eye. Megan let her have it with the Peace sign, in *both* eyes.

Now they were circling each other, chests heaving. Irma in her Pig Establishment bunny outfit and false eyelashes, Megan in her Counter Culture bluejeans and braid.

Irma kicked Megan—*oh wow!*—spike heel to the shins.

Megan lept high, nicking Irma—*kung fu!*—on the chin. Megan slipped on a Bon-Bon. Irma pounced on top of her. Grabbing a box of Sweethearts, she ground it, custard-pie, into Megan's face.

Now, Megan drew up her knee under Irma in a no-rape hitchhiking technique and followed that up with a karate chop to the chest. Megan's hand bounced! *Irma had a heating-unit stuck down there!* Irma was steel-plated!

"*False advertising!*" shouted a joker from the crowd. "*Boo-hiss, Miss Marshmallow Mounds!*"

"Cheater!" shouted someone else. "*False-heater!*"

A bunch of them started shouting.

Irma, spitting tacks, strutted to the edge of the platform, gesturing furiously. Megan, grabbing a leg, yanked her back to business on the mat. They rolled, biting and clawing, over the carpet, and—*thump thump thump*, braless to breatplate—down the steps.

They grappled in the snow, leather boots and spike heels flying.

Some guys started moving in, breathing heavy, as if they couldn't control themselves. Brigitte and the other libbers joined hands around their struggling sisters.

"Stand back, you perverts! Give them a chance! They're raising their consciousness!"

Megan and Irma slugged it out. The crowd, in an orgasm of fantasies fulfilled, oofed and groaned. It was a great bonus for Irma's supporters when Megan's Counter Culture jeans split, from crotch to waist, revealing red bikini pants with LOVE embroidered on one cheek and PEACE on the other. Irma's false eyelash, lodged as a moustache in the runoff from her nose, equalized things quite nicely for the other side.

Brigitte remembered—*oh wow!*—her pamphlets. She began passing out lib. lit. with the fire of a priestess at Holy Rites. She saw—*yikes!*—Bimbo Brown, head down, driving interference for two cops, looking like he was made enough to tear down the whole stadium. Brigitte, tossing her pamphlets, screamed: "Cut it, Megan! the *fuzz!*"

A hiss swept through the fickle crowd, biased in favour of the present entertainment. They joined hands against the cops and the now-radicalized Bimbo, battering, growling, elbowing his way through. They thrust back the invaders from the dais, rhythmically stamping their feet.

The libbers were spirited off by the crowd. They chanted and danced their way down Bloor Street, wrapped in their grey blankets on the end of a long long line of Hari Krishna.

The cops and Bimbo arrived at the dais about the same time as a bewildered Eve Martin, carrying a cup of coffee.

She waved her fox-furred arm over the debris. "What happened?"

She stuck her head, also fox-furred, through the gutted Valentine, just as a photographer from Canadian Press snapped a picture: "FOXY DEN MOM LOOKS FOR MISSING BUNNIES."

Bimbo, still CLOTHED IN THE DIGNITY OF THE MOVEMENT, was trying to dress under his blanket when the photographer caught him, red behind protruding: "PIGSKIN CHAUVINIST GETS BUM'S RUSH FROM LIBERATIONISTS."

Irma Burbank, dabbing at her eyes with Kleenex, her bunny costume in worse disarray than anyone could remember, was snapped by the now-giddy photographer inside the busted Valentine, holding up a broken spike heel like Cinderella's glass slipper: "MISS MARSHMALLOW MOUNDS, BROKEN-HEARTED."

Bimbo Brown, chasing the foolhardy photographer down the street, provided one more mug shot before he managed to break the photographer's arm: "AFTER THE BRAWL, BEAUTY PROMOTER TURNS BEASTLY."

Brigitte Young hated the Computer Control Centre. The one-way mirrors looking in! The flashing red-and-green lights! The whirring dials like eyes! The double row of switches like teeth! The clicking tickertape tongues! Like it was 1984. Big Daddy is watching you!

Brigitte paced the plastic floor. Why would *he* want to meet her in Basil Fitch's den, except maybe because it was sound-proof and he wanted to shout it out!? Why would *he* send her a note instead of phoning? Why wasn't *he* at the fucking Confectioner's Convention like he was supposed to be?

She smoothed a crumpled paper against the nearest computer:

> BRIGITTE—Meet me in Computer Control, Monday, 5.30.
> CXH.

She cast a nervous glance over her shoulder. The bad vibes in this place were getting to her, like really psyching her out! Oh *wow!* Anyone but *him* would have been *glad* of all the women's lib publicity—like it must have been worth a few thou—but *he* was so *straight*, so supergroove uptight Establishment that probably all he could think about was how undignified it would look at his men's club to have everyone coming in off Bloor Street with *his* chocolates stuck to their feet. Or maybe it affected his credit-rating or something. If only she knew what Dragon Lady had told him, then maybe she could cope—like prepare a few answers. As it was, with *both* of them ready to come screaming down on her—*oh, wow!*

Brigitte tossed her braids. *Not that she cared*, but—she glared up the double-row of computers, to XKEM5S1R1 facing her at the end—this place spooked her out.

Brigitte looked at the watch, pinned inside her macrame bag. It was only 5.20. *Oh wow!*

That made her nervous, then angry, like she was letting *him* get to her with his cheesy summons. She thought of leaving then coming back, but that made the whole thing too important, like her mother being afraid to get to a party first, and all that bourgeois crap. She thought of leaving and *not* coming back?

Brigitte frowned.

She chewed her hair.

She squatted on the plastic floor, ballooning her skirt around her and thickening the expression of sullen hostility she always wore when she felt she was over her head.

She chewed her nails.

She spit a piece of cuticle on the floor, and stuffed her fists in her pockets.

The trouble was . . . she hadn't seen enough of cx lately to straighten anything out, and they were always getting their signals crossed. Like three Sundays ago. *She* thought *he* said he could spring loose, so she sat up all evening with a sesame-seed casserole that she ended up feeding to the pigeons. Then last weekend had been Christmas, and this weekend the stupid Confectioners' Convention. Brigitte wouldn't even have bothered coming in today—her horoscope said to keep a low profile—except that old witch-bitch kept track of things like when she had the curse. *She had eyes in the toes of her snakeskin shoes, that one!*

Brigitte played with the watch inside her shoulderbag, feeling it heavy in her palm. Why hadn't she had sense enough to come late? Before the stupid watch, *she* was the one who always kept cx waiting.

Brigitte remembered with resentment now the night cx had given her the watch.

She had admired it in the window of an antique shop on Markham Street, and he had bought it for her "on one condition"—that she learn to tell time. "I know one minute doesn't look very much different from another at *your* age," he said, smiling sadly with his grey-flecked moustache repeating the expression like a tragic shadow, "but if you've lived with Death as long as I have, you wouldn't be so heartless about keeping an old man waiting."

cx always talked that way about his health—mockingly, yet earnestly. He was—to hear him tell it—the victim of some strange hereditary disease, undiagnosable but always present, so that when he was with her he felt "like Lord Byron with one foot on his coffin lid and the other in poetry."

It was really a matter of luck—"a miracle, actually"—that he had survived so long without serious illness. Now, at fifty-five, he felt "all out of miracles." Death, to him, was "like something personal—a bill collector who, at last, has my unlisted number."

cx had looked so *intense* when he had said these things, so *appealing*, that Brigitte had, indeed, accepted the watch, and she had, at last, learned to tell time, whereupon cx himself had lost the knack. Now when *she* complained about *him* keeping *her* waiting, he told her airily, "So young . . . so impatient. . . . *You* think of time as moments of pleasure. *I* think of it in terms of goals. That's the way it is for those of us who haven't abandoned the Work Ethic."

That, to Brigitte, was like being taught a new language so

she could be insulted in it. Time for her had been a great big bubble you blew up till it burst in the sunlight, and then you blew another. Now she heard it go *tic tic tic* like the watch in her hand . . . or *drip drip drip* like water on her forehead . . . . or *tap tap tap* like a bony finger at the window. Now it drove her *crazy* to be kept waiting, especially when she didn't know why, or whether she was to get chewed out, or maybe fired, like waiting in the principal's office and not knowing whether a teacher had found grass in your locker or whether the old geezer just wanted to check your legs.

The thought of grass reminded Brigitte of the joint Morgan Jones had slipped her with the first copy of "Sour Grapes"—an underground mag he had launched to offset the toothache he got from "Sweet Tooth," and what he liked to call his first step toward Larger Purposes. She picked it out of her purse and lit it, remembering with satisfaction that cx had told her he would fire her on the spot if he caught her with any of the stuff on Hunter property. Brigitte scratched her back against a computer: *Well, let him, and who cared!* She had left all that Respect-for-Authority jazz behind her when she had gone up the road with her thumb!

Brigitte smoked with one hand, playing with the tucks in her peasant skirt with the other, enjoying the roughness of the homespun, like patting a mongrel dog. She had woven it herself the summer she had freaked out in Greece, with Moish, on the island of Mikonos. Brigitte closed her eyes, remembering her first glimpse of Mikonos from the skiff—a phosphorescent dazzlement of white with miniature whitewashed houses and churches and windmills tumbling down whitewashed streets to the Aegean. She remembered running down those chalky streets, drenched by mists from the sea . . . so high on fresh air it was like she was on acid . . . blowing her mind the freedom of it and the beauty . . . her bare feet sticking into the wet cement like it was icing . . . skipping downhill, through layer upon layer of icing like she was the bride on a wedding cake, rushing headlong into the sea. . . .

Brigitte opened her eyes, almost surprised to find herself in the steel-and-plastic Computer Centre.

She told the next computer, defiantly: *When I get married—which I never will—I'm going to make myself a wedding cake, like Mikonos, with a windmill on top.*

Brigitte drew a heart, with her bare toe, on the side of the computer. She smudged it out with a Peace sign. *Bah!* She despised hearts and flowers, and all that sentimental bag. Like it was the older generation's substitute for Real Emotion, like their machines were a substitute for Real Human Power.

Brigitte felt dizzy.

She hadn't smoked much since being Employed.

She glared up the double-row of steel cubes, like idols, to XKEM5S1R1 at the end. Morgan was right: XK *did* look like cx. She remembered Morgan's cartoon, in "Sour Grapes," with XK dressed in a pinstriped suit, with a moustache, gnashing his teeth on dollar bills.

Brigitte giggled. She genuflected before XK, then tried to stare him out, right into his whirring pinwheel eyes. *Oh wow!* That was too much! She blinked and fell back. She scrambled to her feet, and kicked XK in the shins, forgetting she had on sandals. *Oh wow!* Brigitte nursed her bruised toe, feeling tears gush into her eyes. How did she get into this mess, anyway? How did this guy, cx, get so deep into her head?

Brigitte squatted on the floor, still rubbing her toe, reflecting.

Like, at first cx had just been a dude she thought she could hustle for some bread. He had picked her up in Yorkville and taken her for a spin in his car—a red Jag, with a dalmatian sitting in the back. It had blown her mind, but nothing she couldn't forget in, say, five minutes. She had him figured for some guy out slumming, right? Like he was probably wanting a freebee, and ready to pretend you were hungup if you didn't jump for it, like it was your debut. Instead, he kept asking her questions about her "lifestyle," till she began to think he might be the fuzz in civvies, but, no, he had too much class for that. When cx had bought her a submarine, then let her out where he picked her up without pitching, she guessed he was just a straight with a fatherly fixation. Or maybe he was queer. Anyway, it didn't matter one way or the other till he came back a week later and started really moving in on her. Like peeling her down, bringing her things, and taking her to classy places, cutting her off from her buddies, and making her dependent, so that when they finally did make it, she was really ready for it, and it was like out-of-sight— really flipping out. Brigitte giggled, remembering. It had nearly ruined her politically! It had nearly turned her on to the whole capitalist system!

Brigitte dragged on her joint.

cx had never actually asked her to give up other guys. He

had just made it impossible for her to think about them, like always calling her at the last minute and asking her if she'd like to zap off here or there. It was a different scene than the one Brigitte was used to being cynical about, and she didn't have any reason to resist—like, it was a new experience, right? And it was kind of a groove to be fussed over and even told *not* to do things. Brigitte had been one of the middle kids in a large bourgeois family, so who cared? And besides, most of her friends had split when the fuzz moved in on Yorkville. Brigitte had just kind of naturally drifted, like a homeless planet, into orbit around cx.

When he had suggested she work for him, Brigitte had been wary, but she kind of dug seeing him every day and, besides, if she had a job she wouldn't have to count on him for bread anymore, and maybe she could even put away a bit for Buenos Aires, so it was really like being *more* independent than less, right? *Wrong!* Brigitte didn't know exactly when she had begun to hang in too heavy, or when he had cooled out, or even if he had. It was just like he was always out to lunch lately, or on a downer, but when she asked him about it, he always said *she* was the one who was in a bad mood, looking for trouble when it wasn't there, or else maybe he'd just say their relationship had settled down "into a comfortable equilibrium." Brigitte had begun to suspect his game had been to break down her game, and that his defence was to destroy her defences, but he'd already done that. . . . If he was tired of her, why did he want to hold on to her? Did he enjoy torturing her, making her squirm? *Why wouldn't he let her go?*

There had never been any future. cx had explained all that casually at the start, and then, once more, at a swank evening he had laid on her when she had panicked and tried to leave him. Though he had nothing in common with his wife Celeste, they had been more-or-less betrothed from the cradle; half of his property was in her name, and she was a good mother to his three dogs and two children. He was miserable. It had been a mistake right from the start, but he was now, had always been, *stuck*. Then, of course, there was his health. He honestly didn't think his heart—"or whatever nameless nemesis I nurture at my bosom"—could stand the upheaval of divorce, and he was too proud to saddle a young woman with his frail constitution. He knew it was selfish of him, but— here, one of those sardonic smiles that so confused Brigitte— he adored her. Her freshness and vitality pumped new blood

167

into an aging constitution, gave him something to look forward to, day by day. If it was not being too unfair, would she—who had her whole life ahead of her—consider spending a little more of it in his rather dreary "garden of Gethsemene" and see what developed?

Brigitte had looked into his melancholy face, gazing at her across a table in the roofbar of Sutton Place against a twinkling backdrop of stars, both real and phony, and—squelching the image she had in her mind of her grandfather, sitting each Sunday, in front of his TV, clutching a different part of his body, and praying "Heal! Heal!" along with Oral Roberts. "Oh, Lord get me through this new day of Pain!"—she had melted.

Afterall, her favourite uncle had died of heart seizure when she was ten.

Her only true boyfriend had been killed in a freak accident when she was fourteen.

Brigitte believed in male mortality.

Sooo . . . she had unpacked her wicker case, completely, for the first time since she had left Sudbury, and she had taken back the watch—her ball and chain—and she had moved from her rooming house to the attic of a triplex, and she had used the dough she had been squirrelling away for Buenos Aires to buy furniture from Crippled Civilians and, when CX had snapped at her twice in one day that they might have more time together if she brushed up on her Office Skills, she had signed up for a nightcourse in typing and shorthand. With their twice-weekly dates having dwindled to once-every-other, that had left Brigitte a lot of free time, which was how she got into women's lib. Megan Mason of Hard Centres had asked her if she wanted to "go to meeting" one night, and being too old for Girl Guides and needing some minds to rap with Brigitte had said, *Why not?* She had already done the U.S. embassy bit, the Campus Riot bit, the Viet Nam war bit—not so much because she was radical, but because she was grooving with this group, or that guy, and it was the thing to do, like going to Woodstock, or hanging around the hockey rink, maybe, if she were back in Sudbury. . . . She'd expected a bunch of dykes cruising for new prospects, and career cats wanting more bread, and activists on a power trip, and they were all there, but, when she tuned into the marathon raps, they really turned her on.

Of course, the "mob" had come down on her, pretty heavy,

about her relationship with Charles. Like, they were always at her about how he was snowing her, and trying to get her to smarten up and cut out. Megan had called cx a Singing Worm—one of a garden-variety, always fishing when they were already hooked—but even so, what was Brigitte to do? Where was she to go? She couldn't go back to panhandling— the market had dried up, and besides, in rubbing off her rough edges, cx had taken off most of her skin. She couldn't work that scene anymore—it was like a meatmarket—and she couldn't go back on the road—the bad vibes coming up from the States about the cults and the crazies made her break out just thinking about it. She couldn't go back to Sudbury. Her mother thought it was "cute" to have a real Counter Culture heroine in the family—like she was supposed to almost get raped every night so her mother could brag about it—and her father had disowned her when she quit school. Besides, what could she do there, anyway—work down the nickel pits?

Brigitte shuffled through her shoulderbag for the hatpin she used to stick her joints.

*Oh wow!* She was sweating all over. Her blouse felt like two clams in her armpits.

She took off her suede vest and blew her nose in a soiled Kleenex to keep herself from crying. The trouble was . . . she didn't recognize herself anymore. She was finding all sorts of strange needs inside herself that she never dreamt existed— like the need for something to do every day, and like having her own place, and maybe a couple of friends instead of everyone just passing through all the time. The humiliating truth was that she liked her job, shitty as it was, and having things expected of her, except now, with *both* Mama and Papa Bear down on her all day, every day, stuffing her basket with joe-jobs and laying traps for her, and acting like her goddamned letters were supposed to be works of art or something, it was getting so she was scared to come in each morning. Why was that motherfugger Eve always picking on her, wanting to cross broomsticks? Why was she leaning on her *so* hard? Couldn't she see she was just hanging on by her fingernails, and they were already chewed past the quick? It wouldn't hurt her to move over a little. She practically *owned* the damned company! And why was cx so mean? She was only trying to breathe in the little air he left her! Why was it necessary to take even that much away? Why was it necessary *to hurt her so much?*

Brigitte cried into her lap. *Oh wow!* She was in for it for sure. She was going to be pitched right out over the beauty contest thing, but what choice had she? Old Dragon Lady had really laid it on her, pushed her right to the wall, and when she kicked over that stinking Sweetheart display, with *his* name all over it, and the chocolates spurting in every direction, it was like she'd finally given *him* the kick in the keester he deserved. Like why should *he* be able to push everybody around, just because he was born with a few extra pennies in his jeans, running over everybody and never letting on, like he thought he had that thing her history teachers used to talk about—*the divine right of kings?* Why shouldn't *he* get it back sometimes, even though she knew he was too selfish and thick-skinned even to notice!

Brigitte began to feel whoozy, like maybe she was freaking out without acid. The room was swirling around, spiralling in to meet her. Like how could that be? She'd been off the stuff for over a year . . . but this was beginning to feel like a bummer. She could feel the machines moving in to get her, like they knew she didn't belong, and pushing their metal sides in, like they were trying to rub her out, and that one at the end with the pinwheel eyes, was telling them to do it, was telling them—

Brigitte dragged her eyes away from the pinwheel eyes of Big Daddy. She had been staring into them, hypnotizing herself, *oh wow!* She hung her head between her knees, trying to calm herself, trying to clear it. It wasn't acid or drugs. It was just the future crowding her—that was the real bummer. Brigitte let her arms, her shoulders, her head droop, relaxing herself. She began to breathe deeply, forcing dead air up from the pit of her lungs, then filling and expanding them. She made her mind into a white blank . . . *white white white* . . . like Mikonos. She intoned her mantra, *oahhhmmmm oahhmmmm,* letting one syllable run over the next till it was a warm buzzing clot in her head, filling . . . expanding . . . lifting . . . *aoooooooooaaaaahhhhhmmmmmmmmmmmmmmmmmmmmmm* . . . like the time they all did it, sitting on the grass outside the Chicago Seven courtroom, practically floating up the whole city like it was a flying carpet . . . *ooooooooooaaaaaaahhhhhhhmmmmmmmmmmmmm* . . .

Eve Martin lay flopped out, like a rag doll, on the chintz chesterfield in the women's lounge, her arms and legs tossed every which way, smoking a cigarette—her usual Cameo but without the holder, letting it burn past the filter . . . scorching her fingers and not noticing.

The women's lounge was a place she never went. She'd been here maybe fifteen times in as many years, but today she wanted a sanctuary.

She'd had it!

The *least* she needed was a vacation, but that wasn't going to solve anything. She was still going to have to come back to the same load of manure.

The tension—meaning Brigitte—had finally gotten to her, snapped her in two.

She and Brigitte had been very careful of each other ever since the first beauty contest memo. It had been clear that Brigitte's relationship with Charles was prickly, and Eve had been hopeful that she might be able to get rid of her, permanently. Brigitte's Storming of the Barricades on Saturday had floored Eve. She had planned her retaliation, all Sunday—exactly what she would say to Charles when he returned from the Confectioners' Convention, and how she would say it. Then she had breezed into the office this morning, bushytailed and confident, only to find Brigitte already at her desk, in her peasant skirt and braids yet, thumping out women's lib literature on her capitalist typewriter.

Eve knew, then, that she was beaten.

She couldn't compete against that kind of gall. It was youth and sex against creaky middleage, and if she won this round she'd lost the next.

Besides, and this was the crux, Eve knew Brigitte was right about the beauty contest. It was, as Danny Steele had said, "corny, tasteless, and from the Dark Ages." The fact that she had pushed such a piece of garbage against her better judgement to get back at Brigitte, proved how demoralized . . . how *sick* she was. What Eve was suffering from was a bad case of self-disgust.

The truth of the matter was her fate had been sealed eight months ago when Brigitte was hired against her recommendation. Eve knew the old plays better than anyone: hire an assistant for someone, with authority to undercut him; or, the more discreet approach, promote the person *over* the job, to Executive Something-or-other, so that the job itself falls into the lap of the new person.

It was the second ploy that had been used on Eve. Despite the gold-plated title—EXECUTIVE SECRETARY—of which she had been so stupidly proud, there was little for her to do these days. That was why she spent her time in silly power plays that were nothing more than childish harassments, like blowing smoke in someone's face. What a fool she'd been! She had seen too many executive-executives reduced to wandering around their departments with the holiday list in their hands to forgive herself for her blindness. She had even typed out their execution notices, congratulating them on their new promotions and wondering how they could be such asses. Now she knew. . . .

Eve took a long drag on her cigarette.

She knew that Charles X. had not *consciously* decided to get rid of her. The part of his mind that was in control of such things had simply seized upon the executive thing as a familiar and convenient way of setting up something he wanted set up. Namely, the presence of Brigitte inside his organization. The fact that it might turn out to be inconvenient, even homicidal, for Eve would neither be predicted by him nor a consideration of his if he had foreseen it. It was simply a question of doing what he wanted, as he always did, and letting the chips fall. Since Eve's job *was* his convenience, there could be no question of *her* convenience over his. If she did not see it that way, then she was not doing her job.

Eve knew he would be surprised, even shocked, when she told him she was quitting. He would—all solicitousness—take her to lunch to find out what was wrong. If she tried to tell him—*really* tell him—he would "not understand," but would, to mollify her, suggest "having a little talk" with Miss Young to let her know she could not be insubordinate—if she had been—to his faithful Eve. And, of course, there would be a salary increase—something he'd been planning for a while but hadn't gotten around to. If, after all that, Eve should *still* talk of quitting, then—here the most marvellous leap of a truly agile defensive mind—she *should* leave, since the fact that she could leave was such a betrayal of the loyalty between them that it automatically disqualified her from the job. "And so, with heartfelt thanks, generous severance pay, glowing references, and a sense of hurt, yes, Eve, genuine hurt. . . ."

Eve felt a disgusting sickness in the pit of her stomach, for she knew the other prong in the set of pincers Charles wielded so dextrously from the presidential suite—i.e., what would happen if she allowed him to persuade her to stay on at Hunter's. The part of his mind that saw and arranged things, the Executioner part, would feel a growing contempt for her for accepting the unacceptable and would begin to undermine her, or, more properly, would give Brigitte *carte blanche* to undermine her, until she was so demoralized she was acting a squirrelly as she felt and as others were beginning to see her. Then—after a period in which she was paraded around on the platter of her own incompetence—she would be carried down to her own special office in the basement ("No one will bother you here, *heh heh*") and given her own special title (Secretary to all the Secretaries) and her own special function (to troubleshoot for the company, beginning, hopefully, with herself). Thereafter, she would be hauled up to the surface, every five years, to be lined up with the other Old Contemptibles, blinking in the sunlight, and presented with a gold pen, or a pin, or a watch, thus demonstrating to the unwitting how good Hunter's was to their old-timers and to the witting how careful they must be.

Eve knew she was not being fanciful. A little morbid, maybe, but not fanciful. She had often heard Charles X., with the puzzled brow of the Innocent and the quirky smile of the Executioner, serve up the fate of one man to the confidentiality of another with such remarks as: "I don't understand what's happened to Old Smedley. He seems to have lost his judgement—not sure of himself at all these days. It's lucky we brought in that new whip Boneycastle as his assistant, or we really would be in a pickle in that department!" Or, alternately: "I'm afraid Jones is turning out to be a disappointment in that executive-head spot. He doesn't seem to be able to produce anymore—it's all falling on that young Smith fellow we hired for good measure. I guess I made a mistake in promoting him, but—" here, a self-forgiving smile "—I always like our older employees to have first crack at the big stuff."

Eve had the desire to retch, but she knew she would not be able to "produce" even in that department.

She hadn't eaten for days.

All *she* had to puke was fifteen years of self-deception, and no toilet bowl would hold that . . . because—let's face it—even when her job *was* her job, it was no great shakes. What was her function, anyway? To reflect Charles X. To protect Charles X. To project Charles X. To preserve his image of himself, to himself, and to others. To housekeep for him. To remember for him the things he didn't think important enough to remember himself. To do for him the things that weren't important enough to delegate to someone else on the power pyramid. To be polite to others so he wouldn't have to be. To keep her mouth shut. To support him, unequivocally, both personally and professionally, even when she thought he was dead wrong. Even when Charles was out of the office and serious decision-making fell on her shoulders, her value to the company—her function—was to use her knowledge of him to second-guess him. She almost never made a decision that had to do with her own assessment of the facts. It was always, "What would Charles X. do if. . . ." Therefore, after fifteen years of dealing at the heady heights of power at Hunter Con., she had little to offer a new employer but her knowledge of the neurosis of the past one and a few rusty office skills.

Eve made one more painful assessment about her personal relationship to Charles X., for, despite what it was *not*, there was still the question of what it *was*: the single most important relationship in her life. There was little doubt it had served her as a type of low-key marriage she despised, syphoning off her masochistic "housewifely" need to be slavishly loyal, while protecting her from deep involvement there or elsewhere. He had been the yardstick by which she had judged other men, choosing only to measure them against his glamour, while ignoring what she knew were his very serious weaknesses. She wasn't so much "in love" with him as she was in love with the power she had given him over herself.

Eve hauled herself up from the chesterfield.

She checked the memo in her snakeskin purse.

MISS MARTIN—Computer Control, tonight at 6.00. Please bring November computer operating figures. CHX.

Eve couldn't imagine why the man was coming into the office this evening, nor what they were supposed to be doing sniffing around Computer Control with the operating figures, but as always . . . her not to reason why.

Eve stubbed her cigarette.

She went into the washroom and dashed cold water on her face.

She freshened her lipstick, trying to decide what to say to

*174*

Charles about the Miss Bon-Bon fiasco—whether to have it out with him now or to let it ride till she had time to think.

She tightened her belt a notch, taking pleasure from the feel of good leather, well-crafted, not like the smelly poorly tanned stuff the Brigittes of the world thought was "cottage industry." She picked up her snakeskin bag and walked around the corner to Computer Control.

Eve was surprised to see a light through the one-way glass.

Certainly, Charles wouldn't have arrived early, and everyone was supposed to be gone from this section for over an hour. Her first thought, as she opened the steel door, was that she must report the light, since it affected the temperature, which affected computer performance. Her second was: *Screw it! Why should I play company stooge?*

Eve sat down by the coffee-machine, just inside the door, intending to have a smoke and a coffee.

She heard a gentle buzz, so subtle and resonant she thought it must be inside her own head. Then she figured it must be one of the computers, and then . . . Eve stood at the top of the Avenue of the Computers, skinny arms folded across her chest . . . looking at the crumpled form of Brigitte Young, her head swaying between her knees, meditating: *oooaaahhhh-hhhmmmmmmm. . . .*

Eve felt surprise, then irritation, and then the contemptuous superiority of the non-believer who catches out the faithful in the vulnerability of prayer.

She nudged Brigitte with her snakeskin toe, as she might something unpleasant on the sidewalk.

Brigitte looked up, eyes unfocused.

"What are you doing here?" demanded Eve. "I should think with the mess you're in you'd think twice about breaking the Unauthorized Personnel rule. If you get out quickly, I won't report you."

Brigitte started to scramble to her feet, like a guilty child caught stealing apples. Then she stopped herself. With one cat-eye on Eve, she yawned, loudly and insolently: "Thanks for waking me. I've got a heavy date, and I slept in."

Brigitte picked up her things, in slow motion, from the floor.

She sauntered to the door.

Under Eve's scrutiny, she reached for the knob. She turned it. She pushed, then pulled. The door seemed stuck.

Eve swept by Brigitte, with her usual martyred air of *Must*

175

*you be so stupid? Followed by the answer: Of course you
must because you are!* She snatched the knob. She twisted,
pushed and yanked. The door held. Had the lock snapped?

Eve scowled.

"Well, we won't have long to wait. *Mr. Hunter* is due any
minute and he's never late." She saw Brigitte flush, and added,
on a hunch. "For *business*."

Brigitte slunk behind one of the computers.

She seemed to be fumbling with something inside that
stringy bag of hers: a wad of paper? . . . *What was going on
here?* Eve's eyes narrowed. *The whole situation was beginning
to smell. Was this another set up?*

Eve saw Brigitte head, once more, for the door.

She cut her off.

"Get back. I'll take care of this."

Eve took a nailfile from her purse. There was no place to
insert it! The door—trust Basil Fitch—was like a walk-in safe.
She fiddled with the knob, becoming more and more impatient.

Eve could feel her tic dancing like a flea.

She smacked her palm against the door.

She kicked it.

She strode to the one-way glass and smashed her two fists
against it.

She bore down on Brigitte, eyes poisonous: "All right. I
don't know what you think you're up to *this* time, but if
you're mixing with me again, you'll wish you hadn't."

Eve turned. She brought up her hand, intending, once more,
to attack the door. Instead, she watched—in fascination—as it
arced like a red-tipped serpent through the air to strike Brigitte hard on the cheek. "You brat!" she exclaimed, putting
eight months' venom into it.

Brigitte reeled backward. She caught her head on the side
of XKEM5S1R1. She slid to the floor.

Eve crouched over her in a stance from her sandlot days,
waiting for her to get up.

Brigitte remained, her head dropped between her knees, as
if meditating.

Eve touched her, gingerly, with her snakeskin toe, almost
expecting her to wake up, foggy from prayers as she had done
a few moments before, so they could start the reel all over
again.

Brigitte slumped further down the computer.

Eve lifted Brigitte's head, warily, as if still expecting some trick. Her face was ashen. She was bleeding profusely from the nose and slightly from the head. *Concussion? Oh God!*

Eve got down on her knees beside Brigitte. She tapped her face, lightly, rapidly, trying to revive her. She felt for a pulse. She felt for a heartbeat. *Too fast? Too slow?*

Eve looked helplessly toward the locked door. Her eye caught the coffee-machine. She bought two cups of hot water and, using her hanky, dabbed blood from Brigitte's head and face, telling herself this was no different from the zillions of times her brothers had gotten into scraps, and she'd done the same for them or their victims.

There didn't seem to be much damage. A burst blood vessel in the nose. A small cut on the lip where Brigitte's bunny-teeth had gone through. And—that knock on the head, hard to see because of the mat of hair.

Eve shook Brigitte. Still she did not open her eyes. Her face was bleached . . . almost transparent.

It had always been painful, even humiliating, for Eve to cry. Her face was computerized for strength. She fumbled in her purse for a hanky, holding her lacquered features tight, thinking how ugly she looked when she cried, and wanting something to hide behind. She couldn't find her hanky. She emptied her purse on the floor—wallet, lipstick, bankbook, aspirins. She saw her hanky. Of course. It was stuck, like a moustache, to Brigitte's nose. Her backup Kleenex was wadded against Brigitte's head. Eve rubbed her eyes with her fists, and then her nose on her arm—a gesture so childlike it broke through the last of her defences. She flung herself, face down, on the plastic floor, and moaned: *Oooohhhhh.*

Brigitte Young opened her eyes. She had no immediate recall of the fight, and she couldn't feel her wounds. She looked at the scene laid out before her as if it were a movie she couldn't quite get the hang of. She wriggled her nose—large and tender, with a hanky stuck to it—and remembered the whole square off.

Brigitte looked at the Dragon Lady, kneeling, her eyes streaming mascara. *Praying! Didn't she know God was dead?* Brigitte grinned, seeing the expensive face running as if it were glue, remembering the exhilaration she had felt when she had tossed a brick through a jewellery window in a Peace riot, and watched it shatter, *oh wow!*

Brigitte investigated her split lip, sore from grinning. Then the lump on the back of her head. She looked sideways at the D.L. She was really giving out with the mumbojumbo now. It was getting embarrassing, especially when Brigitte heard her own name mentioned, *oh hallelujah!* Brigitte thought she should put out a hand or something, the kind of woman-to-woman stuff they stressed in the Movement, but she didn't feel like it. She said, aloud—referring as much to her own face as the D.L.'s: "Boy, are you a mess!"

The D.L. stopped, in mid-confession.

Her eyes flew open.

She gagged back her sobs, mortified to be caught out at the softcore of her privacy, and began stuffing things back into her purse. She snapped the clasp and was getting to her feet when she remembered: there was nowhere to go.

She cursed.

She threw down her purse. It spilled again.

The D.L. tucked pieces of hair back into her french twist.

She tightened her leather belt.

She flung herself down at the computer opposite Brigitte.

Brigitte helped herself to one of the D.L.'s Cameos.

She lit it, with the D.L.'s snazzy silver lighter.

She said, matter-of-factly, in strict women's lib protocol: "Okay, Dragon Lady, do you want to lay it on the line first or shall I? Like, I guess we've got all night."

Eve, still reluctant, took a note, folded once, from her purse, and placed it between them on the plastic floor.

Brigitte topped it with another, torn, chewed, and mutilated. The handwriting on both was the same—*his* handwriting.

"I think," said Eve, "we've been had!"

She no longer sounded angry, or even resigned. She sounded relieved, like at a meeting when someone who has been silent too long is glad to have their hand forced.

Brigitte sniffed the notes: *powdered roses.* She sighed nostalgically. "He's changed his cologne."

# 7. Celeste Hunter

Celeste Hunter stepped from her jasmine bath water onto a white-fur rug, wearing a turban and her Palm Beach tan. Her bathroom was a gold-and-mirror jewelbox. Everywhere Celeste looked, she received gilt-edged reflections of herself.

Celeste adored things that glowed, sparkled, and tinkled. Her palatial Bridle Path home was full of such splendours—crystal chandeliers that flickered in simulated candlelight; rows of cutglass bottles arranged to sliver sunlight; silver polished till it looked transparent, and mirrors, mirrors, mirrors, set in all the unexpected places. It was the sort of house that quickly sifted out those who didn't belong, or, as Celeste liked to say with one of her spangly laughs: "*I* don't have anything to hide, *darlings*, do you?"

Celeste placed her graceful foot against the marble tub, anointing it with a mixture of baby oil, herbs, and hormones that her masseur, Guillaume, had invented for her. Beginning with the last segment of each toe, she worked up her foot, singing, "Oh, What a Beautiful Morning!" remembering the night she and Charles had actually seen *Oklahoma*, with Alfred Drake, Howard Da Silva and Celestè Holm. That was twenty-five years ago, but Celeste Mayfair Hunter made no attempt to be *au courrant*. Why should she when the past had always been so wonderful to her?

Celeste replaced one foot with the other.

It was going to be a busy day, and Celeste liked busy days. The Valentine tea for *Charles'* girls, then cocktails with the Van Allens, then O'Keefe Centre for the New York City ballet, then a late dinner with the Millers at the new little restaurant that had just opened on Marlborough.

Fortunately, Celeste had had a good start on the day! Here it was only nine, and she had already breakfasted with *Charles*, walked the dalmatians and had herself a nice leisurely tubsoak. Half her friends wouldn't be up for hours yet.

They all wondered *where* Celeste Hunter got her *formidable* energy and—here a throaty chuckle—sometimes Celeste wondered right along with them!

Celeste dribbled oil across her stomach, pleased with its tautness. That marvellous *Guillaume* again! All the women in Celeste's "set" told Guillaume that were pregnant before they told their husbands. It was a rigorous program and he charged the earth, but "Voila!" as Guillaume would say, "no stretch marks!"

Celeste oiled her breasts—pleasantly ovular, though a little too "full" for a *Vogue* figure. She had nursed Xavier, III, on the doctor's advice, but against Guillaume's. *Guillaume* had been right, of course, but—here a gentle maternal smile—there are some things a woman must decide for herself.

The thought of young Xavier caused a tiny black stirring in the back of Celeste's head. *Oh, dear: migraine!*

Celeste had awakened with the beginnings of one that morning.

She put her fingers to her temples and massaged in circles, letting her turbaned head fall back, relaxing her neck muscles. She though of . . . how many loaves of bread it would take to make five sandwiches each for seventy people, then how many eggs, tins of salmon, liver paste and cream cheese it would take to make an equal quantity of each.

Celeste loved mathematical problems. They relaxed her. She was the person the head of The Women's Committee of the Art Gallery phoned in a frenzy to ask how many walnuts of butter could be scooped from a ten-pound slab. Provided, of course, Celeste wasn't in charge of the job herself—which she usually was!

Celeste let her head droop forward. Her migraine seemed to have flown off like a black crow into somebody else's garden.

She continued smoothing oil into her hands.

Celeste had lovely hands—each nail a perfect oval dipped in Blush Pink. She flashed a nostalgic smile. Back when she was a deb, her "beaux" always used to say the first thing they noticed about a girl was her hands! Of course, men were so much more romantic in those days, and they expected their women to be more feminine. Celeste congratulated herself for having been born at the right time in the right place. She wouldn't be a young girl today for "all the tea in China!"

Celeste splashed Joy perfume down the crevice of her breasts, into the creases of her arms, and behind her knees.

She pulled off her turban, releasing a gush of strawberry blonde hair. She wrapped herself in a fleece towel, and floated into her bedroom on a cloud of Joy, herbs, and the sense of her own deepdown cleanliness.

People were always surprised when they saw Celeste's bedroom. The rest of the house was decorated with the formality that suited the Hunter name, but in her own room Celeste indulged her taste for the fussy, the detailed, the ultrafeminine—a white spool bed with ruffled canopy; violet nosegay wallpaper; petite-point cushions, depicting Celeste's favourite fairytales; her first ballet shoes, dipped in gold; her collection of China dolls, arranged around one with strawberry hair and a broken nose that Celeste used to talk to until—Celeste giggled—the doll started to talk back! Most people thought the room was Ashley's, but then, most people had always confused Celeste and Ashley until—Celeste grimaced—Ashley had gone "radical."

The thought of Ashley in the centre of one of Celeste's buoyant moods, encouraged her to do something she had wanted to do for a long time, ever since she had visited Ashley at her London flat in fact. Celeste walked to her highboy, took down a picture of her daughter in a sari with a red dot on her forehead, and removed it from its frame, automatically revealing one of Ashley in smocked dress and ringlets. Celeste hadn't enjoyed her last visit with Ashley. The girl had been positively spiteful. When Celeste, trying to avoid making a fuss over her daughter *actually living with an Indian boy*, had asked her how she could stand to stay in such an ugly flat after the beautiful things she had been used to, Ashley had replied, cool as a cucumber: "This is my wipeout stage, Mother. *It wipes out you!*" Celeste had not thought that nice—in fact, totally uncalled for. She put Ashley's preposterous red-dot photo in her dresser. "Until," she told the moppet, "she comes to her senses."

Celeste, closing the bracket on *that* little bit of unpleasantness, returned, humming determinedly, to the business of dressing. She pulled out the bottom drawer of her highboy and selected a pair of orchid panties from a perfumed pastel cloud of lingerie. She turned, catching herself naked, in her vanity, and a strange wistful thought popped into her head: *I wish someone would paint me, exactly like this, before it's too late.*

Celeste broke her pose.

She admonished herself aloud in the "cross" voice her

mother had used on her when she was small and that she, in turn, had used on Ashley: "What a naughty girl you are! Such wicked thoughts to have in your head!" She added in a more ironic tone: "Especially for a Virtuous Wife and Mother, last of a breed!"

Celeste put on her panties (handmade by a foreign woman on Spadina), then the bra, leaning over so her breasts would fall into the cups, knowing that was what you were supposed to do, but forgetting whether it was to prolong the life of the bra or of the breasts.

She selected an orchid slip from a satin hanger. Again, she caught herself in her vanity, and again she had an heretical thought: *I wish I were taller. Then I could have had one of those society-model flings, like Doody, in Paris and New York.*

Celeste stopped, in mid-hum.

She would have burst right out laughing at herself if her migraine hadn't started acting up again. The migraine convinced Celeste she'd better get to the bottom of her present mood—to figure out why, under her almost indecent happiness, she found this plaintive little voice in herself, feeling sorry for herself. Celeste prided herself on being the sort of down-to-earth person who didn't kid herself about things, and now she "took herself to task," quite severely, in her most adult voice: "Are you feeling sorry for yourself—Celeste Mayfair Hunter—because Charles forgot today was your anniversary and didn't leave a little surprise for you at the breakfast table? Now that would be silly! You know *Charles* isn't the sentimental sort. Celeste pursued relentlessly: "Are you upset, *Miss Sulky*, because Charles forgot to remember you were entertaining his office staff today? That would be silly, too! Considering all the work *poor Charles* does you can't expect him to think about your little projects! You know he's grateful for the support he gets at home—*any* man would be!—but you can't expect him to say thank you, everytime. Especially when he's been so *distracted* these days. Why, he's barely home anymore, *and it's been three weeks since—*"

Celeste drew in her breath and smothered the rest of that sentence in a shaky laugh. What a silly billy she was! The reason their marriage was so good—*so absolutely wonderful*—was because support and affection were taken for granted between them. It was true that they might not "sparkle" as a couple the way they used to when they were in their "heyday" and giving parties every weekend, but they were still very much a "going concern," and it was perfectly idiotic for her to expect *Charles* to express himself when it wasn't "his character"!

Now that Celeste had rooted out the deeper causes of this morning's "sulk," she tackled the more superficial manifestation of it: that ridiculous business about *Doody* and her modelling "fling." It was perfectly true—and Celeste would be the first to admit it—that she sometimes regretted she didn't have many *specific* recollections of the past. She had always been so happy that one golden year had flowed into the next without dark patches to set anything off. There were the wonderful years at Bishop Strachan, with vacations in Muskoka! that wonderful year at Neuchatel, with a summer in Rome! the thrill of marriage with *Charles*—a childhood dream come true! ... Why, talk about memories, *she could practically write a book!* Celeste giggled. She could even recall *exactly* what *Charles* had said the night he proposed. They had been dancing to "Some Enchanted Evening" at the Artillery Ball, when *Charles,* in one of his phrase-making moods, had said: "Celeste Mayfair is a beautiful princess, gliding over a mirror in crystal rollerskates. If I marry her everything I touch will turn to gold." Then he had proposed, right there in the middle of the Royal York Ballroom, and his father had announced the engagement two dances later, while the Burt Niosi Orchestra played "The Girl That I Marry," and everyone had toasted them in Mumm's champagne, and both their mothers had cried, and *dáddy* had given them their first home, and *Charles'* daddy had given them the business, and—Celeste caught her breath—*they had lived Happily Ever After!* In fact, the only blight her life had ever known was the terrible lingering illness of her dear daddy and now the temporary estrangement of her two children, which every parent was going through these days till the young folk "came to their senses."

Celeste laid her angel-skin slip on her bed, and burrowed, headfirst, into it. It was true that a lot of luck had gone into her life. Afterall, not everyone was fortunate enough to be born into the social set she was born into, but all you had to do was to look at a girl like *Doody* to see that a lot of *good sense* had gone into her life, too ... *Poor Doody!* Now there was a girl to feel sorry for! She'd had the crystal rollerskates, too, but what a botch she'd made of things: a tragic romance with a French race-car driver, *three* disastrous marriages, a half-dozen attempted suicides and—

Celeste stopped.

She fought her way through her slip, breaking a strap. She lay down on her bed, shaking, feeling the room fall away ... *seeing herself on a narrow ledge clinging with her claws ... looking down into an abyss ... foul, like a black mouth....* She had had that nightmare again last night ... the same one she had had the night her daddy had died, and the night young Xavier had left home and the night—

Celeste slowly, steadily recited the multiplication tables.

She massaged her temples, untying the knot in her forehead. How could she have let her guard down so foolishly? That *terrible* memory stealing up on her like that.... What a treacherous thing the human mind could be!

Celeste recited the facts to herself in a sing-songy monotone designed to take the "bad magic" out of them. There was simply *no* comparison between *her* experience and *Doody's,* just as there was no comparison between *her* life and *Doody's.* Her "experience" had been an accident, a stupid *embarrassment.* She had had a beastly attack of migraine. There had been the tension. Yes, she would certainly admit *Fiona* had caused tension. And the doctor had prescribed pills, more to control Celeste's *formidable energy* so she could get some sleep than anything else. The pills had been on her dressing-table. That was stupid. She always kept them in the bathroom now. Celeste had taken one, then another, losing track until—she took a deep breath—until ... she managed to call *Charles* at his mother's, and he had rushed her to the hospital, and she had ... had her stomach pumped.

Celeste got up from the bed.

She put the torn slip aside for Ruby to mend, and went to the closet for another.

"Fortunately," she confided to the strawberry doll with the broken nose, "*Charles* is the only person in the world who knows that *silly* story. I would have *died* of embarrassment to let anyone think *I* was the sort of *melodramatic* woman who did *that* sort of thing, though you and I both know women who would. Afterall, the way Fiona *flung* herself at *poor Charles* was really *disgusting*—no rules, no decorum, just that wild-eyed way of hers. Any man would have been flattered, and I'm not going to pretend *Charles* is an *angel.* He's a man, and a virile one, and the way some girls deport themselves nowadays—well, it's a bad *joke!*"

Celeste laid out the fresh slip, smiling ruefully. Why, it had got so bad that, just for the laughs, she had taken to naming her migraines after the girls who had gone after poor Charles. There was Migraine Roxanne, Migraine Belinda, Migraine Debra, Migraine—

Celeste felt a warning stir in her head. She slid into her slip, switching her thoughts so smoothly she almost didn't notice the transition. She thought, instead, of how she, Celeste Mayfair Hunter, had helped *other* women in her "set" handle their husbands' flings, for—although she certainly was no authority on the subject—she had done *a lot of frank observing of others,* and her wisdom was much prized. Celeste always gave the sort of sensible directives that helped other women knit up the raw ends of their marriage over the nasty holes their husbands' affairs left, rather like invisible-mending an heirloom bedspread some drunken fool had burned a hole in so it looked almost as good as new. Celeste "got on" with other women, at least those with whom she had things in common, and she went out of her way to be gracious to the rest, *provided they did not betray her trust.* In this regard, and in most others, Celeste considered herself entirely reliable. She never betrayed a confidence, no matter how "juicy," and she would sooner *die* than be so prideless as to admit she had anything to confide herself. This sort of discretion set Celeste off from the other women in her "set." That, and the fact she had never found it necessary to have an affair of her own, either for "thrill-seeking" or for revenge. If sometimes *Charles* gave her a little trouble . . . well . . . she believed that if she gave him enough "rope" while pulling on it just a little, he'd soon "come to his senses," and then they'd both be glad she was unblemished. As a matter of fact, Celeste had to admit—*yes, she did, being an honest person*—that she felt superior to the other women. She knew it was "wicked" of her, but she usually called them—to herself, and maybe, yes, to *stewart,* her hairdresser—the Midol Mafia! Celeste let out a peal of laughter as she sat down at her vanity, feeling much refreshed. It certainly *did* pay to get things "out on the table" instead of keeping them from one's self the way some women did!

Celeste tied a makeup bib around her neck and a white-linen band around her hair.

She took her "magic box" from her flounced vanity, and set it inside a ring of perfume bottles.

Using a puff of cotton, she patted skin freshener from a crystal bottle on her heart-shaped face, then astringent, from another crystal bottle. She rubbed in moisturizer from a gold pot, pushing back her skin from her hairline, and feeling deliciously pampered even though it was her own hands doing the job today instead of *Robert's*. Celeste enjoyed the touch of her fingers to her face, because she could "see" her face better that way than with her eyes. Celeste put down this strangeness about her face to her total lack of vanity about it, though she knew from all the compliments that it must be a pretty face, maybe even a beautiful one. A "spoiled" face, one old beau had called it "with features more perfect than interesting." That had miffed Celeste. She didn't mind the "spoiled" part— she guessed she was, with all the attention she'd always had— but how could something "more perfect" be less interesting than something "less perfect"? That put off Celeste's whole idea of aesthetics, and she didn't like to be put off when it came to something she knew she did well. Everyone agreed, even the "names" at the Art Gallery, that Celeste Mayfair Hunter's "forte" was aesthetics!

With a magnifying glass and a strong light, Celeste inspected her face for blemishes. Her enlarged eye caught her attention. It had tiny crow's feet at the corner. The same bad crow had landed on the bridge of her nose, then had hopscotched to either side of her mouth. She knew his name—Migraine.

Celeste touched the lines. Did they show? All she knew— given her blind-eye—was that she had watched the "net" of expression slide over her friends' faces, almost like a slow enchantment, taking them over, feature by feature, with changes so slight one rarely could tell when prettiness had gone and selfishness had taken over, or fear, or bitterness, or defeat, or greed. The best even her friends who "looked after" themselves had achieved was a kind of bland neutrality. You looked at a face, like the face of an aging movie star, and you knew it wasn't the *same* face, but you couldn't pin down exactly how it was different. It was what was known, in Celeste's set, as "Darling, you're looking simply marvellous!"—meaning, "well-preserved."

Celeste put down her magnifying glass.

She released her strawberry hair, shaking it in the dappled

light from her window. Her hair was her most striking feature, with the colour so close to her "bridal" colour that she almost forgot *Stewart* "did anything" to it.

She picked up her gold brush and began brushing it with long, loving strokes, suddenly catching the eye of her broken-nosed doll in her mirror. She turned in surprise. It looked so much like *Stewart*, with its strawberry hair and "cracked" face, that she couldn't believe she hadn't noticed it before. Celeste turned back to her mirror, enjoying the crackle of her hair as it flew up to her brush. It was strange about herself and Stewart. Of all "her men," he was the only one—the only *person*, actually—she confided in. Together, they "giggled like schoolgirls!" What was really strange was that Stewart was the only one of her men—the only *person*, actually—who was mean to her. Celeste believed in frankness, that was certain, but she didn't believe in being cruel, and there was no question that Stewart was sometimes *very cruel*. Why, just last appointment, Stewart had asked her to close her eyes, and when she had opened them, she had found herself looking at a bouquet of roses to which he *knew* she had a severe allergy, and though they turned out to be *artificial*, the *shock* had left her sneezing for the rest of the appointment. Another time he had glued a piece of her hair over her lip, then, positively sniggering, had announced: "After forty a woman's *crowning* glory turns into her *clowning* glory!" Celeste was very upset about that. It was so much like seeing a picture of herself defaced. If Stewart had meant it was time to start bleaching out the little red moustache on her upper lip, why couldn't he have found a nicer way of telling her?

Celeste put down her hairbrush, but not without giving the strawberry-haired doll with the broken nose a "bad boy" look.

She heard the ballerina on her chime clock begin to pirouette to "Dance of the Sugar Plum Fairies." *My goodness! How times flies when you're busy!*

Celeste put on a pink cashmere skirt and sweater set, just to be cosy while she did the final planning on the Valentine tea. First she would have to check up on the help. Not on *Hannah*, of course. Hannah was the gem of gems, but on Ruby, the girl from the correctional home who was Celeste's latest charity. That girl was *impossible*. Celeste not only had to dust everything after her, repolish all the silver, hold glasses up to the light, and refold the linens, but she also had to *count* everything. Of course, Celeste's friends thought she was crazy to

187

bring *that* sort of person into her home and—here, Celeste smiled fatly with her thin lips—if help weren't so hard to get she'd be inclined to agree.

Celeste switched her mind to more important matters. The icecream bon-bons that hadn't arrived, and the flowers still to be arranged. Celeste *adored* arranging flowers, and she liked lots and lots of them, especially in winter. Today she was planning Bird of Paradise for the hall, carnations in the powder room, white mums for the living room, and then, of course, lilies for the dining-room centrepiece. Celeste always used lilies for her centrepieces when she could get them. She had won a blue ribbon in 1960 at the Garden Club's Spring Show for her lilies, which the judge had called "inspirational in the purity of their transitions. For the first time, I have seen this most difficult flower treated by someone who understands them."

Celeste put on her gold charm-bracelet, as always, then hesitated over the other things in her jewelbox. She picked out a set of tinkly earrings, put one on, then imagined *Adrian* waggling his finger over her shoulder. "No *no*, madame. Ears this season are for *listening!*"

Celeste, with a quicksilver laugh, returned the earrings to their box and settled for more Joy perfume on her earlobes. She paused at her vanity for a security check. She looked good. She felt good, even a little ... *virtuous*. After all, she could be playing bridge with her mother at the Ladies' Club. She could be shopping at Holt Renfrew. She could, for that matter, be with *Doody* at Main Chance, or soaking up the sun in Palm Beach. Instead, here she was, Celeste Mayfair Hunter, in good old Toronto the gritty, preparing to be gracious to *Charles'* girls. How many of the women she knew would bother? Most thought she was crazy to be so charitable, and—given the ingratitude she sometimes found in this world—Celeste was inclined to agree.


Charles X. Hunter sat at his desk in an office that had changed little since Xavier X. Hunter bought its furnishings in an estate sale in 1896.

A wall calendar, with cards rotated daily by a succession of secretaries, stated the day, the date, the month, the year, and the century. A grandfather clock, to which Old Xavier had grafted a third hand, told Xavier, then his son, and now his grandson, time to the second. A double thermometer attached to the single oval window, recorded indoor and outdoor temperatures. The Hunter family motto, over a listing bookcase, gave moral instruction: ALWAYS KEEP YOUR FEET ON THE GROUND.

The office's present incumbent had made only three changes.

In an alcove created by a rickety sherry cabinet was a series of charts that looked like the profit lines of a very stable company, but which, when examined, proved to be graphs of his own blood pressure, temperature, heartbeat, brainwaves, and anything else that could be measured by the physician who visited him every month.

On the wall, over a lumpy horsehair sofa where Old Xavier had hung Queen Victoria, the present incumbent had hung a Karsh portrait of his deceased mother, swaddled in the black crepe in which she had celebrated twenty-three years of widowhood.

The third change was more of an extension. To a wall map of Toronto, marking the location of Hunter's Confectionery, and another of Canada, marking Hunter outlets, and one of the world locating Canada, the present incumbent had added successive skycharts, placing the Earth in the Solar System, then in the Milky Way, then in the Universe, so that if you started with the black-and-gold Charles X. Hunter nameplate, and progressed upward, you would get a fair approximation of the schoolboy game that begins with a name in a flyleaf of a book and ends up positioning its owner at the centre of his Universe.

Now Charles X. Hunter, working in the slot of time between 9.03 A.M. EST, and 10 A.M. EST, February 14, 1974, sat at his desk, in pinstripe suit and half-moon glasses, shuffling papers back and forth as he read the first entry in his Economist Diary:

10.00 A.M. BRIEFING OF LAURA TEMPLE OF QUALITY CONTROL RE U.S. RODENT HAIR. To this was attached a memo from Eve, stating: "Herewith, a copy of the recent U.S. Pure Food and Drug report—widely publicized in Canadian papers—penalizing certain U.S. companies for unacceptable levels of rodent hair and excrement in their products. The Canadian Consumers' Cleanliness Committee has taken exception to the suggestion that there might be such a thing as *acceptable* levels of rodent hair, and has been bombarding various

Canadian food processors with questionnaires demanding information."

*Ahhh, yes* ... Charles remembered the problem now: Hunter's, and a half-dozen competitors, had decided to meet with the CCCC this morning to celebrate—in a united, nationalistic voice—the purity of the Canadian product, using middle-level spokesmen to de-emphasize the issue. Laura Temple of Quality Control, immaculate in lab coat and hairnet, was to be Hunter's spokesman, but before the meeting Charles X. had to ensure she herself had the "larger" picture. Specialists, and especially women specialists, were inclined to get lost in detail. Laurie, for example, like to argue that all foreign matter would, of necessity, be sterile, because of the high processing temperatures—a technicality Charles did not think would sit well with your average militant consumer.

He ticked Laurie's name with his gold Eversharp. A stubborn woman, especially on a matter of principle. Better lean heavily on the Hunter charm: "I understand, my dear, that's why you're so *valuable* to the company, but this time do it *my* way."

Charles X. read the next item:

10.30 A.M. MEETING WITH DANIEL STEELE OF ADS RE LOW-CAL SALAD BARS. This was accompanied by a marketing report stating that the testing of the new lettuce-leaf wrapper in Vancouver, Halifax, and Oshawa had proved negative. Comments were: "Makes me think of garlic." "YUK!" "I thought the green cherries were cabbage worms." Summary: "Only 'green' flavour public willing to associate with chocolate is mint or, in urban centres with population over 110,000, pistachio. Recommendation: Mint-leaf package."

Charles shrugged. He passed on to:

11:00 A.M. MEETING WITH SVEN JENSON RE COST OF AUTOMATION IN CHOCOLATE DEPARTMENT. He skimmed through the estimates, about what he expected, though the production loss seemed inflated. Sven was covering himself there, fighting Fitch all the way.

11:30 A.M. MEETING WITH BEAU WHITEHEAD RE FEASABILITY OF COMPANY COUNSELLING SERVICE. This was accompanied by pro and con reports from a dozen different department heads.

12:00 A.M. LUNCHEON MEETING WITH SALES, ADS. 1973 SALES AWARD TO BIMBO BROWN. FRESH IDEAS RE EASTER PROMO?

Charles started to pass over that, glanced at his grandfather clock, then resignedly took a pad from his desk, drew a margin, and listed digits from 1 to 10.

He tapped his Eversharp against his teeth, and watched the second hand buzz, like an angry insect, around the face of his grandfather clock, with the other two hands drooped like a moustache. *Two minutes.*

Charles X. pulled his eyes guiltily from the clock and focused them on the blank page. He drummed his fingers to drown out the tick, and sucked on his Eversharp like a worried schoolboy. Ten years ago he would have had the page covered with ideas, feeling them gush out so fast he'd have to call in Eve to take shorthand. Now he had to prime himself, but what could be fresh about the chocolate business to Charles X. Hunter after twenty-eight years? Besides—he twitched his own moustache, as if he might have a second-hand whizzing like a fly around it—what was the matter with all the Bright Young Men he kept at vast expense on his payroll? Why should *he* waste time playing hotshot when he needed every second for administration?

Charles considered skipping today's Promo meeting, then recalled what had happened last time he opted out—*Miss Bon-Bon!* He grimaced, then smiled wistfully. Since he'd paid for it, he would have liked to have seen it. Imagine, the latest chapter in the struggle for female dignity fought out, hand to hand, in two hundred pounds of *his* Sweetheart Bon-Bons. The first *he'd* heard of it was when he saw himself burned in effigy on the eleven o'clock CBC news in a Thunder Bay hotel-room, and some young pup from Canadian Press had phoned to ask how he squared exploitation of the female body with corporate responsibility. What he should have said was that next time he'd like the "corporate responsibility" of choosing the program—maybe, Gloria Steinem and Germaine Greer *vs* Raquel Welch and Mae West. Have them start out easy, pulling taffy in a tub of it, stripped to the waist, eyes-blazing, crouched and snarling like a couple of panthers. . . .

Charles grinned. Anger in women excited him. The challenge . . . the promise . . . the *danger.* He recalled, with a prickle of his scalp, someone he hadn't thought of in years: Yalla, the mad halfbreed who hung out with him at the air-base during the war—an ember-eyed beauty with so much rage in her you could feel it burn right through her skin. She was Red Power ahead of her time, so full of vengeance she

191

would attack him as they made love, her teeth sinking deep into his lip, her nails gouging crescents across his back, as he stoked her fury with a young man's lust for excess—rockets exploding! blast-off to Mars! One day she attacked him with a tomahawk and a scalping knife. Just hurled herself at him out of the dark, blades flashing, in full warpaint, whooping as she tried to peel back his scalp. She wasn't joking, either. He had had to fight for his life—his squash-and-tennis muscles against her murderous hatred, an almost even match, ending in the most explosive lovemaking he had ever known, her rage consuming him until—unexpectedly! thrillingly!—it became his own. He could have killed for her, for himself, that night. He could have painted his face ochre and—he glanced up at his mother's picture—parted his mother's blue hair with an axe.

Xavier's clock bonged the half-hour.

Charles started in his chair, carved and heavy like a judge's chair. He stared, eyes glazed, at his name in gold on his memo pad, and the neat column of digits, 1 to 10. *When was the last time he had felt unbridled lust? fury? joy? unbridled anything?*

Charles put a tight, resentful collar around his name. He arranged his spine so the bump in the back of the chair would catch him at exactly his punishing point, and considered, with only a touch of sarcasm: *Lenten chocolate bars? Unleaven wafers dipped in bittersweet chocolate?*

Charles doodled wings and a tail to the oval round his name. Then he added a stream of bombs falling *zip zip zip.* He let his eyes drift out his window, scanning his patch of sky to see if there were any little Cesnas or Pipers from the Island Airport playing around up there, and feeling the ache in his gut he always felt when he looked up into the wide blue yonder.

Charles let his mind wander with his eyes.

He had always wanted to fly more than anything else in the world, but the moment he stepped into the cockpit for his solo it had hit him—the sweats, the trots, the shakes . . . the whole acrophobia thing. Everyone at the base put his failure down to stagefright, then, when it persisted, to cowardice. Charles did, too. It was easier to believe he was a coward than to admit what actually had happened.

The night befoer his solo—the night his brother crashed in Germany, as he later discovered—Xav came to Charles in a nightmare, wearing his flight suit with a parachute cord knotted around his neck, his face bloodless and transparent like a zombie's, eyes curdled in agony, mouth rimed with spittle. Placing an icy finger on Charles' feverish forehead, he repeated over and over, in the exact intonations of Old Grandpa Xavier, the Hunter family motto: "ALWAYS KEEP YOUR FEET ON THE GROUND, my boy. ALWAYS KEEP YOUR FEET ON THE GROUND."

Charles jerked himself out of his reveries with a sharp snap of the neck. He dragged his eyes from his window to his skycharts, then down to the nameplate on his desk. He fastened them on his memo pad and drew an elaborate rocket, covered with stars. He wrote firmly: "How about a Venus chocolate bar shaped like a rocket?" then remembered Mars Bars, and threw the whole thing into the basket.

Charles X. took a brier pipe from his desk and began sucking on it. He wrote on a clean sheet: "Recall success of this year's white-chocolate Santas. Is there an ideas, here, for Easter?" He was about to add: "Why not a white-chocolate Jesus?" when he remembered they didn't have a brown one and in the chocolate business white was the novelty.

He looked at the clock: 9.36. The big and the little hands were closing in on him like a nutcracker. He found his hands shuffling papers as if he were tuning a balky motor. He put the papers aside. He took off his glasses. He massaged the bridge of his nose, then wrote: "Why not Executive Bars? Energy pick-me-ups full of raisins and nuts for the tired exec? How about a pinstriped wrapper with a gold tie?" He drew one. The stripes looked like cell bars. He stared at them accusatively. . . . It wasn't as if he'd even wanted the chocolate business in the first place. He'd just been conscripted as a Chocolate Soldier at age seven when his brother Xav had defaulted by trying to burn down the Candy Factory. After the war, he'd tried to break free, but the failure of his flying career had cut deeper into his confidence than he cared to admit. He hadn't dared risk another failure, or another confrontation with Old Xavier. Far better to pretend he more-or-less wanted what the family expected of him than that he had no choice. To the extent that he felt discontentment, he had rationalized with all the uppercase nouns: Duty, Tradition, Loyalty. And the lowercase one: common-sense.

Charles picked up his Eversharp. He turned it over and over, his moustache twitching. It was still fifteen minutes to his first appointment. He checked the top item in his slush basket, then wished he hadn't. It was the usual sheaf of complaints about the Heat/Cool System, plus the confidential report of a private investigator who had been working to "break" the case.

"After scientific co-ordination and mental analysis," concluded our intellectual Sam Spade, "I can only adduce the cause of malfunction to be in the nature of sabotage or other criminal misdemeanor, since the infraction has been pinpointed to the openings of, possibly, a single upstairs window in the Business Sector, often between midnight and 7 A.M., and lasting less than one minute, indicating an item of convenient size being passed in or out. It is hypothesized by this investigator that a narcotics ring of some size may be operating on the premises, with the possibility of certain batches of export candy being used—" *Oh God!* Charles X. stuffed the report into the crackly yellow stuff at the bottom of his slush file, hoping never to see it again in this lifetime.

He looked at the item now on top: a memo from Basil Fitch, demanding that he "do something" about the woman in Special Accounts. Charles drummed the memo, glowering. The person he'd like to "do something" about was Fitch himself. The Computer Control Centre was—for his tastes—an unmitigated disaster. Instead of replacing employees, it had required Hunters to hire more. The machines made work for each other like the most infuriating of middle-echelon infighters. They couldn't be reached by charm, bluff, or persuasion. What's more, they demanded more coddling than humans required under the most irrational of health services.

Charles scrawled across Fitch's memo: "Eve, make an appointment this week or next with Mary what-was-her-name?" recalling as he did that Eve, along with the rest of his female staff, would not be here this afternoon because of Celeste's Valentine tea.

Charles felt a grateful eruption of hostility. *Damn Celeste and her "little projects!"* Why couldn't she keep her nose out of his business? It was different when they were younger. Then her "I spy" was more of a game. Now, after twenty-five years he was just plain *bored* with—

*Twenty-five years!* Charles put that figure together with another staring up at him from his diary: *February 14. Valentine's Day . . . their anniversary. Damn!*

He imagined Celeste sitting at her vanity with cold compresses against her forehead, playing the whole scene for High Tragedy. *Was it too late to order flowers?*

Charles reached for his phone as his buzzer sounded.

He dropped the receiver, with a satisfied smirk. Sentiment would have to wait. He had business to attend to.

"Miss Temple," announced Eve.

Charles checked his Economist Diary. *Ahh, yes.* The rodent excrement vs the CCCC. He tightened his tie and found, to his consternation, that his hands were trembling. . . . Yalla, the day he had told her he was leaving. . . . They had made love with the easy camaradarie of good friends saying good-bye, and then—laughing, almost gay, the two of them still naked, still warmed by each other's flesh, bathed in each other's scents and juices—she had thrust something cold and heavy into his arms, wrapped in a stained blue blanket. Charles stood in her darkened shack, feeling fingers of apprehension toy with the cords of his neck and watching, in fascination, as the blanket slid from the bundle to reveal . . . *a fishbowl with the foetus of a baby suspended in clear jelly—mouth gaping! eyes bulged! fingers spread! . . . trailing fibres of mould, of decay, like a bloated blue frog in a puddle, and—around its neck—an umbilical cord, knotted like a parachute cord!*

Charles, paralyzed, rooted to the floor by two icy barefeet, groped up through escalating shockwaves of horror, feeling the gruesome chill of the thing in its swollen glass belly pressed against his own.

He read the silver identification bracelet slung round the neck of the bowl: CHARLES X. HUNTER, JUNIOR.

Charles smashed the fishbowl. *She had lied! The crazy bitch had lied!* It was the same ghastly joke she had played on another airman with whom she had once had an affair. He knew she lied, but yet he could never get that macabre image out of his mind. Even today it rose up to choke him when he found something fishy or jellied on his plate. It floated in a crimson puddle behind his eyes, haunting his dreams. And when, years later his own son had been born, he had withheld his name, as if—

Celeste Mayfair Hunter posed in liquid elegance at the end of her mahogany table, her ankles neatly crossed, her silk Pucci unscored by movement, her marquise diamond flashing in the light of her chandelier as she poured *tea? coffee?* and made tinkly chitchat with her husband's female staff who milled awkwardly about her delicate antiques before settling, like burs, on the damask chairs and sofas bracketing her silk-and-crystal living room.

She told Daphne Steele that she thought a woman never looked more radiant than after she had just given birth.

She told Fanny Llewelland, the fat, raspy woman who used to run the Hunter Switchboard, that she would always remember her melodious voice, which made it such a delight to call Hunter's.

She told Irma Burbank—*my god! did they still make that ghastly colour of hair?*—how much she adored her rhinestone poodle-pin.

She told Megan Mason, defiantly wearing bluejeans—*oh, really! one had a right to respect in one's own home!*—that she admired the way young people today stood up for the things they believed in, just like her daughter *Ashley*.

She told Eve Martin how much she counted on her loyal support in keeping Charles from working too hard.

Now, Celeste was talking to Brigitte Young, a smile set like a pink stone on her china face as she withheld Brigitte's cup, preparing to collect her reward for the afternoon's tedium. "You must be *Charles' junior secretary*. Where has he been keeping you?! Such a cute and refreshing thing you are! I'd *adore* you to meet our son, *Xavier*. Imagine! Charles and I have been married twenty-five years today!"

It was a polished performance with Celeste deftly manipulating Brigitte so that both were reflected in the same antique mirror, and Celeste could enjoy, along with her guests, Brigitte's gaucherie framed in her own good taste. By the time the younger girl, flushed with resentment, was allowed to receive her coffee, with the cup too full and the silver spoon tilting it on the saucer, sloppage on the pale gold broadloom was inevitable.

"Oh, don't bother about *that!*" exclaimed Celeste, far too jubilantly to be kind. "*Ruby* can look after it later."

Celeste, her face feeding on her small victory, turned to Laurie Temple.

She told Laurie she always felt sure of the purity of the Hunter product with Laurie as the "watchdog" on Quality Control.

She complimented Lena Petty, the doddery woman with the shrill laugh who used to work in Personnel, on the fine stitching in the misshapen sock she was knitting.

She told Matty Ryan that she thought women should revive

the "street" tradition of wearing flowers in their hair after seeing how pretty one of her own carnations looked in Matty's "do."

Celeste felt herself squirm.

It was a movement so uncharacteristic she wouldn't have believed herself capable of it if she hadn't actually "caught herself" at it in the antique mirror by her sideboard.

She disciplined her elegant bottom to stay put on its Queen Anne chair, but she could do nothing about the sense of internal twitchiness she felt building up inside herself and the fear it would erupt in a fit of sneezing.

Celeste heard a giggle over her shoulder.

She turned to see something else she did not like: Eve Martin and that Brigitte girl "as thick as thieves" on her loveseat.

What was going on between those two?

Celeste hadn't minded so much the way that awkward girl had spilled her coffee—though that *was* a nuisance, coffee was like a dye—but she hadn't at all liked the way *Eve Martin* had rushed to her rescue. The two of them were giggling together with no regard for anyone else, and—*could it be?*—actually sending Celeste hostile glances! Could they possibly be "mad" at *her?*! Celeste went over her conversation with Brigitte, prepared to admonish herself if she had not gone far enough to make that unappetizing girl feel comfortable, but, as fairly as she could recall, she had been graciousness itself. Celeste caught a glimpse of Ruby going about her duties with some efficiency for a change, and felt reassured. If she weren't so *used* to dealing with "recalcitrants," she would begin to doubt herself now.

Celeste poured several more cups of tea, smiling fatly with her thin mouth, careful to put the recipients "at their ease" with compliments and well-proportioned interest.

She caught sight of the Brigitte girl stuffing a ladyfinger into her mouth sideways, leaving a sugar moustache on her mouth, and right then and there Celeste allowed herself to be "provoked." *Such a childish display of bad manners!* She hadn't seen anything so *ghoulish* since ... well, since *Ashley* left home, but Ashley knew better. She was just being "rebellious," whereas this girl clearly had no training at all, no background. Really, what could *Charles* have been thinking of to hire such a girl? She was entirely unsuited to his prestige. Celeste would have a little talk with him this evening and suggest—

*No.* Celeste would *not.*

She would *not* criticize the girl. Maybe her shorthand was a "whizz" or she had some other worthwhile "office trait." Celeste would merely show *Charles* the stain on the carpet and the loveseat that would surely have to be cleaned, if not fumigated, after that girl's sloppiness, and explain to him, in the amusing way she had of "looking on the bright side of things," the trouble the poor thing had had this afternoon, and let him come to his own conclusions.

Celeste, feeling "more herself," returned fulltime to pouring tea—to the fat woman with the coarse bass voice and the thin flutey one with the truly appalling knitted hat. It must be their fifth cup! Where were they putting it? *Ooooh, well,* Celeste reminded herself, charitably, these people hadn't had the opportunities to "broaden" themselves that she had had. She would just have to be more tolerant.

Celeste forced herself to listen to an interminable anecdote about the Switchboard, her eyes glazed, her mouth spread to capacity, holding her laugh for the punchline, should it ever declare itself.

Again she felt the twitchiness build up inside herself, accompanied by a feathery tickle in her throat.

*Oh dear!*

Celeste held her breath as long as she could, then let it loose in a gaggly ripple of sneezes that she stifled, in her lace hanky.

She set herself against the next attack, knowing now—*oh dear, oh dear, oh dear!*—that she had no choice but to face the terrible thing that she had been suppressing—that nasty incident she knew to be the source of her present discomfort.

It had happened that very morning, just before noon, when, flushed with the pleasure of arranging her flowers, Celeste had answered the merchant's bell herself to find the man from Tidy's Florist with another parcel.

At first she thought it must be part of her original order, something that had been forgotten. Then she *knew* it must be from Charles. He *had* remembered their anniversary after all! This was her "little surprise"!

Celeste had unwrapped the parcel, full of happy expectations, only to find an unsigned card wishing her a Happy Anniversary and . . . *two dozen sweetheart roses!*

She had begun to sneeze then, and she had never really stopped. Though she had ordered Ruby to burn them in the incinerator, she could still smell the thorny blooms in her nostrils. And it wasn't just the scent that was bothering her. It was the thought . . . the gnawing suspicion. *Every*body who knew it was her anniversary also knew how severely allergic she was to roses. Who could have done such a *spiteful* thing when she always went so far out of her way to be generous with people?!

Celeste had wondered if it might have been *Stewart*. Had he been miffed when she'd taken him to task for his little joke with the artificial roses?

Then she had been forced to ask herself—*oh, what a ghastly thing suspicion is*—if it could have been her own mother? Bessie had been "off" a little more than usual lately, and roses were her favourite flower.

Now Celeste had a darker and more ominous suspicion. Could the roses have been sent by Eve Martin "in league" with that Brigitte person? Had Charles asked Eve to order flowers for him, and had she done this bold and malicious thing? Were there things "going on" at the office that were far worse than Celeste had dared imagine?

Celeste let loose a gargle of slightly hysterical laughter, hoping it would land in some convenient place in the anecdote. She noted, with relief, that she seemed to have been successful there. At least, the thin woman—the harpy one—had begun her version of the same boring happening, clearly in competition.

Celeste took that opportunity to struggle for control, sucking in her cheeks, clenching her jaw, drawing on every reserve of Mayfair poise and discipline, fighting the irresistible urge to give way to a deep sneeze and feeling now the gathering of discomfort into fury, because . . . because . . . she was *sure* all this allergenic reaction could *not* be just from this morning's incident. *Celeste was sure now she could smell roses somewhere in this room.* Had that ingrate Ruby brought them back and hidden them somewhere? Or was someone, here, at the tea, wearing rose perfume?

Celeste let her green eyes, jagged with dangerous lights, flash in and about the persons clotting her living room, recalling a Valentine tea several years ago when she had had to ask one of her husband's employees—an older woman—to leave because of the unusually strong rose sachet she was wearing, looking for that woman now, but finding—peculiarly for her—that she couldn't remember what the woman looked like, finding, too, that it was becoming increasingly difficult to see through the pall of smoke and the throb of pain that was her migraine, collecting itself in a fist in the back of her head, fed by the slither of tongues against wet smiles, the tinkling of silver spoons, the singing of birds on hats.... *Oh dear oh dear oh dear!*

The smell of roses was becoming stronger now. What were Eve and Brigitte still giggling about on the loveseat? Why was that six-foot amazon looking at the hallmark on her silver—was she intending to steal it? And—*oh God!*—had she actually seen that tart with the unbelievable hair lean over and butt her cigarette in her arrangement of lilies?

Celeste put a hand to her mouth to stifle a sneeze. With the other, she set down her tea. The cup missed the table. It flipped onto her lap. Celeste felt the soak of brown liquid through her Pucci dress, her handmade slip, her orchid panties. She felt a flush of crimson through her cheeks. She crossed her ankles: *Was it running down her legs?*

Celeste looked frantically around her.

Incredibly, no one seemed to have noticed.

The fat woman and the thin one were arguing with vehemence now about some fine point in their anecdote. Celeste recalled, with alarming clarity, almost as if she were reliving it—*oh, this can't be happening!*—the day she had been sitting at the breakfast table amidst dozens of exquisitely arranged roses, listening to her parents argue about ... about ... something very trivial ... their voices topping each other ... until ... until ... her beloved father had pitched over into the roses, clutching his water goblet, calling to her with foam on his mouth to get his pills, and she had had to tell him, shaking her head, *no no no, impossible!* because ... because ... she had just "got her little friend" for the first time, and if she had moved, everyone—the maid, her mother, her father—would see the blood running down her legs.

Celeste started to sneeze. She sneezed and sneezed and—

Celeste fled, shoving past the fat woman and the thin one who had just come to some agreement on their now joint anecdote, hearing the teapot crash behind her as she stumbled up her spiral stairs, convinced she must have blundered into someone else's life by mistake.

She almost screamed with relief when she got to her own room. She flung herself on the bed, sneezing herself into insensibility.

Her dress felt unclean ... gooey.

She thought of the brown stain, spreading over the pale

broadloom with the teapot overturned in the middle, and Ruby making as much fuss as possible scrubbing it up, triumph mingled with distaste as if she were cleaning up for one of the dogs. Celeste punched her pillow. *That bitch! I'll fire her tomorrow!* She had had enough "social consciousness" to last a lifetime!

Celeste got up from her bed. She walked calmly—if dazedly—to the bathroom. She took three tranquillizers. She removed her Pucci dress, swabbing the stain as best she could before throwing it into the dirty clothes hamper, feeling the helpless guilt she always felt when disposing of soiled panties.

She wrapped herself in a white towel and returned to her bedroom.

She rang for Ruby.

She waited, expressionless, till Ruby, face pulled long, appeared. She explained, in a cool-as-crystal voice that she had taken ill, that her guests were to stay as long as they pleased, but that she was sorry she couldn't rejoin them.

Celeste waited till Ruby had left the room. Then she collapsed at her vanity. She felt the numbing pulsations of her migraine, and clutched a perfume bottle in each hand, cutting them into her palms in an attempt to siphon off the pain. *Why weren't the pills working?* She tried to recreate the scene in her dining room, before things "went bad," trying to find enough good threads to knit over the ghastly hole she had fallen through. She pictured the beautifully set mahogany table, with the gleaming trays of sandwiches, dyed pink and green and yellow, and arranged like flowers. She thought of the flowers themselves, her best arrangement so far, classic yet informal, not like the weedy windblown stuff the younger members of The Garden Club tried to foist on the judges.

Celeste felt overwhelmed by weariness. *Oh God, why do I bother? Why do I entertain those lumpen women, with their dowdy hats and linty dresses when they don't know how to better themselves?*

Celeste picked up her hairbrush. She began to stroke her hair . . . *one, two, three.*

She felt a queer pause in the room, as if it were taking stock, and then she heard the laughter—sludgy and gurgling, like mud oozing up over a silken shoe.

"*I'll* tell you why you entertain them," said a nasty voice she couldn't quite place. "You do it to showoff to the less fortunate, *so you can envy yourself.* You do it to brag to your friends about your *social consciousness*. You do it to squeeze into *poor* Charles' life. You do it to spy on whomever he happens to be sleeping with and to demonstrate *your full power and glory as head wife in the harem*. You do it for the same reason you make lists and have massages and chase after auction sales—*you do it to kill time!*"

Celeste put down her brush. The voice stopped.

She picked up the brush again. The voice began again, this time with greater cunning. "You didn't get to that girl today, you know, *darling*—Migraine Brigitte *ha ha*. You made her uncomfortable but you didn't impress her. She thinks you're a *dinosaur from the dark ages*—just like Ashley does. She doesn't need *you*, darling. You need *her*. You were counting on getting the goods on her this afternoon so you could have one holy row with *poor old Charles* this evening. You're *desperate*, darling. You'll do *any*thing to strike a few sparks from him these days, but he doesn't want *you* anymore. He's *bored* with—"

Celeste put down the brush. The voice stopped.

She was sure now that it was not inside her own head. She was sure it was here, in this room, if only she could trick it into revealing itself.

Celeste picked up her brush again.

"He's *bored* with you," continued the voice. "You're a *boring* woman, darling. People don't say what *a nice nice nice* lady that Celeste Hunter is. *You* say that. What *they* say is, 'Oh god, what a bore!' Even your *boring* friends find *you* boring, darling. You at least used to be an expert at holding on, but you're losing your grip. *Dear Charles* doesn't even count on you to flatter his virility anymore by accusing him of spreading it around. He's tired both of *his* Boy Lover and of *your* Jealous Wife. The old games have broken down, darling, and you don't know what the new ones are."

Celeste swivelled in her chair, her hairbrush in her hand.

She heard laughter spew up from every point in the room, *but she could not be fooled anymore!* ... She had been watching the doll with the strawberry hair and the broken nose—the one she used to confide in, because, being imperfect, it had no right to expect her to be perfect! She was almost positive she had seen its lips move, the way it had learned to talk back to her in childhood.

Celeste advanced on the doll with her hairbrush.

She yanked it up by its strawberry hair.

"Such a *nice* lady," crooned the doll, its breath stinking of sewers. "Such a *nice nice* lady, if *nice* means adoring the troubles of others so she looks *sooooo good*! Such a *nice* lady if nice means devoting herself to others so they feel *soo enslaved*. Such a *nice* lady, if nice means keeping herself pure **so** that others feel *sooo guilty*. Such a *nice* lady, if nice means hiding all her ugliness so that—"

Celeste smashed the doll with her hairbrush. *He had no right to tell on her!*

She saw the face splatter.

"Niiiiiiiiiiiiiicccccccce!" shrieked the doll. "Thank Charles for the nice little surprise! Thank Charles for the *nice roses!*"

Celeste looked into the jagged gap where the face should be. She screamed. She threw the doll into her vanity, hearing that smash, too. She leapt into her spoolbed and pulled the covers over her head, feeling herself spiral downward, hopelessly, helplessly . . . down and around . . . through a bright white funnel, throbbing with migraine. Now she was running . . . through a glass tunnel. She was wearing crystal rollerskates, but they were sticky, as if they had glue on them. She could see Charles at the end of the tunnel, at his desk, surrounded by the women in his office. They were dancing round him in harem costumes and the hats they had worn to Celeste's Valentine tea, playing teaplates like tambourines, juggling sugar-cubes and typewriter ribbons, balancing shorthand books on their noses.

Celeste tried to break through the dancers to Charles, but was repulsed.

She joined the group, pretending to be one of them, humming "The Girl That I Married" as she dangled her charm bracelet in front of her, trying to attract Charles' attention . . . holding up one then another of her charms for him to see— her Virgo birthcharm, her harp from the Symphony Committee for the bangup job she did on the rummage sale, her palette from The Women's Committee for her "forte" in aesthetics, the severed heads of their two children, the farm in King, the cottage at Deepwater Lake, their home on the Bridle Path!

Now Celeste was close enough to rescue Charles.

She swung her charm bracelet around her head like a lasso, then let it fly. She caught Charles around her neck. She pulled. He toppled forward. She gasped. *It was not Charles but a wood dummy!* The *real* Charles X. Hunter had slipped his gold tether!

Celeste spun round and round, hearing the women at her tea party laugh. She saw her vanity mirror and plunged through it in a splatter of splintered quicksilver. Now she seemed to be trapped in a mirror house full of corridors and cul de sacs. Again, she could see Charles ahead of her, through a thick glass partition, in a large gold bed, emblazoned with the Hunter crest. Celeste rapped on the glass, but he couldn't hear her. He was smoking in bed. She saw smoke curling out of his ears, and remembered with Granny Mayfair had always said: "Where there's smoke there is fire!"

Celeste banged on the glass.

Now flames were spurting up the bedsheets, licking round Charles' naked body. Celeste screamed. She saw a face in the flames: *Fiona Montrose!* Fiona was striking matches and throwing them onto Charles, deliberately setting him a-flame.

Celeste kicked frantically at the glass.

It spun like a revolving door. Always she could see Charles ahead of her, in one bed or another, consumed in flames, but every time she banged on the glass, trying to warn him not to play with fire, it would spin, creating a whirlwind, feeding the flames. The whirlwinds all had names—Roxanne! Belinda! Debra!

Celeste's head was pulsing. Always Fiona kept pace with her, passing easily where she had to reap the whirlwind, winking at her and offering her tranquillizers on a silver platter. Celeste snatched a handful. She spun round and round and round and. . . .

Now she was running through a cutglass forest with trees that tinkled like chandeliers, and crystal flowers smelling of Joy perfume, and jewelled birds that sang Broadway hits of the fifties when you wound them.

She came to a gold damask curtain, bearing the warning:

THE STATE OF PUBLICO STATUS QUO
Pass At Your Own Risk

Under this was the symbol of state: A blindfolded jackass, bearing the motto:

EVIL TO HEE-HAW WHO EVIL SEES.

Celeste grabbed the hem of the gold curtain.

A crowd of women—many of whom she recognized as

204

members of the Midol Mafia—gathered round her, trying to restrain her.

Celeste pushed them aside.

She tore the curtain.

Celeste stared, stupefied, through the gap. Charles and Brigitte Young, partially dressed in an Indian sari with a red dot on her forehead, were copulating in a patch of brier roses!

Celeste screamed.

She tried to close the curtain, but it was ripped.

She tried to invisible-mend it, but the cloth was so rotten it fell apart in her hands.

Celeste tried holding it together, but everyone was pointing at her and laughing. Some were tossing around her dirty laundry, and making a great fuss about stains.

Celeste heard a blare of trumpets.

Through the tear in the Publico Status Quo curtain came a procession led by the blindfolded jackass of state, carrying a set of brass weighing scales over his back, and a fat powdery woman looking astonishingly like her own mother . . . *reeking of rose perfume!*

Celeste swooned. The members of the Midol Mafia revived her all too quickly. Now she seemed to be in a courthouse. A doll with strawberry hair and a broken nose was leaning over her, his mouth twisted in a sour smile. "I warned you not to get your nose out of joint. This is your last chance to save face!"

He offered Celeste a choice of masks—a beautiful white one, with the eyes closed, or a black one, with the features twisted in a look of outrage.

Celeste reached for the white mask.

There was polite applause undercut by much snickering. Celeste felt her migraine throb. She snatched up the black mask and advanced on the lovers with her features twisted in OUTRAGE.

The court broke into prolonged applause. So many members rushed to support Celeste that the floor actually tilted in her direction. The Midol Mafia raised her on their shoulders in a tasteful arrangement of lilies, "inspirational for their purity," and carried her about the court behind blue ribbons proclaiming: VIRTUOUS WIFE AND MOTHER, BEST IN SHOW, LAST OF A BREED. A woman from the Symphony Committee serenaded Celeste on her golden harp. One from the

Women's Committee of the Art Gallery painted her features "more perfect than interesting" with her gold palette.

Charles and Brigitte were dragged, naked and blinking, into the light of day on their wanton nest of brier roses.

Both floral arrangements were set before the judge, sitting crosslegged on a bridge table, wearing a tea-cosy as a hat.

The judge gestured for the white jackass of state to come forward with the brass scales.

She placed Celeste, in her lilies, on one weighing pan, and the lovers, in their briers, on the other. She brought down the thumb of justice, heavily, against the lovers. She put gold replicas of the Hunter home, cottage, and farm on Celeste's side, adding bags of gold till the pans balanced.

The crowd clapped and cheered.

Celeste looked triumphantly over at the lovers.

They were fornicating, unmindful, in their brier bed.

Celeste began to sneeze.

Her migraine was pulsing worse than before.

She shouted, so loudly she cracked her mack: "Stop! Have mercy!"

The room grew ominously still.

Everyone looked at Celeste.

"Mercy on *whom?*" asked the judge.

Celeste looked into the cynical faces around her. "On the children!" She pressed on the judge pictures of Ashley and Xavier III, ages twenty-one and twenty-four, squeezed into moppet clothes licking lollipops.

"You should have thought of that earlier," said the judge, adding the snaps to the facecards in her bridgehand. "Now you will have to pay a forfeit."

"Forfeits!" shouted the crowd.

"Why?" demanded Celeste. "*I* am the injured party!"

"You *were* the injured party until you turned your domestic affair into an affair of state. You can't expect to enjoy both hypocrisy *and* justice. If you don't want the truth now that you've got it, you'll have to take the consequences. You can't expect the rest of us to wear our masks after you've discarded your own unless you're willing to pay a forfeit."

"Forfeits!" shouted the lustful crowd.

Celeste looked into the hard glittery faces. "*What* forfeit?"

"Whatever the crowd demands," replied the judge. "She who lives by public opinion must expect to be judged by it."

Celeste stole a peek at the lovers, still embracing, hotly, in their briers. Eve Martin was running around, with her derby hat, taking up an office collection for them.

Celeste put her hand to her fevered brow: "Do with me as you will so long as *Poor Charles* has an opportunity to come to his senses."

The crowd snickered.

It wasn't the response Celeste had expected. What would they do to her? Again, she put her hand to her fevered brow. *What could they do that was worse than she had already suffered?*

Celeste felt tension escalate around her.

She looked for the broken-faced doll.

He was grooming the white jackass of state with a golden hairbrush. Celeste remembered that when she was "naughty" as a child her mother would "tan her hide" with a golden hairbrush! She wondered: was that what they were going to do to her?

Celeste saw the broken-faced doll remove the blindfold from the white jackass of state. Moments later, she felt the blindfold being tied around her own eyes. It was scratchy cotton, of the poorest quality. Celeste thought, with chagrin, of the beautiful dresden face she had thrown away. "Is this the only mask I am to get? Do I have to go through life with a blindfold everyone can see?"

The doll giggled: "No, you'll get a proper mask afterwards. The blindfold is just for your protection while you pay the forfeit."

Now, Celeste felt someone take hold of her by an arm and a leg. She felt herself being splayed over a fur stool. *Ahhh, then.* It *was* to be a public flogging. She was—as usual—to be a whipping boy for *poor Charles!*

Celeste bit her lip. She imagined the prickle of the hairbrush as it descended upon her still-firm flesh, drawing jewels of blood through her Palm Beach tan. She imagined writhing, in anguish, across the fur stool ... fainting, then being revived, then fainting again until the jeers of the crowd had turned to moues of admiration. She imagined being wrapped in her new mask—*a martyr's mask of white gauze?*—and carried around the ring on her litter of lilies, spangled with blood. She imagined being carried *down down down* into the bowels of the court, to the slimy cell where Charles would be huddled—sheepish in his tattered wolf's clothing. She imagined reaching out a lily white hand and saying, "*Dear Charles,*

I forgive you," like the time she had had to bail him out for drunk-driving.

Celeste shifted uneasily: What could be delaying things?

She felt her "housewife's knee" act up the way it did when she had to get down on all fours to examine the floors after Ruby had scrubbed them.

She was jolted by a blast of trumpets: *Ahh, then . . .* Celeste felt hands lift her white gown. *Well, then . . .* she felt other hands lower her orchid panties *. . . clean and well-paid for.* She felt a warm glow flush through the cheeks of her all-over Palm Beach tan. *So be it. It is a far far better thing I do than*—

Celeste waited for the brush to descend.

It did not descend.

She felt a queer, not-unpleasant sensation in the area of her Palm Beach tan.

The crowd sniggered.

Celeste waited for the brush/the lash/the cat-o'-nine-tails.

The pleasant sensation continued. When would the torture begin?

Now the crowd seemed hysterical.

Celeste had the urge to peek. After all, the blind eye had always been for her own protection.

Celeste lifted the blindfold.

She gasped. *Her Palm Beach tan was copulating with the white jackass of state!*

Celeste shrieked.

The crowd guffawed.

"Why *me?*" demanded Celeste. "Why must *I*—a faithful servant of Publico Status Quo—be the one to be *buggered* by it?"

The judge shrugged. "The State of Stalemate devours its children as greedily as The State of Revolution, but much less heroically. The cheat of your life was not your husband's infidelity, as you like to pretend, but the lifetime of injury you made of it. You were both each other's excuse for personal failure. How you wept, and gnashed your teeth, and bit your lip, and wrung your hands. You were the longest, wettest soap-opera in town. That was *your theatre,* and how you *gloried* in it, but since you always took your part from the scripts your husband brought home, you have to choose from the parts offered you and, as all aging actresses know, the choices narrow."

"When do I get my new mask?" demanded Celeste.

"You already have it," said the judge.

Celeste's hands flew to her face. "It *feels* the same!"

"They usually do," said the judge. "It's the *look* of it."

"Then what does it *look* like?"

"That depends on who's doing the looking," said the judge.

"What does it look like to *you*?" asked Celeste.

"Why does that matter?" asked the judge. "Why don't you find out what it looks like to *yourself*, since you're the one who's wearing it?"

The broken-faced doll handed Celeste a jewelled mirror.

Celeste stared into it. She screamed. She tried to shout. "*I have nothing to hide, darlings, do you?*" but all that came out was "Hee-haw!"

Celeste bucked about the courtroom, clutching her mask by the ears, trying to pull it off.

"It's just uncomfortable because you're not used to it," said the judge, matter-of-factly. "The truth is there are some people who will like it because they're wearing one exactly like it, and others who won't notice any change, since they think you've been wearing it for a very long time."

"Hee-haw!" said Celeste. "Evil to hee-haw who hee-haw!"

# 8. Charles X. Hunter

Charles X. Hunter collapsed in Old Xavier's chair, finding it almost comfortable. *What a helluva week! What a helluva helluva helluva week!*

He listed its disasters, staring at his blood-pressure chart, defying it to remain steady:

Monday, he'd had to cancel a board meeting because of the missing automation estimates.

Tuesday, he'd had a fight with that crazy detective who was convinced he'd stumbled on an international narcotics ring.

Wednesday, there'd been a wildcat strike in the Production Room, when the girls, who moulded the yolks for the cream-centred Easter eggs, had burned their hairnets because the men, who dipped them, didn't have to wear any.

Thursday, the Starch machine in Soft Centres had gone awry, spraying starch, like snow, all over Irma Burbank, who just happened to have a photographer handy to snap her picture as Miss Snowbunny for "Sweet Talk" and, no doubt, for "Sour Grapes."

THANK GOD IT'S FRIDAY!

Charles glanced at his Economist Diary. He had one more appointment: the woman from Special Accounts. He considered cancelling but Xavier's clock rebuked him. *Better see it through.* The poor old soul had probably worried about it all week.

Charles knew how things preyed on the elderly.

He glanced at his late mother's picture, remembering how she used to call him twenty times a day to see if she should put on her rubbers, till Eve stopped putting through the calls. Besides—he tapped the financial report sitting at the side of his desk—there was still Basil Fitch to deal with, and his insistence on more room for Computer Control.

Charles drew his Domestic Speech file from the papers Eve had placed on his desk. He flipped through Speech for Firing

Employee for Incompetence, Speech for Congratulating Employee for Good Effort, Speech for Rewarding Employee for Good Result, Speech for Reprimanding Employee for Failing to Utilize Channels, Speech for Reprimanding Employee for Failing to Use Initiative, Speech for Promoting Employee a) with pay increase b) instead of pay increase.

He removed Speech for Easing Out the Elderly a) because of change in corporate structure b) because of failing health c) with extra consideration for distinguished service, and noted Eve had already marked the salient portions and attached a copy of the original memo.

He skimmed through the memo: "personal" had been typed "personell"—Miss Young's work, obviously—then went through the speech itself, nodding as familiar phrases came back to him, trying to picture Mary Moon, but failing to pick her face from the dozens that slid, like snowflakes, through his mind, each different, but somehow the same. Oh, well. Charles reassured himself: He wasn't very good at faces. Or names. He felt a flicker of guilt which he projected as annoyance. *That was Eve's job ... Or Celeste's ...* He looked up, defiantly at his mother's picture—*woman's work*—then turned, morosely, to stare out the window, watching the snowflakes spatter, like faces, against the pane.

Charles felt the sudden need to establish his own humanity.

He pushed his desk buzzer. "Eve? You might as well go home, now. And Miss Young. We could be in for quite a storm, by the look of things."

Charles continued to stare out the window. He reached for the financial report, taking instant pleasure from the bulk, the crispness and the smell of it: *Man's work. . . .*

Putting on his half-moon glasses, he settled back as far as Xavier's chair would allow for a few minutes' respite.

He read the first three pages of the report, sucking contentedly on his pipe. By page six his teeth had clamped down on the stem, and by eight they'd almost bitten through. *Damn Celeste!* Her girlish little private-school jottings were sprinkled over every page, making grammatical corrections, seeking clarifications, and, in one case, figuring out the savings in a ton of fudge if it were whipped for a lighter texture!

Celeste was a compulsive reader of anything with figures she could manipulate—from the recipes on cereal boxes to, well, financial reports. This wasn't the first Hunter document she had pilfered and doctored. She did it, Charles figured, to remind him she had given up a math scholarship to become his "child bride."

Charles brought his thumb down on his buzzer before he remembered he had already sent Eve home.

He tried another page of the report, then threw it down in disgust. Every time he hit one of Celeste's little backhand loop-de-loops his thoughts took off in the most disconcerting way. Because that was the real trouble of course, the real reason the week had been such a disaster. He just couldn't get Celeste's disloyalty out of his mind. It was such a bloody bore for her to have taken off in that silly melodramatic way, and simply unfair to a man who carried a corporation on his back, especially when he had to practically will his heart and his lungs to function on a day-to-day basis. No clean shirts this morning. A hardboiled egg, instead of soft. The unwalked dalmatians howling like someone had died—it was bloody eerie. Surely-to-God when a woman had nothing to do but run a house she could set things to work for a couple of weeks by themselves, the way he did his business. God knows, he paid enough for help, though by the look of the last lot, with their foreheads and beetle brows, he felt like Fagan running a halfway house in the wrong direction.

Charles X. took Celeste's postcard from his vest pocket and studied the postmark. Though it was blurred, he was sure it said February 15, and certainly it was from New York. That was reassuring. Celeste couldn't last a week in New York with less than seven hundred dollars. He'd give her another week to spend what she'd cadged before she'd be back with her tail between her legs. What else could she do? If old G.O. Mayfair were alive to look after his Little Princess, Charles could expect trouble, but with Big Bessie guarding the family vault, there was no way Celeste was going to get a nickel she didn't earn across the bridge table. A week was a long time for a woman of Celeste's type, spoiled by luxury.

Charles relaxed, sucking smugly on his pipe. He'd be understanding about her "problems" whatever-the-devil-they-were, while letting her know her little escapade hadn't meant much. Maybe, after all, it was the menopause? They say middle-aged women did crazy things, worse than when they were pregnant. Maybe he should pack Celeste right off, as soon as she got back, to that spa of hers. That would give her plenty of time to come to her senses while proving to her he hadn't missed her too much. What was the name? Maine Chance? Ed Bailey said they treated those women like babies: mud baths, saunas, whirlpools, massages.

Charles felt the acrid surfacing of an emotion he'd been suppressing. Envy, pure, painful and green-eyed. Why the devil should *he* work *his* ass off to move Celeste around from one silk cushion to another? He had a poignant vision of himself lying bronzed and motionless on a hot white beach in the white trunks he'd bought for that trip to Hawaii he'd had to cancel because of the dock strike in South Africa. He imagined himself surfing, playing tennis and golfing—not the kind of golf he played at Rosedale, practically signing up someone on the sixteenth hole—but off by himself, really enjoying it, gracefully, and in slow motion. The kind of vacation he hadn't had since . . . well, when? Since he got married? Since he became president of Hunter's? *Maine Chance be damned!* If Celeste was so bloody keen on whipping fudge, let her come down to the factory and whip up a batch. Better yet, let her sit down on this damned back-breaker of a chair and he'd cadge off her for awhile. If anyone deserved to be pampered, to seize the Maine Chance, as it were, it was Charles X. Hunter!

Charles pushed with both feet against Xavier's chair, trying to make it tilt against its principles. Who-the-devil gave Celeste the right to take off, anyway, when it was tacitly agreed between them that if anyone ever left it should be him? What did *she* have to escape from? Despite her pretensions to culture and charity, she really did little more, since the kids had left, than his mother who had spent her widowhood visiting doctors for her "spells" and taking care of three cats!

Charles treated himself to a corollary outrage. And while he was at it, *what in blazes had that woman done to his kids?* What was his daughter Ashley making of her life? Where was his son? They hadn't heard a word from young Xavier in over a year, while Ashley positively tortured them with details of a life that would make the boys in his stockroom blush! What was going on? How did *he* get left holding the vomit bag for everyone? When he was Ashley's age he was winning a war. When he was Xavier's age, he was running the bloody company!

Charles tapped his pipebowl on his blotter, forgetting it contained neither tobacco nor ashes, just a spattering of saliva.

He threw it on his desk along with Celeste's postcard. If he'd had *his* way he would have become an engineer or an architect and built something solid and lasting, maybe even gone into the space-rocket program! He sniffed his hands. *Pahh!* He was beginning to stink of Hunter's Formula 581 chocolate.

Charles laid down the monthly report, noting a calendar Celeste had drawn on the back. It was a marketing gimmick, with each month illustrated by the glossy of a Hunter specialty tied in with a holiday, and with the appropriate order date circled: "One phone call today, and we will send, gift-wrapped—"

Charles picked up his Eversharp to make a note of that, then put it down, too weary to bother. He slumped in Xavier's chair, hitting his spine, as usual, against the cancerous lump in the back. He rubbed the bruised spot. He rubbed the lump. To his surprise the chair tipped back.

Charles turned in his chair.

He examined the lump that had caused him so much aggravation. Astonishingly, it contained a release mechanism which, when rubbed like Aladdin's lamp, tilted the chair.

Charles leaned way back. Now his feet shot up past the Hunter family motto, ordering him to ALWAYS KEEP YOUR FEET ON THE GROUND. What's more, he could see out the oval window, into the clouds.

Charles, for the first time, felt comfortable in the chair. He felt the blood rush warmly to his head. He rotated in the chair till he was swirling like a kid on a merry-go-round, remembering that glorious afternoon when he had taken Fiona to the midway at the Ex and, drunk on dreams, they had ridden round and round and round on a single unicorn, laughing like children, enchanted! possessed! galloping off giddily into the sunset and not giving a good goddamn who saw them. *Fiona!* the only woman he had ever been in danger of loving—*had* loved! Where was she now? Had she married? Did she have children? Was she plump and matronly? Silly and blue-haired? Tanned to old shoe leather like the stick-women who played golf all day and drank martinis all night?

Charles, still swivelling, pictured Fiona the way she had been the first time he had seen her. The night he had become engaged to Celeste. He saw, again, Fiona's glowing face, cool and sardonic through a slit in glossy blueblack hair as other faces—gross, vapid, smiling hideously—pressed sweatily around, offering limp hands and toothy blessings. Charles, already feeling unreal, like the plaster groom on top of a wedding cake, had for an instant caught Fiona's eye. Pulling her face long, she had tugged at the gold chain around her own throat, as if it were a leash, and then she had winked. Charles was so startled he had almost dropped his champagne glass. Her gesture was so exactly what he had been thinking, even to the fact that his hand was already on its way to loosen his collar. He, too, had laughed, shattering the plaster, feeling the rich relief of it, convinced that this beautiful stranger had seen through the mockery of his life and had forgiven him for it.

Charles didn't see Fiona again for a year—not until he was safely married to Celeste. Then she had become his mistress for fifteen months—fifteen magnificent, tormented months in which she had lived as a vibrant secret buried at the core of his existence, a lodestar against the Hunter system of rights and duties that bound him round in a golden net, trapping him without quite killing him. *My god!* He was out of his mind! over his head! in possession of wings! With Fiona, every moment was separate from every other with its own special taste, colour, transluscence. With Fiona, the future, even the next hour, was uncharted! With Fiona he felt alive, and it both thrilled and terrified him. He would deliberately stand at his office window, feeling the dreadful downward pull of his acrophobia, and defiantly intone the Hunter family motto: ALWAYS KEEP YOUR FEET ON THE GROUND, my boy. ALWAYS KEEP YOUR FEET ON THE GROUND.

Charles stopped swivelling.

He tipped the chair further back, till he was lying flat, his hands folded across his chest like a lily.

It had taken another touch of the Dead Hand to get rid of Fiona. This time, Old Xavier's ambassador was his own father. They met at the Toronto club for lunch and for what, it soon developed, was to be one of those "now my son" chats—the first and last of their lives.

His father was as embarrassed as Charles had ever seen him. He had no rights to speak to Charles in that unctuous way, but from the moment he opened his mouth to remind Charles there had never been a divorce in the Hunter family, Charles knew it was Old Xavier speaking. The stiff neck, the precise nasal twang, the tight mouth were all so unlike his father's usual devil-may-care charm that, at one point, they caught each other's eye and both burst out laughing. Then, although it was still mid-afternoon, they had got drunk together, with Charles Sr. apologizing over and over for what he had said. But the message had been delivered, and they both knew it.

Afterwards, Charles had swept across town in his white Thunderbird, jamming the gas pedal to the floorboards, and he had scooped up Fiona like a knight rescuing a princess, and he had raced off with her to a country inn that had been the scene of their first assignation, and they had clinked glasses under the stars, and held hands in a cherry orchard under drifts of pink blossoms, and kissed in a canopied bed, with a perfect escalation of sexual desire that had mounted through rapturous pulsations to that point of frenzy when Charles slid in fierce commitment between Fiona's thighs, only to find himself entirely impotent—the first of many such humiliations during that long, feisty summer which, often as not, saw him weave the white line in a drunken dash back across town to make love to a groggy Celeste, with the fire of an eighteen-year-old stud, imagining her to be Fiona, before locking himself in his study and crying like a baby.

Charles rotated slowly, methodically, counter-clockwise in Xavier's chair, remembering the last time he had seen Fiona, that afternoon he drove her to the airport, through autumn leaves more vividly poignant, in their last hours of life, than any he had ever seen before, his body stiff with inexpressible emotion, his hands stuck to the wheel, his throat choked with words he could never speak, but already composing in his head the letter he would send begging her to return, denying the present with the future. He stayed up all night writing it—a long, heart-wrenching confession in which he poured out his love for her, telling her unreservedly all those things he had withheld, and promising to begin divorce proceedings the instant he heard from her. He waited like a lovesick schoolboy for her response. His reply came two weeks later—his own letter back. He had misaddressed it.

Charles did not hear the door open, or close. He simply looked up, dizzy to the point of nausea, to see a small woman, smothered in black, sitting on the horsehair sofa under the picture of his mother, exuding an old woman's smell of powder and dead roses. *Mary Moon? Good God! He'd almost forgotten.*

Charles leapt to his feet in overweening graciousness. He felt the room spin, and steadied himself, smiling in embarrassment. "Well, well, well . . ." Would she think he was drunk, just like his father?

The room was much darker than it should be. Charles started toward the lightswitch, but the woman waved him back. She was wearing both dark glasses and a veil. The blind had been pulled over his single window. Charles remembered how his mother had sought the shadows in her last years because of failing eyesight. Did Mary Moon have the same trouble?

Charles, all accommodation, strode to his leather armchair and settled himself with authority—his arms along its arms, his back straight against its back, his feet firmly planted like the famous statue of Abraham Lincoln. It was a pose—he discovered, after he had assumed it—suitable for confronting bank managers but scarcely appropriate to the "personell chat" Brigitte had promised Mary Moon in her memo. He shifted position under the guise of reaching for his pipe, crossing one pinstriped leg over the other to reveal an expanse of blue sock. He remembered his socks were not clean. *Damn Ruby!* And then, shifting blame to where is belonged. *Damn Celeste!* He remembered also that he was wearing an undershirt for the second day. That, like the socks, made him feel grubby and unsure of himself, as if his surfaces were crumbling, his hair falling out, his jowls dropping, his teeth decaying, as he stepped over the border from Shangri-la. He felt his companion's eyes fastened, unblinking, upon him, and had the first clear premonition that this interview was not going to go as he intended.

Charles sucked on his pipe. The sound appalled him. What could he be thinking of? He put the pipe distastefully away, realizing it was not so much the smoking he missed as the hand movements: the filling and tamping, the fussing and cleaning. He clasped his hands around his kneecap.

"Miss Moon," he began in a solicitous voice, "how are—" He glanced at the memo, where Eve normally jotted the next of kin, finding only the word DECEASED "—*you* keeping these wintry days?" he amended, rocking back in his chair and seeing his pants rise up his white leg, luminous in the darkened room. He let go of his kneecap and lurched forward, almost knocking his chin. He reached for something—anything—from his desk, as if that had been his intention, and found himself staring at a bill from Tidy's for two dozen sweetheart roses. *Where the devil had that come from? His slush basket?*

Charles distinctly remembered having *considered* sending Celeste flowers on their anniversary, but he did *not* remember

217

sending them, and certainly not roses! What could it mean? A bouquet of roses had figured prominently in Celeste's garbled going-away note.

Had he sent them?

If not, how did this bill get into his slush basket?

It wasn't the first puzzle of this sort Charles had had to deal with in the past few months. Both Eve and Brigitte claimed to have received notes from him that he swore he didn't write. The last investigative report of the Heat/Cool System had practically pinned the presumed sabotage to *his* window. What was going on? Was someone playing jokes on him?

Charles, much perplexed, forced his attention back to his companion.

She seemed to have answered his question and was awaiting his response. Charles wondered. Had she claimed good health or bad? Was he to be sympathetic or glad for her? He slurred over the next few moments, his mind still on that damnable bill, before plunging ahead with: "I guess you're wondering why I invited you into my office today, *heh heh. . . .*"

The chuckle came out as a leer. In fact, the whole sentence sounded, in the dark, like the opener for a Grade B seduction scene.

Charles fumed at his own incompetence, then, as usual, projected it on the person nearest. Why-the-devil *had* he invited her anyway? Why, considering the fragility of his nerves, couldn't he have dealt with the whole bloody thing through Personnel? Brigitte was right for a change—a "personell chat." It was these bloody human problems that drained his strength.

The woman, perched like a frail bird on his sofa, prompted him, gently. "You were wondering, I believe , why you invited me?"

Charles started to find his thoughts so accurately read.

"Yes," he affirmed, deftly remoulding the sentence between them: "*You* were wondering why I invited you here."

He glanced at his nameplate, as if for reassurance, and, pulling himself up by the dirty socks, as it were, launched his Speech for Easing Out the Elderly, clauses b) and c), as if reading from a mental photostat, in the same confident voice he had used on the Harvard debating team, pausing at all the stipulated places for emphasis, fumbling as if groping through emotion for the appropriate word, shamelessly enjoying the "con" of his performance, as if life itself were a play he had scripted, giving himself all the best lines: "... Changes in an organization we didn't believe possible ... life is bigger than Hunter's Confectionery .... while we still have our wits and our will about us .... an opportunity to read, to garden, even perchance, to travel. I don't mind telling you—" here he leaned forward, unfortunately fumbling for the name "—Miss Mary Moon, that I secretly envy you!"

Charles turned away, discreetly, to let the woman collect herself. After a decent interval, he turned back, prepared to deal firmly, yet compassionately, with what was likely to be a difficult human response.

The woman seemed strangely unmoved. He could still feel her eyes, unyielding upon him, seeming to pull him out of his skin. Charles began to have a most peculiar feeling about this visitor. He glanced from her to the picture of his mother—a thing he had avoided doing. The resemblance was ... uncanny, but then—he smiled indulgently—*all old women swaddled in black looked alike!*

The woman was still staring at Charles—waiting?

He noticed, now, that she kept an ear cocked. Was she hard of hearing? He glanced at Eve's memo. There was no notation. He raised his voice, experimentally, intending to repeat only a few key phrases. However, once launched, he seemed unable to stop. He listened, in horror, to his own voice repeat the speech from the top, fumbling at all the same intersections like an electronic dummy on whom a switch has been thrown.

Mary Moon listened, politely, for a few paragraphs, then waved her hand, as if giving him permission to stop. Charles' teeth clamped down on the word "sincerely," leaving the last two syllables wriggling in his mouth like the end of a severed worm.

"I understand all that," she said, not unkindly, "but the reason I was silent—and I'm sorry if I seemed rude after all you've gone through to put us both at our ease—but I was trying to do some plotting in my head, and I'm not as good at tying loose ends as I used to be."

*Plotting? Loose ends?* Charles felt a comforting rush of sympathy. Once more he assumed control. The poor old soul! She was probably worried sick about finances. Even his mother, in her declining years, periodically had her accountant up all night tying up "loose ends" despite the money *she* had stashed in gilt-edged cooky jars. Had he run through c)with extra stipend for distinguished service, or had he forgotten that clause in his confusion? Charles decided to risk repeating the sense of c) while avoiding the original wording.

"Don't forget when doing your 'plotting' to add in our special consideration for special employees. Hunter's has always appreciated your family's long record of service to our company."

As soon as Charles said the word "family," he remembered. *Of course! Old Phil, the nightwatchman!* Was this woman still living in the loft? He had assumed when the old man died that the family had moved out, but—

"You needn't worry about a roof over your head, either," he added delicately. "I'm sure your present living arrangements can continue indefinitely."

The woman stifled what sounded startlingly like a chuckle. "I'm not sure I would *want* my present living arrangements to continue," she said, her voice flirting with irony. "The 'loose ends' I was referring to have to do with the completion of my Special Accounts to which you yourself are my only major obstacle."

Charles started. "I?" He was not used to being taken to task by an employee, and certainly not under such absurd circumstances. Ever since this woman had entered his office, he had felt like a child called to account. He looked indignantly up at his mother's portrait, and then to Xavier's clock by way of higher appeal. Surely, he had done both his corporate *and* his personal duty? At any rate, he simply did not have more time or energy.

Charles X. arose, looking pointedly toward the door.

His companion remained seated.

He *walked* toward the door.

The woman did not move.

Charles returned and, with ingrained politeness, perched on the arm of his chair.

"Miss Moon," he said, carefully. "I don't think you understand. If you have any problems, don't hesitate to call on my secretary, but I'm afraid your retirement date must be considered fixed and firm."

Still the woman did not react. Was she senile? Charles felt a familiar surge of guilty tenderness, quickly overtaken by an even-more-familiar sense of being manipulated by deadly frailties. He heard himself say, in a flat voice growing cold: "As you probably know, Miss Moon, there has been a move a Hunter's, spearheaded by Basil Fitch, to computerize as much as possible of the Hunter operation. The truth of the matter is we need the Special Accounts office for expansion. The truth of the matter is the office of Special Accounts will be abolished on your retirement. The truth of the matter is the accounts you have been keeping have, for quite some time, been entirely superfluous ..."

As soon as the words were out, Charles felt self-disgust vomit up from his dirty socks to his coated tongue. What had come over him to say such a cruel thing? He saw the woman's chin drop to her chest, and her gloved hand fly to her face.

Charles bolted for the sherry cabinet.

He poured a stiff brandy for himself and a light sherry for his companion, humiliated to see his hands shaking. *Women! The damned silly things.* Always falling apart in a crisis. Or running away. Not like a man, having to stand there and take it, no matter how he was cracking up inside. He had a long guilty memory of his mother perched on their hepplewhite sofa, twisting him and her hanky around her finger, crying because he hadn't phoned her ... crying because he forgot her birthday ... crying because he hadn't introduced her to his latest girlfriend. *My god!* He hadn't even cried when his drunken brother had run over his dog and the poor wretch had bled to death in his arms, or when he got his leg crushed under his horse Wild Lady and thought he might lose it.

Charles consulted his health charts, taking courage from the steadiness of the *noblesse oblige* heart line. He carried the brimming sherry to the woman and set it on the table beside her.

Her chin was still on her chest. Her shoulders were shaking inside her black shawl. Charles heard the sound of ... *laughter!*? He studied the woman with indignation. She seemed convulsed!

Charles sank back in his chair, at first relieved, then trembling in exasperation. Why should he, Charles X. Hunter, have to put up with this bloody nonsense at the end of such a rotten week? Maybe Ashley and her Indian seer were right in their hocus-pocus about electrical impulses flying about the zodiac! Maybe there *were* times when a man was not master of his own fate.

Charles looked with reproach at the woman who seemed to have calmed herself.

"You'll have to forgive me," she apologized, "but having

my retirement announced to me is not without its amusement."

Charles nodded stiffly, not understanding, and not even trying to. The woman was clearly dotty. In a few minutes he would call Eve at home and have her devise some ruse for getting rid of her without offending what was left of the proprieties.

In the meantime, he steeled himself for a few sentences of polite chitchat, looking toward his window as if he hoped to escape out it, feeling the overwhelming need for light, fresh air, contact with the *real* world.

Charles put down his brandy.

He *strode* toward his window, as if pursued.

He reached for the catch, remembered the Heat/Cool System, turned away, then spun back and—*damn Basil Fitch!*—threw wide the window and poked his head through the blind.

Charles gulped air, in great draughts, like ice water.

He looked up into the sky—a shrill blue with a spitting of snow—and watched as a jet split it cleanly in two. Charles X. felt a pain in his chest so exquisite he had to clamp it to keep it from cracking open. He looked down at the fresh fall of snow, thickly covering the juniper bushes two floors below and, feeling his acrophobia, drew back.

He turned from what now seemed like a gaping hole in the wall, and strode to his desk, then to the window again, across the fudgy broadloom sticking to his feet like melted chocolate, breathing deeply and jerking his arms and his legs as if pulled by strings, exaggerating the movements with an actor's satiric control, adding comic bits such as the raising of a leg that caused an arm to fall and even, at one point, pretending to beat a drum, taking a dogged satisfaction from his performance, and reciting—*oh god*—his Easing Out the Elderly Speech, with pauses and gestures in all the wrong places, like a dummy working against its own mechanism, until, in a final shudder of truth, he blurted: "I don't mind telling you, Miss Mary Moon, that I secretly envy you!"

Charles X. Hunter slumped in Xavier's chair a full minute in stupefied silence before picking up his brandy and gulping it. He began to speak calmly, matter-of-factly:

"Would it surprise you to know, Miss Mary Moon, that I used to make marionettes of professional standard?

"Or that the Hunters have one of the world's finest collections of toy soldiers?

"Or that I have seen the *Nutcracker Suite* once for every year of my life?"

There was no response.

Charles hadn't really expected one. It seemed to him that the last few times he had looked over to the horsehair sofa there hadn't been anyone on it . . . just the shadows . . . just his mother's picture, hanging over it. *Was this it, then? Was he breaking up—completely, irrevocably, at last?*

Charles dropped his head into his hands. He let despair sweep over him, *wave upon wave upon wave*. Again, he smelt the stink of Hunter's Formula 581 chocolate, oozing in slimy worms from his pores. Is this what a lifetime of achievement had netted him? This sense of self-nausea? Did other men feel this . . . this cheat? this inner hollowness? How could this be? He'd accomplished everything anyone had ever asked of him, in a style that had attracted much admiration. He'd made all the money he had time to spend. He'd had more than his share of friends, women, prestige, good times! If he wasn't happy, who could be?

Charles stretched his hand, flat, across his memo pad. The flesh was becoming pallid, the cords more prominent. The freckles were spreading into liverspots. An *old* hand. Older than his father's! Charles Sr. had dropped dead in a bar, at fifty-two, *officially* the victim of heart attack. His brother had died at twenty-five. *Was there such a thing as a family curse?*

Charles doubled his hand into a fist. He stared, in fury, into the shadows clinging to his horsehair sofa, then up at the portrait of his mother, almost seeing a flutter of black lace hanky, almost hearing the hurt, perfumed voice, each word bearing the weight of civilization from the Greeks to the Astors, exhorting him to godliness and cleanliness, *to be a Good Boy.* He looked at Xavier's clock, compulsively pumping into the silence, its pendulum swaying back and forth in its glass case, its brass disk gleaming, *back and forth, back and forth,* stealing seconds from his life!

Charles snatched up his gold Eversharp. He wrote, in slashing strokes, across his memo pad:

> Dear Celeste,
> The first few days you were gone were an agony. I tried to convince myself that I didn't care. After that, things got much worse. I tried to convince myself that I *did*! How the hell can a man live with a woman for

twenty-five years, have two children by her, and know or care so little about her? Even now my strongest feeling about you is HOW MUCH I ENVY YOU! How did *you* manage to survive? Where did you hide your anger? In the chinoiserie umbrella stand? under the bed? Where did you find the guts to leave me?

I never loved you. Our marriage was something both incidental and inevitable. You were part of the Hunter package as carefully trained for your role as I for mine, and it made no more sense to balk at marrying you than to fiddle with the terms of any other contract once it has been agreed to in principle.

I know I've always appeared to be a selfish person, entirely wrapped up in my own concerns, and that is something I deeply regret, but the truth is, my own survival, in the terms laid down for me, has always drained off so much of my energy that there was never anything leftover for anyone else, except—for a little while—Fiona. With Fiona, for the first time, I felt energy flowing back in. Fiona was REAL in the way we, the two of us, were never allowed to be. With Fiona life was real—a gamble in which the dice were never loaded, whereas the Hunters and the Mayfairs never approached the gaming tables any other way.

When you found out about Fiona, our affair had already been over for six months.

It wasn't necessary for you to know, but I think bringing you into it was my cowardly way of asking for help.

I was drinking heavily. I could hardly drag myself through a day. The only part of myself that I valued had been surgically removed. It wasn't something I dared express, but I thought, maybe, with my gut opened up, you and I might find a path into something more meaningful. I tried to explain that to you, but you would not, or could not, come to grips with the reality of Fiona. It did not satisfy you that the affair was over, only that it should never have been. You had to see it as a "little fling," engineered by Fiona, and when I tried to tell you the truth, as the start of a new relationship between us, you became convinced the whole messy business must still be going on, but that if you held on tight to all the old terms I would eventually "come to my senses"— meaning I would see things your way, or pretend to.

That night you attempted "suicide" I know you believed you saved our marriage, but that was the night you killed it for good. I realized then how desperately you would fight to preserve your illusions. Anything about our marriage that couldn't be framed and passed around the Ladies' Club didn't exist, including the suicide, so that after a few weeks that didn't happen either.

After that, I gave you only what I thought you could handle—a beautiful home, beautiful clothes, beautiful children, myself as a gracious mannequin to be trotted out for social events and, since there was nothing at stake and we could afford to be generous, a good sex life. This is the period you like to say the happiest of your life and, to be fair, this is the period I, too, have been taught to think of as my Golden Age. Though I couldn't say I was happy, there was a kaleidoscopic excitement to my professional life that kept me hopping from project to project, and what our personal life lacked in depth, it made up for in shimmer. Though I had many affairs during this period, you were never in danger. I suppose it could be said that I transferred the fiercest part of my sex drive to the business world. There was nothing strange in that. All my friends were doing the same thing. We were expected to be tycoons, world-fuckers. It was the North American Way. Women were still important, but strictly as recreation, another area of buddy-to-buddy competition, with me as a robot, well-trained to remember that I had to get up to work in the morning, and to believe that was the most important thing.

I can't believe that you left me over Brigitte Young.

The day I met Brigitte I was driving around in my Jag—bored, frustrated, sick—wondering if I should head off Scarborough Bluffs, when I saw this girl—a child, actually—crosslegged on the sidewalk in the midst of some of the most disreputable punks I've ever seen. She was barefoot, playing a flute, and I have no hesitation in saying that what attracted me was her utter slovenliness combined with the assurances of a queen! I picked her up, and it was better than I dared hope. She was so prickly pear! so sourgrapes! so bitterlemon! so downright unappetizing and, as a bonus, she hated candy. She told me she saw the whole candy business as a capitalistic pacifier, and that when her mother had tried to bribe her with sweets as a kid, she had washed her mouth out in dirt. I was enchanted! Here was a weapon of the highest potency. All she had to do was to walk through the Hunter Production Sector with those filthy feet of hers, and the whole place would close down from sanitary shock!

On our first assignation, she cooked for me in a borrowed pad that was done up in sleezy red velvet, candles, and cheesecloth like a French whore gone buddhist. We had wheat germ, organic watercress, ginseng root sprinkled with a sauce made of ground-up recycled peach pits and, for dessert, one whole lemon, unpeeled and unsweetened—*a girl utterly without compromise!* We made love on a leaky waterbed, patched like an old innertube, and it was like being a stowaway on a tramp steamer and twenty-one again!

For six months I was in Captain's Paradise. Brigitte was so raw, you so overprocessed that I was a happy man coming and going between. Unfortunately (fortunately?) to bring Brigitte into my organization was to kill the thing that attracted me to her—her reality. Like Fiona, she is a "no shit" artist. When I knew Fiona, it was the part of me that was still alive that yearned after her. With Brigitte, it was the part of me *that still remembered what it was like to be alive!* I've faked everything else in my life, but even I couldn't fake being real.

It's an ironic thing. When you left me, I was never more willing—you could even say eager—to accept your view of our enduring marital bliss. The hollow image of the wonderful husband, father, and provider who took his little flings to show the world how lucky you were might have been just the golden sarcophagus I was ready to lie down in, in hopes that, with the pretty features painted on the outside, no one would smell the rot, but—*oh god oh god oh god oh god oh god!*

Charles Lay, face down, on his desk, feeling himself consumed by guilt, overwhelming and corrosive, the burden of guilt he had carried since he was a small child, but *worse now, worse and worse and worse, much worse,* the guilt of a man who has committed a major crime for which there can be no expiation.

Charles struck the side of his head with his fist. *What*

226

*crime? What had he done that was so terrible?* When had he ever *failed* to do what was expected of him? *God!* He'd always been manipulated by strings of guilt that grew from his body like hair from a rotted corpse, as if begging people to pull on them. *When had he ever done anything in this life but obey?*

Charles picked up his pen and began to write, dispirited now, not really caring anymore but trying, with some honesty, to get it all down.

He felt something brush against his ankle. He kicked at it absently, as if it were one of his dalmatians. He continued writing, thinking, recollecting. He felt it again—something cold, something sticky, clinging to his ankle.

Charles felt his hair rise and his scalp prickle. He froze, bolt upright, staring at Xavier's clock . . . . It was around his leg now, wet and slimy. He felt it creep up the side of his thigh and then move across his back. He felt the weight of it on his back, clammy and whimpering. He felt it slip its tiny hands under his collar, its fingers paddling and pressing, as they found his Adam's apple and, ever-so-gently, began to squeeze. . . . Charles heard a baby voice pule in her ear: *Daddy!*

He felt the air clot in his windpipe. He felt himself begin to choke. The hands were an icy ring around his throat. Charles was gasping for breath, struggling with his whole body but seeming to be clamped into Xavier's chair, paralyzed, immobile. He closed his eyes, feeling them bulge like marbles from their sockets, still gagging, slipping down into darkness like a drowning man . . . *down once . . . down twice* seeing it again, as it had been . . . seeing Yalla, her face ugly with hate, hearing her laughter—*insane!*—crackling round her head like a nest of electric eels.

He had smashed the fishbowl.

He had thrown it down between their naked feet. He had watched it splatter, releasing a plop of something oozing and obscene that nuzzled against his ankle as hands of jagged glass slashed both their legs, spewing Hunter and halfbreed blood over the mess between. He had seen the jelly split and quiver, with the tiny corpse inside seeming to struggle for life, splashing in a pool of aspic, as it later struggled, nightmare, after nightmare, in the blood behind his eyes, its face contorted, its eyes popped, its mouth rimed with spittle as it tried with tiny, perfectly shaped hands, to pull the umbilical cord from its neck . . . whimpering . . . pleading for life . . . begging to be spared . . . promising to obey, to work hard, to be a Good Boy if only it would be allowed to live.

Charles pitched forward in his chair. Using his feet and the forward propulsion of the chair, he catapulted himself, head first, arms outstretched, out his open window.

For one blissful moment, Charles X. Hunter—guiltless, weightless—hung suspended in the black jelly of the universe, his body gracefully arched toward the stars. Then, with the night sky still several lightyears over his head, he felt his body dip and the earth tilt.

# 9. The Candy Factory

It was one of those magical thaws.

Hidden decay had weakened, rotted, and carved out the underbelly of the dying snow. Overnight came a massive collapse. Winter slid like a great white whale into the gullies and the ravines of the city, where it lay, shivering, for a few more days before the first shoots of green turned it under.

Crocuses opened in Hunter park.

Robins returned to the fountain.

The Candy Factory moved into Spring-Summer production.

Celeste Mayfair Hunter sat crosslegged on her lumpy bed at the Ford Hotel, making neat jottings on hotel stationery. She looked at her Piaget watch, then pushed aside her papers. What was the point of belabouring something she knew so well?

Celeste stood up, uncurling from the waist in her blue Courrege pantsuit. She took a cigarillo from her alligator bag, and lit up. Smoking was something new for Celeste. She had always been taught that ladies didn't, and—Celeste gave a throaty chuckle—maybe they *didn't*.

She sat down again on the bed, this time with her arms flung back against the iron headstead, blowing smoke through her dainty nostrils in a long cool stream . . . enjoying the schizophrenic look of the hotel room. Her mirror jewelbox on the chipped walnut dresser . . . her tweed travel ensemble by Adrian on a wire-hanger in the closet-without-a-door . . . her charcoal Ballenciaga on the straight-back chair by the broken wash-basin . . . her gold charm bracelet tossed on the sill of the sooty window through which you could see the bus terminal where she had arrived last night from New York.

Even in her panic to leave home, Celeste had packed diabolically well. For example, the Courrege suit. . . . She had bought it last year on impulse in Paris, and Adrian had disap-

229

proved. "Not your style. Too aggressive. As wrong for you, in one way, as the froufrou in another." The Courrege had been pushed to the dark side of her closet, and yet, when she had packed, it had been the first and most suitable thing she had snatched.

Celeste ran her fingers through her strawberry hair, now cut into a sleek helmet. As soon as she had put on the Courrege, her fluffy matron's hair had looked wrong. The suit had stayed. The hair had come off. Celeste felt—and looked—ten years younger. Men whistled at her now instead of opening doors.

The *inside* redesign of Celeste had not been so easy.

It had taken place—was still taking place—in stages, as new conflicts surfaced, accompanied by bouts of depression, panic, much heavy thinking, sometimes frenetic planning, a little ecstasy, some sense of growth-through-pain, and frequent backsliding.

First, and worst, had been the nightmares. Most often Celeste had dreamt she was inching along a slippery mountain ledge, sometimes with her father, sometimes with Charles, sometimes by herself. Below her was a gaping pit, smelling of sewage and shrieking with moans. Sometimes she would fight with whoever was with her on the ledge, and they would try to push each other down. Toward the end she had dreamt, over and over, that there were crabs all over Charles, and she was trying to beat them off. Then it was only one large red crab, tearing at his flesh with claws and pincers—every bit of it clamped onto every bit of him.

It had taken an analyst—and the pawn money from her marquise diamond—to sort out the dreams. The ledge, the analyst had meticulously explained, was the precipice on which she lived her life. Her father and husband were interchangeable, because she had married her husband hoping for a continuation of the same protected relationship she had had with her father, failing to see that in both families, as in so many others of their type, the men loved-hated their mothers, then carried the love to their daughters and the hate to their wives. The clinging red crab, he explained, was herself, feeding on her husband. Her attempts to free him from the crab were an expression of her concern for her own security, projected as concern for him—the same hypocritical device she used in real life. The abyss, he explained, was her fear of falling, of losing the approval of others, and especially of her husband

and father, but mostly the abyss was the emptiness she found inside herself.

It had all seemed absurd, but after one or two sessions the nightmares had ceased, and then—deep down—Celeste simply *knew* it was true. That, incredibly, this information had always been filed in her gut, waiting for her when she dared look for it, along with a lot more.

Celeste was supposed to go back to the analyst, but she had broken her appointment. She wasn't ready yet to replace one set of authorities with another. She wanted to think things through on her own.

She had holed up in New York at the Bellamy Hotel. Its slumminess had pleased her. She had enjoyed living on a budget, hawking jewels and juggling accounts. She had enjoyed being a renegade, and the luxury of forgetting who she was supposed to be while she figured out who she really was. Celeste understood now what Ashley had meant by her "wipeout" stage though now that Celeste was having one, Ashley had turned positively upper-middle class. In fact—here Celeste laughed jubilantly, as she puffed her cigarillo—the last letter she had received from Ashley was so full of motherly homily and advice to the wayward that she had found herself checking the handwriting to make sure she hadn't written it to herself.

Celeste took the picture of Ashley dressed in Indian sari from her handbag. She felt closer now to her daughter, though, technically, more estranged. She also understood, or at least accepted without such bitterness, the disappearance of Xavier. The pain was there, even more now that she could no longer pretend that, any day, he would fall on her neck with love and gratitude, having "come to his senses." It was quite possible that he hated her, and that she had given him cause. That was not a subject she was willing to cope with yet.

Mostly Celeste had spent her time in the past few weeks brooding about herself and Charles and their marriage and, because the two seemed intertwined, her parents and their marriage, for it seemed to her now that they, too, had been inching along a slippery ledge with an abyss below, that she had known it and had gone on blithely, to repeat their mistakes. Why had she accepted so docilely the "wisdom" of the past, when clearly it had not been wisdom? Why, when she saw the world changing so quickly about her, when she saw the changes in her children's lives, had she thought her own couldn't, or shouldn't, change?

Celeste had thought a good deal about Charles' infidelities. *Had* they been important? In themselves, or just because she had made them important? She had assumed, from her parents' marriage, that she was supposed to feel angry, threatened, and betrayed, so she *had* felt angry, threatened, and betrayed. What if she had decided, from the start, that they didn't matter? Would they have mattered less to Charles? What if she had taken them as an indication that something was missing in their own marriage, and had moved in to fill the gap? Could she have done that? Or did both she and Charles need that gap—the inadequacy in their marriage—to protect themselves from facing the inadequacy in themselves? She had always cherished the illusion that she yearned for total love while Charles denied this to her. Now she wondered if it wasn't the *illusion* she had needed rather than the love.

Celeste listened to streetcars rattle by her window.

Maybe preserving that illusion had been what the failure of their "reunion" in New York had been about. They had talked for a while, and then Charles had made love to her, with an edge of desperation she had never felt in him before. For the first time, she was unable to respond. The most passionate he became, the more outraged she felt. Invaded. Violated. *She was a different person! Couldn't he see that?* She had wanted to slam her fists against his chest, vomit in his face, bite his tongue. Instead, she lay rigid and glassy-eyed, while Charles, becoming more mechanical, had performed. Afterwards, he said, quite phlegmatically: "I asked you for understanding twice in my life. Both times you refused."

Celeste lit another cigarillo. She twisted the marquise diamond on her finger, then remembered it wasn't there.

In a way, she and Charles had corrupted each other by asking too little while pretending to ask too much.

They had never been able to get beyond appearances, to do more than join mirror images. A marriage was not based on one or two bad decisions, or good ones. It took thousands of them, played out over the years—a carefully charted course, approved by both parties. Celeste had been on solid ground once, with powerful weapons—her youth, her looks, their children, their property, their common background, and—if not Charles' love—at least his affection. She should have used these weapons to fight *real* battles, for *real* stakes, instead of the sham battles they had fought. She should have used them to fight for her own life and dignity, so she would not have had to claw for what didn't belong to her—Charles' life. The trouble was, Celeste had not know *how* to fight, or what was important, so their marriage had deteriorated into "getting away with" and "putting up with" . . . at least, on the surface. Celeste was beginning to believe that in any marriage—given enough time—the accounts were more exquisitely balanced than most participants would dare imagine.

For this, she went back again to her parents' marriage.

For most of it, her father had treated her mother with indifference bordering on callousness. Then old G.O. had had his first stroke. Overnight, Bessie Mayfair had assumed the driver's seat. She wheeled her husband everywhere in his wheelchair, showing him off like a new baby in a perambulator. While old G.O. shrivelled down into senility, looking more and more like a hairless mouse, Bessie Mayfair had become more saintlike. She fed him, gave him his pills, and enemas and—Celeste remembered this very clearly—always talked babytalk to his little "weenie," while keeping it very very clean. The more Bessie insisted on doing for old G.O., the less he was able to do for himself. Celeste sensed in him a queer acquiescence, as if he felt relieved he was, at last, getting what he deserved, as death, and Bessie, stroked him, finger by finger, into the grave.

After the funeral, no one could figure out the change in Bessie Mayfair. Before she had seemed the embodiment of feminine charm. Now she was gross with jewels and warpaint. Her silent partnership in her husband's holdings became very vocal indeed, as Bessie reversed all his policies. The Mayfair sons—it was now clearly seen—had always belonged to Bessie. Old G.O. Mayfair was left without an empire or an heir, and more than one person wondered how much he had really controlled when he was alive.

Celeste had come to understand—as she watched her mother's hostility surface, layer by layer—that she, too, had deposited her resentment of Charles in dark ways. She no longer believed that a marriage could produce one winner and one loser . . . nor that it could really be a union between exploiter and victim. She believed now that when you tallied all the secret deals, all the hidden pockets of resistance, denial and revenge of the "wronged" party, and especially when you measured the hostility deposited in the children, the thing came out more or less equal; that, in fact, both parties wanted it that way, and continued to manoeuvre till this was true, and that it was this scrupulous equality of wrongs and rights, more than happiness, that made for a stable marriage, and that when this balance could not be achieved, or was broken, that the marriage itself broke up.

Celeste had, by way of metaphor, imagined a marriage to be two containers joined down one side.

A "good" marriage was one in which there was a high level of liquid in the joint container, and a "bad" marriage was one in which there was a low level, and a growing relationship was one in which the liquid level was rising, and a deteriorating relationship was one in which the liquid was leaking out.

Agitation from within, or without, created troughs and peaks, but the liquid always worked toward an equilibrium, and it was impossible to have a stable situation with a high level of liquid in one beaker, and a low level in the other, and that the person who *thought* he was "getting away with it" lived only under the *illusion* that he was getting more, and that the person who thought she was "putting up with it" lived only under the *illusion* that she was getting less, or was giving more, and that all any "exploiter" had to do to get the true measure of his "gain" was to look at his "fool" and to credit himself with half the other's loss, and that all the "martyr" had to do to get the value of her "sacrifice" for the other person, was to look at the pool of blood she thought she had shed, and to know that half had been drained off from the other side.

Well, what did all that add up to? A sense of sadness, yes, and waste, but this, too—a release from guilt. If the sides were equal, then the partners could choose to renegotiate on even footing, or they could choose to separate, with only the pain of parting, and not with the addition of guilt. The cheat was mutual. The debt had, in the living, been paid.

Celeste stubbed her cigarillo. Two months ago, she couldn't have imagined life without Charles. Now she couldn't imagine life with him . . . on the old terms. Their marriage had become a leaky container with very little liquid in it. She no longer had external pressures. She was not the mother of small children, or economically oppressed. There was nothing to hide behind "for the sake of." Their personal relationship had to stand or fall on its own merits and, despite the panic, the depression, the nightmares, Celeste had the feeling that, already, the pain was becoming less.

She got up from the bed.

She exchanged her Courrege suit for a chic black dress, dark stockings, hat and gloves.

She ran a bronze lipstick over her mouth, fussed with her hair, then doused herself with rose perfume—a perverse favourite of hers since the Valentine tea.

The phone rang. Celeste picked it up, smiling thinly. Basil Fitch, of course. Come to fetch her to the meeting.


Charles X. Hunter sat in the boardroom under the portrait of Xavier X. Hunter, amidst the lush ferns which, like all Hunter greenery, had burgeoned into jungle condition since he had order the removal of the Heat/Cool System.

Maybe it was a trick of the lights.

Maybe it had always been an illusion.

Charles X. no longer resembled his founding forebear.

His grey hair, turned white, had grown into a scruffy mane over his crumpled collar. He had shaved off his moustache. His clothes bent, lumped, and creased when he bent, lumped, and creased, rather than setting an impeccable standard his body tried to live up to. He no longer wore a vest or a watch. A handkerchief, posing as an ascot, replaced his tie. His pinstripe jacket had the sleeve torn out to accommodate the arm cast he had acquired in his *jump? fall? flight?* from his office window, and one of his legs, crossed over the other, revealed a white leg and drooping stocking.

But it was the expression on his face that now shattered all resemblance: whereas old Xavier had been pickled in oil at the point in time when, eyes like pitchforks, he was about to fire the whole sales force for an 0.01 drop in sales, Charles peered through his renegade ferns into the Standing Room Only boardroom with the vague bemusement of an aging circus lion putting in the last few moments before showtime. In one hand, he held a pipe that he smoked with sensuous pleasure, occasionally blowing a smoke ring that would hang, haphazardly, over his right ear, till he twirled a finger inside it in the gesture which—more than one person in the room noted—meant *crazy.*

On Charles' right sat his wife Celeste.

On his left sat Basil Fitch.

Down the Antique Original table were the other members of the board, and some of the more important department heads—Sven Jenson of the Chocolate Department; Bill Fontana, Production Manager; Danny Steele, acting head of Promo.

Seated back from the table were Eve Martin and Brigitte Young, and such department representatives as Bimbo Brown of Sales, Laurie Temple of Quality Control, Megan Mason of Hard Centres, Joh Greenlaugh of Public Relations.

Standing were Irma Burbank, Sam Ryan, Zeve Ross, Beau Whitehead, Morgan Jones.

It was 4.30 P.M.

Charles arose from his fern fronds.

He fixed the room with a look that could only be described as vintage Xavier and, slipping a thumb into a non-existent vest, announced: "We are assembled here today with pleasure mingled with regret to say goodbye to Charles X. Hunter, President of Hunter's Confectionary, who has been an important part of this company for twenty-eight years. . . ."

Charles smiled.

In fact, he grinned.

He broke his pose, adding almost jovially: "That is the first line of a speech I have been delivering, with eleven variations, for twenty-eight years. It is the last line of that speech, or any other, that I intend to deliver. I shall also dispense with the anecdotes, illustrating how the company could not have gotten along without Charles X. Hunter, or how Charles X. Hunter could not have gotten along without the company, with the emphasis on whichever is least true."

Charles heard an uncomfortable murmur through the room.

"But Seriously Now," he said by way of comfort, "as most of you have heard, I've chosen today to announce my retirement. To put it another way, I am intending to 'fly the coop'—a journey I began a few weeks ago, when I flew out my window in my heavier-than-air craft, and one of you"—here a sly grin at Sam Ryan, nudged in the doorway—"was kind enough to repay a similar favour by digging me, feet first, out of the juniper bushes."

Charles brandished his cast, almost proudly.

"Whatever I've been able to accomplish for this company has been done. Whatever this company has been able to do for me, has also been done. I hope to be phased out as soon as possible."

Charles, looking down at the tight faces, resisted the whimsical impulse to flap his arms and make propeller noises. "I have no intention of talking about my plans for the future, but I do wish to assure you that *your* future at Hunter's is in good hands.

"The woman who for twenty-five years has been my wife as of five minutes from now will be your acting president, an appointment I am sure the board will confirm after seeing her in action. She is young, ambitious, talented, and she combines an historical sense of this company with a fresh viewpoint and formidable business acumen.

"For those who view this appointment as being a little too convenient, I merely point out that my own major qualification for this job was that I happened to be the son of the former owner, whose big brother died before he could be harnessed. It is, though we often deny it, the way of the world.

"That is all the special pleading I intend to do on Celeste's behalf.

"The only *serious* regret I have, from a business point of view, is that I was unable to persuade Eve Martin to stay on with the company as Secretary to the Board. Eve has been consistent in refusing this appointment to fulfil a long-time ambition to attend university in the fall, and for this I know we all wish her well."

Charles nodded to Eve. There was a generous round of applause.

He turned to Celeste. There was expectant silence.

"I would like to introduce Celeste Mayfair Hunter, and to urge you all to stay a few minutes longer to hear the quite remarkable first report of your president, *Celeste?*"

Charles, grinning, gave up his position in front of the Throne Chair. Celeste, frowning, accepted it.

She looked down the gantlet of cynical boardroom faces, puffing smoke towards her from a dozen Montecristo cigars.

She opened her mouth to speak. No sound came.

She felt for her charm bracelet. She had apparently forgotten to put it on. . . .

She felt for her marquise diamond. It was gone. . . .

Celeste spun round, looking for Charles. She caught, instead, the pitchfork eyes of Xavier X., so much like Granny Mayfair's. Turning a stiff back to the portrait, Celeste leaned forward, her weight evenly balanced on either side of her report, and, challenging the room with eyes like emerald canape forks, began, in a silky voice: "Members of the Board, Department Heads, all other personnel. . . ."

Charles faded back into the jungle foliage. He listened, for a few minutes, head cocked, nodding polite assent, as Celeste showed how the profits of Hunter's could be raised 5 per cent in less than a year, simply by good housekeeping.

At point eleven—whipping the fudge for a lighter texture—Charles slid his hand behind his back. He fumbled through fetid fern, then along the gilt-edge of Xavier X. Hunter's portrait till he found the nameplate.

He pressed the middle X in his grandfather's name—which, like the lump in his chair, was a release mechanism—and, hearing a gentle whirr, examined, with a scuffed golfshoe, the hole newly opened in the wood-panelling.

Under cover of Throne Chair, ferns, portrait, new president, and the ample backside of Basil Fitch who, ever since Charles had stepped back, had been easing into position beside Celeste, Charles ducked through the opening. No one except Eve, who touched two fingers to her forehead in the Old Warrior's salute, saw him leave. Nor had he expected anyone would. From the moment he had confirmed Celeste, the eyes in the room had shifted to her, at first covertly, then in obvious curiosity and sycophancy, till she was the power focus and he was divested. It had hurt a little. He had not expected it to happen so baldly, or that he would feel the stripping away of his corporate identity as acutely. By the time Celeste had begun to speak, he had felt himself so lacking in substance he was almost convinced he could have passed through the wall *without* the secret panel.

Charles sighed. In a month or two he'd be reduced to the status of an occasional anecdote, so that when he chanced to meet anyone in the halls, the eyes of the other would glint in surprise. *What, aren't you dead yet?*

He waited for his own eyes to adjust to the murky light.

He had explored the secret room, by flashlight, when he had discovered it last week, feeling like one or other of the Hardy Boys discovering a Secret Treasure. The Treasure, in this case, had turned out to be a horsehair sofa, identical to the one in Old Xavier's office, a spitoon full of unsmoked cigars—old Xavier, apparently, liking them as little as himself—and one of the gaudier collections of pornography this side of Sodom and Gomorrha, beginning with turn-of-the-century ladies in corsets, and progressing up through the more explicit works of the liberated twenties.

Charles heard prolonged applause on the other side of the wood-panel.

He lay his eye against a peephole.

Basil Fitch, jowls in motion, was toasting Celeste, unctuously, effusively, with his waterglass. Celeste was responding with the glittery patronage of one who, while accepting the compliment, reserves judgement on the source. Charles made a grimace which he forced into a grin: *Mayfair & Fitch—why not?* It was time, in the history of Hunters, for consolidation, computerization, "good housekeeping." *His* contribution had been creative expansion. Celeste and Fitch could live off his innovations for a dozen years yet.

Charles focused his attention entirely on Celeste, letting her profile fill the oval peephole. She was dressed, uncharacteristically, in black. Charles mentally added dark glasses, a dark veil, a hat brim, and black shawl, recalling that he had noticed, while standing beside her in the boardroom, the scent of cheap rose cologne. He drew back abruptly from such a dangerous vision. *That way true madness lay! All small women swaddled in black looked and smelled alike!*

Charles removed his eye from the peephole.

He groped for, and found, the button for the secret panel on the other side—a rather obvious placement in a nude which, on the subject of airbrushing, ranked well ahead of its time.

He crawled on hands and knees through a fake ventilator which opened—with what original intention on that part of his founding forebear he dared not think—into the women's washroom. He crawled to the door (best to let them think he was mad rather than a pervert) and into the hall.

Charles strode through empty corridors, hearing his heels echo on wood, then gag on broadloom of increasingly plusher textures, so that by the time he reached the fringes of presidential influence, he was labouring uphill.

He passed through Brigitte's office, feeling a guilty pang. *What was there to say? She was young and resilient and already, it seemed, taking solace from that Morgan fellow in the Chocolate Department.*

He passed through Eve's office, giving her shrouded typewriter the Old Warrior's salute.

Charles stepped into his own office. He paused on the

threshold, expecting to feel ... nostalgia? regret? At least some emotional monument to the years he had spent here. Instead, he felt only ... *chafement* ... as if the room were already too large in some ways and too small in others—a hand-me-down suit that had never quite fit. In fact, the office had always been old Xavier's, which was why Charles had stamped his name on everything: *his* gold pen, *his* ruler, *his* memo pads, trying to hold the damned thing down.

Charles spun his nameplate. How many people would put their name on *both* sides? Actually, it had been a wise precaution. He had always been in danger of forgetting who he never really was.

Charles poured himself a brandy without permission from Xavier's clock. *Ahhh, yes, the clock.* He registered now what he had noticed the moment he stepped into the office. *The clock had stopped.* The hands stood in a lopsided moustache at 10.20, with the second hand hanging below like a red tongue.

Charles walked toward the clock, staring into its face with the tactless courage one uses on the face of a corpse. He ran his hands down the glass case, then along the walnut sides, recalling the last time he had seen Old Xavier alive ... that tragic night, almost fifty years ago ... on a cruise ship ... along with his father and brother. Fire had broken out, their second night from port. Grandad had awakened them, fully dressed even to his spats, carrying wet towels. He led them in a human chain through smoke so thick they couldn't see the hands they were holding. People were screaming and breaking glass. Some were jumping from the top deck, only to crunch on the deck below. Some were stuck by their lifejackets in portholes, too dazed to take them off. Some were swinging down knotted sheets into the water. One woman, naked, with fire instead of hair, arced like an arrow into the sea. A man with charred skin sat in a stairwell peeling himself.

Grandpa Xavier was a hero. He helped people into lifejackets. He beat with his cane some crewmen who were trying to escape in a lifeboat, making them give up their seats to women and children. He made others string ropes into the sea.

Charles, his brother, and his father were the last into the lifeboats. They looked around for Grandpa.

"Look!" shouted Xav. "He's up there!"

Charles looked up. There was Grandpa, his back stiff as his

cane, his cane across his knees, in a lifeboat still up in the ropes, dangling grotesquely over a puddle of flame.

They called: "Grandpa! Grandpa!" till their lungs ached. Grandpa wouldn't come down. He wouldn't even answer. He was in *his* seat, in *his* lifeboat—the one he was assigned the first day at sea, and that would be his seat or none.

Charles huddled in his lifeboat seeing flames spurt like blood into the sky, hearing the sizzle of steam as the boat sank into the icy water, calling: "Grandpa!" He saw the flames creep up his Grandpa's coat, then into his hair. He saw his face, illumined in flame. He saw it melt—the skin actually run from the bones like wax from the face of a mannequin. He saw the body slide down in slowmotion into the flames.

Charles, feeling the last of a lifetime's hostility melt away, patted the face of Xavier's clock. He reset the hands, and gently started it working again. No man would choose to die in the ghastly way Old Xavier had died. His grandfather was not—never had been—the villain of his life. He had just been a convenient "scape-ghost"—the projection of Charles' own fears, his own sense of inadequacy, his own need for security. It wasn't Old Xavier who had driven away Fiona, or who had prevented him from flying. It was Charles himself, afraid that if he tried to break away from the Hunter system of props and strings that there would not be enough of himself that was real to survive. The Hunters were a family who, over the generations, had come to favour clan survival over individual survival. Old Xavier—and Charles, and his father, and his brother—had been the victims of a system which had bribed and bullied them into killing off their own feelings, hopes and dreams in favour of family ambitions. Charles understood now the source of the crushing guilt which had always oppressed him. He knew, now, his crime. It was not failure to live up to the strict family code, as he had suspected, but the opposite: self-murder, the slow strangulation of the real person striving for existence within himself. The foetus knotted in an umbilical cord. The flier twisted in his parachute. It had been his own hands, around his own throat, that last day in his office.

Charles took the family motto from the wall, and jammed it by golf shoe into the wastebasket.

He loped to his desk, piled with papers, prepared to deal benignly with the tag-ends of his past, feeling a sense of buoyant release. He gave Xavier's chair a playful spin, humming calliope music as he seated himself, finding, for the first time in his life that he was able to carry a tune. He looked out his window. *Who knows? Now that he had the time and the inclination maybe he would learn how to fly.*

Charles attacked his backlog with vigour, taking advantage of his last day to make a number of appointments: Danny Steele, confirmed as Head of Promo. Beau Whitehead, Head of Personnel. He even transferred Irma Burbank to Public relations.

Charles yawned. He leaned back *impersonally* in Xavier's chair and looked *impersonally* at Xavier's clock. It was 8.15. Though the sun had almost set, the sky was still bright with reflected light. The stars were only now beginning to poke through as pinpoints of light. Soon, with the blindfold of daylight removed, he would be able to see Infinite Time and Infinite Space ... light beamed forth billions of years ago; galaxies hurtling through the universe—the discus game of the gods!

Charles tipped forward in Xavier's chair. He had one more thing to do before he could properly put aside the past and embark on his future. He had been planning it ever since he had awakened in the hospital.

Charles searched through his junk drawer—the one where he sometimes stashed his galoshes. He drew out a ring of rusty keys of the sort a dungeon-keeper might carry.

He fingered the keys. Well, did Mary Moon still exist? Did she ever? Did she still live in the loft? Was she the Lady in Black or had everything during that last curious appointment been a part of his breakdown? And what about the other strange and inexplicable things that had been happening this year all through the Candy Factory? Had *he* been responsible? Did the madness of one person trigger madness in another? Had *she? Why?* Had they been planned? coincidental? fated?

Charles had begun investigating the facts, first thing that morning. The results had been mixed—entirely baffling.

Mary Moon existed on some official company records, but not on others. Her pay, for many years, had been made over to the Save the Children Fund, and was still deposited monthly with that organization.

Some persons who worked near Mary Moon claimed to have seen her recently. Others swore she hadn't been near her office for several months. A few insisted she had retired years ago. One or two said they thought she was dead.

Mary Moon's Special Accounts office afforded few clues. Her "out" basket was empty. Her "in" basket held the usual clutter of company circulars going back over a year, but not Charles' own memo inviting her to a "personell" chat.

Charles closed his desk.

He turned out his light and shut his door.

He strode through the empty corridors of the Candy Factory, past the other executive offices and the boardroom. He paused in front of a firedoor at the end of the hall ... *just as he remembered*.

He opened the door.

He stepped into a vestibule, dimly lit by light from the fire-escape.

Charles looked up the stairs to the Candy Loft. He hadn't been there for forty years—not since he and his brother Xav used to sneak up on rainy days to rattle chains and groan down ventilators and release rats dipped in phosphorescent paint, resulting in one near-heart attack, several resignations, a severe whipping for both Xav and himself, and the myth that the Candy Loft was haunted.

Charles felt for a light switch.

He found a gap in the plaster where it had been.

He started up the stairs, slowly, feeling anticipation build.

He stood on the top step, breathing deeply.

He rapped on the loft door—gently.

There was no response.

He rapped again ... more forcefully.

He put his ear to the keyhole. Not a step, not a rattle, not a flutter ... *dead air?*

He tried the porcelain knob. It turned easily. He pushed open the door.

Charles stepped inside, waiting for his eyes to adjust to the darkness. . . .

## About the Author

Sylvia Fraser was born in Hamilton, Canada, educated at the University of Western Ontario and now lives in Toronto. She has won two Women's Press Club Awards and the University of Western Ontario President's Medal for magazine writing. This is her second novel, the first being PANDORA.

## More Bestselling Canadian Titles from SIGNET

## Have You Read These Big Bestsellers from SIGNET?

- [ ] **EARTHSOUND by Arthur Herzog.** (#E7255—$1.75)
- [ ] **THE DEVIL'S OWN by Christopher Nicole.**
  (#J7256—$1.95)
- [ ] **CARIBEE by Christopher Nicole.** (#E6540—$1.75)
- [ ] **THE GREEK TREASURE by Irving Stone.**
  (#E7211—$2.25)
- [ ] **THE KITCHEN SINK PAPERS by Mike McGrady.**
  (#J7212—$1.95)
- [ ] **THE GATES OF HELL by Harrison Salisbury.**
  (#E7213—$2.25)
- [ ] **SAVAGE EDEN by Constance Gluyas** (#J7171—$1.95)
- [ ] **THE FINAL FIRE by Dennis Smith.** (#J7141—$1.95)
- [ ] **SOME KIND OF HERO by James Kirkwood.**
  (#J7142—$1.95)
- [ ] **A ROOM WITH DARK MIRRORS by Velda Johnston.**
  (#W7143—$1.50)
- [ ] **THE HOMOSEXUAL MATRIX by C. A. Tripp.**
  (#E7172—$2.50)
- [ ] **CBS: Reflections in a Bloodshot Eye by Robert Metz.**
  (#E7115—$2.25)
- [ ] **'SALEM'S LOT by Stephen King.** (#J7112—$1.95)
- [ ] **CARRIE by Stephen King.** (#E6410—$1.75)
- [ ] **FATU-HIVA: Back to Nature by Thor Heyerdahl.**
  (#J7113—$1.95)

---

**HAR-NAL DISTRIBUTORS, LTD.,**
**100 Steelcase Rd. E., Markham, Ontario L3R 1E8**

Please send me the SIGNET BOOKS I have checked above. I am enclosing $_____(check or money order—no currency or C.O.D.'s). Please include the list price plus 35¢ a copy to cover handling and mailing costs. (Prices and numbers are subject to change without notice.)

Name_____

Address_____

City_____Province_____Postal Code_____
Allow at least 4 weeks for delivery